Under the Watchful Sky

by

Roger Thomas

TUMBLAR HOUSE
'Bona Tempora Volvant'

Arcadia
MMXVI

Printed in the United States of America

ISBN 978-1-944339-10-4

Under the Watchful Sky
Copyright © 2018 by Roger Thomas
All rights reserved.

Visit our website at www.tumblarhouse.com

The Thumb Region of Michigan

Angelus

The phone chimed with an incoming message.

Case OPEL 12182 ideal. Action cleared. Accelerate at your discretion. Details follow.

Charon's teeth bared – at last. He'd been pushing this for over a year, but those old women at the department had been too timid. They must have finally gotten desperate enough. "Porcher!" he hollered as he tapped up the e-mail that contained the case details.

"What?" came the reply from outside the office door.

"Get in here – good news," Charon called back, scanning the e-mail.

"What good news?" Ron Porcher stuck his head in, looking scornful and sounding as sullen as always.

"We finally got clearance." Charon shoved the phone at him. "Seems they found the perfect case."

"Well," mused Porcher, as he examined the message. "Looks clean – but all the way over in Port Huron?"

"What do you mean?" Charon scoffed. "We can drive over, do the job, and get back within three hours."

"Okay, but..." Porcher trailed off.

"But what?" Charon goaded. "Don't tell me you're wimping out on me. You've got plenty of field experience."

"It's not that," Porcher protested. "It's just that – aren't we both getting a little high-profile for field jobs? I mean, if something goes wrong..."

"We're going to ensure nothing goes wrong," Charon interrupted. "This is the trial balloon, the proof of concept. I've been prodding them on this for months. If it goes smoothly – which it will – they'll give the go-ahead for the second phase, and we'll start seeing some real progress."

"Well – okay," Porcher replied skeptically. "When do you want to do this?"

"Tomorrow," Charon said.

"Tomorrow!" Porcher exclaimed.

1

"Sure, tomorrow. Why wait? It's not like conditions are going to get more prime than they are," Charon pointed to the text on the screen. "All we have to do is drive over, execute the simple plan, and drive back."

"All right, let's do it," Porcher said without enthusiasm – as if he had any choice.

"We're on, then." Charon started to compose a reply regarding various arrangements that had to be made.

Luciana's phone rang, and she saw it was the agency. Puzzled, she answered.

"Hi, Luciana?" came an unfamiliar voice.

"Yes?"

"Just to let you know, Mr. Holmes won't be needing you today. He called to let us know. You're still set for Friday, though, unless you hear otherwise," the voice said.

"Oh – okay," Luciana replied. "Thanks. Do you – are there any other jobs for me?"

"Not sure," the voice said. "Let me look into it and get back to you."

Hmm, thought Luciana as she tucked the phone away. That was odd. She'd been helping them for over a year now – first both of them and now, of course, just Mr. Holmes. During all that time, he'd never contacted her through the agency when there'd been a change in plan – he just called her directly. Part of her wondered if she should call him to see if everything was all right. But if he'd called the agency, he'd probably had his reasons, and wouldn't appreciate a call from her. Maybe she'd find out on Friday. In the meantime, it was a bother to lose the hours, but it freed up the afternoon. Maybe she'd get that haircut she'd been trying to find time for.

Glancing up, John Holmes saw that noon was approaching. With effort, he levered himself out of his chair and worked his way to the back door with the help of the quad cane. Luciana was starting to hint that a walker might be more suitable, but he wanted to hold off on that as long as he could.

He undid the chain and threw back the bolt with a little pang of sadness. He remembered when they'd never locked the doors, day or night. Even when the neighborhood had started to decline, they'd still kept them unlocked during the day, more as a sign of defiant hope than anything. But now, with him alone in the house in his condition, it wasn't prudent to leave the doors unlocked. And "decline" was no longer the word for the state of the neighborhood – "decay" was more like it. There were no more kids playing in the streets, just lost youngsters driving noisy cars with the bass thumping.

He hobbled back to the living room. Shortly before noon now – almost time for the Angelus. Sometimes Luciana was here and would say it with him. He and Angie had always tried to stop to say the brief devotion, wherever they were. Of course, it had been easier once he'd retired and they could stand side by side. Now he was standing alone again, for a while, though he tried to imagine her pausing wherever she was to pray the familiar words with him.

He lowered himself into his chair. Luciana should be along any minute. He had a bit of an appetite today, which should please her. She liked cooking for him, and on the increasingly rare occasions he felt like eating, she'd go out of her way to make something delicious.

The back door opened – there was Luciana now. "Good morning! I'm in here!" John called.

But instead of Luciana, two strange men walked through the archway from the kitchen. One was large, with close-cropped black hair and a heavy jaw dark with stubble. The other was shorter – thin and gangly with stringy brown hair and a weak chin.

"Who – who are you?" John asked, alarmed. From their clothes alone, these men didn't look like street thugs, but there was something even more menacing about them, something about their eyes. The brown-haired guy never looked directly at him, but the eyes of the black-haired man were cold and dead.

"Luciana couldn't make it today, Mr. Holmes," the black-haired guy said, placing a small duffel on the dining room table and zipping it open. John noticed that both the men were wearing vinyl exam gloves. "So we'll be helping you instead." He tossed a handful of what looked like straps to the brown-haired guy, who swiftly walked behind John.

"What – what do you want?" John's voice squeaked as he tried to rise, but they were too quick for him. A heavy hand on his shoulder forced him back into the chair, and a wide band of some sort was thrown around his chest. The brown-haired guy pulled the band tight, pinioning his torso and upper arms, and he heard the ripping sound of heavy Velcro being secured. Then swift hands reached around his sides, pulling his wrists down to the chair arms and securing them with smaller straps.

"We're happy to fill in, though," the black-haired guy kept talking as he pulled more things out of the duffel, arranging them on the table. "As it happens, today is going to be a big day for you, Mr. Holmes. A really big day."

John's heart was pounding and his mouth was dry. Whatever was going on was serious – much more serious than a simple robbery or even a beating. Whatever these briskly efficient men had come to do was bad – very bad.

Yet as even as this realization fully dawned, and his body began sweating and shaking, calmness rose within him. Something was clearly going to happen, but he could do nothing about it. It was out of his hands. There was nothing these men could do to him, anyway, not really. Peace suffused his mind and heart, and he stopped struggling against the bonds.

The black-haired guy was busy prepping something which John recognized when he handed it to the other guy. It was an old-style jet injector. He'd used those when he was a corpsman back in his Navy days. The brown-haired guy brought it over and pulled up John's sleeve. This was all about whatever was in the vial loaded in the gun, and John couldn't do a thing to stop the injection. But as he felt the cold tip press against his skin, he tightened his arm muscles, just as he'd once instructed his patients not to do. The gun gave its muffled pop, and his tensed muscles stung a little. There. Whatever it was, was now done.

"Yes, Mr. Holmes," the black-haired guy said, coming over and putting a prescription bottle on the small table beside the chair. "Today is the day you commit suicide."

John's heart was hammering, but he said nothing and just looked at the man.

"Yes, suicide," the man continued as if John had spoken. "It's been a hard few months for you. Luciana's been quite concerned."

"She has, has she?" John almost whispered. Over at the table, the brown-haired guy was breaking down the gun and packing it away.

"Oh, yes," the black-haired guy said. "You've seemed so depressed, what with your wife's death, and the advance of the Parkinson's, and your arthritis. You haven't been eating or sleeping well. You seem to have lost all interest in life."

John said nothing, but kept looking at the man. He was starting to feel lightheaded, which certainly meant that whatever they'd injected him with was starting to take hold.

"Water. From the kitchen – any glass will do," the black-haired guy instructed the other as he picked up the pill bottle. "Yes, Luciana was glad when you took your neurologist's advice to go see Dr. Daniels. She even drove you to a couple of the appointments."

"She did, did she?" John slurred.

"Oh yes – at least, that's what she'll tell any investigators, should they ask. She was also concerned when you called to tell her not to come today, but she figured you had good care."

John's vision was blurring and his muscles were starting to spasm.

"But Dr. Daniels, Dr. Daniels," the man continued theatrically, shaking his head. "Forgot that amitriptyline isn't the first choice for a suicidal patient. But then, he might have discerned what you were truly seeking: relief from the trials of life, relief that would reunite you with your wife – relief that your archaic morality would deny you." The man turned and smirked at the crucifix hanging on the wall.

Following the man's gaze, John spotted the two frames on the mantel and had an idea. Though his throat was tightening and he was losing control of his muscles, he jerked his head toward the frames.

"Picture," John croaked.

"What's that, Mr. Holmes?" the man asked.

"Picture," John repeated. "Give me picture."

"Picture? You want the picture?" the man asked, picking up the frame holding the photo of John and Angie at their fiftieth anniversary party. "Oh, that's a nice touch – slipping away while holding a picture of your wife."

"No," John struggled, shaking his head jerkily. "Other picture."

"Other picture?" the man asked skeptically, putting down the anniversary photo and picking up the other frame. It held a picture of a round-faced smiling man wearing some outfit thick with gold embroidery. "You want this picture?"

John nodded, his neck muscles tightening painfully. They'd given him more than just amitriptyline – it was working far too quickly. His vision was nearly gone and his hearing was fading. He felt the man tuck the picture frame beside his leg.

"Not a full glass, you idiot," the man was berating his partner. "Drink about half of that, then go dump most of these pills down the toilet and flush it twice. This needs to look convincing."

John's vision had whited out now, and he could feel his muscles straining against the straps. Roaring was beginning to fill his ears when another sound cut through. It was the chimes from the clock on the mantel, the chimes sounding noon. Then he realized they weren't just the clock chimes. These were tower bells, a full set of them joyously pealing out the call to prayer. Reflexively, John bowed his head as best he could and recalled the familiar words.

"The angel of the Lord declared to Mary," he whispered through quivering lips.

"And she conceived by the power of the Holy Spirit," answered a beloved voice, strong and clear. In joy and shock, John jerked his head straight up, his eyes wide open, searching for the voice.

"Angie?" he whispered.

"Hail Mary, full of grace, the Lord is with thee," the voice continued the familiar words, and he could dimly see a figure descending the steps to his right. "Blessed art thou among women, and blessed is the fruit of thy womb, Jesus."

"Holy Mary, Mother of God, pray for us sinners," John gasped, "now and at the hour of our death."

And there she was, his Angie, coming across the room to him, not hunched over with arthritis or swollen with diabetes, but straight and strong and smiling and beautiful.

"Behold the handmaid of the Lord," John whispered with his last earthly breath.

"Be it done to me according to thy word," Angie sang, reaching her loving arms out to him.

"Wow," Porcher said as he put the pill bottle on the table next to the glass of water. "More convulsing than I expected."

"Good to know," Charon noted. "Next time we'll pad the straps. We don't want any strain bruises."

"How – ah – quickly is this supposed to work?"

"Straight to the bloodstream? The tech said ten, fifteen minutes. Listen to his breathing – he's going already," Charon replied.

"What's with the picture?"

"He wanted it," Charon explained. "No harm, and a nice touch of authenticity – fading away holding a favorite photo. I don't know why he wanted that one instead of the one with him and his wife."

The two men watched in silence as the spasms slowed and their victim finally slumped over against his bonds.

"Is that it?" Porcher asked. "I can't hear any breathing."

Charon took one of his wrists. "If there's a pulse, it's too weak to detect. He's gone enough for us – he won't recover from here." He began stripping off the straps.

"Will he – fall out of this?" Porcher asked as he undid the chest strap. The upright hard-backed chair didn't seem the best for holding a corpse. "Should we lift him into the recliner?"

"Nah – the less we mess with things, the better. He died here, we prop him here. If he falls out, he falls out. Let's go."

Back in the car, they stripped off their exam gloves. "There you go," Charon announced as he backed the car down the drive and headed for the expressway. "Less than twenty minutes from entry to exit, without a hitch or delay. We haven't lost our touch."

"Should we have locked the door?" Porcher asked.

"No matter," Charon shrugged. "The worst thing that could happen is some local punks walk in. If you were a punk who walked into an unlocked house and found a corpse, would you stick around?"

"Not hardly," Porcher admitted. "What if someone runs a full tox eval of his blood and finds more than the amitriptyline?"

"Will you stop fretting, dammit?" Charon snarled. "You're starting to sound like those spineless pukes in D.C. When they find this case, they'll see a depressed old man with a degenerative illness who couldn't take the grief anymore and put himself down. They might do some cursory investigating, but that's what our covers are for. We show them what they expect to see, and nobody's going to want to look any further."

"All our covers are in place, then?"

"Just one more, and I'll tackle that tomorrow," Charon assured him. "You message in and tell them we're clear."

The next morning, as Charon was finishing his post-job writeup, he remembered his final task. He picked up his phone and tapped up the application that allowed him to overlay the source number with one of his choosing. Using that, he dialed Luciana's number.

Luciana was cleaning up Mrs. Jamison's breakfast when her phone rang. The display said it was the agency again. Answering it, she heard another unknown voice, a man this time.

"Listen carefully," the voice said, sharp and harsh. "Do not interrupt and ask no questions. I will say this only once. If you do not follow instructions, the consequences for you and your family will be severe."

"Who is this?" Luciana asked instinctively.

"No questions!" the voice barked. "If you are asked, John Holmes called you yesterday and told you not to come. He had seemed depressed, and had been going to a doctor who had prescribed medicine for him. Just say that, and nothing will happen to you. Say anything else, and trouble will find you." The line went dead.

Luciana gasped and leaned against the sink, her heart pounding. Mr. Holmes! She'd known something was not right!

Who was that menacing voice? Suffocating fear rose within her. Someone at the agency? That made no sense. The only men at the agency were Tony, Philippe, and James, and none of them sounded like that. The voice had threatened her and her family. What should she do?

Luciana bustled about tending Mrs. Jamison, barely thinking about what she was doing, her mind was racing so quickly. Trouble had found her. She'd done her best to live quietly and not make a fuss, but trouble had found her regardless. What should she do? Nothing? But would that cause even more problems? And what of Mr. Holmes? Might he be in danger? She was scheduled to visit him on Friday – what would she find? She didn't want to walk in on more trouble.

Something was wrong, she just knew it – something was badly wrong. Luciana felt she should do something. Should she call the police, or would that just make things worse for her? Didn't they have an anonymous tip line? No good, no good, they could always tell the number you called from. Wasn't there some way to make a call that masked the calling number? She thought there was, but didn't know how. What could she do?

Gary! Gary who worked at the Community Food Depot. He was friendly and helpful and knew everyone and everything. He could be discreet. She'd call him, and then he'd call the police, and then he'd forget that she'd ever been involved. She pulled out her phone and keyed the number for the Food Depot.

Preliminary Exam

It was shortly before lunch when the phone at Derek's elbow rang. "County morgue," he answered.

"Yeah, this is Stacie down at PHPD," came a voice that Derek recognized.

"Hey, Stacie, what's up?" Derek replied.

"We got a possible suicide at 1729 Walker. Anonymous tip. Squad car and EMS are there now."

"On my way," Derek said. He stopped long enough to fire off an e-mail to his boss and grab his field kit. Lunch would have to wait. He hoped it wasn't a messy suicide, or lunch would wait longer. At least it was close; the address was only a couple miles from his office in the hospital. Calls from the county sheriff sometimes meant drives to Algonac or Yale.

The house was one of those increasingly rare enclaves of order in a neighborhood that was going to hell in a hand basket. Decades ago, this had been a trim residential area, but now it was primarily run-down rentals and vacant houses. This house was an exception, with a well-cut lawn, clean siding, and a few neatly tended small shrubs. There was a squad car at the curb but the EMS was backed up the driveway. He went in the back door.

Derek walked into the familiar smell of death. The EMTs were sitting at the table next to their gurney, which was taking up much of the kitchen. He handed his ID to the policeman.

"Derek Stevens, deputy medical examiner. Stacie called me."

"Good. In here," the cop led the way into the living room, where the smell was stronger. It was easy to see why. A man's body was sprawled on the floor in front of a wooden chair. On the table nearby was a prescription pill bottle and half a glass of water.

"We found him just like this, clearly dead, so we didn't touch anything. No attempt at resuscitation," the policeman explained.

Derek nodded. He put his kit down and pulled on exam gloves. He felt the man's neck – no pulse, and the flesh was at room temperature.

"Anything out of order? Forced entry? Theft?" Derek asked.

"Back door was unlocked. His wallet is in the drawer of the desk by the door – has a few bills in it."

"Did the tipster give any details?"

"Nothing," the cop said. "Just that there was something suspicious and we should check it out. Could have been a neighbor, could have been anyone."

Derek nodded. "I concur with the initial assessment that this appears to be a suicide or other non-suspicious death. I'm going to start taking pictures and moving things around. He should be ready to remove in about ten minutes."

"Right," the policeman said, making some notations on his tablet. Derek took out his phone and snapped some shots of the body, the chair, and the table. He picked up the pill bottle and glanced at the details. An anti-depressant. Well, that made sense.

"All these specs will be in the police report, right?" Derek asked as he handed the bottle to the policeman.

"Yup," the man confirmed as he tucked the bottle into a plastic bag and labeled it.

Derek was taking pictures of the body from a couple angles when he noticed something. "It looks like he's lying on something. Can you help me roll him over?"

They did, and the thing turned out to be a picture with cracked glass. Derek got a shot of it where it lay, then flipped it over for another, then propped it against the chair and took a full-screen snap of it.

"Who is this guy?" Derek asked, pointing at the picture.

"No idea," the policeman admitted. "Someone official, I'd guess – that looks like a professional shot."

"Why would he be lying on that, I wonder?" Derek mused.

"I'd guess it meant something to him," the policeman answered. "Suicides will do that sometimes – hold something meaningful when they go. Kids, especially girls, will occasionally be found clutching a stuffed animal. That's sad.

Adults will hold letters, pictures of loved ones, that sort of thing."

"Hmm," Derek said, looking around. "That's odd. There's a picture of him and his wife on the mantel, yet he chose to hold this picture. Any idea why it's broken?"

"Most likely it wasn't," the cop explained. "He probably died in the chair with that on his lap, and then slumped over and fell forward onto it."

"Right," Derek replied, a bit chagrined at having missed something so obvious.

"You guys ready?" one of the EMTs called from the kitchen.

"Just about," Derek said. He snapped a couple more shots of the man then grabbed some sampling bags from his kit. He swabbed the man's mouth, then the rim of the glass on the table.

"Okay, he's ready," Derek waved the EMTs in. As he bent over to tuck away the DNA samples, he discreetly swabbed his own cheek and labeled that as the third sample.

"Any idea who this is?" Derek asked the cop.

"ID says John Holmes. Looks like he lived here alone, though it seems his wife lived here until just recently. She may have died, which might be a factor in the suicide. There's a card pinned to the board in the kitchen for a local care operation called Homeward Angels. We're checking that out," the policeman explained.

"Thanks," Derek said as he tapped a few details into his phone. "I'm heading back to the morgue. I'll do a prelim on him, but I doubt anyone will want a full autopsy. Looks pretty straightforward."

"That's what I think. Where should I send a copy of the report?"

"Medical examiner. I'll be the one he forwards it to," Derek replied.

Derek made it back to the morgue to receive John Holmes' body, but postponed the exam until after lunch. The delay meant he was plenty hungry, and he'd missed the worst of the lunch rush. He glanced around the half-empty cafeteria for a spot to sit, and caught sight of a familiar face who happened to be sitting by herself. He worked his way over.

"Hey, Janice!" he greeted her. "Mind some company?"

"Derek!" Janice stood to give him a hug. "What have you been up to?"

Janice Boyd was a nurse whom Derek had met during some continuing education seminars. She had curly, reddish-brown hair which she kept cut short, brown eyes, and a round face with just a hint of freckles across her nose. She had a sunny smile which changed her whole appearance when she wore it, which in Derek's opinion was far too seldom. It wasn't that she was morose, it's just that she was often – well, somber.

But Janice wasn't somber now. Her delight at seeing Derek brought out her most brilliant smile, which cheered him in turn.

Derek explained what he'd been doing lately, and told her of the suicide he'd just picked up. Janice shook her head sadly.

"I just got transferred to Geriatrics," she explained. "It can be so depressing. So many old people with nobody to care for them. They just sit there for hours, staring at the walls or the television, with nothing to look forward to but their next meal."

"Don't they have visitors?" Derek asked.

"Some do. Many don't. There are a surprising number whose kids live far away, or who don't have any kids. Those are the saddest. Some just stare at you when you come in, but others want you to sit and talk to them – for hours, if you'd let them."

"That does sound sad," Derek admitted, though he could understand part of the problem. He'd have a hard time visiting his mother over in New York if she were to go into the hospital.

"Hey, Janice," came a voice from over Derek's shoulder. Derek turned to see a large-framed woman with cropped brown hair.

"Melissa! Have a seat," Janice said. "Derek, this is Melissa Bateman, shift supervisor on my floor. Melissa, Derek Stevens, the deputy medical examiner. He runs the morgue."

"Derek, good to meet you," Melissa said in a husky contralto, gripping his hand firmly. "I got Katie to cover for me so I could slip away for a bite."

"Katie? Then they must be short-handed – maybe I should go," Janice started, but Melissa waved her back down.

"Relax. It's after lunch, and lots of 'em are taking naps. We've got time."

"Y'know, Melissa," Derek asked, his curiosity piqued, "maybe you can explain something to me. I see your ID badge has all sorts of pins and things stuck around the edges. Are they just decorative? Or do those things mean something? I've seen that around the hospital here and there – some people have them, some people don't."

"Well, it depends," Melissa explained, holding out the badge which hung around her neck on a lanyard. "Sanitation regulations discourage wearing a lot of pins and such on our clothing, which leaves the ID badge or lanyard. We can't stick anything through the badge itself because of the embedded circuitry, and festooning your lanyard with shiny things that could have poky edges is a recipe for trouble. That leaves this quarter inch of laminate around the edge to work with.

"Some people do nothing with that, like you two. Others put one or two little decorations, like flowers or flags pins. People like me, we go whole hog, pinning as much on as we can. Like this is my gallon donor pin, and this is my honors pin from when I got my Masters. This is a pin from a conference I attended in Vancouver."

"What's this?" Janice pointed to a gem in one corner, and Melissa grinned sheepishly.

"That's half a set of diamond studs that I had. I lost one of them, and couldn't bear to have the remaining one sit in a drawer, so there it is."

"What's this one?" Derek asked, pointing to a pin along the bottom edge of the card. He thought he saw a curious expression flash over Melissa's face as she glanced at it.

"That? Oh, that's just a pin from an association I belong to." She held it up so he could get a better look at it. The pin was three capital letters – XCV – gold hued with a tiny red jewel in the upper left, embedded in the X, and two tiny blue jewels in the C and the V. It reminded Derek of the Greek letters used by campus organizations.

"So this is – a sorority of some type? A professional organization?" Derek asked.

"A little of both," Melissa said. "Fraternity/sorority, with both men and women. But sort of like a professional group, too. But enough about me – what are you two up to?"

Derek glanced at the clock and remembered that a job awaited him back at the morgue. He excused himself, leaving Janice and Melissa to finish their lunches.

"Seems like a nice guy," Melissa said.

"He is, but I wouldn't want his job," Janice replied. "He was telling me how he's got to do an exam on a suicide victim. Older guy, lived alone, his wife may have died recently."

"Too common a story," Melissa said, shaking her head. "I remember the warnings fifteen or twenty years ago: as the Baby Boom generation began to hit true old age, it would stretch every resource we had. Now that time is here, clogging our support channels and taxing our facilities. You see it every day up on the floor, and we don't see the worst. You know what it's like out there in the homes and assisted living facilities."

Janice grimaced. No matter how tedious and frustrating work was on the geriatric floor, she knew she was far better off than those nurses who had to take jobs in the foster care homes, ALFs, and nursing homes that littered the area. Those were thankless jobs with erratic schedules, minimal pay, scant benefits, and just few enough hours to avoid full-time status. Janice knew classmates who'd had to take two of those jobs just to make ends meet.

"It's terrible, just terrible," Janice acknowledged.

"And if you look at the demographics, it'll continue like that for at least another five years," Melissa pointed out. "With new life-prolonging treatments, possibly ten or fifteen."

Janice's heart sank. She knew that government reimbursement for senior care just barely covered the cost of treatment, and sometimes not even that. As a result, senior care was sucking up ever more of the hospital's resources. Geriatrics had once taken up an entire floor of the old section of the hospital, now it also occupied a wing of the floor beneath. She hadn't gone into the medical field to get rich, but she'd hoped for a raise from time to time, and maybe a chance for advancement. Already there were rumors that the pay freeze, in effect for two years already, would be extended for another year. Between her student loan payments, rent on the house, and her car payment, she was barely keeping her head above water. Would she never get a break?

Melissa was watching carefully as Janice pondered these depressing details. "So, tell me," she asked. "Are you from this area? Is your family around here?"

Janice was taken aback by the abrupt change of subject. "Um – not any more. It's just me now."

"'Not any more'?" Melissa asked.

"It's complicated," Janice sighed. "My mother works in the charity industry..."

"The 'charity industry'?" Melissa interrupted.

"Yeah," Janice confirmed. "Non-profits and charitable organizations are huge, handling billions of dollars. Most people don't realize it's possible to make a career out of them. They need managers and grant writers and press secretaries just like corporations do. My mother was one of the careerists. We moved to this area when she got a job with a local foundation. I was in later elementary school at the time. My mother climbed the ladder here for a few years, then got offered the directorship of an agency down in the Houston area.

"By then I was in high school, and didn't want to move, and my father had had enough. He's an accountant, and got tired of having to fold up his practice and start from scratch every time she got a new position. So she divorced him and moved to Houston."

"That's a shame," Melissa said.

"Not really," Janice shrugged. "We weren't particularly close, especially during my junior high and high school years. I have some dim memory of happier times when I was very young, but by the time I was growing up, she seemed more interested in her career than me. I think I was a disappointment to her."

"A disappointment?" Melissa asked.

"Yeah," Janice confirmed. "My mother's idea of girl time was shopping for clothes. Since she liked to shop for and wear the latest fashions, she figured all women wanted to. What made things worse was that she was one of those slender, willowy types who was only one size above petite, while I was big and chunky."

"You? Chunky?" Melissa snorted. "Now me – *I'm* chunky."

"Well – in comparison to her I was," Janice explained. "If she was like – a stalk of celery, I was like a big baking potato. She'd keep choosing outfits that would look good on her, but didn't suit me at all. She'd drop hints that if I watched my diet more carefully, the clothes she liked would work for me. She kept urging me to try them, and when I put my foot down, she'd say I had an attitude problem and was ungrateful. We used to get in the most terrible fights. Sometimes I wonder if she moved to Houston as much to get away from me as to take the new job."

"What about your father," Melissa asked. "Is he still around?"

"Sorta," Janice said. "After the divorce, his practice dwindled. He stuck around here until I graduated from high school, then took a job as a staff accountant with a firm up by Saginaw."

"Didn't you want to move with him?" Melissa asked.

"Nah. Dad and I are like – cordial. I think he thought I was supposed to be my mother's responsibility, so when mother and I were at odds, he didn't know how to deal with me. I go visit him every few months. We spend the weekend watching movies and eating take-out pizza. I can do that here."

"Any siblings? Other relatives?" Melissa asked.

"No," Janice replied, growing curious about Melissa's persistent questioning. "Just me. I get the impression that there was some problem or issue with conceiving me, but I never figured out what. Um – if you don't mind my asking – is there some reason you want to know all this?"

"You're new to the floor," Melissa replied casually, gathering up her tray. "And I like to get to know the people I'm working with. I don't mean to pry. I'll tell you about my family sometime – but right now, we have to get back, or Katie will have my head."

Back in the morgue, Derek had Mr. Holmes' body on the exam table. Looking over the police report, he saw that Mr. Holmes had suffered from Parkinson's, arthritis, and mild emphysema. The home caretaker had reported that he'd called to cancel her visit that day, and that he'd been seeing a doctor for depression. That must have been the doctor who'd prescribed the antidepressant that he'd used to kill himself.

Derek skimmed the report for other pertinent details. Married fifty-four years to a wife who'd died a few months earlier from complications of diabetes. No children, it seemed – next of kin was listed as some trustee. Veteran – the guy had been a hospital corpsman in the Navy, then had gone to a local college and then worked in sales most of his life. Plain vanilla guy who'd lived to a good old age and, it seemed, decided he'd had enough.

Derek tapped up the notation app on his tablet and started his walkaround. Some chafing around the wrists – he wondered if that went with the condition. Otherwise unremarkable, except for that small contusion on his upper left arm. It was the kind of thing you might get from clipping a door frame or walking into the corner of a cupboard, but it was very small and surprisingly round. Odd. Probably nothing, but he took a picture and made a note of it, if only to demonstrate that he'd done his job.

Then he removed the three swabs from his kit and put barcodes on them. He drew a vial of blood and, on a hunch, drew a second. He coded both but only tucked one into the lab bag with the swabs. He thought about requesting a full toxicology workup on the blood sample, but those were more expensive and Dr. Stout had been leaning on him to keep costs down. So he just marked the sample to be tested for – what was the drug? – amitriptyline. Dropping the lab bag in the pickup box, he rolled Mr. Holmes to the cooler to await whatever arrangements the next of kin made.

Back at his desk Derek assembled everything into his preliminary finding report. He attached his write-up, the photos he'd taken here and at the site, the codes for the lab samples, and a link to the police report. He didn't recommend a full autopsy, but flagged the case with a Numchucks code of 93 – self-expiration – with a "tentative" modifier. He recommended closing the case upon receipt of the lab results.

Certainty and Uncertainty

"Mr. Schaeffer?" came the voice on Kent's phone.

"Yes – who's calling, please?" The number was a local one which Kent didn't recognize.

"This is Officer Doug Talmadge of the Port Huron Police Department. You're listed as next of kin for John Holmes of 1729 Walker Street – is that still true?"

A chill shot through Kent and he sat back down at his desk. "Yes, that's still true. Is something wrong?"

"I'm sorry, Mr. Schaeffer, but Mr. Holmes was found dead in his home this morning..." The voice continued for a while but Kent didn't hear. His eyes blurred with sudden tears.

John Holmes, dead. Kent had dropped in on him just two days ago, and he'd seemed as fine as a man with mid-stage Parkinson's could be. He was missing Angie, of course, but otherwise his only complaint was that he often had no appetite for Luciana's wonderful cooking. What had happened?

"Sir? Sir?" the voice on the phone was saying.

"Yes, yes," Kent said, forcing himself back to the moment. "I'm sorry, it's – this is a bit of a shock."

"I understand, sir," Officer Talmadge said sympathetically. "It would be helpful if you could make it down to the morgue sometime soon for positive identification."

"Yes, of course," Kent said. "Where is the morgue?" He realized that he'd grown up in the county but didn't know where the morgue was.

"Port City Hospital, sir. First floor. Just ask at the desk and they'll direct you."

"Thank you, officer. I'm on my way," Kent said, grabbing his jacket. He dialed Linda as he walked to his car.

"Hi, sweetie," Linda answered. "What's up?"

"Are you sitting down?" Kent asked.

"Oh no – what's wrong?"

"I just got a call from the police. John Holmes is dead."

Linda's mouth opened in shock, then she covered her eyes and bowed her head. "Oh, no," she whispered through her tears. "So suddenly – what happened?"

"I don't know," Kent replied, his own tears now flowing freely. Somehow telling his wife brought the loss home. "I'm on my way to the morgue right now to ID him – I'll learn more then."

"Oh, sweetheart," Linda said. "First Angie and now John. Do you want someone to meet you there?"

"I'll be all right," Kent said. "Just – call Gil, and Ruth. They'll get the word out. I'll update you as I learn more." He pulled out of the lot and pointed his car toward the city.

The Walker Street Irregulars. That's what they'd called themselves – the collection of neighborhood children who had gathered around the home of John and Angie Holmes through the years. Though the couple had never had children of their own – always a source of quiet grief to them – they'd adopted every child had come into their home, touching countless lives with their love. There had always been good food and kind words and books to read and games to play at the Holmes's house. John had been handy in his workshop, teaching the boys how to craft wood and hardware into skateboards and hockey sticks. Angie had shown the girls how to bake and sew and comport themselves like ladies. Both of them had shown all the children how to work hard and tell the truth and respect themselves and others.

Kent counted himself among those whose lives had been saved by the simple charity of John and Angie Holmes. Most of the boys Kent had grown up with had wasted their lives – no direction or focus, stumbling from one low-paying job to the next, in and out of meaningless "relationships". Now, many were in prison and not a few were dead. Kent's life had been on a similar trajectory – roaming the streets, neglected by his mother, ignored or belittled by the string of boyfriends or stepfathers, no guidance or protection or formation from any adult until John Holmes had stepped in.

John had gently but firmly taken Kent in hand, showed him what love was, taught him the value of discipline, and demonstrated how real men behaved. It had been John who'd encouraged him to graduate from high school, to join the Marines to learn what he was capable of, and to choose a good college. In so many senses, Kent owed his life to John Holmes.

Now John was gone – abruptly, with no chance for last goodbyes. Oh, they'd all known the time was near, and had laid plans accordingly. No wise man could help his own wife through her final days, while suffering Parkinson's himself, and not be keenly aware of his own mortality – and John Holmes had certainly been a wise man. One of his favorite sayings had been, "Nobody's guaranteed a tomorrow." Yet they'd all hoped for a little more warning.

The hospital information desk directed him to the morgue, where he found a slight, dark-haired young man in a lab coat behind the desk.

"Hello, I'm Kent Schaeffer. They called and asked me to come down to ID John Holmes."

"Hello, Mr. Schaeffer," the young man replied. "I'm Derek Stevens, deputy medical examiner. This way, please." They walked back to the brushed metal doors in the wall, one of which Derek opened. He pulled out the drawer and folded back the sheet.

Tears formed in Kent's eyes as he looked on the face of the closest thing he'd ever had to a father. "That's him," he confirmed. Derek slid the drawer back in and made a notation on his tablet.

"My condolences, sir," Derek said. "I'm sorry, but could I see some ID? Just a formality."

"Sure." Kent pulled out his wallet and let the lad scan it. "So – do we have a cause of death?"

"Well," Derek said, jotting a few more notes on the tablet. "I've written up a preliminary report and sent some samples to the lab. Once the results come back and the medical examiner signs off on the report, we'll release the findings."

"That's great, but it doesn't answer what I asked," Kent said. "Do you even have a presumed cause of death? Do you plan to do an autopsy?"

"Not – not unless the lab results indicate something unusual," Derek replied cagily.

"Well, then, what's your guess?" Kent pressed. "Heart failure? A stroke? Did he fall down the steps?"

"We...ah...it seems the cause of death was a drug overdose," Derek said miserably. He hated this part of the job.

"Drug overdose?" Kent asked sharply. "Which drug?"

"An anti-depressant, sir. It was – self-administered."

"You mean – suicide?" Kent asked, his vision narrowing.

"It would seem so, sir," Derek confirmed. "The lab results should confirm it, but that was the preliminary finding."

Kent was still for a moment, then started shaking his head. "No. Not John Holmes. He'd never do that."

"I – I'm sorry, sir," Derek said a little nervously. "I was at the house; I saw the circumstances of his death. It was – there was little question." He wondered if he should call the hospital social worker. Unexpected deaths were always difficult, and suicides especially so. People expressed shock, rage, denial – all sorts of things. Derek hoped this guy wouldn't get violent.

Kent pinched the bridge of his nose and took a deep breath. It wasn't the kid's fault. He was just doing his job. "Son, you may have seen the circumstances, but you didn't know John Holmes. He would never commit suicide."

"Well, sir, he had suffered the loss of his wife, and had Parkinson's," Derek offered lamely. "Grief can do strange things to people." He didn't know why he was talking – this was definitely a job for the social worker or a grief counselor.

Kent took another deep breath and prayed for patience. "I know all about his wife's death and his numerous ailments. But I'm telling you that John *would not* kill himself. Not only was it against his faith, it was completely against his character. Never in a thousand years would John Holmes quit his duty station on his own authority."

Derek said nothing, a bit taken aback by Kent's statement.

"Look – you said there was an anti-depressant," Kent said. "John wasn't taking anti-depressants."

"I'm sorry, sir," Derek explained. "The bottle was right there."

"Which doctor?"

"Ah – those details are in the medical report, which has not yet been approved," Derek explained.

"When will it be approved?" Kent asked.

"I'm not sure, sir. That's up to the medical examiner. Tomorrow at the earliest, more likely the day after that."

"All right – Derek, wasn't it? I need to look at that report the minute it becomes available," Kent said. "Here's my card. I'm the named next of kin, the trustee of the Holmes family trust, and the executor of the estate. That should be all the authorization anyone needs. If someone wants paperwork, I can provide it. Will you call me immediately when the medical report is approved?"

"Yes, sir," Derek replied, taking the card.

"I'll certainly be back in touch when we get the funeral arrangements squared away. Is there a problem with him staying here for a day or two while I take care of that?

"None at all," Derek assured him.

"Thank you. Sorry if I seemed a little sharp, but something's not right here. Something's definitely not right," Kent said.

"No worries, sir."

"Then I'll await your call. Thank you," Kent said, heading for his car.

Once Kent had left, Derek stood thinking for a long time. He'd seen a lot of reactions to death, including several suicides, but he'd never seen anything like the unshakeable certainty that Kent had displayed. It wasn't even like he'd been upset about the death, but he'd rejected out of hand the idea that Mr. Holmes would – how had he put it? – quit his duty station. Derek had never heard anyone talk about death like that.

Derek tried to shrug it off and get back to his paperwork, but Kent's final words kept nagging him. 'Something's not right here.' Derek realized that a similar feeling had been haunting him since he'd first walked into that house. The whole situation seemed too tidy, too canned. On a hunch, he keyed in a search for amitriptyline and suicide.

Out in the parking lot, Kent sat in his car and tried to gather his thoughts. His grief at John's death was being held at bay by his shock at what he'd learned, as well as his distress at the implications. Finally he pulled out his phone and punched up Gil.

"Kent," Gil answered, his voice thick with grief. "Linda told us. How terrible!"

"Yeah. Gil, are you alone?" Kent asked.

"I can be – give me a minute," Gil said. "I am now – what's up?"

"Gil, what I've got to tell you can go no further. We have some real problems here. They're trying to claim that John committed suicide."

"What?" Gil barked. "How?"

"Overdose. Anti-depressant," Kent said.

"But John would *never*," Gil began, but Kent cut him short.

"I know that, but the preliminary report has already gone to the medical examiner with a finding of presumed suicide. My guess is that if that becomes the official determination, the police aren't going to do a thing no matter what we ask. I'm going to need every tool I can find to get behind the official reports and learn what is actually going on. Is Fitz available?"

"I'm sure he can be," Gil answered.

"Give him a call, will you? Also – do we know any good canon lawyers?"

"I'm sure we can hunt one down," Gil assured him.

"That just leaves the scariest question of all," Kent said.

"What's that?"

"Think about it," Kent urged. "John died under circumstances that looked so much like suicide that nobody is questioning them. But we know that John would never suicide, which means – "

"Somebody killed him," Gil finished.

"Precisely," Kent affirmed. "Which leads to the question: who would kill John Holmes, and why?"

"More to the point, who would kill John Holmes and make it look like a suicide?" Gil asked.

Both men were silent for a while before Gil spoke again in an ominous whisper. "Are you wondering what I'm wondering?"

"Probably," Kent answered.

"I hope we're wrong."

"So do I," Kent said. "Because if we're right, it would be a disturbing development."

"A very disturbing development, indeed," Gil confirmed.

Irregularities

When Derek showed up for work the next morning, the lab results were already in his inbox. He'd sent in several samples, but he skimmed through the results looking for those pertaining to the Holmes case.

There was one – the blood analysis. Positive for amitriptyline, no surprise there. DNA analysis – he lined up the results side by side. Sample one, patient's cheek swab. Sample four, blood. Match there, no surprise. Sample three, the dummy sample of Derek's own cheek tissue: no match. Again, no surprise. Sample two:

No match.

What?

Sample two was from the rim of the glass of water Holmes had used to wash down the pills. But, if the lab results were right, the DNA from the lip prints on the glass didn't match the DNA of the patient's blood.

Stranger and stranger.

Derek pulled out his phone and brought up the images of the sample bags he'd taken. It was a trick he'd learned from a forensic specialist: take a good image of every sample the minute you bagged it. That way you not only had an image in case any questions arose, but a date/time stamp of exactly when you'd done it.

There was sample one in the bag on the floor – you could just see part of the patient's shoulder in the corner of the shot. Sample two was on the table next to the glass it was taken from. Sample three was on the floor next to his own foot. Of course, he had no image of the draw vial.

Derek looked from the images on his phone to the lab results. The cheek swab and the swab from the glass should match, but they didn't. He picked up the desk phone.

"County medical examiner, Shaundra speaking."

"Hi, Shaundra, this is Derek. Is Dr. Stout in yet?"

"Not yet, Derek. Should I have him call you?"

"No, I'm coming over," Derek said. "Has he any appointments?"

"A meeting with an HHS rep at 9:30."

"Can you squeeze me in real quick before then? I just need five minutes," Derek asked.

"Sure," Shaundra replied. "I'll let him know you want to see him."

Technically this wasn't true. Derek never truly wanted to see his boss, who was stuffy, supercilious, and couldn't be bothered with the duties of his own office. Dr. Stout loved reporting to the county commissioners and playing golf with local legislators and getting interviewed by the media, but he hardly ever darkened the doors of the morgue. This was fine by Derek – the less he saw of Dr. Stout, the better. The mile that separated Derek's desk from Stout's office was just about the right distance.

But in this case, Derek felt obligated to communicate his concerns directly to his superior, irksome though it might be. He printed out some hard copies, taking a moment to compose his thoughts and jot down what he wanted to say. Then he grabbed his jacket and headed out.

Dr. Stout's office was on the second floor of the county building, just a couple doors down from the county administrator. Shaundra greeted him with her usual cheery smile.

"How's my boy today?" she asked.

"Hey, Shaundra!" Derek replied. Regardless of what he thought of his boss, Derek always appreciated how Shaundra brought a ray of light into his life.

"He's in now," Shaundra nodded. "He allowed as how he could grant you five minutes."

"Ooh," Derek grinned. "I'd better be fast. Thanks!"

"That's another coffee you owe me!" Shaundra taunted.

Dr. Stout was seated behind his desk, reviewing something on his tablet. He looked up briefly when Derek entered.

"Ah, Derek," he said, gesturing toward one of the chairs facing the desk. He returned his attention to the tablet while Derek settled in to wait. After much more than five minutes, Dr. Stout looked up and spoke.

"So, what can I do for you?"

"Well, sir, it's about a case I forwarded to you yesterday. The Holmes case, which I marked a presumed 93."

"Yes, I've just been reviewing it," Dr. Stout said, gesturing at the tablet.

"Ah," Derek said. "Well, then, I wanted to go over a few details with you before you finalized the findings."

"Go over?" Dr. Stout asked. "What's to go over? It looks cut and dried."

"I thought so as well," Derek admitted. "But there are a few irregularities about the case – "

"Irregularities?" Dr. Stout interrupted icily. "What irregularities?"

"Well, sir," Derek continued, feeling less confident than he had back at the office and despising himself for it, "there were a couple of things about the physical exam. There was some chafing about the wrists, and a small contusion on the upper left arm."

"You are aware that this case suffered from Parkinson's disease?" Dr. Stout asked.

"Yes, sir," Derek answered.

"And you are aware that a symptom of mid-stage Parkinson's is postural instability?"

"Yes, sir," Derek said stonily.

"And you are aware that people suffering postural instability are prone to staggering and falling, causing them to strike objects, leaving contusions?"

"Yes, sir," Derek said through clenched teeth. "But this contusion was unusual enough that I didn't think it likely to have been caused by impact trauma."

"Unusual? In what way?" asked Dr. Stout.

"It was small and regular – a circle about five millimeters in diameter – on his lower deltoid. There was no indication of other bruising in the area. It would take a very unusual fall to leave such a contusion – and nothing else – in the center of the upper arm."

"In your opinion," Dr. Stout added.

"In my opinion," Derek affirmed.

"I see. I presume the information about these physical markings is in your preliminary?"

"Yes," Derek confirmed. "And there are pictures – "

"You mentioned," Dr. Stout interrupted, "other factors."

"Well, there's the blood work," Derek said, laying a hard copy on the desk. "It confirms lethal levels of amitriptyline, but that was the only toxin I tested for."

Dr. Stout said nothing, taking the paper and glancing at it before laying it aside.

"But here is the strange thing," Derek said, laying the printout of the DNA matching tests on the desk. "Samples one and four match. But sample two there doesn't match. That was taken from the rim of the glass Mr. Holmes supposedly used to take the pills, so I swabbed it as a matter of course. But the DNA on the glass doesn't match that of the patient."

"I see that sample three doesn't match, either," Dr. Stout observed.

"Ah, well, I wouldn't have expected that to match," Derek replied.

"Why not?"

"Well," Derek said a little sheepishly. "That sample was a known irregular, sent in for test verification. Those were my cells."

"Your cells? Why would you submit your own cells to the lab for testing?"

"It was something one of my college profs recommended," Derek replied. "he was explaining how labs sometimes zip through a set of samples by patterning the first and then marking the remainder as matches. He suggested occasionally throwing in a known irregular just to keep them honest."

"I see," said Dr. Stout stiffly. "Have you had any reason to suspect any of the labs we use of being dishonest?"

"Well, no," Derek admitted, "but it's just a minor check."

"I see," Dr. Stout continued. "And have you ever sought permission to perform these self-initiated lab integrity verification tests?"

"No, sir," Derek replied.

"I see," Dr. Stout said. A chill silence filled the room for a minute before he spoke again. "With our county's current financial condition, and the county administrator asking me to pare our budget to the bone, I discover that my assistant has been ordering frivolous and unnecessary tests."

Derek clenched his teeth and looked at the floor. This was ridiculous. Random check tests like this were routine in the industry, and the cost of a test was trivial. "I haven't done it all that often," he finally said.

"It is the fact that you have done it at all, upon your own authorization, that is at issue," Dr. Stout pronounced.

"All right, I won't do it again," Derek said.

"I hope not," Dr. Stout said. "Now, is there anything else you wished to bring to my attention?"

Derek paused. They hadn't actually attended to the real issue, which was the second sample not matching. But he knew that if he tried to return to that topic, it would get Stout carping about the unauthorized sampling again. He moved on to his next point.

"This isn't so much a question of a test result as an observation of the site," Derek explained. "Specifically, what wasn't there."

"What wasn't there?" Dr. Stout asked, with raised eyebrows.

"Yes. The patient had been a hospital corpsman in the Navy years before. He would have known the effect that an overdose of amitriptyline would have had – intense nausea and vomiting. Even sites that instruct people how to use amitriptyline to commit suicide warn of this, and recommend taking an anti-emetic before using it." Derek paused, but Dr. Stout waved for him to continue. "There's no evidence that Mr. Holmes had any anti-emetic nearby. He would have known what would happen if he'd dosed himself and then vomited most of the drug back up."

The room was silent for a long while before Dr. Stout spoke. "I see. So now you consider yourself qualified to speculate about the psychology and thought processes of a suicide?"

"All I'm trying to say," Derek replied, exerting all his control, "is that this man would have known his drugs. Had he wanted to poison himself, he would have at least done it properly. He would have taken precautions against vomiting.

He probably would have taken a cocktail of drugs instead of just amitriptyline by itself.

"In your opinion," Dr. Stout repeated.

"In my opinion," Derek said.   The room once again fell silent.

"Tell me," Dr. Stout said at last. "What do you recommend we do?"

"Well, all I've got are some irregularities," Derek began. "We don't know much – "

"Clearly," Dr. Stout interrupted. Derek bit back a response and continued.

"I recommend we do a full toxicology workup on a blood sample. I also think we should do a full autopsy and GI content analysis."

"I see," Dr. Stout said, steepling his fingers and looking over them at Derek.   "If I understand you correctly, you are suggesting, based on these perceived irregularities, that I should spend some of our office's scarce budget – which I have even less of, because my assistant has been ordering unauthorized lab work – to perform expensive procedures that will probably tell us nothing that we don't already know."

Derek stared at his hands, biting back what he desperately wanted to say. "Yes, sir," was what he finally managed through clenched teeth.

There was a moment's silence before Dr. Stout responded. "Very well. I will take your opinions into consideration when drawing up my final notes. Did you have anything else you wished to bring to my attention?"

"No," Derek replied.

"Very well, then," Dr. Stout said dismissively, and Derek bolted from the office, seething so badly that he didn't even acknowledge Shaundra's cheery farewell. He cursed under his breath all the way back to the morgue. This kind of petty humiliation was one reason he so hated dealing with his boss. He resolved to start searching sites for job postings that very evening – seriously this time, not just idly browsing for what was out there.

Back at his desk, Derek saw that Dr. Stout had wasted no time – the death certificate was complete, marked 'Suicide', and the UDR was coded a 93 with no modifier. He'd also removed most of the pictures of the scene, leaving only the image of the body sprawled on the floor and the pill bottle on the table. Derek's notes had been mostly removed. There was no mention of the contusion or pretty much anything else Derek had written. Bastard! Not only had he dismissed Derek's concerns, he'd ignored his legitimate observations.

Derek was still glaring at the workstation, fuming, when the door opened and Kent Schaeffer walked in. Derek's heart sank – Kent wasn't going to like Dr. Stout's determination.

"Morning, Derek," Kent greeted him.

"Morning," Derek said. Kent was the executor, and so was going to need some copies of the death certificate. He unlocked the drawer which held the blank certificates and counted out six sheets.

"That didn't sound very cheerful," Kent observed.

"Yeah, well, it's been a trying day," Derek replied, dropping the blanks into the printer and sending six copies of the death certificate to print.

"And it's only begun – this doesn't bode well," Kent replied cautiously.

"No, it doesn't," Derek said. "And neither does this." He took the top certificate, embossed it, and handed it to Kent. "Notice the manner of death down there – Box 41."

Kent examined the certificate gravely. "So, this was the medical examiner's final determination? Suicide?"

"Well – yes, as it turned out," Derek said somberly as he sealed the other five copies of the death cert. "That's part of what's made my day so hard so early."

"How so?" Kent asked.

"Here," Derek said, handing the copies to Kent. "If you think you'll need more than six of these, let me know and I'll print them up. I went over this morning to try to convince Dr. Stout to hold off on the determination and do a bit more investigating. He was...not receptive to the idea."

"Really?" Kent asked, eying Derek sharply. "Why did you make that suggestion?"

"Well," Derek hesitated. He was on thin ice here – as deputy ME, his job was to simply hand people the death certs and explain the findings.   He was not supposed to discuss procedures, speculations, or any internal operations.   But right now he wasn't feeling much loyalty to Dr. Stout and his precious protocols.   Besides, the truth mattered – certainly to Kent, but to him as well.   He reached over and sent the UDR to the printer.

"Okay, here's the death cert, and here's the UDR," Derek began.

"Excuse me – 'UDR'?" Kent interrupted.

"Unattended Death Report," Derek explained.   "When someone dies with nobody observing, we have to file one of these.   Relatively new thing, within the last ten years, primarily to satisfy Fed requirements.   It provides a place to put a lot of stuff that isn't on the death cert, most notably the Numchucks code..."

"Numchucks?" Kent asked.

"Sorry – jargon alert.   National Unified Medical Coding System – NUMCS for short.   Another federal innovation rolled out some years back.   A consolidation of several industry coding schemes like ICD, CPT, and DSM into one standard base," Derek explained.

"You're killing me, Smalls," Kent said.   "What does this have to do with this report?"

"The critical thing is this code here," Derek tapped the printout.   "This is the resolution code.   It identifies how the patient departed your care.   The 90 range is what we call the exit codes.   They're terminal codes, indicating that you don't ever expect the patient back, usually because he's dead.   A 93 indicates suicide, so that matches the death cert.   But here's the weird thing: normally UDRs have attached to them all the evidence about the death circumstances – photos, site notes, exam observations, the whole smash.   But in this case, Dr. Stout stripped off all but two of the photos and many of my site and exam notes."

"Why would he do that?" Kent asked.

"Spite, probably," Derek said.   "I'd just been over suggesting he look more closely at the case because of some irregularities, and when he rejected the suggestion he also removed any evidence of the irregularities."

"What kind of irregularities?" Kent asked.

Derek didn't even hesitate. To hell with Dr. Stout and his regulations. He grabbed his phone from the desk.

"The first thing was the drug itself – amitriptyline. The more I thought about it, the odder it was. It was the only drug at the site, and the blood test confirmed lethal levels. But if you take that much at once, your body senses 'poison' and throws it right back up. He would have known this. Even the suicide groups recommend taking an anti-emetic first, but there was none in evidence.

"The other oddity was the markings on the body," Derek added, starting to pull up the photos on the phone.

"What markings?" Kent asked.

"Very small ones, almost too minor to notice, but strange. One was a small, circular contusion on his upper arm. See here?" Derek pointed to the photo. "No explanation for that. To my thinking, an impact contusion would have been larger and less regular. And then there's the chafing about the wrists," Derek flicked to the next photo.

"Chafing?" Kent asked, squinting at the screen.

"Yes. See this pink just here? The other wrist matches it. The sort of thing that tight socks or ill-fitting shoes might do – but wrists?

"But none of those were the biggest anomaly. The strangest thing was the DNA matching issue."

"Matching issue?" Kent asked, intensely interested now.

"The samples didn't match," Derek explained. "At least, all of them didn't. The blood sample and a cheek swab I took matched. A verification sample I took didn't match, but I didn't expect it to. But the swab I took of the drinking glass didn't match, either. It should have matched the blood and cheek swab, but it didn't."

"Really?" Kent asked. "Do you have a picture of this drinking glass?"

"Yes – just flick back a few shots," Derek said. "There it is – and the next one is my shot with the swab sample in the bag."

"And you pointed this out to the medical examiner?" Kent asked.

"Yes. I suggested more extensive testing, including a full tox workup and a GI tract exam. The blood sample we sent in confirmed the amitrip, but we didn't check for anything else."

"Was that sample the only one you drew?" Kent asked.

"No – I took another. That's sitting over there in the fridge. But he didn't take my suggestion, citing budget constraints."

"Wait a minute," Kent said, pointing at a picture on the phone screen. "What's this?"

Derek peered at the screen. "Oh, that. That's a picture that was found at the scene. I don't know who that is…"

"I know who he is," Kent interrupted. "That's Pope St. John Paul the Great. Why is the glass all shattered?"

"The policeman at the site thought he fell over on it when he toppled out of the chair," Derek explained.

"Fell on it? John?"

"Yes, it was under his body where it was sprawled on the floor," Derek said.

"Under his body?" Kent mused. "What was the picture doing on the floor?"

"The policeman speculated that it wasn't – at least until he fell on it. He thought it was probably in his lap. Come to think of it, that was another anomaly about the scene."

"How so?"

"The cop said suicides will sometimes hold something of sentimental value while they – go. There was a framed picture of him and his wife on the mantel…"

Kent looked up with sharp intensity. "You mean that there was a photo of him and Angie standing right there, but he died holding a photo of John Paul?"

"It seems that way," Derek said.

"Wow. Wow," Kent muttered, agitated and pacing. "That's important. That's very important."

"Really?" Derek asked. "Why would that be?"

Kent stopped in mid-stride and eyed Derek critically, as if evaluating him. He seemed to come to a conclusion, and walked over to Derek.

"Do you know who John Paul was?" Kent asked, tapping the close-up of the picture on Derek's phone.

"Not really," Derek admitted.

"He was a Catholic pope and a very holy man. He died about thirty years ago – of complications of Parkinson's Disease."

"Oh – well, that makes more sense," Derek admitted.

"But he also wrote an encyclical – kind of like a long essay, but with authority – called *The Gospel of Life*. In that, he affirmed the beauty of the gift of life – and firmly restated the Church's longstanding condemnation of suicide.

"John and Angie Holmes were keen admirers of Pope St. John Paul the Great, so much so that they kept a picture of him on their mantel. They were both faithful children of the Church and knew her teachings well."

"Okay," Derek said slowly, still not seeing a connection.

"Think about it," Kent urged. "If you were taking your own life, in contradiction of your entire moral framework, would you want to do it holding a memento of a man whom you not only deeply admired, but who firmly condemned what you were doing?"

"I – I guess not," Derek admitted.

"That's why it's so important," Kent explained. "Can I get copies of these photos? And this – UDF?"

"UDR," Derek corrected. "Sure, let me print you up some."

"Any possibility I could get a copy of the police report?" Kent asked.

"Umm," Derek paused. That was trickier. "It used to be easier, particularly since you're the executor. But lately they've tightened up, particularly on suicides. These days you almost always have to secure a lawyer, and petition the court, and so on."

"Oh," said Kent, looking a little distraught.

"However," Derek said, feeling more rebellious than ever. "I can pull up a copy right here," he tapped through the UDR to the police report. "If I were to print it out for my reference, like this, and lay it right here, and turn away, I don't suppose I'd notice if it disappeared."

"You're a big help, Derek," came Kent's voice from behind him as he made the report disappear. "You have no idea of how much this means. One last thing, though."

"What's that?"

"That second blood sample you drew – will you be using it?" Kent asked.

"Well, since nobody but me knows I have it, nobody will notice it missing, will they?" Derek asked, fetching the sample and handing it to Kent.

"Thank you, Derek," Kent said. "Thank you very much. You may have...thank you. I've called the funeral home and they should be coming by to pick up John's body later today. Do I need to sign anything?"

"No, it's routine from here," Derek replied.

"All right, then. Thank you again for this information, and your work, and your concern," Kent said earnestly, shaking Derek's hand. "I'll get back in touch with you." He was already pulling his phone from his pocket as he backed out the door.

Derek sat down at his desk and stared at his workstation screen, feeling battered and numb. He could hardly believe this was happening. A chill started growing inside him. If John Holmes hadn't committed suicide, and if it hadn't been an accident or natural death, that left only one alternative.

Derek had handled murders before. Not many, but a few street killings and a couple of domestic violence deaths. It was never easy, but at least everyone knew what they were dealing with. But this – this looked like it was going to be ignored, swept under the rug. A surge of indignation rose within Derek. This wasn't right! This was – unjust, that's what it was! Someone had probably committed murder, then masked it by making it look like a suicide, and the mask was working! Nobody was attending to this man's death because it was easier just to write it off as what it appeared to be. Somebody was going to – literally – get away with murder.

But what could he do? He laid his head on the desk, feeling small and impotent. He'd done his best this morning with Dr. Stout, and had gotten scorned and humiliated for his pains. The death certificate was the medical examiner's final ruling. Unless there was some clerical oversight or substantial evidence came to light, it was almost impossible to overturn an ME's decision. He could take his evidence to the police or the prosecutor, but they'd defer to Dr. Stout, and he'd lose his job in the process.

Suddenly, Derek felt very alone and very frightened. This wasn't like a movie or novel. A man was over there in a drawer because some other man had decided to put him there. That was different than an outburst of rage in a bar fight. The thought of such deliberate malice scared him to the core. It made no sense – why would someone do that? And to a sick, harmless old man? He couldn't comprehend it.

Derek sat still for some time before proceeding with his duties in a mindless, mechanical way. All day long he wrestled to find some mental anchor point, some scrap of meaning that would help him come to grips with what had happened. It was useless. He felt like he was trying to climb uphill during a mudslide, or like he was a scrap of litter being blown hither and thither across a parking lot. He had no appetite for lunch and no desire to chat with anyone, so he skipped the cafeteria, remaining alone in the morgue with his workstation and his lab results and the corpse of Mr. Holmes. Toward the end of the day the funeral home guys showed up to take even him away.

When Derek clocked out, he headed north to hit a drive-through before turning back south to his apartment. He gobbled his burger as he drove, simply to fill the emptiness in his middle rather than out of any enjoyment of eating. He entered his darkening apartment under the cloud of depression that had shrouded him all day. He pitched his keys onto the counter and collapsed into a chair, dreading the long, empty evening that stretched before him. He had no money to go to a bar or a restaurant, and nobody to go with. He had no enthusiasm for the self-improvement book he was gutting through. He flicked through a few show sites, but couldn't take the flash and the noise.

Maybe he could work through a few more levels of his current video game. That would be a distraction that wasn't too taxing. Of course, part of him knew why he wanted to play the game, and which level he would load. He loathed himself for it, but tonight he had no resistance.

He folded up the card table to clear his tiny dining room. The sensor grids were already fastened to the walls. He tapped up the game and then dropped his tablet into the cradle. Slipping on the goggles, he saw the initial menu hanging before his eyes.

He donned the sensor gloves and other gear then reached into the field of vision. His hand appeared in the display, allowing him to flick up and down through the list of saved levels until he found the one he wanted.

The game, Rogue Hunt V, had much more sophistication than his modest equipment supported. He could play, but if he had the more advanced tactile feedback gloves, he'd be able to feel more of the game. Their nanotechnology enabled you to feel hot and cold, or rough and smooth, and some models were so sensitive they said you could feel the breeze. But such toys were beyond his meager budget, so he had to make do with standard sensor gloves.

He stepped into the sensor field and selected the saved level he'd been looking for. The goggles flickered, and suddenly he was standing on a ridge road that led down into a valley. He'd become a burly, grizzled warrior with a saber at his side, a dagger in his belt, and a bow and quiver at his back. Off to his right stood a grove of trees. He knew what lay in there – a band of thieves around their campfire. If he wished, he could go thrash them and plunder their camp. Or he could venture into the thicket down the ridge to the left. It was infested with pixies who might steal some of his gear, but if he could capture one, it might come in handy later.

But neither of these options were what he had come for. What he wanted lay down in the village, where there was an inn. He swift-ran down the road and was at the inn doorway shortly. He went in and paid the innkeeper for a mug and a meal, which he "ate", boosting his strength and stamina. He looked around the room and saw a shadowed figure in a corner. He knew he could approach the figure, strike up a conversation, and end up with a useful traveling companion – but that wasn't what he was interested in just now.

There! In the back of the room, just passing through a doorway: the slightest glimpse of a slender figure, a quick glance over a disappearing shoulder. He got up and went through the door into a darkened hallway. There was the sound of a door closing ahead of him, but the hall was lined with several doors. He knew which one he wanted: the third door on the left. It was locked, of course. You could go to the vendor's site and pay for a key that would fit the lock, but Derek was cannier than that. He'd researched the hacks for the game, and knew that if you knocked on the door with just the right pattern, a voice from within would inform you that the key was in the usual place. Then you could reach into a little alcove to the right of the door and find a key.

This Derek did, and when he'd entered and locked the door behind him, he turned to see the innkeeper's daughter, half undressed. Sometimes she was a blonde and sometimes a redhead; tonight, she was a long-locked brunette. She gazed at him with a sultry smile.

"I'm glad you came," she purred, walking around the bed as she untied the neck of her blouse. She stood before him, looking up with her perfect eyes in that impossibly beautiful face. He slipped the blouse from her shoulders and let it fall around her feet. Her skin glowed in the candlelight, and she moaned as he caressed her shoulders, her arms, her breasts –

He was definitely going to have to upgrade his gloves and other gear.

Investigation

Kent fairly ran from the morgue, keying his phone as he went. Disturbing as it was to get more evidence confirming his hypothesis about what had happened to John Holmes, it also simplified some things. He conferred briefly with Gil, then called the parish to set up an appointment with Fr. Alex, then called the funeral home to arrange for them to pick up John's body. It was looking increasingly certain that the funeral could proceed according to schedule, but a bit more evidence was needed to confirm matters – and for other purposes.

Like Derek, Kent was upset that John Holmes' death was being written off as a suicide instead of being investigated as the murder it certainly was. But Kent wasn't nearly as distraught as Derek that John's killer would probably never be brought to justice. Not only was Kent older and thus more attuned to how the world actually worked, he also knew that there was a bigger picture to consider. John's death was a tragedy and an injustice, but they needed to concentrate their efforts where it would do the most good, and John would be the first person to tell them that. It was the others that they should focus on – and if Kent's suspicions were correct, there might be many others.

Kent sat in his car, looking over the UDR and the police report. He made a few notes as he mentally arranged the sequence of things he'd have to do. The first was a call to Dr. Vaidya.

"Thumb Area Neurology Associates, Janet speaking," came the familiar voice.

"Hi, Janet, this is Kent Schaeffer." He'd had many opportunities to talk with Janet over the past year or so as John's condition had worsened.

"Hey, Kent," Janet replied. "How's John doing?"

"Um – he's dead," Kent explained. "Found yesterday in his home."

"Oh, no," Janet whispered. "What – what happened?"

"Well, there's some question about that, at least in my mind," Kent replied. "That's why I'd like to talk to Dr. Vaidya, if I can. Just briefly, no more than five minutes."

"He's not here at the moment, but he's due in shortly," Janet said. "Should I give you a call when he arrives?"

"Please," Kent replied. "And as trustee, I'll want any outstanding claims you have for John, so the trust can settle them."

"I'll have them ready," Janet said.

Kent drove the few blocks to the medical office building where Dr. Vaidya practiced. He stayed in his car, thinking and jotting notes, until Janet rang letting him know the doctor had arrived. He grabbed his folder and headed in. She was waiting by the door leading to the exam area and gave him a sympathetic hug. "Kent, I'm so sorry. None of us expected this. The doctor's in his office – you can go right in."

Dr. Vaidya was seated behind his desk, and greeted Kent with grave sympathy. "I am so sorry for your loss, Mr. Schaeffer. All my staff is mourning. Please, take a seat."

Kent smiled inwardly. John had been like that, and Angie in her time: even beset by severe illness, they made even the medical staff feel loved and appreciated. "Thank you, doctor."

"If – I may ask," Dr. Vaidya began haltingly. "Is the cause of death yet known? Death can always come unexpectedly, but I was not aware of any conditions he had that would strike so quickly."

"That's part of what I'm here about, Dr. Vaidya," Kent answered. "His death is being attributed to an overdose of a prescription he was taking."

"A prescription?" Dr. Vaidya scowled.

"Yes," Kent confirmed. "One that was prescribed by a Dr. Daniels." He handed over a scrap of paper on which he'd written a few details. Dr. Vaidya scanned the paper with unreadable eyes, but Kent thought he saw the slightest hint of something – alarm? fear? – flicker across the doctor's face.

"As his primary care physician, you would have made that referral, would you not?" Kent asked.

"Um – yes, yes, of course," Dr. Vaidya stammered, handing back the paper as if it was a live snake.

"Do you remember why you referred John to Dr. Daniels?" Kent asked.

"Ah – yes, Dr. Daniels," Dr. Vaidya fumbled. "The details escape me – I should consult the records – "

This was hardly convincing. Dr. Vaidya could recall minutia of complex treatment plans off the top of his head. "What little I could find on Dr. Daniels lists his specialty as geriatric psychiatry," Kent prodded. "Does that ring a bell?"

"Yes, yes," Dr. Vaidya said, suddenly intensely interested in the papers on his desk. "The burdens of his illness, the loss of his wife – beyond my ability to help, you understand. Now, if you'll excuse me – a very busy schedule – "

"Of course, doctor," Kent said, standing. "Thank you for seeing me on such short notice, and for the superb care you provided John during the final months of his life."

"Certainly, certainly," Dr. Vaidya said, rising and extending his hand, though without quite looking Kent in the eye. "An honor. Again, my condolences on – for your loss."

Out in the hall, Janet still looked subdued. She handed Kent a folder full of printouts. "Here's the last six weeks of activity. Most of these claims are still in process. If you'd like, I can send you a balance outstanding summary once everything clears."

"That'd be great," Kent said. He fished in his pocket and pulled out the blood sample Derek had given him. "Favor to ask – could you slip this into your next lab run? I need a full toxicology workup. Let me know the cost and I'll pay you in cash."

"Okay," Janet replied, raising her eyebrows a little. "Do we have a patient name?"

"John," Kent said. "John Doe."

Janet looked at him for a moment, then nodded and slipped the sample into her pocket.

Back in the car, Kent pondered the encounter with Dr. Vaidya. He could understand him being surprised, but – frightened? What might elicit that? He flipped through the printouts of the medical claims. Sure enough, no reference to any referrals, to Dr. Daniels or anyone else.

Time to deal with this directly. He dialed the number that was listed for Dr. Daniels' office and, unsurprisingly, got voice mail. He left a message about wanting to see the doctor. Only after he'd hung up did he realize that the message hadn't given office hours or any other details common for medical practices. Glancing at the address, he saw that it was only a mile or so away. Worth a drive.

The office was in a small, run-down office complex on 10th Avenue overlooking the Black River, just by the drawbridge. It had one of those signs on the door that looked like a clock, telling the visitor that the occupants were gone until one o'clock. Kent glanced at his phone and thought it rather early for lunch. Peering through the glass door, he saw a small, dingy waiting room devoid of any decorations or even magazines on the racks. Hmm. Looked just like the office of a geriatric psychiatrist. Well, he had some errands to run.

When Kent returned shortly after 1:00, the office was open but empty except for a receptionist whose nametag said "Jennifer".

"May I help you?" Jennifer asked.

"Yes, my name is Kent Schaeffer, and I'm trustee and executor of the estate of the late John Holmes," Kent replied handing her a copy of the death certificate and the trust paperwork. "I'm here to get copies of any unpaid claims for Mr. Holmes' care. We'd like to settle up any copays or deductibles as quickly as possible."

"Of course," Jennifer said with a smile. She turned to her workstation and tapped some keys. "Ah, yes, Mr. Holmes. Referred by Dr. Vaidya. Three visits over the past two weeks. Prescription for an anti-depressant." She keyed some printouts.

"Yes," Kent confirmed.

"I'm terribly sorry for your loss," Jennifer said sympathetically. "I remember Mr. Holmes. His caregiver would drive him. He was a pleasant gentleman. Unfortunately, this is something we see far too often."

"I imagine you do," Kent said, taking the printouts and his documents. "Thank you."

Back in the car, Kent was interested to see that Jennifer hadn't given him copies of claims, but printouts of appointment confirmations. Everything looked kosher, but –

Time to contact Brady.

Few people contacted Brady at all, and hardly anyone contacted him directly, at least when he was at work. Brady worked in information technology support at the Regional Medical Administration office out in the township. The RMA had been one of the big cost saving and efficiency boosting initiatives encouraged by the federal government. Health care providers had to use it if they expected to get paid. The benefits were many-fold: no longer did small practices have to bear the expense and trouble of maintaining their own computer systems. All they had to do was access their applications over the network. The RMA managed everything for them in a secure, centralized, virtualized environment.

Brady worked in that environment, and knew it like nobody else, even the director. He knew the hardware and the network devices and the hypervisors and the instances and the packages that ran within them. He was comfortable with the complexity, moving with ease among the disparate components of the center. When a medical office, or a department of one of the area hospitals, experienced problems, it usually took Brady no more than fifteen minutes to isolate and fix them. Brady had often been told that someone of his intelligence and skill could be making a lot more money elsewhere, but that didn't matter to him. He was where he was supposed to be, and was doing what he was supposed to do – which occasionally involved a bit more than his official duties.

As it proved early that afternoon, when his phone chimed with a text message from one of his regular buddies. This "buddy" was not a real person, but an e-mail account on a publicly available e-mail service. The account was set up to send him innocuous messages at random intervals through the day. These were a cover to establish a harmless looking pattern of banter. Very few of the messages included the key phrases that indicated there was a message awaiting that held real content.

Brady checked his phone casually. A Chesterton quote. Urgent but not critical. He paused the task he was working on and pulled out his tablet – the one that was never connected to the RMA's network. Using the phone system's data connection, he connected to the secure website to pick up the e-mail that awaited him.

Hmm. It was from Gil – or, rather, from Kent through Gil. It had all the data he needed: NPINs, dates, patient demographics – though he hardly needed the latter. This had to be about John. News of his sudden death had spread like wildfire among the ranches. Brady hadn't known John personally, but many had, and they were stunned, not least by the rumors that kept circulating. That had to be what Kent was chasing down.

Well, Brady could certainly help there. He propped the tablet by his workstation and started keying in commands. It was the work of a minute to find the instances which were hosting the two providers. Since he was system administrator for the entire site, logging onto them was no trouble. Some discreet querying quickly fetched the data he needed, and he was logged out within five minutes, having touched nothing that would leave an audit trail. Quickly transferring the results of his queries to his tablet, he took a walk outside, bringing both his phone and his tablet. Gil had said it was all right to call Kent directly, so Brady did.

"Hey, Brady," Kent answered.

"Hey, Kent," Brady said. "Got your results here. Yes, the provider database shows three appointments for John with Dr. Daniels, on the dates specified, as well as a prescription sent to a local pharmacy. But there's an odd thing about all those records."

"What's that?" Kent asked.

"They were all created today, within three minutes of each other, right around 11:15. Same user for all three."

"Hmm," Kent said. "And the other record?"

"Good guess there," Brady confirmed. "There is a record in Vaidya's data indicating a referral to Daniels on the 23rd of last month – but that record didn't exist before about 10:43 this morning."

"Doesn't surprise me," Kent said.

"Another odd thing about the Daniels data," Brady added. "There's no billing associated with any of it. Not the appointments, not the prescription, nothing."

"Well, that'd prove it if nothing else did," Kent said. "Could you write up a brief summary of all this and e-mail it? I'll add it to the pile of stuff I'm presenting to Father and the canon lawyer tomorrow."

"You got it," Brady replied.

"Thanks, Brady," Kent said, and rung off. He tapped his phone against the steering wheel as he pondered this new data. It didn't tell him anything he hadn't strongly suspected, but it implied some very disturbing things about the resources and sophistication of whatever party had killed John. The first layer of deception, the scene itself, bespoke organization and determination that was troubling enough. This second level of cover-up was beyond anything they'd expected.

As Kent sat there, he saw "Jennifer" come up the steps, get into a car, and drive away. No surprise there. He guessed that if he were to go back down, he'd see that clock sign on the door again. Very disturbing. He wondered if there was a real Dr. Daniels, and decided there probably was, though it was doubtful he practiced geriatric psychiatry and certain that he didn't inhabit that dingy little office.

Kent had only one more call to make, and one contact beyond that, if the call went well. He decided to drive out to John's house before making it. It took less than ten minutes. The house was in the same simple order; there was no sign that anyone had died there a couple of days before. He dialed Homeward Angels and made arrangements to close out the service contract for John's care. He asked if he could get Luciana's number, but the rep told him that privacy restrictions meant that information couldn't be given out. She offered to pass Kent's contact information along to her so she could call him. Kent said that would be fine, though he guessed that Luciana would never call him if she could avoid it.

That finished, Kent walked quietly about the house, looking for anything helpful. There on the mantel was the photo of John and Angie, and next to it the picture of Pope John Paul. Sure enough, the glass was cracked across the whole face, seemingly from an impact in the upper left corner. He decided he'd bring that, and took it into the kitchen to lay beside his tablet. Looking around the kitchen, he saw the big wall calendar.

Ah, yes, the wall calendar.   Where all the birthdays and
events and practices and recitals of all the "kids" got written.
Whatever John or Angie had committed to was written on that
big wall calendar.   Even with a quieter household, events were
still marked here and there in John's precise but increasingly
spindly handwriting.   Kent noticed that all the doctor's and
therapy appointments were diligently noted.   As expected, there
was no record of any visits to Dr. Daniels, and the days of the
supposed appointments were blank.   He didn't need query results
– a glance at John's calendar would have sufficed.   He decided
to bring those calendar pages as well, so he tore them off and lay
them next to the picture.

Then he noticed that on the spine of the calendar, above
where the pages tore off, was written the name 'Luciana' and a
phone number.   Ah, here was what he'd been looking for.   He
composed his thoughts and keyed the number.

"Hello?" came the hesitant answer.

"Hello, Luciana.   This is Kent Schaeffer, and I'm a friend of
John Holmes.   How are you?"

"Good, good.   Why are you calling?"

"I wanted to tell you personally that Mr. Holmes is dead.   I
called your office to take care of the formalities, but thought you
should know directly," Kent said.

There was a silence on the other end of the line for so long
that Kent wondered if the connection had dropped.   "Luciana?"
he asked.   "Luciana?"

"Yes?" came the breathy response.

"I know this must come as a shock," Kent said gently.   "I
know John was very fond of you, and spoke highly of you."   He
guessed that John had treated his caretaker with the same respect
and charity he'd shown toward everyone, so she must have loved
him in her way.

"Wh – when did he – " the voice trailed away.

"He was found at home yesterday morning," Kent explained.
"The medical examiner guesses that he passed away between
noon and six the day before."

"He – he called me!   He called me that morning, and said
not to come!" Luciana blurted out.   "I wasn't there, because he
called me and told me not to come!"

Kent was taken aback, not just by her abrupt volunteering of information he already knew, but by the frantic, almost panicked edge to her voice. "Yes, I saw that on the police report," Kent said calmly. "I was hoping you could tell me if he said anything else when he called."

"He wasn't feeling good – very sad," Luciana continued in a rushed voice. "Wanted to see the doctor. I took him, once or twice. I drove him. Very depressed."

"To Dr. Daniels?" Kent asked.

"Daniels, yes, yes. Dr. Daniels. Appointments. I drove him a couple of times."

"Yes, they remembered you," Kent reassured her. "So you drove Mr. Holmes to Dr. Daniels office in the old medical office building, on Stone Street just behind the hospital?"

"Yes, yes, Dr. Daniels' office, two times," Luciana repeated.

"Thank you, Luciana," Kent said. "John's funeral will be sometime next week. Details will be published."

"Thank you. He was a good man, a good man," Luciana was sobbing now.

"Thank you, Luciana. Good-bye," Kent said, hanging up and thumbing the voice recorder off. The recording would never be admissible in a court, but he wasn't trying to persuade a court. The terror in Luciana's voice had been palpable. He guessed she never wanted to hear the name John Holmes again, no matter how much she'd loved him. Something or someone had frightened her to the core. What she'd blurted out so frantically sounded suspiciously like a rehearsed alibi or a canned spiel she'd been given – and he suspected the latter.

Poor woman. She'd just been in the wrong place at the wrong time. Well, she'd get no more pressure from him. He was certain that what he'd already gathered would more than suffice for what he needed.

Homeless

"Hey, kid," Melissa's voice interrupted Janice as she was finishing up some paperwork at the nurse's station.

"Hi, Melissa," Janice replied, rubbing her eyes. Janice was more than ready for the shift to wrap up.

"Got anything going after work?" Melissa asked. Janice was a bit surprised at the question, but it wasn't hard to answer.

"Not a thing." All Janice had planned was going home, where she might or might not find her roommate Brenda, but almost certainly would find Kenny, Brenda's next-thing-to-a-live-in boyfriend.

"A friend of mine is in town, and we were getting together at The Shillelagh for drinks after work. Want to come?" Melissa offered.

Janice thought for a minute. She wasn't much of a drinks-with-coworkers type, but that was mostly because she was never asked. She thought about the state of her finances – it was another week until payday, and the electric bill was due. Maybe if she just ordered an appetizer and nursed a small beer...

"Sure, I'd love to," Janice answered.

"Great!" Melissa beamed. "See you at 5:30. I'm buying."

The Shillelagh was an Irish-themed bar downtown that was renowned for its extensive selection of draft beers and hard ciders. Melissa was already there when Janice arrived, sitting in the bar area with a nurse who looked vaguely familiar and a guy Janice didn't recognize at all. Melissa smiled and waved her over.

"Janice, glad you could make it," Melissa said. "Guys, this is Janice Boyd, who works with me in geriatrics. Janice, this is Kendra Myers, who works up in Rehab. Kendra and I go way back. This grumpy sourpuss is Ron Porcher, who should approach agreeable once we get a couple beers in him. Don't even try to talk to him until then."

"Ha, ha," Porcher said, then waved. "Hiya, Janice."

"Ron and I have been colleagues over the years, though now his job is more regional," Melissa explained. "He gives me a call if he's going to be in town, and he's never been to The Shillelagh."

"Try the house chips – they're legendary," Kendra advised. The waiter arrived with menus and took Janice's drink order. They were looking over the selections when Ron gave a snort of derision.

"There it is," he slapped the back of the menu. "The 'Children's Menu'. And Tuesdays are Family Nights – kids under 10 eat free with an adult entrée. How disgusting!"

Janice was baffled. "What's so disgusting about that? Lots of places have kid's menus."

"Ron, finish your beer and we'll get you another," Melissa said, then placed a motherly hand on Janice's arm. "Word of advice, dear – don't get him started."

"I just get a little pissed off sometimes about our culture's prejudice about stinkin' kids," Porcher grumbled.

Janice, who had worked in restaurants, was even more mystified, and thought he just needed educating.

"Prejudice? It's just a business ploy to get families in on otherwise slow nights," Janice started to explain. But Ron sat forward sharply with a scowl on his face, pointed at Janice, and turned to Melissa.

"See? Textbook example. Precisely what I'm talking about," he said. Janice was taken aback and a little put off, but Melissa turned a sympathetic smile on her.

"You got him started," she said with resignation.

"A textbook example of what?" Janice bristled.

"Look, I'm not saying it's your fault," Porcher continued. "You're just reciting what you've been taught, what our world has been steeped in for centuries – no, millennia. You learned it, they learned it – hell, I learned it. Most of my education has been unlearning. But it's all a scam. A ploy by some to get a free – or reduced price – ride on the backs of the rest of us."

Just then the waiter returned, interrupting what was clearly a well-rehearsed monologue. Janice shot Melissa a puzzled look, who returned an indulgent smile and patted her arm while Kendra rolled her eyes. Porcher drained his beer and started on another while they all ordered, and when the waiter departed he clearly intended to pick up right where he'd left off. Fortunately, as Melissa had hinted, more alcohol made him mellower, not more combative.

"Think about this, Janice," he began in a more reasonable tone. "We all know there's no such thing as a 'free' anything. If kids, or blondes, or plumbers, are getting free dinners, then that means the rest of us non-kids, or non-blondes, or non-plumbers are paying more. See that?"

"Well, sure," Janice answered. "But as far as the business is concerned, it's a small amount, and offset by the increased traffic from the families."

"Granted, granted," Porcher replied. "And if it was just dinners once a week at a restaurant, it wouldn't be a big deal. But it's far, far more than that. It's a cultural prejudice that touches every corner of our lives. The damned breeders constitute a privileged class. They get discounts at businesses and breaks from the government ranging from special deductions to tax credits to outright handouts. Plus, a huge percentage of state budgets go to education."

"Well, I understand that raising children is pretty expensive," Janice offered.

"So is owning a boat," Porcher shrugged. "But if you got a boat, would you expect the government to provide you all sorts of deductions and credits? Would you expect the state to pay a percentage of your docking and fuel costs?"

"Well, no," Janice replied, smiling at the thought of her being able to afford a boat.

"It didn't used to be like this, you know," Porcher continued. "In colonial times – those golden years of fond memory – teachers would stay with the families of their students, and meals would be part of their pay. Parents would help with the upkeep of the school buildings, painting and roofing and all. That made sense – the people who used the service paid for it, one way or another. It wasn't until later that they thought of using the laws to milk the entire society to help support their brats."

"Look, Ron, there's one thing I don't understand," Janice began, but Porcher suddenly waved her to silence and discreetly pointed toward the restaurant's main seating area, which was at a lower level than the bar.

"Another prime example," he whispered.

Janice looked in mystification. There were no children in sight, though there was an old lady in a motorized wheelchair being followed by a silent, sullen-looking middle aged man. The lady was trying to navigate her wheelchair through the too-narrow space between two tables where other diners were seated. She kept bulling forward, canting in a shrill voice, "Excuse us, please! Excuse us, please!" She was actually hitting chairs in her haste, and the other diners were having to quickly evacuate their seats to make way for her. Finally, she got clear and rolled to the door, with her dour escort trudging behind.

"Arrogant old bitches like that think the world rotates around them," Porcher muttered angrily. "I'd bet that wheelchair cost more than my car, and she's probably going to her Lexus parked in the handicapped spot to drive to her house on the lake. Yet she gets all kinds of tax breaks, and we pay for her health care and social security with our taxes. Probably left a lousy tip, too."

Janice sympathized a bit with his frustration, given some of the treatment she'd had to endure from her geriatrics patients over the past few weeks. Not all of them, to be sure, but some behaved like the woman in the wheelchair. Just then, their orders arrived, and they were busy with their dinners for a bit. Porcher was well into his fourth or fifth beer when he began holding forth again.

"It's a scam, I tell you," he assured them gravely. "A ploy to use the government to get the rest of us to pay their expenses."

"Here's what I don't understand," Janice replied. "You keep talking about 'them' and 'their', as if there was one sinister group pushing for all this. But you've talked about both kids and old people, and I know for a fact that the educational lobby and the 'gray' lobby are often at odds from state capitols all the way to D.C. How can you say it's all the work of one group?"

Porcher waved his hand dismissively. "Lobby groups are nothin'. Smokescreen. Bickering over pennies. The damage was done long ago, bending the very structure of society to their benefit."

"Again, 'their' benefit," Janice pointed out. "Who are 'they'?"

Porcher put his hand on her arm and looked at her with the soberest gaze he could manage. "Families," he said gravely.

Janice looked quizzically at the two other women, who simply raised their eyebrows. "But – in a sense – isn't that what society is for? To help families?"

"That's what you've been taught – we all have. It's part of the scam. Oh, it may have been true once, though it's never been as true as the cultural legends would have it. We've all been raised on the Norman Rockwell, Currier and Ives images of the boisterous, happy family gathering for the holiday feast. Though reality hardly ever matches that image, we still write our laws and mold our society as if that was the norm. As a result, the rest of us pay to subsidize a small and shrinking part of our society."

Janice pondered for a bit. It was hard to argue with what Porcher was saying, because she knew much of it to be true. But something still wasn't sitting quite right, and she struggled to articulate her disquiet.

"But – even if all this is true, don't we all benefit at some point? Aren't we all members of families, so these structures help all of us some time in some way?"

"Again, that may have been true once," Porcher granted. "Even until a couple generations ago, you could have argued that. But these days it's hardly true at all."

"What do you mean?" Janice asked, baffled. "We all came from families – "

"Did we?" Porcher challenged her.

"Well – I certainly did, and I'm sure you – "

"Did you?"

"But – of course I did," Janice sputtered. "Granted, my folks are divorced now, but they're still my parents – "

"Are they?" Porcher pressed.

Janice looked from Melissa to Kendra, who both looked back noncommittally. She didn't know whether to explode in indignation, burst into laughter, or just change the subject. Porcher saw her uncertainty and continued.

"It was our grandparent's generation, the Baby Boomers, who started to cast off the old conventions protecting the monopoly of families. Easy contraception and divorce dealt lethal blows to the fertility and permanence of marriage. No longer were two people presumed to be shackled together for life, with the social expectation of bearing and raising a herd of kids.

"The next generation was raised in that environment, and lived accordingly. They didn't consider sex to be restricted to marriage, they delayed marriage or didn't marry at all, and they considered kids optional not mandatory. Unfortunately, preventative medicine had yet to catch up with the new social norms, so there were still problems with STDs and abortions, which had the expectable adverse effect on fertility – "

"Wait – " Janice interrupted. "I've never heard that abortion had an adverse effect on fertility."

"Well, you wouldn't expect to hear that out there, would you?" Ron asked rhetorically.

"But that's – how can – " Janice struggled to digest this, but Porcher rolled over her.

"Look, we're medical professionals, not political spinmeisters. We know that you can't intrude into a human body to violently interrupt a normal physiological process without occasionally doing damage. That damage has consequences, especially for a delicately balanced affair like a woman's reproductive system. It doesn't matter a bit to me. I don't care if a woman aborts every brat she conceives. But the point is that a certain percentage of those abortions are going to damage fertility.

"And so it proved for our parents' generation. When they finally got around to wanting kids, many of them found out they couldn't due to their racked up reproductive systems. That's why that generation was the first to make wide use of ART – assisted reproductive technology."

"Are you talking, like, *in vitro* fertilization?" Janice asked.

"I'm talking the whole smash – IVF, artificial insemination, surrogacy, any dodge they could come up with, they tried. It was a lot more widespread than anyone imagined," Porcher explained. "The problem was that the cultural ethic was still stuck in the past. Everyone was walking around with this 'Little House on the Prairie' image of the family that they didn't want to abandon, so nobody talked about it very much. That's why I prod people of our generation to take the DNA challenge."

"What's that?" Janice asked.

"Do a DNA test of yourself and your parents to see if you're a match on both sides. Hell, maybe you already know you're not. But if you think you are, get some samples and get it all tested."

"Without – asking them?" Janice said.

"You can ask if you want. Or not. Hey, if you've been told all your life that you're the daughter of Sam and Jenny, what's the risk of testing everyone's tissue? You just may find out that you're the daughter of Sam and Jenny. Or you may find otherwise."

"How often have you found that to be the case?" Janice asked.

"Around here? About thirty percent of the people learn something interesting. Some places I've been its topped fifty percent."

"Fifty percent?" Janice asked in amazement. "I find that hard to believe."

"DNA doesn't lie," Porcher shrugged. "I told you that people kept it quiet. Sometimes it doesn't even take a test. Someone goes home to Mama to ask her for a sample for matching, and the next thing they know Mama's sitting down at the kitchen table to tell the real story of the conception.

"The point of all this is that the old concepts and ideals are strained to the breaking point. We've got an entire civilization built on the assumption of a particular institution. Government, laws, economics, and social structures are all designed to protect and promote the stereotypical family. Meanwhile, that family is going the way of the dodo. Only a thin, crumbling façade remains. Something's gotta give."

Janice drove home feeling slightly depressed. The topic of conversation had been distressing enough, but there was also something about Porcher that put her on edge. It was more than just his cynical and superior manner – there was something unsettling about his eyes. She didn't at all like his insistence that families were an obsolete institution headed for the dustbin of

history.   Granted, her own family had split, but she still
cherished the ideal, and hoped to have a family of her own
someday.

She pulled onto her street and immediately her eyes
narrowed. She could see her driveway, and it was clear she
wouldn't be able to get into it because there were several strange
cars parked there. She had a good guess what that meant. Her
blood pressure started rising.

Janice banged through the back door of her own house to
find three strangers in her living room. They'd pushed back the
furniture to clear the center of the floor and had their tablets in
cradles around the room. They were wearing video gear – two
in goggles and one in a helmet with full facial screen, and
everyone with the special gloves – and were moving with the
odd, jerky movements of people immersed in their virtual
reality.   There was nobody else in sight, though Brenda's
bedroom door was closed.

"Hey!" Janice shouted, but got no response – the audio feeds
were clearly on full. She looked around for something to throw,
but could see nothing other than a can from the cupboards.
Enraged, she leaned over and yanked one of the tablets from its
cradle.

That got a response. All three sets of headgear came off,
and one of the wearers barked, "Hey, bitch, who said you could
do that?"

"This is my house – I live here," Janice snapped. "Where's
Brenda?"

"In there," the guy pointed to the bedroom door. "With
Kenny."

Gritting her teeth, Janice stomped over to the door but
stopped two feet short, seething. Things had reached the tipping
point with Brenda, but even in her fury Janice wasn't sure she
had the moxie to barge into that room right now. The burst of
mocking laughter from the video gamers behind her further
eroded her confidence.

Janice and Brenda had met in school, and had hit it off
famously. They'd studied together, commiserated over coffee,
shared their lives and playlists. When they'd graduated, it was
an easy fit for them to go in together on a rental. It wasn't much

– a small house in an older section of town – but it was theirs. Brenda had gotten a job at a residential home while Janice had landed the hospital position, so their shifts rarely meshed. But they'd remained good friends, leaving each other pleasant notes and relishing their occasional movie-and-popcorn evenings.

Then, several months ago, Kenny had come into Brenda's life. Janice had no idea how they'd met, since she and Brenda had done little communicating since he'd shown up. Janice had just come home one day to find a sullen, ill-groomed man sitting in the kitchen drinking a beer. Brenda had bounced out of her room and started talking to him, without even introducing them.

Since that day, Kenny had become a fixture around the place. Janice would get up to find Brenda off at work and Kenny sitting in the living room in his underwear, talking on his phone. On the rare occasions that Janice would be home at the same time Brenda was, Kenny would be there, too – and they'd usually be in the bedroom, where they were none too discreet about what they were doing. When they weren't at that, Kenny sat around like he had every right to be there. He ignored Janice, though occasionally she caught him glowering at her from beneath his dark eyebrows.

Only once or twice had any of Kenny's friends come by, and then only to hang around by the back door and talk. This distressing new development of having a gang of them come over, parking in the drive and essentially taking over the house, was something Janice had no idea how to deal with. If she stormed into the bedroom, it would certainly provoke a scene that Janice would find herself on the losing end of – perhaps dangerously so, with four unruly men around. But she couldn't just pretend everything was normal, and go about with her evening shower.

Stomping her foot and crying out in frustration and humiliation, Janice stormed into her room followed by another chorus of mocking laughter. Flying around the room, she snatched clothes off hangers and out of drawers, stuffing them into an overnight duffel while bitter tears streamed down her cheeks. Then she burst out of the bedroom and into the bathroom to hastily gather her toiletries. She slammed her bedroom door, wishing the door locked from the outside, and flew out the back door as one of the gamers hurled some inaudible taunt at her back. Pitching the bag into her car, she roared away from the curb.

The problem was, Janice didn't know where to go. Brenda had been her only close friend. She couldn't afford a hotel. There was one option – she checked her gauges. Yes, she had enough fuel, but barely. She pulled over and dug out her phone. It was a call she was reluctant to make, but she had no choice.

Please answer, please answer, Janice thought as the line rang. There was the sound of someone picking up.

"Jan?" came the voice on the other end.

"Hi, Dad," Janice said.

"This is – this is unexpected," Janice's father replied. "Good – good to hear from you. How have you been?"

"Actually, not so good," Janice admitted. "I'm in a bit of a jam with my roommate, and I was wondering if I could ask you a favor. It's not – it's not about money, Dad, honest it isn't. I was just wondering if I could stay at your place for a couple of days."

There was a silence on the line for a bit. "Oh, I see. You – I see. Well, I suppose – rather unexpected – but perhaps – "

"I wouldn't be in the way, I promise I wouldn't," Janice pleaded. "I could sleep on the couch and I'll live out of my duffel. I don't have shift until Monday, and I just need some time to check some sites and make some calls. You wouldn't even know I'm there. Please, Dad, please." She couldn't keep the sob out of that last part.

"Oh, well," her father answered. "I suppose if you – sure, sure. It's a bit of a mess, but if you don't mind – "

"I won't even notice, Dad," Janice assured him. "I'm heading out now."

"Okay, bye."

Janice's father lived south of Saginaw, about an hour and a half away. They'd talked less and less over the years, not least because Janice always had to initiate all the calls, and could never shake the impression that she was imposing on her father whenever she contacted him.

And now, she pondered as she drove westward, she was going to impose on him for an entire weekend. Tears streamed unhindered down her face – who cared if she cried while she drove? This whole evening had gone from bad to worse. First that disturbing dinner conversation with that creepy Ron guy, then being effectively run out of her own house, the final nail being driven into the coffin of her once-fruitful friendship with Brenda—and now having to deal with the hassle and expense of finding another place to live. Why was her life such a mess?

When Janice arrived at her father's apartment, she was surprised to see the place littered with boxes. She knew Dad had a propensity for clutter, but she'd never seen it quite this bad. The fact that some of the shelves were bare led her to wonder.

"Dad, are you moving?" she asked as she moved a box off the couch.

"Oh – here, let me get that – " her father replied. "As a matter of fact, I am. They're – they're closing the Saginaw office. They offered me a position in Grand Rapids or Columbus, and I chose Columbus. I'll – I'll be moving at the end of the month. There's a truck going down next weekend, so I'm sending most of my stuff then."

"I see," Janice said, wondering when, if ever, she would have been notified of this change. "Well, you needn't trouble about me – all I need is a place to sleep and wash for a couple of days. I can take care of myself."

They spent some time catching up, during which Janice unloaded her frustrations with her now destroyed living situation. Her father responded with his usual vague, impotent bewilderment, as if having a daughter was totally beyond his abilities. Then he patted her arm and headed to bed, leaving her to shower and stretch out on the reasonably comfortable couch. She hoped she'd crash right out – she was certainly exhausted enough – but her mind kept gnawing on what she should have said to Brenda, or could have said to Ron, or should have done about the house, or wanted to say to Dad. She finally sobbed herself to sleep.

For the next two days, Janice busied herself checking sites, sending e-mails, and making calls – most of which involved leaving messages, since it was the weekend. She found a hotel in Port Huron that offered weekly rates and figured she could just manage a week while she ran down the other options. The status of the house was difficult – both her and Brenda's names were on the lease, but she knew Brenda couldn't afford it alone and doubted Kenny would be much help. She also doubted that the eventual departure would be clean and orderly, which meant the security deposit was a lost cause.

Her father went to his office in the morning. He returned in the early afternoon and puttered about packing boxes. They ordered in a pizza for dinner and spent the evening watching a movie, which had always been Dad's idea of a perfect father/daughter evening.

On Sunday morning after her shower, Janice noticed her father's electric razor lying on the vanity. A thought came to her which only took a moment to act on. She pulled out a tissue, popped the head off the razor, and dumped a good amount of beard and skin clippings onto the tissue. She wadded this up, slipped into the kitchen for a small plastic bag, and tucked the sample into her duffel.

She'd been chewing on Ron's 'DNA challenge' since he'd given it. She didn't expect it to reveal anything, but taken as a challenge she'd been mulling over how she could pull it off. Getting her mother's DNA wasn't a problem. Buried at the bottom of a drawer was her only souvenir of her mother: a mother-of-pearl handled hairbrush which Janice had admired so much that her mother had one day given her. She'd never used it herself, but had kept it all those years. The hairs and flakes among the bristles would provide her mother's tissue sample. The challenge had been figuring out how to get a sample from her father, but she'd just solved that.

Over coffee and donuts later that morning, Janice gave her father an update on her situation. She explained the biggest challenge she faced: scraping up a security deposit to move into an apartment while staying at a hotel, even at a weekly rate. Her father grew fidgety.

"Of course, I'd help you if – that is, my current situation – a bit overextended myself – and the move – " he trailed off.

"Oh, Dad, I wasn't thinking of asking *you*," Janice assured him.

Later that day, she packed her gear and got ready to head back to Port Huron. She needed to check in at the hotel and swing by the house for more necessities – something she wasn't looking forward to. Her father carried her duffel bag to the car.

"Well – best of luck with the apartment situation," he said clumsily at the curb.

"Thanks," Janice replied. "Best of luck with the new position in Columbus. When you get there, call me with your new address."

"I will. You come and visit me, okay?"

"I will." Janice reached up and gave him a hug, which he returned stiffly.

"Here," he said abruptly, reaching for her hand and tucking a few bills into it. "For gas."

"Thanks. Bye, Dad."

"Bye now."

As she pulled away, she watched him in the rear view, waving at her departing car. A tear seeped down her cheek – she couldn't shake a feeling of finality.

Farewells

Derek was dealing with some forms when he heard the door open. Looking up, he was surprised to see Janice standing there. They usually only bumped into each other at lunch.

"Hey, Janice, what's the matter, get lost on the way to your floor?" Derek asked, jokingly. Janice didn't laugh – in fact, he'd never seen her look so drawn and bedraggled.

"No," she replied. "I came down here looking for you."

"Oh," Derek said, wondering what Janice would want in the morgue. "Here, have a seat. How can I help?"

"Well – " Janice began, as if reluctant to come to the point. "I was wondering – I don't even know if you can do this – how much does a DNA test cost?"

Derek was puzzled. A DNA test? "What kind of test? Simple matching?"

"I – I'm not certain," Janice admitted. "The kind that can tell if different people are related."

"Related how? Cousins? Within a line?"

"If one person is the child of two other people," Janice explained.

"Ah," Derek said. "Parentage testing – that's one of the easiest. I presume you have samples?"

"Right here," Janice patted her handbag.

"Okay, then," Derek said, pulling out some sample bags. "Give me the paternal sample –" He slipped it into the bag and labeled it. "Now the maternal sample – now the child." Derek deliberately avoided asking or even wondering what all this was about. That was Janice's business. "These are all set, so now you can tell me how you're doing. If you don't mind my saying so, you look a little wrung out."

"Well, it's been a rough weekend," Janice acknowledged.

"Rough?" Derek asked, realizing he was uncertain ground. 'Rough' might mean many things, and he might not want to pry too much. But Janice looked so forlorn that he ventured a question. "Is there – can I help in any way?"

69

"Oh, it's sweet of you to ask, Derek, but I don't see how," Janice replied, and suddenly she was pouring out her woes to him – the mess with Brenda, her father's tepid support, the hassle of having to find a place to live. Derek listened sympathetically, but a little helplessly. He didn't see any way he could help with any of that.

"And just this morning I did some figuring, and what with staying at this motel and eating all my meals out, I won't be able to set aside enough for a security deposit for even a cheap apartment," Janice almost cried. "So unless a miracle happens and I get some of the deposit back from the house, I'm pretty much trapped where I am."

"Well," Derek jumped on that. "How much would the security deposit be?"

"At least seven hundred," Janice said resignedly. "And then there's moving my stuff out."

Derek did some rapid calculating. He'd been saving up for that gaming gear, but –

"I could loan you that," he told Janice. "If you could wait until after next payday."

Janice's head snapped up in shock. "You – Derek, I couldn't. You hardly know me."

Derek couldn't see what that had to do with anything. "Are you telling me you wouldn't be good for it?"

"No, that's not it," Janice replied. "It's just that – I – why would you do something like that?"

Derek was puzzled in turn. "Why not? That's what friends do, right? A friend once helped me out with the down payment on a car loan. You and I are friends, I can help, so why shouldn't I? It sounds like you're in a real bind here."

Janice looked at him, blinking quite a few times. "Yeah," she finally said. "I'm in a real bind here."

"All right then," Derek said with finality. "You line up some apartment walkthroughs. When you find one that looks good, let me know and I'll send you the cash. Then we can set up a time to move you in."

"You...you'd help me with that, too?" Janice gasped.

Again, Derek was bewildered. "Of course – why wouldn't I?"

Janice just shook her head and wiped her nose. "Thanks, Derek. Thanks so much."

"Bah." Derek waved, feeling a bit embarrassed.

"Oh, goodness, I've got to get going," Janice exclaimed, looking at the clock. "I'll call you!"

Derek was left looking at the sample bags. Why on earth would Janice – no, he shook his head. Her business, not his. His business was how to get these samples submitted. Unauthorized testing was currently a sore subject with his boss, but there was no provision for him to have the lab bill for a test separately – if he sent it in, it got billed to the morgue. Derek thought for a bit, then pulled out his tablet and tapped up the calendar. He picked up the phone and dialed Shaundra.

"Medical examiner's office, Shaundra speaking."

"Hey, Shaundra, Derek here. What does Dr. Stout's golf schedule look like over the next few weeks?"

"The doctor currently has field consultations scheduled for this afternoon, Wednesday morning weather permitting, Friday afternoon, the following Tuesday, and the next Friday," Shaundra relayed. "Do you need to see him?"

"Nah – just wanted to know when to stay off the links. Thanks!" Derek hung up – his guess had been correct. His boss was trying to cram in as much fairway time as he could before cold weather set in. With luck, that meant he wouldn't have time to scrutinize expenses so closely, especially trivial ones. He printed off some sample tags, stuck them on Janice's bags, and put them in the lab bag.

The phone rang, and Derek grabbed it. "County morgue."

"Derek?" came Kent's voice. "Do you have my phone number handy?"

"Sure – right here," Derek confirmed.

"Could you call me from your personal phone? I've some things to ask you."

"Sure," Derek said. A bit puzzled, he keyed in Kent's number.

"Thanks," Kent answered. "I wanted to thank you again for your concern and effort on John's behalf. I also wanted to invite you to his funeral. It'll be Wednesday at 10 a.m. at St. Andrew's in Port Huron. We hope you can make it."

"Well – I'll try," Derek replied, feeling bewildered but honored. "I'll have to see if I can get time off work."

"There'll be a lunch following, which we hope you'll attend as well. It should all wrap up by 1:00, though you don't have to stay for the whole thing," Kent continued.

"I'll do my best to be there," Derek said.

"Great! God bless." Kent rung off. Derek tapped his phone on the desk, thinking, and then pulled up the county personnel information page. He had to try to finesse this, given his current standing with his boss. He read the relevant paragraphs and then dialed the county building.

"You again?" Shaundra answered.

"Yeah, different question this time," Derek said. "Regarding time off for funerals, I see that the policy is that it's permitted if the request is made in 'reasonable' time. What constitutes 'reasonable' time?"

"I think the policies permit a certain discretion by the office in that. Did someone you know pass away?" Shaundra asked sympathetically.

"A – very casual acquaintance," Derek assured her. "Friend-of-a-friend sort of thing. The funeral is at 10:00 on Wednesday. If I were to submit a request at, say, 8:00 that morning, would that be in 'reasonable' time?"

"You mean while the medical examiner was out on his field consultation? I think I'd have to use my judgement on such a request, and it would probably seem reasonable to me," Shaundra replied.

"Thanks, Shaundra." Derek grinned.

Wednesday was sunny and just warm enough for good autumn golf, so Derek was clear to head for St. Andrew's midmorning. The church was only a couple miles from the office, so he got there in plenty of time. He parked in the parking lot on the side of the church, but noticed that almost everyone else was getting dropped off under the canopy that reached out to cover the circle drive that looped up to the front. He supposed that would be the entrance he should use. He hadn't been in many churches in his life, and had never been in a Catholic one.

Derek made his way toward the front doors, noticing that almost all the adults were wearing broad-brimmed hats. He wondered if this was a Catholic thing or a funeral thing, and felt a little self-conscious without one until he noticed that all the men removed theirs once they were inside.

Kent was lingering in a vestibule area just inside the doors, and when Derek entered he broke into a broad smile and bustled over, a round-faced woman with brown hair following behind.

"Derek, so glad to see you. This is my wife Linda – Linda, this is Derek, the deputy medical examiner who was so helpful."

"Um – hi," Derek nodded.

"A pleasure to meet you, Derek," Linda said kindly. "Kent mentioned that you'd probably not been to a Mass before?"

"No, I haven't," Derek admitted.

"If you'd like, I could stay with you in the back," Linda offered. "Kent has some responsibilities during Mass, so he needs to be up front, and our kids are old enough to manage themselves. A Mass can be a bit confusing if you've never seen one, especially a funeral Mass, which is a little more involved than a regular Mass."

"That'd be great," Derek replied with relief. He'd been uncertain how he'd manage in this strange environment. Linda walked him into the hall-like church, pointed to one of the bench-like seats at the back, and did a little quick-kneel thing before joining him.

The coffin was in the aisle between the benches up at the front of the church. Many people were coming in now, and Derek was struck by the variety: white people, black people, Hispanics – all of whom were friendly toward each other and most of whom seemed to know one another. Many of them made their way to the casket and paused by it briefly before making their way to their seats.

"They're praying – silently," Linda explained, sensing Derek's puzzlement.

One of these people stood out in a rather unusual way. He was a younger man, perhaps a few years older than Derek, but he came in with a walker. But he didn't move with the plodding, shuffling gait that Derek had seen older people use. He was quite vigorous, lifting and moving his walker easily and almost swinging along with it. He clanked his way to the foot of the casket, set aside the walker, and almost collapsed on the floor, sobbing and nodding. This gave Derek a chance to see why he needed the walker: his hips and legs were twisted at odd angles, clearly unable to support his weight unassisted. Derek guessed that he was seeing a moderate case of cerebral palsy.

Derek felt a little uncomfortable, almost embarrassed, looking at the man's stricken frame. Though his training had taught him about such conditions, he realized that he'd hardly ever seen anyone like this. He felt disquieted by the man's presence though he couldn't understand why.

Those around the man didn't share Derek's unease. After allowing him a few minutes of quiet mourning, some men stepped from a pew and tapped him on the shoulder. They helped him up and into one of the pews and folded his walker at the end of it.

Shortly thereafter, the service started. Some of the funeral home staff put the lid on the casket and draped a white pall over it. Some music started, and the priest and some assistants wearing robes and carrying candles came up the aisle while everyone sang. Derek just listened, but was impressed by the quality of the singing. The service proceeded with ritual prayers and responses that Derek didn't know, though Linda explained things quietly from time to time. At points the priest used some kind of shiny metal vessel on a chain from which poured fragrant smoke. Derek presumed this was incense, which he had never seen used before. Some people, including Kent, got up and read from what Derek presumed was the Bible. Then the priest read, and talked for a while about John Holmes and Jesus. Then followed a part of the service that was very ritualized and ended up with a lot of people going up to the front of the church for what Linda called 'communion'. She said he should stay where he was, which was fine by him. He noticed that about half the people, including the cerebral palsy guy, stayed in the pews for this.

Afterwards there was a stirring moment when a lot of younger people, ranging in age from the early teens to the mid-twenties, circled the casket and sang a hauntingly beautiful song. Derek saw many weeping unashamedly during this, including

Linda. When the song concluded, the priest gave a lengthy prayer and then he and his candle-bearing assistants went back out of the church down the center aisle, with the casket being rolled behind.

Derek was wondering what to do next when Kent stood up and gave some brief instructions. He explained that there wouldn't be a graveside service, but the casket would be in the vestibule for a while so people could pay their final respects. He asked everyone to file out, starting with the front pews, which meant Derek was stuck in the back for a while.

Derek didn't mind waiting. Linda was pleasant company, and explained parts of the services to Derek while they waited. Derek realized that even though he was in the 'death business', he hadn't been to many funerals. To him, death lay in the realm of medical study and analysis. The people here treated death as a transition, focusing on who John Holmes had been to them, and where he was now.

Eventually, enough people filed out that it was time for Derek and Linda to do so, as well. Derek noticed the guy with the walker working his way down the aisle with everyone else. They seemed to think nothing of it, but Derek was torn between an urge to stare at this twisted specimen of humanity and a desire to avert his eyes in embarrassment. For some reason the man's awkwardness made *him* feel awkward, and Derek was glad when he passed through the doors. Derek and Linda followed the last few people out into the vestibule, where many mourners were still milling around. To Derek's further discomfort, the cerebral palsy guy was nearly collapsed by the side of the coffin, sobbing and wailing. Others were also grieving, but none so expressively as he. Nobody seemed to think it odd. Linda looked on the man with pity, and knelt to stroke his shoulder and whisper something in his ear. He hugged her and kept sobbing until two men came over, helped him to his feet, and walked him away down a hallway. Linda returned to Derek, wiping her eyes.

"That was Sam," she explained. "He was very close to John, like a favorite grandson. He's taking this hard."

"Looks like it," Derek muttered.

Linda paused for a moment beside the casket before leading Derek down the hallway and out under a canopied walkway, which led to a set of outbuildings. Derek didn't know what to expect – he hadn't been aware that lunches followed funerals. They followed the flow of people passing along the buildings under the surprisingly deep eaves until they came to a large dining room in which many were already gathered. Various people came up to greet Linda, but she stayed by Derek's side until Kent and another tall, black-haired man arrived. Everyone turned toward them, and the talking died down. The black-haired man punched a code into his phone and spoke into it, his voice now coming through the room's PA system. He thanked everyone for coming and said a brief prayer, then instructed everyone on how to come through the line for lunch. Kent and Linda steered Derek to a table near the back of the room while the families with children went first. Derek hoped they wouldn't take long – he was acutely hungry, and the dishes steaming on the line smelled delicious. Many people swung past their table to greet Kent and Linda, but Derek was only introduced to a few of the visitors, which he appreciated.

While Kent and Linda chatted, Derek looked around the room. Two things struck him. One was how many children were in attendance. He hadn't seen so many children in one place since he'd left elementary school. The second was how cheerful everyone was. He hadn't known what to expect of a meal after a funeral, but he would have guessed that it would be a somber, mournful event. He wouldn't have expected this laughing, chatting crowd of friends engaging in joyful conversation.

At last it was their turn to go through the line, and Derek's unspoken concern about the earlier diners taking all the good food proved unfounded – there was plenty, and he loaded his plate. When they returned to their table, they were joined by the black-haired guy who'd come in with Kent, who was accompanied by a red-haired woman with a ready smile.

"Gil, Jan, I'd like you to meet Derek Stevens," Kent said. "Derek, this is Gilbert and Janine Peterson. Gil helped me plan the funeral."

"A pleasure," Gil said, shaking Derek's hand firmly. "Kent told me about all you did for us. It's good to meet you at last."

Derek looked at him, puzzled. "All I did?"

Gil looked at Kent. "What, you didn't tell him?"

"No time, really," Kent shrugged. "This is the first chance we've had to talk since I left the morgue."

"Tell me what?" Derek was now utterly lost.

"That you're for a large part responsible for all this," Gil replied, waving his hand toward the room full of cheerful people. "Without your help, this probably wouldn't have happened."

Derek furrowed his brow. "How on earth do you figure that?"

Gil was poised to explain when Kent interrupted him. "I'm going to grab Ruth and take these kids outside. It's getting too noisy in here." With the help of a woman from another table, he proceeded to herd the crowd of rambunctious children out a back door.

"There's a playground out there," Gil explained. "We'll all be happier this way."

"So – what's this all about?" Derek asked.

"John Holmes was a faithful Catholic, as are many of us. For centuries, the Church so frowned on suicide that those who committed it weren't permitted a funeral Mass, or to be buried on sanctified ground. It was, essentially, murder, but since you couldn't confess it, you faced God with that sin on your soul.

"During the last century, the Church loosened her stance somewhat. Suicide is certainly a sin, but grave sin requires full moral understanding of what you're doing. Many who commit suicide are not in a sound mental state, and thus are not completely responsible for their actions. The severely depressed would fall into this category. So the Church began allowing funeral Masses for suicides, leaving the judgement to God, Who knows all.

"But toward the end of the last century, the social trend toward assisted suicide began gaining momentum. There was vocal public support for loosening laws so doctors could prescribe, or family members administer, lethal doses of drugs to end someone's life. This is in clear violation of God's law, since only He can determine when we live or die. Nonetheless, even some professed Catholics began advocating for this 'right', and pressing for legal changes.

"The Church spoke out clearly against this, but few in the culture paid attention. It got so there were Catholics who would openly defy the Church, actively encouraging suicide, publicly promoting it, even committing it themselves – and then their families would show up demanding a Catholic funeral.

"So about ten years ago, the Pope and bishops published new guidelines, tightening back down on funerals for those who had committed medical suicide. It wasn't popular, but it was necessary for the Church to be consistent in her teachings. Unfortunately, John's death looked just like such a suicide, especially after the death certificate was issued. We were concerned that the pastor would rule that John couldn't have a funeral Mass or be buried at Mount Hope next to Angie.

"Those of us who knew John were fully aware that he would never end his own life, but that wasn't enough to go on. Kent suspected there was something fishy about the death, but it was the evidence that you provided – the unofficial evidence that didn't make it into the reports – that enabled us to make the case that John's death wasn't what it appeared."

"How could that be?" Derek asked. "If it wasn't officially released, how could it be admissible?"

"You're thinking of a court of law, where standards for evidence are stricter," Gil explained. "All we had to do was demonstrate to the pastor that there was a reasonable supposition that John didn't take his own life. We got a specialist in Church law to help us present the evidence. Thanks to your help, we were able to establish that there was an overwhelming suspicion that John didn't kill himself, so the pastor allowed the funeral Mass."

Derek was disturbed again. "I'm glad for that, but – if it wasn't a suicide, that means it was a murder, and a very cleverly concealed one. Doesn't that bother you?"

"It bothers us very much, at several levels," Gil said grimly. "But our most immediate concern for the past few days has been getting the funeral arranged. Now that it's over..." Gil trailed off.

"Do you plan to go to the police?" Derek asked, a little apprehensive that he might get in trouble if it came to light how much he'd let Kent know.

"You tell me, Derek," Gil asked. "In this resource-strapped area, do you think the police are going to pick up the case of a childless widower whom the medical examiner has already ruled a suicide? What evidence could anyone bring to the prosecutor's office?"

"But – but," stammered Derek. "That's not fair! That's not right! Murder is murder! Somebody should do something!"

"'Not right' is precisely correct," Gil agreed. "And be assured, things are being done." He said this with a finality that left no doubt in Derek's mind that it was true, but left him wondering what that might be.

"Oh, damn – sorry," Derek said suddenly, glancing at the clock above the kitchen door. "I'd better get back to work."

"Of course," Gil said, rising and shaking his hand. "Thank you for coming, and thank you again for all your help. How can I get in touch with you?"

"Kent has my number," Derek said. "Or call the county morgue." He took one last look around at the chatting crowd. He spotted the guy with cerebral palsy sitting surrounded by others, laughing with the rest. Derek was mystified how everyone could be so lighthearted after burying a dear friend.

Out in back, Kent and the woman who had helped him manage the crowd of children stood under a deep eave, watching them play on the school playground.

"I'd like to invite Derek out, Ruth," Kent said. "At least for dinner, maybe for a whole weekend if he feels comfortable."

"You think that wise?" Ruth asked. "You barely know him."

"I don't know," Kent admitted. "But I think it needs to happen. We can't get so cautious that we neglect our main mission."

Ruth eyed him steadily. "We have several 'main' missions. Do you want to risk endangering the others for the sake of a dinner invitation?"

"We owe this kid," Kent answered. "He helped us when he didn't have to, at some risk to himself. He seems decent and trustworthy – and lonely."

Ruth pondered this and then nodded. "Do as you deem fit – but be careful." They were silent for a while, watching the children, before she spoke again. "How long do you think we'll be able to keep doing this?"

Kent said nothing at first, but took off his hat and gazed over at the church. "'Walk about Zion, go 'round about her, number her towers, consider well her ramparts, go through her citadels, that you may tell the next generation that this is our God.' It's their heritage as much as it is ours, Ruth. We shouldn't stop coming until we absolutely have to."

"I feel the same way," Ruth admitted. "But we both know what's at stake. All it would take would be the wrong child to take a tumble and be run to the hospital, and we'd have all manner of complications we can scarce afford. And there's the inherent danger of so many of us assembling in such a public and predictable place."

"Everyone's taking precautions," Kent pointed out, waving toward the parked cars. "The hats, canopied or back-to-back parking, borrowed cars, staying under cover. If we keep up the discipline, we should be okay for a while yet."

"Precautions," Ruth snorted. "You know full well that if they wanted, they could have one hovering among those trees right now, reading the pattern on your tie."

"I know they could, Ruth," Kent replied, putting his hat back on. "Ultimately, they're going to do whatever they like. But I'm sure not going to make it easy for them."

Revelations

Derek made a point of visiting the hospital cafeteria the next day, where he searched diligently for Janice. Spotting her at a table, he angled over just as she was finishing lunch.

"Hey," he greeted her. "Glad I caught you. Your test results came in yesterday, and I didn't know how to contact you – I don't have your number."

"Oh – well, why don't you give me yours, and I'll call you, and then we'll have each other's," Janice suggested, so they did. Then Derek pulled a folded printout from his pocket.

"Here are the results," he said, spreading the sheet out on the table. "These numbers here are probabilities. Here's the paternal sample and here's the maternal. The child sample indicates a high probability of a match with the father – effectively a certainty. It indicates essentially no match with the mother – near zero probability. This would be typical of stepparent and adoptive situations – " Derek rattled on for a while, but Janice had tuned him out. She was staring at the numbers on the paper, which were starting to blur. Her hands were beginning to shake as the words echoed in her mind. No match with the mother. No match with the mother.

"Janice, are you all right?" Derek's voice cut through her reverie.

"I – sorry, I'm a bit distracted," Janice stammered. "Listen, I need to get back to the floor. Thanks for this – catch you later." She walked her tray to the drop-off and wandered out the door. Derek looked after her with concern. Though it wasn't any of his business, he had his suspicions about those samples. It was clear that the results had shocked Janice, but he didn't know what he could do. He sat down and started eating his lunch distractedly as he pondered. Lately, life sure was handing him a lot of situations that made him feel completely helpless.

Janice wandered numbly back to the floor, her mind racing. Could she have been mistaken about the hairbrush? No, that was

81

mother's hairbrush, one of her few anchors to the more pleasant years of her childhood. Mother used to let Janice brush her hair with it, until Janice ended up insisting that only she could use it, and only on mother's hair. That had been back when her mother had been willing to sit long enough to have her hair brushed.

Except that it seemed that she hadn't been Janice's mother at all. That certainly explained a lot. Janice stopped in the hallway and leaned against the wall, holding her head as she tried to make sense of this. Could she be adopted? But no, that would mean she wouldn't be related to father, either. A child of an earlier marriage? No, she'd seen their wedding pictures and knew the date – she was younger by several years. Impulsively, she pulled out her phone and dialed father. It rang and rang, then rolled to voice mail. Of course. He was at work, and never picked up at work, not even for her. She hung up rather than leave a message. Just as well – she needed to think out how she was going to broach the topic with him. If she just charged in with hard questions and accusations, he'd run for cover.

The afternoon passed in a daze, with Janice doing her duties robotically, her mind frantically trying to assimilate the reality. *She was never really my mother.* Memories came flitting back, and Janice examined them in light of this revelation. Certain incidents made more sense, but others were even more confusing. *She was never really my mother.* But if she wasn't, who was? And who was Janice, if not her mother's daughter?

Sometime in the middle of the afternoon, she came to the revolting realization that that creepy Ron guy had been right. That, more than anything, goaded her to call her father when she got off shift. She couldn't let Ron have the last gloat. There had to be some explanation for this, some rationale that would enable her to reassemble her world.

When her shift ended, Janice made her way back to her dingy little hotel room. She'd have to make it out to the laundromat tonight – and she still had the whole living arrangement thing to sort out. She sprawled on the bed, having no strength to deal with any of that just now. She barely had the strength to call her father, but she had to. She couldn't go through another day like today. She grabbed her phone and checked the time – Dad should be home by now. At once desiring and dreading the conversation, she keyed the number.

"H – hello?" came her father's voice.

"Hello, Dad? It's Janice."

"Hello, Jan. Good to hear from you."

"Dad, I'm sorry to bother you, and I promise I won't take long, but I have some questions that only you can answer."

"What – what kind of questions?" her father asked guardedly.

Janice took a deep breath, tried to calm herself, and blinked back some tears. "Dad, is mother my real mother – my biological mother?"

There was a pregnant pause before father replied in an artificially dismissive tone. "What kind of question is that? Of course she's your real mother. Whatever makes you think –"

"I had some DNA tests done, Dad. They were clear. You're my biological father, but I'm not related at all to mother. What's going on?"

"DNA tests? But why would you – "

"Dad," Janice interrupted. "Answer the question. Is mother my biological mother or not?"

There was a very long pause before he answered in a weary voice. "No – but she is your legal mother. The adoption papers were part of the packet, and we filed them – "

"Packet? What packet?"

There was another pause and a sigh. "I – I meant to tell you. I intended to tell you when you got old enough – "

"Dad, I'm twenty-four," Janice erupted. "When were you going to get around to telling me? When I'd turned fifty and you'd moved to Anchorage?"

"We – your mother put off having children until we settled in Port Huron. Then we – well, it turned out to be hard. Your mother had difficulties – conceiving. We tried what we could – the treatments were very expensive – but nothing succeeded. There were no babies to adopt, and your mother wanted a baby. We eventually got in touch with a lawyer who could make arrangements for us."

"Arrangements?" Janice asked. "What kind of arrangements could a lawyer make?"

"A contract with a – a party, someone to bear a child on our behalf. A surrogate. It was completely anonymous, we never met her, we just signed papers and showed up at the hospital to take you home. Legally, it was an adoption."

Janice felt like her insides were being slowly scooped out with a jagged-edged spoon. "So, my real mother is out there somewhere, but nobody, not even you, knows who she is?"

"Jan, your mother is your real mother," her father said in an exasperated tone. "The adoption papers were completely in order. She raised you – "

"When she could take time from her career," Janice snapped. "Until she got fed up and left me."

"Jan, we've been over this," her father said weakly.

"If you never met my real mother, I presume you didn't – what did you do? Supply sperm?" Janice asked sharply.

"We looked into IVF, using our own – tissue – but there were issues with your mother. The lawyer lined up the egg donor, and found a surrogate to carry you. I – contributed – what I could. It was the best way – it was – "

"Cheaper," Janice concluded. Her father sighed and there was a long pause. "So – how much did I cost?"

"I – I beg your pardon?" her father stammered.

"You said there was a contract. There must have been some negotiated compensation. How much did I cost?"

"Jan, I don't think – what purpose would there be – "

"How much?" Janice barked.

"It was – twenty thousand, plus legal and medical fees," her father admitted.

"Good to know how much I'm worth," Janice said bitterly. "I bet mother ended up thinking she got a real raw deal. Probably wished she could trade me in."

"Jan, it's not that, it was never that," her father nearly cried. "Your mother – your mother and I – we wanted you, we really did."

"Sure, she wanted me right up until I got to be too much trouble, at which point she sought other career opportunities," Janice interrupted.

"Jan, Jan, there was so much more to it than that," her father assured her. This time Janice wasn't sure he wasn't crying.

"Well, that hardly matters now, does it?"

"Jan, I'm sorry. You shouldn't have had to find out like this. I meant to tell you, I really did."

Janice fought the urge to continue venting her pain and frustration. This conversation was going nowhere. "Dad, I'm – I'm really tired. I've been on shift, and it's been a rough week."

"Of course," her father answered. "You – you take care of yourself, okay?"

"Right, Dad," Janice said, and rung off. She sat on the bed staring at the wall, her phone hanging limply in her hand. Hollow. That's how she felt: scooped hollow. It had all been a lie. Everything. The mother/daughter teas, the shopping outings, the stupid matching barrettes. Even the baby book had been a lie – the coming home from the hospital pictures, the nursery, all of it. There'd even been a prenatal section, complete with ultrasound picture, that had been carefully filled in. Apparently, her parents had gotten regular reports on her development.

So who was her mother? An anonymous functionary somewhere out there who'd taken her pay and done her job. What did that make Janice? A market commodity? Her mother had gone off to pursue her career, and her father his career. Where did that leave her? She had never felt so alone.

While she was sitting there in a daze, trying to absorb all this, her phone rang. Who could that be? If it was Dad, she wasn't answering – she couldn't deal with him just now. But it wasn't Dad, it was – Derek?

"Hello?"

"Hi, Janice," came the familiar voice. "Hope I'm not bothering you. I meant to ask today – how's the apartment search going? I'll have that money to lend you tomorrow, if you need it."

"Money?" Janice was having trouble assembling the pieces.

"You know," Derek replied in puzzlement. "For the security deposit. The loan I offered you."

Janice shook her head and struggled to come back to the present. "Oh – ah, right. Well, I've looked at some listings and made some calls, but haven't had time to schedule any walkthroughs. And I'm going on afternoons this weekend, so I guess – I guess I'm stuck here another week at least."

On the other end of the line, Derek was mystified and a little concerned over Janice's listless, uninterested tone. Earlier in the week, her housing situation had been her foremost crisis. Now it seemed to barely warrant notice.

"Um – sure," Derek answered. "Whatever works for you." He paused a little then continued. "Janice, are you all right? Is everything okay?"

"Everything's fine," Janice lied. "It's just – I've had some things on my mind lately."

"Okay," Derek said, not wanting to intrude. "If there's anything I can do to help, let me know."

"Okay," Janice replied, and hung up. Derek looked at his phone with a furrowed brow. Something was going on with Janice, that was certain, something even more disturbing than the mess with her roommate. He wondered if it had something to do with those test results. It wasn't his business, and she was little more than a passing acquaintance, but he wanted to help as much as he could. Then something struck him, but even as he reached to dial Janice back, his phone rang. Only it wasn't Janice, it was Kent.

"Hello?" Derek answered.

"Hey, Derek," Kent said. "How are things going?"

"Well enough, for me at least," Derek replied.

"Great. Listen, Linda and I felt like we barely got a chance to talk with you at the funeral lunch the other day. We were wondering if you'd like to join us for dinner tomorrow evening."

"Oh – well – " Derek hadn't been expecting that at all.

"If you have plans, we can make it some other time," Kent assured him.

"No, no – no plans, just a wide-open weekend," Derek said. "I'm free after 4:30."

"Great. Let me give you directions on how to get here. The guidance systems don't send you by the best route."

"Okay," Derek said, grabbing a piece of paper and scribbling down what Kent told him. It was an address in the middle-western portion of the county. "Got it. I'll swing out tomorrow after work."

"Looking forward to it," Kent said.

Derek again looked at his phone, bewildered. Not that he minded, but what was that about? Now, something was nagging him, something he'd had in his mind that Kent's call had driven out. Oh, that's right – call Janice back. He keyed her number.

"Hello?" Janice answered dully.

"Hi, Janice. Sorry to bother you again, but I had an idea. Even if you don't have a new place lined up yet, I could help you move your stuff out of your old place. You could stash it at my apartment for the time being."

"Oh," Janice said, a bit more firmly. "Oh, yes. Um – thank you, Derek. That sounds – I hadn't thought about that – that's very helpful."

"I don't know the details, but from your description it sounded a little sketchy at your old place. I just thought you might want to get your stuff out of there," Derek added.

"Yeah. Yeah, come to think of it, that's a good idea," Janice said. "I just don't know when would be a good time."

"Do you have much stuff?" Derek asked.

"Clothing, kitchen utensils, a writing desk," Janice explained. "The bed and frame came with the place, and I got the dresser second-hand – I don't care if I ever see it again. The place came semi-furnished, so most of the furniture either belongs there or is Brenda's."

"Well, that makes it easy," Derek said. "What day works? Is there any reason we couldn't do it over the weekend?"

"I suppose not. Why don't I call you Saturday morning and we'll work out a time?"

"Sounds good," Derek replied.

"Derek – " Janice added, "thanks for offering. Sorry I've been so out of it. There's been – a lot going on."

"I understand. Anything I can do to help."

The next day after work, Derek turned his car out of town and headed for Kent's place by way of roads he'd never used before. Though he'd lived in the city for a couple of years, the few occasions he'd had to travel outside it usually took him down toward Metro Detroit on the expressway. Occasionally, his work would take him to other places within the county, but then he'd taken the expressway as much as he could. This route followed rural highways and side roads, and he enjoyed the beauty of the land, which reminded him a bit of the hills and farmlands around where he'd grown up. He drove past fields of corn, dried brown and rustling. Often, he passed through towering stands of trees, their branches waving in the wind. Why hadn't he driven out this way more often?

The Schaeffers lived on a dirt road overhung with trees, and when Derek turned into the drive, he saw Kent sitting in a rocker on a porch that spanned the front of the house. He waved cheerfully and directed Derek to park beneath a huge, spreading oak.

Kent came down to meet Derek accompanied by a lad who looked to be about ten and a girl who had the gangly appearance of an early teen.

"Derek, glad you could make it," Kent said with a grin. "Let me introduce my eldest daughter Martha, and my second-oldest son Jude."

"A pleasure," Derek said, shaking their hands. Both the youngsters greeted him as 'Mr. Derek', and were open and at ease with him. This impressed Derek. When he'd been Jude's age, he'd been painfully shy and awkward around any adult but his mother.

They all went inside where Derek was assailed by a variety of tantalizing aromas. A long table was set, and people seemed to be milling everywhere. Kent paid no attention to the merry turmoil, escorting Derek to the table while older children hustled or carried younger ones to their places, or assisted Linda with bringing dishes to the table. In short order, all were seated, and Derek discreetly counted six children around the table, ranging from a tall, teen-aged lad named Philip to a toddler in a high chair named Matthew. Kent led a brief prayer, during which Derek looked at his lap and tried not to feel out of place. Then his plate was filled with a delicious stew, which Linda explained was made with lentils, and the best macaroni and cheese he'd ever had. There was homemade bread with butter and crusty cornbread with honey and cold, fresh milk.

Next to Derek was seated Tabitha, who was six and chatted nonstop. Derek had little idea how to converse with children, but that didn't matter since Tabitha was more than willing to carry the conversation. Derek kept eating the most delicious meal he'd had in ages, while nodding and agreeing with the steady narrative about how the cat had shredded the doll's dress and how she could read chapter books now and how someone had let her toad escape.

Then dinner was finished and everyone was pushing away from the table and tidying up the dishes. Derek started to help, but was shooed away by Kent because guests weren't expected to clear the table. Tabitha was assigned the task of escorting Derek to the family room, where she sat him down and went to fetch a "Little House" book, whatever that was, to demonstrate her reading prowess. She sat right next to him and showed him the pictures and carefully worked her way through the words. Derek found himself thinking that if all kids were like this, they wouldn't be that hard.

Then the tow-headed toddler was standing in front of him, clutching a book to his chest and staring with expectant eyes.

"Matthew wants you to read to him," Tabitha explained. "That's his favorite book and we're all *so* tired of reading it. You don't have to if you don't want to."

"No, no, it's fine," Derek replied, reaching for the book, but not knowing what to do beyond that. Matthew, however, knew how to manage adults, and handed the book over with a gleeful grin while he scrambled onto Derek's lap, nestling into the crook of his arm with eager anticipation. Derek read the book, which had brightly colored pictures and involved a green frog and a blue cow and a rainstorm. When Derek finished, Matthew climbed down and scampered off – to return a minute later with an armful of similar books.

"Matthew, no!" Tabitha cried, but Derek just laughed, took the books, and let Matthew settle in contentedly while he started working his way through the stack.

Derek wasn't quite finished with them, and was just beginning to think that Matthew was feeling a little limp, when Jude came up.

"Come on, you little hobbit," he said, picking the drowsy baby up off Derek's lap. "Time to get you ready for bed."

Derek stood up, a little stiff, to see that the kitchen and dining room were clean and tidy. Martha was hanging up some towels and preparing to leave the room when Linda reminded her.

"Have you done chores yet, young lady?"

"Not yet – I'll call Chris to see if he's ready." She dialed someone and had a quick conversation.

"He'll be there in five. Oh, Mr. Derek, do you like horses?" Martha asked eagerly.

"Ah – yes, I do," Derek replied. "Haven't had much exposure to them, but always interested in learning more."

"Would you like to see mine?" Martha bubbled.

"Along with some of the less glamorous aspects of horse ownership?" Philip chimed in.

"Sure," Derek replied, and followed Martha out a side door. They went across a porch and along a path covered by some kind of awning until they passed under some trees.

"The Big House is over there," Martha explained, pointing through the trees to their left. "Chris and his family live in the house beyond that. But we'll meet him at the big stable, which is along this trail." Sure enough, within a few minutes Derek, could smell what was unmistakably stable.

A dark-haired young man awaited them, whom Martha introduced as her cousin Christopher. The teens strolled into the stable with easy familiarity while Derek followed more slowly. There were stalls in which stood five or six horses. Martha and Chris walked right in among them while Derek hung back, a little intimidated by how big they were when you stood next to them.

"Here she is," Martha grinned, holding the head of a glossy chestnut-colored horse with a roughly circular white blotch on her forehead. "We call her Daisy. She's gentle, but can move quickly when she has to."

Derek didn't want to be shamed by a couple of kids half his age, so he stepped up to Daisy and patted her nose. She looked at him with liquid brown eyes and then startled him by shaking her head.

"C'mon, Martha," Chris urged as he reached for a pitchfork. "I'm guessing you haven't been around horses much, Mr. Derek?"

"Not really," Derek admitted, grateful to be able to come clean.

"Most people haven't," Chris acknowledged. He and Martha were now busy flinging dirty straw into something that looked like a small trailer. "In a way, that's good, because you can learn to work with them properly. Those of us who grow up with them sometimes forget how big and strong they are, and that they need to be treated with respect. For instance, you don't want to linger behind them, and you'll want to avoid making loud noises and sudden movements."

Grateful for Chris's consideration for his inexperience, Derek listened and watched as the farm youngsters gave the horses their evening care. He learned the difference between hay and straw ("Hay is what you put in front of the horse, straw is what you put behind it"), helped fill the troughs with oats, and tried his hand at brushing them. Martha was aghast when she heard that he'd never actually ridden a horse.

As they were working, Derek heard other noises toward the back of the stable and asked if it was more horses.

"No, those are cattle," Chris explained. "We've about a dozen head of our own, and are keeping about half a dozen for others."

"Dairy cows?" Derek asked.

"No, these are all beef. We tried a few head of dairy cows a few years back, but it was too much trouble. We know how to do beef. There's a family up Brown City way who does a lot of dairy; we grow feed and trade them for milk and cheese."

"So – do you slaughter them yourselves?"

"No, we cart 'em up to a guy near Marlette. He slaughters, skins, and quarters them. We butcher the quarters into the cuts we want. Butchering weekend is busy around here!"

Derek tried to imagine that as the youngsters wrapped up their chores. Martha took him back to the house, which had grown much quieter. Philip was reading a book, and Elizabeth and Jude were at some board game. Derek watched them for a bit, then started looking around for his jacket – it was probably time for him to be going.

"Ah, Derek," Kent said, stepping through the front door. "Looking for your coat? We hung it in here." He reached into a closet by the door. Derek donned it and stepped out onto the front porch with Kent.

"A beautiful evening," Kent commented. "A pity there are so many clouds. On a clear night, you can see the sky filled with stars. We aren't totally free of light pollution, but there's a lot less of it out here."

"I'm sure it's beautiful," Derek said. "I'd love to see it sometime."

"I want to thank you for coming out," Kent continued. "Especially on such short notice. It's been a privilege to have you."

Derek looked at him in surprise. "I'm the one who should be thanking you. Your whole family was so generous and hospitable that...well, thank you." Derek trailed off, unable to articulate what he was thinking. He'd found the whole evening delightful, without a trace of the edginess or discomfort he usually felt in the midst of strangers. He realized that this was because he hadn't felt like a guest at all – he'd felt like a member, like he belonged.

"Pah." Kent waved his hand dismissively. "The honor is all ours. Truthfully, after what you did for John, we owe you a debt of gratitude that we'll never be able to repay. In fact, Linda upbraided me a little for inviting you out on a Friday, when all she could set before you were lentils and bread. She wants me to have you back out when she can prepare a proper dinner in your honor."

Derek was amazed. He didn't know what Friday had to do with anything, but that meal had been the most delicious he'd had in years. "I assure you, Kent, dinner was wonderful. Please thank Linda for me."

"I will, but she still wants to get you back out here for a proper supper. She was talking about her slow-roasted beef loin and peach cobbler, and take my word: you don't want to miss either. The kids love you, though you thoroughly scandalized Martha."

"How so?" Derek asked.

"She can't believe you've have never had the chance to ride a horse," Kent replied. "She wants to rectify that as soon as possible. How soon will you be able to come back out?"

"Oh." Derek was surprised, yet in that moment, a keen longing rose within him to do just that – to return to this warm and welcoming home so full of busyness that wasn't chaos. In fact, he suddenly realized that getting into his car and driving away felt like going into exile, returning to bleak and barren lands. "Well, I –"

"How does next Saturday look?" Kent asked. "In fact, if you're not busy, why not come out for the weekend? We have a guest suite where you could stay away from the noise. Give you a little taste of real country life."

Part of Derek instinctively recoiled. Why, he couldn't, he had – but then he realized that there was no good reason he couldn't accept. Sure, it would disturb his normal weekend routine, but what of it? "Well, I'll have to check my busy social calendar," he quipped. "But I think that'll be fine. In fact, it sounds wonderful. Thank you."

"Believe me, Derek, the pleasure is ours," Kent grinned with a firm handshake. "Drive safely, and we can touch base later in the week regarding details."

As Derek drove back along the dark country lanes, the clouds parted a bit and he caught a glimpse of the star-strewn night sky. It was an impressive sight. Maybe next weekend the sky would be clear, and he'd get to see it full of stars. He grinned – another reason to return. Plus, he hoped to fulfill a lifelong dream.

He was going to ride a horse.

New Friends

Janice was just stepping out of the shower when her phone chimed with the message from Derek.

Got a time to meet?

Janice glanced at the time, sighed, and messaged back: *1 hr?*

OK. Where? Derek returned.

Janice sent him the address. She sighed again and resumed drying her hair. She'd been dreading this day – but then, she'd dreaded yesterday and she dreaded tomorrow and she dreaded her future as far as she could see. At least by the end of today she should be clear of the hassle of the house and Brenda. She blinked back sudden tears of mourning for the loss of the friendship she and Brenda had once shared.

Derek met her at the house at the specified time, and it took them less than an hour to clear out her belongings. Brenda was off at work, and though Kenny was lounging on the couch smoking, he didn't do anything beyond glare sullenly at them as they cleaned out Janice's room. Both cars packed, Janice followed Derek a couple of miles to his apartment, sniffing and wiping her eyes the entire way. When they arrived and started lugging boxes, Janice managed to carry in two before breaking down in sobs at the kitchen table. A distressed Derek fetched her some paper towels and asked what the trouble was. Since "everything" wasn't a reasonable answer, Janice just waved her hands while Derek hovered, wondering what he'd done wrong. Eventually she managed to convince him that it was nothing he had control over, and accepted his offer to bring in the remaining boxes by himself while she regained her composure.

Janice was comforted and a little amused by Derek's gallantry. He brought in all her stuff and piled it neatly in a corner that had been set aside just for her. He washed the dishes which they'd had to bring dirty, because Brenda had left them unwashed in the sink. He even kept bringing her new paper towels. When all that was finished, he offered to take her out for a pizza.

"Y'know," Derek ventured tentatively over a deep-dish Meat Monster, "I sure hope all this – distress – isn't connected to those test results. I'd hate to think I had any part in upsetting you so badly."

"No, no." Janice waved aside his concern. "Yes, the tests told me some things, but they were things I should have learned long ago – my dad said so. It's just – so much coming down at once." Grateful for his sympathetic ear, she talked about how sad she was at losing Brenda like this, and how her father was moving and hadn't even told her about it, and what she'd learned from him about her parentage. "So, it's like – I've been living a lie all these years," she concluded, slurping her pop. "My dad said he was going to tell me, but he was also going to tell me he was moving to Columbus – at some point."

"Wow," said Derek. "Wow – that is a lot going on at once. No wonder your life is so stressful. I sympathize, particularly with learning about your – parental situation. It was hard for me when I learned the truth about my conception."

"Really?"

"Yeah – I don't know who my father is," Derek admitted.

"You don't?" Janice asked, then realized the delicacy of the topic. "You – you don't have to tell me anything you don't want to."

"Oh, it's not an issue," Derek said dismissively. "I was raised by my mom, who identified herself as 'a single mother'. Just that, never a reference to a husband or the father of her child. I thought that was just the way it was until I got old enough to learn that there had to be a father in there somewhere. Mom dismissed my questions, saying that she didn't want to talk about my father. But she didn't reckon with the determination and technical skills of a curious fourteen-year-old. I went rummaging in her old files and found that decades ago she'd kept a 'blog' – short for weblog, kind of an online journal. It was full of a lot of whining and complaining about men and relationships and how she 'couldn't get lucky'. Just before she stopped updating it, she made some cryptic comments about 'going it alone'.

"That made me even more curious, so I snuck into her paper files and found the big envelope from the fertility lab."

"Fertility lab?" Janice asked.

"Yeah. She went in for artificial insemination from an anonymous sperm donor. The papers had all the details – except, of course, the identity of the donor. There was just a numeric ID that she could use in case of any questions on genetic issues. So – the only thing I know about my father is an eight-digit number, which puts me in a similar situation to you."

"Wow, Derek," Janice said. "Did you ever – bring it up with your mom?"

"No," Derek shook his head. "I was hardly going to confront her as a teenager, and by the time I got older, I'd come to peace with the idea. My mom has enough problems without my deliberately causing more."

"Well, at least you share some genes with your mother," Janice muttered.

"It doesn't make much difference," Derek shrugged. "I suspect that having me wasn't the key to happiness that my mother thought it would be. Not so much me in particular, but the whole concept of having a kid. I used to wonder what it was about how she treated me. Looking back, I now realize what it was: I was always a nuisance, a hindrance, a problem to be dealt with."

"I know what you mean there," Janice sighed. "I got the same vibe from my mother, especially as I got into my teens and we started butting heads more often. Turns out it was buyer's remorse – literally – on her part."

"So I understand how you feel," Derek assured her. "I may seem calm now, but I was pretty upset at the time. I'd fantasize about storming into my mother's room and demanding the truth, or contacting the lab, but I never did any of it. Instead my mom and I just drifted apart. That big secret, plus the fact that she's made no attempt to come clean with me about it, have been like an invisible wedge between us. That's why I had no compunction about taking this job here, leaving her in New York."

"What does she do?" Janice asked.

"She was a financial counselor of some type," Derek replied. "She's semi-retired now, I think. She spends a lot of time in the community garden."

"Ah," Janice said, picking a piece of pepperoni off the pizza. "Which just leaves me to figure out what do to."

"With what?" Derek asked.

"Oh, my life," Janice answered. "Since I'm not who and what I always thought I was, who and what am I?"

"Oh," Derek replied quietly, "That sounds a bit profound for me to help with. But I can help with something more immediate, if you'd like."

"Like what?"

"Apartment hunting. I can do searches and send you links to likely rentals. If time is a big problem, I could even do some walkthroughs for you, just to weed out the rat holes."

Janice looked at Derek and blinked a few times. "Really?" she asked. "You'd do that for me?"

Derek looked back in confusion. "Why, sure – it's not like you're asking me to build you a house or something."

"Well, of course not," Janice said. "But still – "

"Look, I can't help you much with these big issues you're grappling with," Derek pointed out. "But I can be your friend, can't I?"

"So – you're an Ishmael," Melissa said.

"I'm a what?" Janice asked.

Melissa was still on days for the week, but she'd caught Janice at the start of the afternoon shift. Picking up on Janice's distress, she'd cajoled her into telling about the DNA test and aftermath. Once she'd heard the story, she made that immediate pronouncement.

"An Ishmael. It's a story from the Bible. Of course, Ishmael was a guy, but the principle applies. Turns out that Abraham couldn't sire a son with his wife. Since that was the all-important thing, he started getting nervous. So he took a servant and bedded her, and she got pregnant with a boy they named Ishmael," Melissa explained.

"That's in the Bible?" Janice asked.

"Sure it is," Melissa replied. "That's how they did surrogacy in the old days. But it gets better. Eventually, Abraham's real wife gets pregnant by him, so Ishmael and his mama are

suddenly *persona non grata*. At his wife's instigation, Abraham
pitches them both out of the tribe to wander off into the desert."

"Wow," Janice said, amazed.

"Yeah, and that was Abraham, the big father of faith that so
many religions look up to. Your situation differs in only a few
details – sounds like your mama wanted you at first but
eventually tired of you. She didn't have to kick you out into the
desert. She could just take a job in another city and move away
– gets rid of you just as effectively."

Janice's heart sank. It was bad enough to learn she'd been
lied to all her life, and Melissa's treatment made her feel like a
piece of shoddy merchandise that couldn't be returned and so had
been abandoned. But, in a sense, that was what had happened.

"Do me a favor, please," Janice pleaded. "Don't tell Ron
about this. He was so – snide. I don't want him crowing over
how right he was."

"I understand," Melissa said, patting her arm. "Ron's an old
friend and can be helpful, but what he lacks in tact, he makes up
for in sarcasm. This'll just be between you, me, and the wall."

"Thanks. Gotta go," Janice hurried off.

Melissa waited until she was well out of sight before pulling
out her phone and keying Porcher's number.

"Yeah. About Janice, the one we met at the bar? Direct hit.
Yup. Took the challenge, discovered she's an Ishmael. Not a
clue – she's totally gobsmacked. Her dad was going to tell her
'when she was ready'. Yeah, that's what I'm thinking. We're
back up, aren't we? Next Saturday night, Burton site? No, I'll
ask her tomorrow, and I'll ensure she's not scheduled."

The next afternoon Janice again bumped into Melissa at shift
change.

"Hey, kid, how are you doing?" Melissa asked. "A little
better?"

"A little," Janice admitted. "Of course, I've also got the
hassle of finding an apartment, but a friend is helping with that."

"Wonderful. Listen, I was wondering if you'd like to come
with me to a little gathering over near Flint this Saturday
evening?" Melissa asked.

"Gathering? What kind of gathering?" Janice replied.

"It's hard to describe," Melissa said. "It's like a rally, but it's an educational and motivational thing, too. They have speakers come in. But mostly it's a mixer for like-minded people to gather and get to know one another. I thought you'd like it."

"A rally?" Melissa mused, wrinkling her brow. "I don't know, Melissa."

"Just a thought," Melissa said, gathering up her things. "You just seemed a little – lost and alone, with all the developments in your life. I thought you might like the chance to broaden your horizons a bit, make a few new friends. But if you're all set, then – "

"Oh, no, Melissa – I appreciate your thinking of me, and I do want to meet new friends. It's just that the new schedule isn't out yet, and I'm not sure I won't have shift that evening."

"Well, depending on your work schedule, of course," Melissa allowed. "I think you'd find it a fun gathering. You probably have a lot in common with many of the people who'll be there. Many of them are medical workers. Could you give me a ride over?"

"Um – sure, if I can make it," Janice agreed.

"Super! See you!" Melissa bustled off, leaving a puzzled Janice wondering what she'd just agreed to.

The week crawled by, with Derek searching for apartments and forwarding links to Janice, who made the calls did the occasional visit. The problem was the usual one, striking a balance between affordability and livability, particularly a suitable location. Finding a decent place in a decent neighborhood was challenging, given what Janice could afford by herself.

As the week drew toward its close, Derek's innate shyness began to rear its head. Why had he agreed to go spend the weekend in the home of virtual strangers? What did he know about these people, anyway? He had almost decided to message Kent and beg off, but Kent beat him to the punch by calling to confirm the visit. Once Kent explained that Linda was already thawing the beef loin, Martha had located a saddle for him, and Matthew had a stack of books all ready, Derek couldn't back out.

So Friday morning he threw an overnight bag into his car and he headed out to the Schaeffers after work.

The weather report called for clear skies and sun all weekend, so Derek hoped to get a view of the stars one evening. He pulled up under the tree and Martha, Tabitha, and little Matthew all tumbled down the porch steps to greet him. They escorted him to his room to drop off his gear and then to the dining room for dinner. The table was piled high with corn on the cob, a variety of vegetables, and plates of fish fritters (which Kent pronounced "hardly penitential", mystifying Derek.) Everyone treated him like family, and he stuffed himself with the delicious meal.

Afterwards, there was the inevitable reading to Matthew, and playing a board game with Elizabeth and Jude. Then Kent took him outside to see the last of the sunset and the stars coming out against the deep blue sky. It was an awe-inspiring sight, and Derek wondered why he didn't just stop and look up more often.

"You're our guest, and under no obligations," Kent said. "But some of the guys will be haying tomorrow morning as soon as the dew's off. You're welcome to join them, or not, as suits you. Martha will have you out on at least one ride this weekend, but she has responsibilities in the morning and won't be free until after lunch."

"The haying sounds good," Derek said. Now that he was here, he was determined to throw himself into this life as fully as he could. "What does it entail?"

Kent explained the basics of baling and stacking as the stars brightened overhead.

Derek awoke before his alarm, the morning sunlight streaming through the window. He could hear voices down the hall, and pulled his clothes on to go see who was awake.

Everyone, as it turned out, especially Matthew who ran to Derek, shrieking with excitement as he entered the kitchen. The kids were helping themselves from steaming platters laid out on the counter. Derek poured himself some coffee and grabbed a biscuit.

"Morning, Derek," Linda greeted him. "How did you sleep?"

"Very well, thanks," Derek replied as Philip sat down next to him.

"So – coming haying today?" Philip asked.

"I thought I'd give it a try, if you don't mind a rookie hanging about," Derek answered.

"Sure, welcome along," Philip said. "The more hands, the better. But – ah – is that your breakfast?"

"Sure," Derek said, looking at the biscuit. "I'm not much of a morning eater."

"Well," Philip grinned, scooping a generous portion of eggs onto a plate, adding some sausage, and placing it in front of Derek. "If you're working in the fields with us, you'll need more fuel than that."

After breakfast, Philip took Derek to the stable, where they met a couple of guys who were hitching the hay wagon to the baler.

"Guys, this is Derek, our guest for the weekend," Philip introduced him. "Derek, this is Cletus and Sixtus Winters, they live over at the Big House."

"The fields look to be drying nicely, so we should be able to get going soon," Cletus said. "The Wizard fixed the kick arm release for us, so we shouldn't have any problem with that."

"Um," said Sixtus a little hesitantly, looking at Derek. "Were you thinking of going out like that?"

"Like what?" Derek asked, looking at himself. He was wearing his usual knock-around garb, a t-shirt and jeans.

"You're right, Six," Philip admitted. "I hadn't even thought of it. Derek, you won't want to be haying with bare arms. Hold on – " He rummaged in a locker just inside the stable door. Returning with a tattered flannel shirt, he pitched it at Derek. "Try that. It'll be warm, but it's better than getting your arms scratched to pieces and sunburned on top of that."

"He'll need a hat, too, or his neck and face will be toast," Cletus added, grabbing a broad-brimmed hat from a peg. "How's that?"

"A bit snug, to be honest," Derek said, tugging at the brim.

"Okay, try this," Cletus throwing him another.

"That's better," Derek said.

"Which leaves – the shoes," Sixtus said. Derek glanced down to see that the others were all wearing sturdy leather boots, with which his light fabric running shoes contrasted sharply. The guys were shaking their heads and thinking.

"Is there a problem with wearing these?" Derek asked.

"More like a risk," Philip explained. "If someone lets a bale slip, you're going to want more than open weave fabric between it and your toes. At the least you'll have to deal with hay dust and scraps in your socks, which is scratchy. But I don't know what to suggest. Either of you guys have a spare pair of boots?"

"All I've got is my dress pair," Cletus said. "What shoe size you wear, Derek?"

"Ten, ten and a half," Derek said.

"Yeah, too large as well," Cletus shrugged. "You'll just have to wear what you have. Be sure to keep your feet away from any machinery. Let's get going."

Feeling completely rustic and a bit excited, Derek rode on the wagon out to the field where the cut hay was lying in long windrows. Sixtus lined the tractor up on one of them, engaged the baler, and started down the field. Philip explained that they were using a very old-fashioned kick baler that packed the hay into rectangular bales and then, by means of a strong spring-loaded arm, hurled the bale up onto the wagon. If the wagon had tall sides, the thrown bales could just pile up randomly, enabling one man to bale by himself if necessary. But if hands were available, the bales could be caught and neatly stacked, doubling the amount of hay that could be placed on the wagon. Even as he was explaining this, the first bale came flying up. Cletus caught it in midair and swung it back to them. Philip, who'd been expecting it, grabbed the bale and swung it in a smooth arc neatly into a corner of the wagon. The next bale came Derek's way, and Philip pointed to where he should drop it. The bale was lighter than Derek had been braced for, and simply swinging it into place wasn't all that strenuous.

"That wasn't so bad," Derek said a bit smugly.

"The first ones never are," Philip said with a grin. "This is an endurance game."

By the end of the third windrow, Derek was learning just how true that was. Though he quickly picked up the midair handoff trick that the other guys used, which used the thrown bale's momentum to help swing it into place, his arms and shoulders were feeling the unaccustomed strain. The flannel shirt made him hot, but he didn't dream of taking it off – given the scratches he'd taken through the long sleeves, he dreaded to think what his arms would look like without them. He was thirsty, too, but wasn't about to ask for a break before one of the teenagers did.

Derek was relieved when someone finally floated the suggestion of a break at the end of the fourth windrow. The wagon was nearly half full of bales stacked higher than their heads. They walked around the rig, stretching and joking and passing around a jug of lukewarm water, which tasted far better than Derek expected. Then they washed the hay particles off their necks and hands and prepared to get back to work.

As they got ready to resume, Sixtus suggested that Derek take a turn driving the tractor. Trying to hide his excitement, Derek listened carefully as Cletus explained the basic controls and how to position the tractor relative to the windrow, so the baler would sweep up all the hay. He let Derek start the tractor, make the turn, and align for the run. Once he was certain that Derek was steering true and geared for the proper pace, he jumped down and joined Sixtus and Philip in the wagon. Not wanting to make a fool of himself, Derek concentrated on following instructions and keeping the tractor properly aligned with the windrow. A few times he glanced back to watch the guys catch and stack the bales. Their more experienced handling looked almost like a dance, beside which Derek's best handling looked clumsy and jerky.

As they approached the end of the windrow, Derek was confident that he could make a smooth turn and line up on the next one. But he never got a chance, because a few dozen yards before the turn there came a grinding and thumping noise from the baler, and suddenly all the guys were jumping off the wagon and hollering at him to stop the tractor. Near panic, Derek slammed on the brake and fumbled with the clutch. He gladly slipped aside when Sixtus leapt up, threw the shift into neutral, and disengaged the power take off.

"Did – did I do something wrong?" Derek asked.

"No – you just had the bad luck to be driving," Sixtus said. "Can't be certain, but I think it's that release giving us problems again. This is one of the drawbacks of working with equipment that is just about antique. He said he'd fixed it, but he also said it was a quick patch. We should've allowed him time to fix it properly. "

"So – what do we do?" Derek asked, wondering who 'he' was.

"You and I will dash back to the stable for a tool kit," Sixtus explained, looking down to where Philip and Cletus were detaching the baler from the tractor. "They'll open up what they can while we're gone. Then we'll remove the release and pray that nothing got damaged when it failed."

So Derek endured a bumpy ride hanging on the side of the tractor while Sixtus drove it full speed back to the stable to fetch the tools. This enabled the men to open up the side of the baler and partially disassemble the internals. Derek just watched this evolution, impressed at how mechanically adept all the guys were. Bringing along one of the extracted parts, they piled on the tractor for the ride to the shop, where Sixtus and Derek stayed while the other two rode back out to take the wagon to the stable and unload what they could.

The shop was a long single-story building made of cinder blocks. "Hopefully he'll be able to fix this quickly, so we can get back out there today," Sixtus said, holding the part as he opened the door. The interior was dominated by several long tables which reached down the middle of the room. Something about the tables struck Derek as odd, and he swiftly realized that it was how low they were – the tops were several inches closer to the ground than was typical. Above the tables hung a surprising number of what looked like cables or ropes. Some of these hung straight down, but others swept from the crown of the ceiling to anchor points on the walls. There were ladder-like extensions dropping from the rafters. The sides of the room were crowded with cupboards and shelves full of random stuff.

"Hello?" Sixtus called. At first there was no answer, but then a voice called back:

"Did it break?"

Derek could scarcely make out the words, they were so slurred and oddly accented. He was just trying to recall where he'd heard such stilted speech when his question was answered. A short figure banged into the room, grabbed a low-hanging cable, and swung himself onto a table.

With astonishment, Derek recognized Sam, the handicapped man who'd mourned so deeply at the funeral. With even greater astonishment, he watched as Sam swung himself from the far end of the shop with astonishing agility using nothing but the hung cables and ladder-like things. He dropped on the table in front of them and held out his hand.

"Yeah, it broke, Sam," Sixtus said, giving him the part. "Didn't damage anything, but I'm not sure the part can be salvaged."

"Everything can be salvaged, with enough work," Sam slurred, turning the part over in his hands. "May have to machine a new one of these." He tapped a component that looked rather twisted.

Derek was struggling to adapt his hearing so he could follow Sam's indistinct speech, but Sixtus didn't seem to have any difficulty.

"Great, Sam," he said. "Any idea how long? We'd like to get that hay in today, if we can."

"Do my best – couple hours, maybe," Sam granted.

"That's terrific, Sam – call me when you're set," Sixtus said, turning to go. Derek started to back away, too. As at the funeral, he found that even the sight, much less the proximity, of the crippled man made him uncomfortable.

But Derek was not to get away that easily. "You!" Sam nearly barked, smacking the table with something that looked like a short cane. The cane was pointed right at Derek, and Sam was eyeing him from under dark brows.

"Ah – yes?" Derek asked, wondering what he'd done wrong.

"You're Derek, right?"

"Yes," Derek answered tentatively.

"You help with John Holmes, right?"

"Well – yes, in a way," Derek began, but Sam cut him off.

"Thank you," Sam barked, thrusting out his hand. Surprised, Derek took the hand and found his seized in an almost shockingly powerful grip.

"Just doing what I could," Derek stammered under that piercing gaze.

"Thank you," Sam repeated solemnly, then released Derek's hand and turned his attention back to the broken part.

"Thanks, Sam – let us know," Sixtus said as they departed. Once outside, Derek shook his hand and Sixtus grinned. "Yeah, Sam's a bit of a surprise when you first meet him."

"And he's...he's your mechanic?" Derek asked.

"And metalworker, and electrician, and plumber, and electronics tech, and pretty much everything else," Sixtus explained. "His disability fools everyone. He's got a genius grade intellect and is the cleverest guy with his hands that I know. Because his legs are crippled and his speech is slurred, people underestimate both his mind and body. But the palsy only affects his lower body, so he compensates by using his arms and shoulders, which is why they're so strong."

"That's why he swings around like that?" Derek asked.

"Exactly," Sixtus confirmed. "He's rigged those lines and braces all over his shop – you'll see some in the barns and garages, too. He can whip himself around on those with amazing speed."

"Wow," Derek said. "If that's how he gets around, no wonder his arms are so strong."

"Yeah," Sixtus said. "Do *not* try to arm wrestle him. Hey, you're planning to ride with the kids after lunch, right?"

"That was the plan, but – " Derek began, not wanting to appear to be shirking.

"It's fine," Sixtus waved him off. "It's almost lunch now, so you go in. I'll go help the guys until they ring the bell for us. Hopefully Sam will have that part soon – he always overestimates the time it'll take him – and we can clear that field this afternoon. Thanks for your help."

Derek headed in to Kent and Linda's place, catching a glimpse of a sprawling ranch house beyond a bank of trees. He guessed that was the 'Big House' to which everyone kept referring. It looked like quite a complex, with ponds and big decks and a gazebo. He wondered if one family occupied all that space.

Linda and Elizabeth were bustling about the kitchen preparing lunch, and Derek chatted with them about how the baling had gone. Linda chuckled when she heard his account of visiting Sam's workshop.

"He's a caution, isn't he? Don't be put off by his gruff speech – it's part of his condition. He lacks the ability to add the modulations and inflections we all learn as part of speaking. Most of what he says comes out sounding like something between a bark and a growl. You have to work with him a long time, and learn to read his eyes and mannerisms before you can pick up on his subtleties. He really has quite the sense of humor, once you figure out his communication style."

Lunch was a brisk affair, with those who were present sitting down at a table heaped with sandwiches and cheese and deliciously fresh vegetables, with fruit afterwards. Everyone chatted about what they'd been doing all morning, except Martha, who focused her conversation on the afternoon's ride. Derek was puzzled, because it looked for all the world like Martha had been starting to speak, but had been quelled by a quick glance from Kent, after which she'd been happy to focus on horses. She was champing at the bit to get out to the stable, so as soon as she and Derek were finished they were given permission to go.

Chris was already in the stable, prepping and saddling the horses. Derek got the impression that they'd both escaped an afternoon of chores in order to accommodate the guest, and were eager to get out on the trail before anyone changed their mind. But there was nothing flighty about their instructions to Derek. They had for him a dapple grey horse named Kilroy, whom Martha described as "lively enough, but won't go crazy." They showed him how to hold the reins and sit in the saddle and how to stop and turn the horse. Then the sore topic came around again.

"Are those," Chris asked hesitantly. "The best shoes you've got, Mr. Derek?"

Derek again looked down at his running shoes, noticing that the kids both wore thick-soled work boots like the guys had worn for haying.

"I'm afraid so," Derek admitted, resolving to rectify the situation before he came out again. "Does it make that much difference with horses?"

"Sometimes you have to kick them to get their attention, and soft soles don't make much of an impression," Chris explained. "And if the horse runs too close to a branch or tree, you won't want your foot caught with no protection."

Derek was beginning to wonder if his poor choice of footwear was going to derail his first ever horseback ride. He needn't have worried. Derek was Martha's ticket to an afternoon of riding, and she was hardly going to let a triviality like his shoes hinder that.

"He'll be okay, Chris," she said confidently. "We'll make sure Kilroy minds, and we'll keep to the center of the trails. Let's go!"

They walked the horses out of the stable and, to Derek's surprise, didn't head directly out over the fields. Instead they skirted the outbuildings until they came to a band of trees. There they had Derek practice mounting and dismounting a few times before everyone mounted up and they turned toward the woods. Derek was puzzled, as Martha appeared to be headed toward a dense thicket of bushes, but at the last minute she skirted and went behind them. Following her, Derek saw that indeed a trail began there, but you had to know it was there to find it.

Once behind the bushes, they found themselves on a wide, well-groomed trail that seemed to run up the center of a narrow strip of trees. Chris explained that these long woods were mostly windbreaks, planted along the edges of fields to block the wind and prevent soil erosion. There were also larger stands, sometimes five or ten acres, that hadn't been cleared because the soil was unsuitable or the farmer didn't need the ground. The trails cut through these, enabling them to ride quite a distance in the shade. Derek appreciated that, though he didn't appreciate the flies and mosquitoes that swarmed about. He was again grateful for the hat and flannel shirt.

"Have these trails always been here?" Derek asked Chris.

"No," Chris explained. "These are relatively recent – ten, maybe fifteen years. But you can go for miles on them. If we had to, we could go nearly to Yale in the north or Capac in the west without substantially breaking cover."

When they'd walked long enough they trotted for a while. Martha wanted to try cantering and galloping, but Chris thought that would be best on the way back, near home, when Derek was more accustomed to riding. For his part, Derek was satisfied just getting the feel of rising and falling with the horse's gait, sitting up and gripping with his knees. He may have once entertained some fantasies of leaping into the saddle and galloping off, but now that he was up here, he realized that it would be a while before he could do that. There was a lot more rider participation in horseback riding than he'd ever appreciated.

Walking and trotting, they passed along many miles of trails with which the youngsters seemed quite familiar. Occasionally, they'd cross roads, but always to plunge back into woods on the other side. Derek mostly rode quietly, concentrating on his posture and avoiding low-hanging branches. He chatted intermittently with Chris, though not so much with Martha, who stayed out ahead. At last they came to a spot where they turned onto what appeared to be a side trail, where there was a stand of small trees and bushes. Seated on the horses, they could see over the thicket, and spotted a cinder block building that looked abandoned.

"What's that?" Derek asked.

"The old factory," Martha explained. "Though Daddy says it was probably a tool and die shop. It's been empty for decades. There are old abandoned buildings like this all over the area."

"Ah – I was wondering if it was your school," Derek said, nudging Kilroy forward to get a better look.

"Oh, we don't go to school," Chris replied. "We're off the grid kids."

"Christopher!" Martha nearly barked. Derek wasn't certain he'd heard Chris correctly, and turned in his saddle to see Martha holding Chris' horse by the bridle and talking quickly to him in a fierce whisper. Chris looked chastened, but Martha looked alarmed, almost terrified.

"I'm sorry," Derek said. "I didn't quite catch that."

"I just meant – we don't get into town that much," Chris said quietly.

"Ah. So, how far is this from the farm?" Derek asked.

"Almost twelve miles by trail," Martha said. "Though about fifteen by road."

"Listen," Chris said. "Someone's coming." They all went quiet, and sure enough, they could hear the sound of something motorized on the trail behind them.

"Trail bike?" Derek asked.

"Wonder who it is," Martha said, looking a bit nervous. They hadn't long to wait – a strange looking motorcycle came into view, ridden by a strange looking rider.

"Mr. Sam!" Martha cried. Sure enough, it was Sam, riding a three-wheeled cycle with two of the wheels in front. They were narrow-set, making the scooter only a little wider than a motorcycle.

"He made that himself," Chris informed Derek. "He can't ride a motorcycle because of his balance, but he sometimes wants to go places too narrow for a four-wheeler."

"Hey, guys!" Sam called, stopping his bike far enough away that the exhaust didn't spook the horses. He unhitched two canes from the bike and made his way toward them. They dismounted to greet him.

"Part fixed," Sam said to Derek. "Haying done today. I decided, go for ride!"

"We were just looking at the old factory, Mr. Sam. Do you think it was a tool and die shop?" Martha asked.

"Maybe," Sam agreed. "Tool and die, machining, maybe casting or pattern. See the heavy power lines?" They looked at the decrepit building for a while before Sam announced, "In use again."

"Really?" Chris asked skeptically. "Still looks empty to me."

"Only once in a while," Sam explained. "Meter running again, fresh tire tracks in dirt."

"Do you come here often?" Chris asked.

"Time to time," Sam replied, then pointed with one of his canes. "Weird. Meter running, but never lights. Tire tracks, but never cars parked. Weird." To Derek, Sam seemed affronted by the strange behavior around the empty factory.

"Mr. Sam, do you have any plans for dinner tonight?" Martha asked.

"Sandwich. Shop. Work to do," Sam grunted.

"Mom's making loin," Martha coaxed. "It's been roasting all day. You should smell it."

"Loin? Your mom?" Sam asked with bright eyes. "Maybe dinner there!"

"Plenty of room at the table," Martha assured him.

"And we'd better get going, if we're going to make it back in time," Chris added. Sam climbed back on his scooter and roared away while the riders followed.

They rode a little more quickly on the return trip, which was a mixed blessing for Derek. He felt more confident in the saddle, and appreciated the breeze and leaving the flies behind, but his hips and legs were starting to remind him that he'd never done this before.

Back at the farm, the dinner table was a merry cacophony, especially after Sam showed up. The kids all treated him like a favorite uncle. The slow-roasted loin was like nothing Derek had ever tasted, and the roasted potatoes made a superb complement. Everyone excitedly chattered about their day while Derek listened, gorged himself, and flexed various parts to ease stiff muscles.

"What?!" At the other end of the table, Linda's voice rose in a tone of amazement and rebuke. "Martha Therese, you didn't!"

Derek looked down to see Martha looking guiltily at her plate under Linda's stern gaze, but Kent and Philip were looking at him with wonder and a little pity.

"Wow – did you really?" Philip asked.

"Did I really what?" Derek replied.

"Ride to the old factory this afternoon?" Kent said.

"Um – yes," Derek confirmed. "Is that a problem?"

"Young lady, you knew full well that this was our guest's first time riding," Linda admonished Martha sternly. "I had expected you to demonstrate far more prudence and consideration than that! Five miles, maybe, but not almost to the next county! That was completely irresponsible!"

"Yes'm," Martha said to the table.

"A bit *into* the next county, actually," Philip added, *sotto voce*.

Derek felt surprised and a little awkward on Martha's behalf. "Please, nothing happened, and I only feel a little stiff now."

Kent and Philip gave him sympathetic looks. "Now isn't when you feel it," Kent assured him.

Bastards

Janice's day was trying as well, though in different ways. She visited the laundromat in the morning and spent the rest of the day touring potential apartments. Only three were even close to acceptable. She returned to the tiny hotel room feeling wrung out and discouraged. Part of her was tempted to message Melissa and beg off the meeting that evening – gas costs were a factor as well – but the alternative was sitting around the room staring at the walls. Also, she'd promised to give Melissa a ride.

Janice picked Melissa up at the hospital. She threw some sort of duffel in the back seat, muttering something about staying with some friends. On the ride west, they chatted about work and Janice's apartment search and other trivialities. Janice subtly probed for more information about the group hosting the meeting or rally or whatever it was, but Melissa was maddeningly vague. It sounded a bit like a professional association and a bit like a fraternity and a bit like a club, but no specifics were forthcoming.

"You'll like us," Melissa assured her. "We're really fun and open, and have a lot in common. You'll fit right in."

"Okay," Janice conceded, not wanting to press too hard. "When does this – gathering – begin? Should we grab a bite along the way?"

"Oh, no, there'll be a buffet," Melissa explained. "Plenty of food and drinks, too, and I don't mean fruit punch."

"Oh," Janice said, a little surprised. "Is there – a fee, or something?"

"Nope. You're my guest, and we love guests."

They eventually came to Burton, an eastern suburb of Flint. Flint had once been one of the prominent cities in the state, but decades of job losses and urban decay had left it a shell of its former self. Janice couldn't remember ever having attended anything around here. Melissa directed her to a building whose parking lot was filling up, with many people heading inside.

Janice's spirits lifted a little – maybe this wouldn't be as boring as she feared, and at least she'd get a dinner out of it.

Melissa grabbed her duffel and they headed in. Just inside the door there was a reception desk staffed by what looked like security guards. As people came in, they passed by the desk and swiped cards past a reader, after which they were welcomed and waved in. Melissa walked right up to the desk.

"Sherri, Alex, this is my friend Janice," Melissa introduced her. "She's my guest tonight." Melissa pulled out her hospital ID and tapped the reader.

"Janice, what a pleasure," Sherri said with a broad smile. "We're so glad you could join us."

Alex, who'd been rummaging in a drawer, pulled out a loop woven of thick yellow ceremonial cord. "Glad you could make it, Janice," he said, handing her the loop.

"You wear it, dear," Melissa explained when she saw Janice' mystified expression. "It's so everyone can welcome you properly. Here," she took the loop and draped it around Janice's neck. Janice wasn't sure she liked being so prominently identified, but could hardly object.

"Do you have your hospital ID?" Melissa asked.

"Um – yeah, it's in here," Janice said, fishing in her purse.

"Any ID will do, but since so many of us are medical we often use our staff IDs," Melissa explained. "That's good, just tap it there." Janice tapped her ID while Alex fiddled with a keyboard.

"And you're set," he pronounced. "Have a great time."

Melissa steered Janice through the large lobby area wherein clusters of people were standing around holding drinks or little hors d'oeuvre plates and chatting. Everyone looked very familiar with everyone else – just the kind of social milieu in which Janice was least comfortable. Even Melissa was calling out greetings and hailing people as they passed by. Janice fingered her bright yellow token and felt excluded.

"Well, kid, the food is right here – snacks and such on this table, sandwiches and wraps down there," Melissa said as they approached a long buffet. "The bar is that way. If you'll excuse me, I have *got* to run to the ladies' room. Be right back." Melissa patted Janice on the arm and bustled off. Janice looked at the mob crowding around the buffet and decided to wait until it thinned out a little. She didn't want to try the bar without Melissa at her side, not while wearing such a prominent badge of outsider-hood.

Melissa did visit the restroom, then tucked her duffel in a cloak room and sent a message. She lingered in the hallway outside the cloak room, occasionally glancing out across the lobby. Eventually, a man came around the corner.

"Where have you been?" Melissa asked with exasperation. "I messaged you on the way over, and was expecting you at the door!"

"I was tied up," the man answered nonchalantly. His outfit was a masterwork of understated elegance, his hair perfect, his stubble neatly trimmed, and even in the dim lighting he was wearing the tinted wraparound glasses which he favored. He clearly thought a lot of himself and was just waiting for the rest of the world to come around. "So – where is she?"

"There – by the buffet," Melissa nodded to where Janice stood alone while the chatting crowd swirled around her. She was stroking the yellow cord and looking around nervously.

"Sheesh," the man grimaced. "I know how important nurses are, but why do they have to be so dumpy?"

Melissa looked at him with contempt. "Because the good-looking ones have already married doctors," she sneered.

The man looked back at her with indifference. "I don't care – bring 'em anyways."

"Just do your damn job," Melissa snarled in disgust, stalking away. The man glanced after her, shrugged, and sidled into the crowd.

"I didn't know whether you preferred red or white, so I brought one of each," came a voice from right behind Janice, causing her to nearly jump with surprise.

"Oh – you startled me," Janice said as she turned to see a nicely dressed man standing there with a glass of wine in each hand. He was clearly speaking to her, but she'd never seen him before. "Is – are those for me?"

"If you wish them both, you're welcome to them," the man smiled.

"Oh, no," Janice stammered. "One – one will be fine, Mr. – "

"Logan Thompson, no mister," the man said, stepping closer and holding out both glasses. Janice tentatively took the red wine. "And you must be Janice."

"Yes, I am," Janice said weakly as she sipped the wine. The man was standing very close, holding the glass of white and looking down at her.

"Melissa is a friend of mine," Logan explained. "She mentioned she'd be bringing a guest, and I've been looking forward to meeting you."

"You have?" Janice asked, taking another swig of wine. Why was it so warm in here?

"Of course," Logan said. "We always love guests. Though I would have come sooner had Melissa mentioned – say, let me get you something to eat. You'll be wobbling where you stand if you keep drinking that on an empty stomach." He handed Janice his glass and headed for the buffet, leaving Janice feeling confused and a little woozy – her wine was nearly gone.

Logan returned shortly with a plate piled with delicious looking goodies and another glass of red wine. Clearly, he wasn't intimidated by the crowds.

"Come on – there are some coffee tables over here that should be empty by now," he gestured toward a corner of the room which Janice hadn't noticed. There were some sofas, so they perched at the end of one, unnoticed by the two women carrying on an animated conversation at the other end. Janice and Logan shared the plate, with Janice trying not to be too greedy, which was difficult because she was hungrier than she'd thought. Logan questioned her about her job and her living situation, and fetched her another glass of wine when she'd finished her second. He was really quite nice, helping her feel much more welcome.

"It's about time for the program," Logan said as she was finishing. "You drink up while I clear this away. The restrooms are down that hall – why don't I meet you by those doors?"

"Sure," Janice agreed. "I wonder where Melissa went?"

"She's probably tied up," Logan explained. "She has a lot of responsibilities."

Janice tried to spruce herself up as best she could in the bathroom mirror. She wished she'd worn a nicer outfit, and a bit more makeup. She half-wondered if Logan would still be there when she came out, but there he was, right where he said he'd be. He held open one of the doors with a charming smile.

"What's – is this what happens next?" Janice asked, a little confused.

"Oh, didn't Melissa tell you?" Logan asked, following her through the door into a wide semicircular area that sloped gently down toward a stage-like platform, on which stood a solitary lectern. Chairs were arranged in rows facing the platform, and people were making their way in through doors around the edge of the room. "We usually have a program of some type – a lecture, or an inspirational talk, or a panel. Don't worry, it won't take too long, and it's usually pretty interesting."

"Okay," Janice said, wishing she hadn't accepted that third glass of wine. "What is this place? Is it a theater?"

"No, it used to be a church," Logan explained.

"A church?"

"Sure. They've been folding up all over the region for the past twenty years, particularly after they started having to pay taxes. They pose a real problem for the cities, because they'll just be abandoned and start to decay, but they don't sell easily because they're not good for much other than their original purpose. We found out about this one and picked it up for a song."

"Y'know," Janice said, shaking her head to dispel some of the fuzziness and trying to fix Logan with a serious gaze, "there's something I keep trying to pin Melissa down about, but she never quite answers."

"What's that?" Logan asked.

"Who's 'we'?" Janice pressed. "You – and she – keep talking about 'we'. 'We' have a problem, 'we' got the building. What kind of organization or club is this?"

Logan smiled and patted her hand. "Melissa might be vague because it's a little hard to tightly define us. I'd call us a brotherhood, but many of us are women. Perhaps 'fellowship' is a good term."

"But – what do you *do*?" Janice asked. "What are you about?"

"Quite a few things, actually," Logan replied. "Professional development, for one – seminars, networking, things like that. Oh, and plenty of opportunities for hanging out, like social events, parties, outings, and the like. You'll see some of that later."

"Okay," Janice said, still confused. "Does this – fellowship – have a name?"

"Shh – he's starting," Logan patted her shoulder and pointed to a where a man was walking to the lectern. "Hopefully you'll understand better by the end of the evening."

Everyone applauded politely as the man welcomed them. The way he spoke gave Janice the impression that these gatherings were resuming after a recess of some type, perhaps a summer break. He made some announcements about matters that meant nothing to Janice.   Then, to her surprise and embarrassment, she was introduced.

"I understand," the man announced loudly. "That we have some guests in our midst tonight. Would you be so kind as to stand so we can welcome you?"

There was general applause, and Logan was levering her up by the elbow. Another guy on the far side of the room also stood, wearing the yellow cord necklace and looking around shyly. Now Janice really wished she'd worn a better outfit, and washed her hair for that matter. But the welcome she was getting was more than warm – people were applauding for the guests more enthusiastically than they'd applauded for the man at the lectern. Logan was among them, looking up at her with a big smile and clapping loudly. She reached down for reassurance and he clasped her hand. When the applause started to fade and she sat down again, he still held it, smiling reassuringly at her.

"See? We don't bite," he whispered, his lips brushing her hair. She blushed and smiled, gripping his hand more tightly.

The man at the lectern was doing some kind of brief introduction, and then everyone was applauding as a tall man with jet-black hair came striding out. He had a heavy jaw and dark eyes that Janice found a little unsettling. They were so black that for a brief moment she thought they looked like empty voids in his face. But he was brisk and confident in his manner, and there was something grimly fascinating about those eyes.

"Who's that?" Janice asked Logan.

"Charon Strom. One of the higher ups."

Charon set his tablet on the lectern, gripped the edges firmly as he looked out over his audience, and then spoke in a crisp baritone.

"Good evening, bastards."

There was a moment of heavy silence in which could be heard a few halfhearted laughs as well as the faint hint of some gasps. Janice was a little startled herself, but guessed that the speaker had reason for such a provocative opening. Nor was she wrong.

"Yes, I called you bastards, and I'm sorry if anyone is offended, but I do not recant," Charon continued. "The time has come for frank, even brutal, speech, and if you cannot take that, then you'd better leave now. For we stand on the threshold of the greatest change in human society since the Industrial Revolution, and possibly since civilization began.

"That's an audacious claim, so let me support it. Many have tried to understand why we humans do what we do. Particularly in the last three centuries, as the human race has moved into the age of reason, humankind has sought to examine and critique history in order to avoid our past mistakes. Unfortunately, the solution still eludes us – in fact, we now seem to be in worse shape than ever.

"I'd submit that the reason for that is that we haven't examined deeply enough. We've been like men standing on a watchtower, scanning to the horizon for the tallest structure in sight – yet we've never thought to look down at our own feet.

"I've lately been reading the works of some daring and insightful scholars, thinkers who have looked deeper than any who have come before. They've published some interesting theories and are proposing some challenging solutions. I'd like to share some of them with you bastards, because they have particular relevance to you."

Janice was impressed. So far Charon hadn't referred to whatever notes were on the tablet. He was walking about near the lectern, keeping his voice and delivery controlled, but she could see that he was containing tremendous passion. She wondered where he was going with this.

"Since the dawn of history, what we call civilization has been bent toward one thing: protecting and enhancing the power of families. Politics, economics, law, religion, and other social structures have all been constructed to that end. Principles of inheritance, bloodlines, and marriage have stood at the center of our civilizations as unexamined, unquestioned goods. In fact, some of you are probably wondering what the problem is with that.

"The problem is strewn across history, in plain sight for those with the guts and intelligence to look for it," Charon's delivery was intensifying now, and all eyes were upon him. "Even today – the unrest of Asia, the meltdown in Africa, the implosion of Europe – all these can be traced to political and economic policies designed to protect and prop up families. In fact, even the moral code which has been so central to civilization has been a blatant attempt to shield families. 'Honor your father and mother', 'Do not commit adultery', 'Do not covet your neighbor's wife'. Even the most central prayer of the Christians begins 'Our father'. See the deep-seated bias? Understand how central, how foundational, this orientation is?

"But there have always been outsiders, those with a different viewpoint. The outcasts, those on the margins, the ones who, according to the moral code, shouldn't even exist! The bastards. Dreaded, despised, shunned – from Ishmael to Mordred to Don John, their very existence was a threat to the social order, their very title an insult.

"These days, things are more complex. While it used to be a man bedding the wrong woman, now there are many ways to have children – as all of you know. Every one of you is here because you break the rules. Some of you are simple bastards, some are Ishmaels, some are petes – there are as many stories as there are of you. But even if you were conceived within the framework of a family, make no mistake – you're an outsider. The whole social order has been constructed from the ground up to protect the interests of families. Even if you've been ceded a place within the expected construct, you're still a threat.

"Here's the collision: medical technology has freed us from the bonds of reproducing like animals. That genie is out of the bottle and there's no getting him back in. But the foundations of civilization are still aligned with an outlook that's millennia old. Our society has yet to catch up with our technology, and until it does, folk like us are shoved to the margins.

"But there's an advantage to being on the margins—it gives us a distinct perspective. We can see things that those inside can't or won't see. We can spot weaknesses and failures others cannot. We have no sentimental attachments to how things are. We can dream of new, better ways because we have nothing to lose.

"By 'better ways' I mean things much deeper than political action or legal change. I mean nothing less than a radically new social order, a dramatically different basis for human relations, one that neither presupposes nor protects the traditional family."

Charon was well into his stride now, walking about the stage, punctuating his message with emphatic gestures. Janice was totally entranced, so she was all the more surprised when a hand went up in the audience off to her left, about three rows back from the platform. Charon noticed it and walked over to hear the woman's question, which Janice couldn't quite catch. There were quiet murmurings in the crowd as Charon stood with a pensive look, listening.

"Yes, that's an excellent observation, Becky – Becky, right?" Charon finally continued, walking back to the lectern. "Becky there, who clearly knows her history, asked if the Soviet Union didn't try something similar in the early days of the Communist Revolution, just over a century ago. She's right, they did – breaking up families, eliminating the distinction between legitimate and illegitimate children, and so on. They ultimately failed, but this stands as a testimony to just how radically we need to think. The problem with the Soviet Union was that the changes they implemented were too superficial. They sought to transfer people's loyalties from the family to the state, essentially trying to leverage the existing social orientation for their purposes. That's why that experiment broke down – they tried to build a new house on an old, crumbling foundation. The same is true for all the other great political experiments of recent centuries. The American Revolution, the French Revolution, the Revolutions of 1848 – all trying to implement the nation as the family writ large.

"In fact, this is why nothing has worked in the long run. Capitalism, communism, fascism, socialism – all have failed because none of them have been radical enough. They've all tried to build on the same faulty foundation. All these solutions have been surface patches, attempts to make a broken system work. That's why history has been a series of noble experiments followed by spectacular collapses."

Janice sat enthralled. It was like seeing for the first time – but it made such sense! It explained everything! Charon was striding about the platform now, his voice thundering with passion.

"But we – we can dare to dream, dare to envision, for we have nothing to lose! We're already outside, already excluded, so we can cry out that the emperor has no clothes. We can forge a new moral order, we can imagine a fresh future – one that respects individuals for who they are and what they hope for, not for which family they belong to. A future that treats everyone with an equality that transcends privileges of birth or security of economic position.

"You are the bearers of that future! You are the prophets of the new dawn! You are the leaders who will guide humanity out of the wreckage of millennia into a new beginning! You are the ones who will free them from the shackles of the past!

"I give you – each other. We have no place in this society, oriented as it is toward safeguarding families. We are the bastards, the outcasts. Embrace that, and embrace one another. Find unity in your common exclusion. You stand on the threshold of a great future, if you have the courage to seize it!"

The auditorium erupted. People were jumping and screaming and hugging each other in ecstasy. Janice stood with tears streaming down her face. Finally, she knew. At last, she fit. She turned to Logan and hugged him tight, sobbing into his shirt. Then a woman from the row behind hugged them both, and suddenly Janice was surrounded by people hugging her and kissing her and bidding her welcome.

Charon had descended from the stage into the crowd, shaking hands and accepting hugs as he worked his way through. Janice even didn't see him coming down the aisle until she turned and found herself facing him.

"I wanted to bid you a special welcome, guest," he said, taking her hands.

Overwhelmed, Janice sank to her knees before him. Sobbing with gratitude, she kissed his hands. He laid one hand gently on her head then moved on. Janice knelt still, letting the experience wash over her, contented yet at the same time tingling with excitement. Then people were leaning over her, gentle hands were lifting her. Whispers around her, "he came over just to welcome you!" Then she was hugging and kissing and sobbing on everyone she encountered, her heart overflowing with – was this joy?

Then Logan was by her side, escorting her out with the rest of the crowd that was leaving the auditorium. The large vestibule area, which had been set up for the reception when they'd arrived, had been transformed. The lights were dimmed, and moveable panels of dark fabric had been set up around the edges of the room, forming little alcoves. Low chairs and sofas had been placed in the alcoves, creating a room full of intimate little nooks in which people were already gathering.

Janice was interested to see that part of the transformation was that the walls now had prints hung upon them. She wandered over and saw that some of them looked familiar – classic scenes from the likes of Norman Rockwell. She recognized the one of the family gathered around the Thanksgiving table while the grandmother placed the turkey at the head of it. But there seemed to be something odd about the picture. Looking closer in the dim light, she saw that what she'd thought was the turkey looked more like the festering carcass of a small dog. Recoiling and wrinkling her nose in distaste, she looked at the next one. She'd seen that one before as well – a scene of a girl and a boy seated, with a dog lying in the background. Then she noticed that the girl's basket, instead of holding daisies, was full of multicolored condom packets.

Another was of a plain-looking man standing to speak, but his pockets were stuffed with cash and the hands around him were holding out more.

Janice's ecstatic mood was a bit punctured. "Logan, who did this to these paintings?" she asked.

"Not sure," Logan admitted. "Maybe someone tired of saccharine propaganda intended to sanitize an unjust social order."

"Oh," Janice said, deciding not to look at any more prints. "What comes next?"

"Socializing," Logan explained. "Let's sit here, and I'll get you a drink. What's your pleasure? Wine? Cocktail? They make an excellent daiquiri."

"That'd be fine," Janice replied. She usually felt lucky to get cheap beer. Logan went off while the two women chatting at the other end of the couch greeted her warmly. One of them took a vial out of her purse and tapped some pills into her hand. She gave one to her friend and offered one to Janice, who declined. She then took one of the pills herself. Looking around the room, Janice could see that many people seemed to be taking pills of some sort. It made her feel squeamish – she didn't care what other people chose to take, but she wasn't used to frequenting parties where there was a lot of drug use.

Logan returned with a beer and a cocktail glass. The daiquiri was tasty and very smooth. Logan sensed her more subdued mood.

"Something up?" he asked.

"No, not really," Janice equivocated. "It's just – well, this woman offered me some kind of pill, which I declined, but it seems like a lot of people are popping."

"Oh, that," Logan waved his hand dismissively. "Muscle relaxants. Know that laid-back, easygoing feeling you get after three or four drinks? Those just accelerate that."

"Oh," Janice said, not mentioning that for her that threshold was about two drinks.

"Probably best you didn't accept, given that you have to drive back tonight," Logan said. They sipped their drinks for a bit before Janice remembered the question she'd meant to ask.

"Logan, what's a 'pete'?"

"What's a what?" he asked. His mind appeared to have been elsewhere.

"A 'pete'," Janice repeated. "He said that some of us were Ishmaels, and some were 'petes'. I know what an Ishmael is because I am one, but what's a pete?"

"Are you, now?" Logan said. "Well, 'pete' is short for 'petri dish' – in other words, *in vitro* fertilization. Conceived in a petri dish, and then implanted, sometimes in the natural mother, sometimes in a surrogate. I'm one."

"You are?" Janice asked, wide-eyed.

"Yup," Logan spread out his arms. "You're looking at the finest human money can buy and technology can provide. All things considered, I'm happy to have made it."

"Happy to have made it?" Janice asked, puzzled.

"Oh, sure," Logan said casually. "Tricky stuff, being a pete. Usually three or four eggs are fertilized at once, and they're watched. The one that seems to be developing best is chosen for implantation. The others are either thrown away or frozen for possible later implantation or donated for experimentation. Or they might implant all of them to see which one takes. That means there might be a multiple pregnancy – twins, or even triplets – but that's okay, because they'd probably do a selective reduction."

"Selective reduction?" Janice asked.

"Clinical term for a carefully targeted abortion," Logan explained. "They take out the surplus, leaving one perfect, expensive, and exquisitely wanted child. Hell, for all I know I've got siblings on ice somewhere, or maybe who were killed within inches of me while I floated, blissfully unaware, in the warmth of my mother's womb. Sobering thought – that maybe the chance positioning of a needle, or the arbitrary decision of a technician, meant that I lived while my sibling died."

Janice looked at Logan, a little set back by this bleak perspective.

"But enough about me," Logan said casually. "You said you were an Ishmael – what's the story there?" So Janice told him what she'd learned about her own conception and birth. Logan nodded knowingly.

"Yup – classic surrogate situation. More common than us petes these days, especially on the coasts. It's a booming market, with so much trouble and so few opportunities overseas. Entire apartment complexes full of women from Latin America, India, Eastern Europe, and Africa, just bearing kids for couples. Rent-a-wombs. Usually it's because of some fertility issue, but increasingly people just don't want the disruption and risk of a pregnancy. Easier to arrange for some young foreign woman to do it – that way you can focus on decorating the nursery and researching the day care."

"Is that – legal?" Janice asked.

"Maybe not." Logan shrugged. "But who's enforcing?"

Logan's casual cynicism left Janice feeling drained and cheapened, like she really had been some commodity purchased in a marketplace, fit in somewhere between the boat and the summer cottage.

"Of course, it's not completely safe being an Ishmael," Logan continued. "Most contracts these days have termination clauses. If the product is defective, or the couple decides that they don't want it for whatever reason, they can require a termination."

"Like – what reasons?" Janice asked.

"Divorce is common," Logan said. "Couples think they want a baby, but when they start to face the reality, it strains the relationship. Or just splitting – that happens to gay couples a lot. Or the baby is the wrong sex. Sometimes it's just a change in a life situation – I've heard of cases where the mother got a better job, one where a baby would have been inconvenient, so they just made the call and killed the contract."

Janice felt chilled – she could very much see her mother doing that.

Logan suddenly seemed to notice the effect his words were having on Janice. "Here, let me get you another drink," he offered, rising and taking her glass. "They should be starting the music soon – want to dance?"

"Dance?" Janice asked, a bit startled. "I'm – I'm not very good."

"Neither am I," Logan confided with a wink. "So at least you won't show me up."

Sure enough, before Logan returned, some music began playing, and couples began moving into the open area in the middle of the room. Janice guzzled her daiquiri and let herself be led out onto the floor. Logan was a better dancer than he'd let on, but did a good job of not making her feel too self-conscious. They did a fast dance followed by a slower one. Then they sat down and Logan fetched a couple of waters. Janice was once again feeling relaxed and comfortable. She noticed that the occasional couple would trickle off the dance floor and down a dimly lit hallway. She also noticed that Logan was glancing down that hallway from time to time and playing with his beer bottle.

"What's – down there?" Janice asked as casually as possible, feeling warm but emboldened by the drinks.

"Down where?" Logan asked, coming out of another reverie.

"That hallway," Janice pointed. "Where those people are going."

"Oh, that," Logan said dismissively. "That used to be offices and classrooms, but they've been turned into lounges and salons – places for more private conversations. In fact, there's a whole second floor of them. Less noisy, more – intimate." He took another swig of his beer and looked at her with a keen glance. "I'd ask you to go, but I'm afraid that's for members."

Janice mindlessly fingered the yellow cord, feeling self-conscious, as if she was standing between Logan and that hallway. "You – you can go by yourself, if you wish," she blurted out. "I'll be fine."

"No," Logan said, nonetheless casting a longing glance toward the private rooms. "I'd rather stay with you tonight." He caressed her bare arm with two fingers, sending shivers up her spine. Then he glanced at his phone. "It's getting late. No more drinks for you, since you have to drive home. Got time for another dance?"

They did one more quick spin around the floor, after which Logan ducked off somewhere and returned with a plate of munchies and a cup of coffee for Janice. He walked her out to her car.

"Thanks for taking care of me, Logan," Janice said sincerely. "I have no idea what happened to Melissa. She just – vanished. I haven't seen her all night."

"She has responsibilities," Logan said vaguely. "I'm kind of glad she wasn't around, though – it meant I had you all to myself." He smiled warmly, his face just inches from hers, and Janice trembled with anticipation. He slowly raised her hand to his lips, then opened her car door.

"It was a delightful evening, Janice," Logan said after she got in. "Thank you for your time."

"Oh, thank you," Janice replied clumsily.

"You drive safely, now," he admonished, closing the door and waving.

"I will," she assured him, then pulled away. She forced herself to concentrate on the roads, for her insides were quivering, and her hands as well. She felt wrung out by the tumultuous events of the evening, and turned over and over in her thoughts all that had happened. Her mind felt full to overflowing with all she had learned and the new perspectives to which she'd been exposed. Everything seemed turned upside down. Plus, she felt flushed and tingly from the attention Logan had lavished upon her. She'd not known that feeling since – oh, since Darrin Martin had pulled together the courage to ask her to junior prom, though that hadn't turned out so well. But Logan – he made her feel shy and giddy and womanly all at once. She smiled and savored the memory of dancing with him.

She'd been on the expressway half an hour, and was east of Imlay City, when she realized that she was still wearing the yellow guest cord. She fingered it, then took it off and hung it from her rearview.

She'd have to get rid of that.

Back in the parking lot, Logan watched Janice's car pull away. Once her taillights had vanished, he pulled his phone from his pocket and keyed a message as he walked back toward the building.

Bait taken. Good enough?

The response came back soon. *We'll see. How many drinks did you down?*

Logan rolled his eyes and typed back, *You want results, you pay for them.*

He opened the door and stepped back into the darkened lobby. There were only a few couples still on the dance floor. He pulled a vial from his pocket, tapped out a couple of pills, and downed them. His phone chimed again.

just a reminder: over quota = you pay. We have a budget to mind.

"Cheap bastards," Logan grumbled, grabbing his beer from the table and heading down the hallway in search of action.

Learning Pains

The morning sunlight shining through a gap in the curtains slowly awakened Derek, and he rolled to turn away from it.

And nearly cried out in agony.

There was a noise in the hallway and Philip stuck his head in. "Ah, you're awake. How are you feeling?"

How was he feeling? Derek lay as still as possible, since even the slightest movement sent stabs of fire through his limbs and torso. A dull groan was all he could manage in response.

Philip smiled sympathetically. "I know how you feel. I was a mite sore this morning from tossing all those bales yesterday, and you're totally unused to it. The riding would have strained your legs and rear as well. That's why Mom about skinned Martha last night."

A 'mite sore' hardly described Derek's condition. To lie still was excruciating but to move was agonizing – it seemed like every muscle in his body was screaming. Philip came into the room and took his arm.

"Mom assigned Martha to be your personal servant all today, so you can take your time recovering. But they're all over at Mass right now, so I'm all you've got. Probably best, since you'll want a hot bath, and Martha could hardly help with that."

"Hot bath?" Derek gasped. "I can't even get out of bed!"

"I know, it's tough," Philip said. "But trust me – the only way past this is to get those joints and muscles working. C'mon, let's work on sitting up."

After about ten minutes of cajoling and assisting, Philip had Derek seated on the edge of the bed. He gave Derek some aspirin and went off to draw a bath, returning shortly to help Derek totter to the bathroom. Though every movement took its toll, Derek could feel himself getting marginally more flexible, and it was better to be moving than just lying still in pain.

Getting ready for the bath made Derek a little self-conscious. It was the first time he'd been naked in the presence of anyone else since high school gym class, but Philip took it in stride. As

Derek eased into the steaming water, assisted by Philip's strong grip, he nearly screamed when his thighs hit the surface. Philip winced.

"I saw that chafing, and knew that it was going to hurt. Once I get you settled, I'll fetch some herbal ointment that Mom has. It doesn't sting, and it really helps."

Derek soaked until he felt waterlogged. The warmth did help loosen things up, and the painkillers did their part, but when it was time to apply the salve he was still too stiff to do it effectively and had to ask for help. Derek felt humiliated, but Philip was sympathetic and apologetic and behaved like applying ointment to sensitive and private areas of a near-stranger was a normal part of life. Then Philip found him a pair of loose shorts, an overlarge shirt, and some sandals.

"It's a warm day, and you won't be going anywhere for a bit," Philip explained. "No use trying to squeeze into trousers just yet." He sat Derek on a couch in the living room and went to get some coffee.

While Derek was seated there, twisting and stretching, the rest of the family came bustling back in, clustering around him and solicitous about his condition. Linda had Martha stand before him and apologize for being so careless and promise to help in any way she could. Derek assured her that he was feeling better already and was sure he'd be fine.

"I'm telling you, Mom, it wasn't just the riding," Philip said, putting a big mug of coffee and a sandwich at Derek's elbow. "That'll work the legs and lower torso, but the baling was what got his arms, shoulders, and upper torso. The combination was lethal."

Little Matthew came around with an armload of books, and though the others tried to shoo him away, Derek insisted he stay. When Matthew was made to understand that Mr. Derek had an ow, his little face grew grave and he soberly showed Derek a healing scrape on his leg. Thus comforted, Derek read the books to his comrade in suffering, grateful for the distraction from his pains.

The household bustle swirled around Derek as everyone busied themselves with one thing or another. Sunday dinner was being prepared, which was apparently the day's large meal and was served in the early afternoon. Everyone was kind and considerate, and Derek continued to be amazed that they could make him feel like an honored guest and one of the family at the same time.

When dinner was ready, Linda offered to have a plate brought to Derek, but he wanted to sit at the table, so he limped his way over with a minimum of groans and winces. The dinner was incredible, and Derek again stuffed himself, amazed at how hungry he was.

"It's the muscle work," Kent explained. "Your body's screaming for protein. Be sure to drink lots of water, and go light on the alcohol for the next few days, if you're a drinker."

By the time dinner was over, Derek's soreness had subsided to an overall dull ache – something he never would have believed when he'd awakened just hours earlier. He decided to take a walk outside, grabbing a jacket but sticking with the loose shorts. Martha came along, offering to walk beside him, but he waved her off to attend to the horses. He hobbled along, trying to stretch his legs. The sky was still clear and the sun was warm, but the breeze was from the northeast and held just a bit of the off-the-lake coolness that would intensify as autumn progressed.

Not following any definite direction, Derek wandered around the end of the long building that was Sam's shop. He found Sam just coming out, working his walker through the door at the end.

"Hey, Sam," Derek called with a wave, then winced as his arm muscles complained.

Sam looked at him for a while, then barked with what Derek guessed was laughter. "Riding, eh?"

"And haying," Derek admitted.

Sam barked again. "Sore man. C'mere." He gestured with his head and went back into his shop. Derek followed, to find Sam rummaging beside a desk. He pulled out a cane and handed it to Derek. "Here. Extends at bottom."

Derek adjusted the cane to a good height and leaned on it. He immediately felt the strain on his legs and torso lessen.

"Wow, Sam – that's great! Thank you!"

"Just for few days, till muscles heal. Walker, if you need," Sam said, tapping the desk with the short cane he seemed to always keep with him.

"Hey, is that an arc welder?" Derek asked, looking around the shop.

"Arc welder. Brazing torch. Cutting tips," Sam said, tapping each setup in turn. "Anything you need."

"I always wanted to learn to arc weld," Derek said. "We were supposed to learn back in shop, but we never got to it."

"What did you learn?" Sam asked.

"Basic stuff," Derek explained. "Grinding, drilling, cutting, lathing. A little bit of soldering. I always wanted to learn more, but my mom thought shop was too dirty. She wanted me to go into a clean profession, so medicine it was, which is why I'm a physician's assistant. Of course, now I work with corpses."

"You come back," Sam assured him. "I teach you."

"Teach me what? Arc welding?" Derek asked.

"Sure, if you want," Sam.

"What, today?" Derek asked.

"No work today," Sam scowled up at him. "Lord's Day. Just going to see cows."

"Can I watch?" Derek replied.

"Sure, come along," Sam said, so together they headed for the stable where the small herd resided. Derek noticed that hanging from the front of Sam's walker was what appeared to be a coil of black wire. It banged against the walker frame as Sam worked his way along, but Sam took no notice of it. After puzzling for a while, Derek finally asked.

"Sam, what is that?"

"What's what?"

"That coil on your walker."

"Oh. Whip."

"Whip?" Derek was astonished. "What are you doing with a whip? Are you going to whip the cows?"

Sam stopped and turned to give Derek a look of mild scorn mixed with amusement. "Whip cows? Why whip cows?"

"I don't know," Derek replied, a little embarrassed. "I just wondered…"

"Whip cows!" Sam snorted in laughter as he resumed his clunking progress toward the stable. "No, never whip cows. Used for getting around. You'll see. Whip cows!"

The stable was mostly open, with stalls about the edges that were all empty. Most of the floor was enclosed in a semicircular fence made up of corral panels that stood about five feet high. The flat side of the semicircle was the stable wall, in which were doors that stood open, allowing the cattle to pass in and out from the barnyard, which was also enclosed by a semicircle of panels. Hanging from the ceiling of the stable were a few long cables draped from the rafters in broad arcs, hanging about ten feet above the floor at their lowest points.

Sam made his way to a gate where he folded his walker and lay it against the fencing. He took the coil from the front and, looking over his shoulder at Derek with a mischievous grin, called out, "Okay, cows, time for your whippin'!" The cows took no notice, but Sam climbed up the pipes of the corral panel with surprising agility. Propped at the top of the gate, he deftly flicked the coil so that it trailed out behind him, then with amazing speed and accuracy snapped the whip so it flew up and wrapped around one of the cables hanging from the rafters. He quickly scrambled up the whip to the cable and, clambering onto that, whipped the next cable so he could swing down to a feeding station on the far side of the pen.

"Wow, Sam, I didn't know you could play Tarzan!" Derek said with a grin.

"Easier than walking," Sam pointed at his walker and then at the stable floor thick with mud and straw. He inspected something about the feeding station, then swung back up and over by the door where he looked over some of the hinge mechanisms. The cows shied from him just a little, but didn't seem overly alarmed by his presence or activity. Finishing his work, he used his whip to catch the cables and swing back to where Derek stood by the fence.

"See? Whip cables, not cows," Sam grinned.

"You rigged those cables for that purpose just like you did the ones in your shop?" Derek asked.

"Yes. For big whip, easy to get around. Small whip back in shop – for extending reach," Sam said as he coiled the line back up. He then explained what he'd been inspecting at the feeder, and about the care and nurture of cattle and calves.

When Derek took his leave, it was a slightly heavy heart, for he knew he'd soon have to head back into town. Aches and all, he had immensely enjoyed his time and hoped it wouldn't be his last visit. Back in the house he found that there was not any common suppertime for the day, but there was plenty of food laid out for people to nibble as they desired. Derek grabbed a plate and then remembered to dose himself with another round of aspirin. The minute Matthew saw him stationary, it was book time again. After that round of books, Linda looked in from the front porch.

"Derek! It's such a lovely afternoon, we were wondering if you'd join us on the front porch for a bit."

Levering himself up with effort, he made his way out to where Kent and Linda were sitting. The breeze was refreshing and the view took in miles of fields and woodlands.

"Looks like you're feeling a little less sore," Kent said. "Again, our sincere apologies for not being more careful about overexerting you."

"It's nothing," Derek assured him. "Shows how far I have to go to get in shape."

"I must say, it's been a delight having you," Linda added. "The children all want to adopt you immediately, and are already wondering when you're going to come visit again."

"As soon as possible, I hope," Derek admitted with a smile. "This has been the most wonderful weekend I've had in a very long time, muscle aches notwithstanding."

"Consider yourself as having a standing invitation," Kent pronounced. "Even if you weren't a good friend to have around, we'd owe you at least that for your help with John."

That thrilled Derek, for he'd already been harboring hopes about the next weekend. They chatted for a while about riding and cows and farm equipment. It seemed to Derek that he'd never seen a more natural and fitting environment than that home, nor a more contented place to be than on that front porch talking to these people.

At a lull in the conversation, Derek gathered a bit of courage to ask a question that had been nagging him. He hoped it wouldn't be a sensitive topic.

"Y'know, I was wondering," he said, trying to affect a casual tone. "What's an off-the-grid kid?"

Silence fell so swiftly and deeply that the air almost crackled. Derek looked up to see Linda shoot Kent a quick glance. "Why do you ask?" she asked, also trying to sound casual.

"It was a term Chris used when we were out riding," Derek explained. "Martha cut him short pretty quickly, so if it's something you can't talk about, that's okay."

Linda and Kent looked at each other soberly. Linda gave a little nod, and Kent cleared his throat.

"Well, Derek, it seems you are intended to be bound into our lives whether we wish it or not," he said. "Not that we mind, but it's all happened rather quickly.

"As you can probably infer from the term, off-the-grid means not known or about or accessible by standard communications means. An off-the-grid kid is our term for a child not known about by the government – particularly the federal government. All but one of our children are off the grid. They were born at home and their births were recorded with the county clerk, but that was all. We didn't apply for social security numbers for them, we didn't enroll them in the health care system, and they don't have a government advocate appointed. We do not claim them on our income taxes, we school them privately, and they receive medical care like vaccines through different channels. As far as the state and federal governments are concerned, they don't exist."

"Wow," Derek said, pondering this. "Is that legal?"

Kent and Linda shifted uncomfortably and exchanged looks. "That's a gray area that's growing blacker," Linda said. "Technically, it is still legal, but there's what the law says, and there's what actually happens. Some contend that not enrolling a citizen in the national health care system is illegal, but the courts have issued contradictory rulings on that. Assignment of a child advocate is automatic but technically voluntary – though it's like pulling teeth to have children removed from the system once they're in. Private schooling is not yet illegal, but that may change at any time.

"What's of most concern to us isn't law, but policy. Some government agencies have dictatorial powers in certain arenas, particularly where it pertains to children. Our biggest worries are HHS at the federal level and Child Protective Services. They're a state agency with local offices, but they're bound about with federal guidelines and directives, making them essentially a branch of the federal government. When it comes to the welfare of children – as they define it – they have unlimited powers and answer to nobody. If they decide to target your children, there's almost nothing that can stop them. Additionally, the very thought that any children might be eluding their control infuriates them, so having off-the-grid kids marks families for special attention."

"We know a couple families in this area," Kent said soberly. "One family has three children. Their door was kicked down in the middle of the night by agents with machine guns. The children were swept away in their pajamas and the parents were hauled off to jail on a warrant for suspected child neglect and endangerment. The happiest, most loving family you could find, but a CPS worker decided to harass them. They had to defend themselves against false charges while their children were placed in foster care. They managed to beat the charges, but because they were 'suspect', their children weren't restored."

"Wow," Derek whispered.

"Most people have no idea how much power these people wield," Kent continued. "When you're arguing against a government agency for the return of your children, you can offer all the testimony you like, but the judge examines psychological profiles of the children prepared by agency workers – profiles that you aren't allowed to see. There's no appeal of their decision. This family is still fighting for the return of their children. It's been four years. They have no idea where they are."

Derek was dumbstruck. Linda was quietly sobbing in the gathering dusk, and Kent sounded a little husky as he continued.

"Another family we know had a similar thing happen, though it was in broad daylight – sheriff cars pulling up all around their house. Four kids, vague and unsubstantiated charges. We got lucky with that – we found out where the kids were taken. We staged a rescue and got them back."

"What – happened then?" Derek asked, considering the ramifications of that.

"They had to flee, as a family," Kent explained. "Leave the country. But best not to talk about that too much."

"If you don't mind my asking – why?" Derek asked. "If there's so much potential for trouble, you must have good reason for running the risk."

"A complex set of reasons," Kent agreed. "Increasingly, especially over the past generation, the government has been intruding into family life to override the decisions of parents, particularly in the areas of education and health care. There are things we teach our children – morals and ethics right from the Bible and Church teaching – that someone could get jailed for even saying in a public school. Other things which are morally forbidden are taught as acceptable and good."

"Our sons and daughters would be taught things and subjected to medical procedures – without our knowledge – that would violate them and their faith," Linda chimed in.

"Another factor is kind of circular," Kent continued. "These days the government examines all kinds of things to decide who they're going to watch carefully, such as income, communications patterns, and travel. One of the factors they look for is family size. Larger families trigger suspicion."

"Really?" Derek asked.

"Yes," Kent assured him. "It's so dramatically countercultural that, in their minds, it's associated with other suspect behaviors."

"Which puts us in a difficult position," Linda added. "If we were to report all our children, it would be like raising a red flag to say, 'come inspect us more closely'. And if government inspectors want to find problems, they usually do. We've seen it happen."

"It is these circumstances that force us to skate close to the edge of the law," Kent said. "Something our faith forbids without grave cause."

"Holy smokes," Derek said quietly, imagining the horror of black-jacketed agents sweeping in and making off with the Schaeffer's delightful children. "I had no idea. Of course, I won't say anything to anyone. I –"

"We know, Derek," Linda assured him. "If we thought you untrustworthy, we wouldn't be telling you all this. But once you overheard the term, we could hardly ask you to forget it. We'd rather explain matters so you can take basic precautions."

"What kind of precautions?" Derek asked.

"There are only a few," Kent explained. "One is, try not to use the term 'off-the-grid' at all, or only around us if you must. Particularly in your position as a county employee, if the wrong people heard you even use the phrase, your job security would only be the start of your troubles.

"For that matter, don't talk about us. Don't talk about going to a farm, or where we're located, and especially how many children we have. Get into the habit of saying you were 'with friends'.

"Another thing is to always come here by back roads, especially tree-lined ones. The expressway would be quicker, but all the traffic on it is under constant video surveillance for miles inland."

"Really?" Derek asked. "I didn't know that."

"Part of the blessing and curse of being a border community," Kent explained. "It's been that way for decades. Initially the explanation offered was border security, but now the scope includes 'domestic terrorism'."

"Okay," Derek said, mentally cataloging these suggestions. "That sounds simple enough."

"Actually, there's one more thing," Kent added. "If it's not too much trouble, when you come, could you leave your phone behind, as well as any other device with communications capabilities? If you don't want to leave them behind, could you remove or drain the battery while you're here?"

"Um – sure," Derek agreed. He hadn't even touched his phone since arriving.

"All phones and other wireless network devices have locator circuitry," Kent explained. "Even if they're turned off, that circuitry will respond to an interrogative signal with the location of the device. Not that we expect anyone to send your phone such a signal while you're here, but it's just basic precautions. In time, we can take your phone over to Sam and get that feature dealt with, but that has ramifications, too. For now, it's best to just leave it behind."

"Sure," Derek said, pulling out his phone and looking at it as if it was radioactive. Then he noticed the time. "I'd better be going. Let me go get my stuff." He headed off to the bedroom.

Linda and Kent sat silent for a while in the dusk. "Well," Linda said finally. "That was unexpected."

"I don't know," Kent said, shaking his head. "Quite sudden, I know, but I can't shake the impression that our lives are intertwined with his in ways we can't see just yet."

"I notice you didn't mention the biggest danger," Linda said.

"Yeah, well, I didn't want to tax him with that until I absolutely have to," Kent explained.

Seduction

Despite the lingering soreness, Derek came into work Monday morning the cheeriest he'd been in a long time. He'd slept like a rock, woke up refreshed, and got himself a proper breakfast rather than a donut and coffee. Linda had given him a jar of the salve and assured him that the soreness from the chafing would subside quickly, which it was already doing. Even the message to call his boss didn't dampen his spirits, especially when the actual interaction took less than thirty seconds before he was shunted off to Shaundra.

He was sorting through the day's tasks when his phone rang. It was Janice.

"Hey, how was your weekend?" Derek answered.

"It was...okay," Janice replied. "Look, I walked around a few apartments over the weekend, and yesterday settled on the best one I'm likely to find. I want to call the landlord today, but I was...was hoping to take you up on your offer...you know, about the security deposit."

"Sure, sure," Derek answered. "Why don't we meet for lunch so we can make plans for that and for moving you in?" After agreeing on that, Derek felt nagged by some unsettled issue, but couldn't quite identify what it was. After racking his brain for a minute, he remembered. Keying in a quick search, he furrowed his brow at the results. Not much there, but it was a start – he'd have to check it out after work.

Apparently, the closest place for him to find proper riding footwear was some tractor supply place on the north side of town.

Janice's answer to Derek notwithstanding, her weekend hadn't been all that good. After the thrill and glamor of the gathering Saturday night, spending Sunday in her dreary hotel room was even more depressing. All the shows she found were just banal, and she didn't have the gas to drive anywhere or the money to do anything once she got there. The "Service Engine"

145

light in her car was flashing again, and the last time that had happened it had cost her over four hundred dollars. She tried to alleviate her weariness by replaying some of the highlights of Saturday evening, and indulging in some fantasies involving Logan, but in the end all that did was highlight the drab disappointment the rest of her life had been over the past couple weeks. Coming into work Monday morning to face bedpans and bedsores didn't relieve her depression. To cap it, the new schedules were out, and she saw that she went back on afternoons this weekend.

"Hey, kid," came Melissa's voice as Janice was finishing up some notations. "How'd you like the gathering?"

"Well, I had a good time," Janice replied a little tartly. "I hope you did, too – wherever you were."

"Yeah, well, sorry about that," Melissa said a bit sheepishly. "An old friend buttonholed me and wanted to talk my ear off. I was unable to escape no matter how hard I tried. I hope you didn't have to spend the evening sitting by yourself."

"Oh, no," Janice said with exaggerated nonchalance. "This guy came by and kept me company."

"Oooh, a *guy*," Melissa grinned. "What was his name?"

"Logan," Janice replied. "He said he knows you."

"Logan?" Melissa's eyes widened. "Yeah, I know him. Decent enough, but kind of stand-offish. Keeps to himself. You say he talked to you?"

"Yeah. In fact, he kind of stayed with me the whole evening," Janice said, flushing a little.

Melissa gave a low whistle. "Wow, lady, whatever you got, I want some. Anyway, what did you think of the talk?"

"It was great – provocative and challenging. It made me look at things in a new light," Janice replied. "That Charon guy is amazing."

"He's quite the speaker," Melissa admitted. "We only get him periodically, but he's well worth it. He's speaking at the next one, too, which is next weekend."

"That's just my luck," Janice grumbled. "I start afternoons again next weekend."

"Well, that is your luck. The next one is on Friday night."

"It is?" asked Janice.

"Yeah, they try to move them around so people on steady shifts can attend the ones they can," Melissa explained. "In fact, how does your whole Friday look?"

"I've got it off, though I may be moving into a new apartment," Janice said.

"Well, Friday's gathering will be preceded by some seminars in the afternoon. I can set it up so you can attend, if you're interested and available," Melissa explained. "They're free."

"Seminars? On what?" Janice asked.

"The gatherings serve a lot of functions: social interaction, networking, motivational talks, and such. As you saw, we want to effect change in the culture. But there's a lot of solid research and thinking behind it all. Occasionally, we have seminars where there are presentations and panel discussions that explore some of the theories. They're open to everyone, though usually only the leaders attend. It's by invitation, though, so let me know if you'd like to go."

"Where are these workshops?"

"Same place. They just use some of the conference rooms. When the seminars conclude, attendees just come over to the gathering."

"Will you be going?" Janice asked.

"Not this week," Melissa said ruefully. "I've got afternoon shift on Friday. You'd be on your own, but I think you can handle yourself. You might even bump into Logan again, if he can make it."

Janice tried not to make it obvious that this was the very eventuality she was hoping for, but the seminars did sound interesting. She knew she was smart enough, and she wanted to learn more about this organization and the ideas underlying it. Besides, it wouldn't hurt to have the leadership, whoever they might be, see her around.

"I don't know if I'll be free, because I don't know if I'll have to be moving then," Janice cautioned. "But if I am free, I'd like to go. The in-services around here lately have all been about coding scheme changes, and I'd like something more substantial."

"These will be – I've always found them interesting," Melissa said as she punched up some program on her phone.

"Here, let me see your badge." She held Janice's ID up to her phone, which gave a chirp. "There – you're cleared to attend. Just wave your badge at any scanner and you're good."

"Thanks, Melissa," Janice said sincerely.

Janice met up with Derek for lunch and they planned to move her in on Wednesday afternoon, providing there was no problem with the lease signing, which Janice hoped to take care of on Tuesday. Derek seemed unusually cheerful, though he occasionally winced when he moved. She gathered that his weekend had been great, but didn't learn much beyond the fact that he'd stayed with friends and had engaged in an unusual amount of physical activity, which explained the wincing. He transferred the funds for the security deposit, waving away her offer to write up a promissory note and telling her she could pay him back when and how she could.

This so relieved Janice that she returned to shift feeling like the dark clouds which had overshadowed her life of late were starting to break up. Her spirits weren't even dampened when her phone chimed with a call from Brenda. She let it roll to voice mail, then listened to the profane rant about an eviction notice and Janice's responsibility to pay something. Janice took dark satisfaction in deleting the message and adding Brenda's number to her blocked list. Let Kenny help her. She'd already explained the situation to her old landlord, which reminded that her she needed to contact her new one regarding that lease signing.

Derek found the tractor supply store without any trouble, and found a good pair of sturdy boots. He also picked up some work jeans, long-sleeve shirts, and a properly fitting hat while he was there. He took it all back to his apartment and, deciding that he had enough dirty clothes to make it worthwhile, headed out to the laundromat. That finished, he found himself back at his place with a long evening in front of him. Never had his apartment seemed so drab. He'd far rather be cleaning out stables with Chris, or helping Sam with a project, or even reading to Matthew, than watching some inane program or playing a game. At least sleep came easily – his overworked body was still recovering.

The week sped by. Everything worked out with Janice's new place, so she and Derek moved her few belongings in on Wednesday after work. On Thursday Derek got a call from Linda, wondering if he was planning to come out over the weekend, and if so, could he pick up some goods 'in town' and bring them when he came, thus saving a family member the trip. Derek was happy to – he'd been hoping to come visit that weekend, but suggested that he just pick up the items and run them out that evening. Linda was grateful for this, and a bit tentatively read off the list to him: about thirty gallons of cooking oil, ten industrial rolls of aluminum foil, a dozen twenty-pound boxes of soap – the list went on. Derek was a little surprised at the quantities, but took it all down before asking Linda where he could find all these items. With embarrassment she realized she'd just assumed he had a membership in the local warehouse club, and suggested he scrap the whole idea. He countered by offering to get a membership, since the club was just west of town, not far from his apartment. So it was that the afternoon found him in his new jeans and boots piling jugs of oil and bags of nuts into his trunk, reflecting on how much life could change in just one week.

Derek's drive out to the farm felt like coming home, and nearly all the kids tumbled out of the house to greet him. Many hands stacked the goods onto a trailer which was towed away, and Derek was tugged inside where dinner had been held pending his arrival. He savored the delicious meal while Philip asked after his muscles and Martha passed judgement on his boots (she approved) and the middle ones deluged him with updates on their week. They made him promise to come back for the weekend because they'd be picking grapes and making jam. Then Matthew appeared with his pile of books, and Derek was able to pull out his surprise – two *new* books he'd grabbed at the warehouse club. Matthew was beside himself and wasn't satisfied until each new book had been broken in with three readings.

An evening of bustling family life made Derek more reluctant than ever to head back to his empty apartment, but the hope of returning the next day buoyed him. Linda made sure to reimburse him for the groceries, in cash, which Derek found quaint, and thanked him profusely for his service. This amused Derek, who almost thanked her in return for providing an excuse to come visit.

The following day Derek dashed home from work, packed up his gear for the weekend, and did something he'd not done for years: powered down both his phone and his tablet and left them behind. He'd forgotten to do this the night before, but wanted to respect Kent and Linda's request. Out at the farm the kids still greeted him gleefully, just as if he hadn't been there twenty-four hours before. Dinner was meatless, but still better than some steak dinners he'd had in his day. He read the obligatory books to Matthew, got dragged out for an impromptu game of soccer in the yard, helped Martha with the horses, and went to bed tired but looking forward to a full Saturday.

Janice spent Friday morning shopping for groceries to stock her new kitchen, but headed toward Flint in time to catch the seminars. There were far fewer cars in the lot, but enough to let her know that something was going on. She remembered to don the yellow cord that identified her as a guest, though she didn't know if it was necessary for the seminars.

Inside the door there were no signs or placards, just a young man sitting behind a table with a tablet and a scanning pad. Once Janice had swiped her ID, he gave her a binder and directed her to a conference room. She found the room about a third full of people milling about, chatting and munching snacks from a table in the back of the room. Trying not to feel self-conscious, especially about her yellow cord necklace, Janice got herself a cup of coffee and a croissant and lingered about the edge of the room. Nobody took any notice of her until a woman who looked familiar detached herself from her conversation to walk over. It was Kendra from Rehab who'd been at the Shillelagh with Melissa and Ron.

"Hi, Janice," Kendra said. "Melissa said you might be coming, and asked me to watch out for you. Come on, let's sit down – the talks are about to begin."

They sat facing a lectern with a screen behind it on which were projected the slides for the presentation. There was still no information about the group sponsoring the event – the first speaker just stepped up and began talking. Janice supposed that everyone knew who they were and why they were there.

The first speaker introduced himself as Dr. Steve Jansen. He spoke about the growth in government spending and borrowing. He said that the efforts begun twenty-five years earlier to contain health care costs hadn't delivered on their promise, and these costs were now consuming a larger and larger share of the government budget every year. He had graphs and tables showing the growth of health care spending as a percentage of total spending, and how it was crowding out vital services such as education and homeland security. He used a measurement which Janice had never heard before: "days per dollar spent". This figure measured how many additional days of life each dollar of health care spending provided at various ages. Examined this way, the outcomes were stunning: the older a person got, the more spending it took to extend their lives by even a few days. For children, each dollar of spending could buy a day or more of life; for those nearing the upper end of life expectancy, the cost was in the hundreds or thousands of dollars per day.

"Which means, economically," Dr. Jansen emphasized. "That we as a society are saying that aging people far past their productive years are worth hundreds or thousands as much as healthy children with a lifetime of potential before them."

That got Janice's attention. What seized her attention more firmly was a summary slide that followed, showing a graph of increasing life expectancies over recent decades. She'd seen this sort of thing before, and though the upward trend had leveled off somewhat, it was still gently climbing.

"This metric is universally acknowledged as a positive thing," Dr. Jansen explained. "Average life expectancy is one of the ways we judge how advanced a nation is. But there's the idea of too much of a good thing. This next slide puts this laudable figure in a whole new light." He overlaid a bar chart upon the life expectancy graph that had to do with spending. The effect was dramatic – a couple people even gasped. For as the life expectancy line rose gradually higher, the spending bars jumped dramatically, especially over the past few years.

"As you can see," Dr. Jansen went on. "The cost of these minor increases in life expectancy is staggering. For example, during this period, when average life expectancy increased by one year, corresponding costs for health care increased by thirty percent. Thirty percent! That's a lot to ask society to pay just so grandma can be around for one more Christmas."

The presentation then moved into territory with which Janice was more familiar: the variety of ailments suffered by people as they got older. There was a chart that broke the population into age brackets and showing what percentage of them were diagnosed with conditions such as diabetes and dementia. Janice hardly needed a graph to tell her this, working as she did with geriatric patients every shift, but she'd never made the connection with the economic impact. The presentation went on for a while, further substantiating the contention that the cost of extending a life for one year included not only the cost of the immediate care, but all the consequent costs treating all the secondary conditions the patient might have during that year.

"To summarize," Dr. Jansen concluded "We may boast of figures like constantly increasing life expectancy as if those metrics existed in a vacuum. But if we are to evaluate overall social good, we must consider them alongside other figures to appreciate just how much we are paying to attain these lofty numbers. We must frankly consider how much we're willing to pay to increase the unquestioned, unexamined good of things like sky high life expectancy – and, indeed, whether we're already paying too much."

There was polite applause and a guy who appeared to be the meeting facilitator stepped up to announce a twenty-minute break. Many people clustered around Dr. Jansen while Janice and Kendra headed for the restroom and then grabbed a couple bottles of water.

"Well," Kendra said. "That was a lot to absorb."

"It was," Janice echoed, glad that Kendra had admitted it first. "I mean, I followed some of it, but he was moving a bit fast at times."

"Especially for those of us without advanced degrees in macroeconomics," Kendra added. "But he did grab my attention with some of those points. I mean, I'm in the industry, so I've got a rough grasp of the expense, but I had *no idea* it cost that much."

"Especially those figures on how much it costs to extend life by one day. Those early life figures are reasonable, but when you get to those final years of life, it's unbelievable! I noticed that for near end-of-life patients, adding one day to their lives costs more than I pay in rent for a month!" Janice exclaimed.

"And for what?" Kendra asked. "You work with cases like that every shift – what kind of days are they?"

This kept Janice going for quite a while as she groused about how miserable and irascible the patients could be. She also recounted stories she'd heard from nursing homes and care facilities of lonely men and women marking out meaningless hours, unvisited, forgotten, living for their next meal, impatient with the overworked and underpaid staff.

Then the facilitator reconvened the meeting. He had what he called a "legislative report", most of which was lost on Janice. There was talk of bills and committees and lobbying efforts, none of which meant anything to her. But the impression she got was that things were moving forward at the federal level, but there was still resistance at the state level that it was impeding progress. This surprised Janice, who'd thought the president had enough power to do whatever he wished, but apparently that wasn't the case. States could have laws that hindered advancement. Janice felt frustrated – what were these little tin-pot politicians doing, obstructing vital progress? The facilitator concluded by encouraging people to contact their state representatives and senators, and Janice realized that she didn't even know who they were.

Then the facilitator introduced the next speaker, who turned out to be Charon. Janice felt a little thrill at this. This was a slightly different Charon than the one who'd spoken last Saturday night. This Charon was scholarly and authoritative, speaking with firm confidence.

Charon explained how he'd recently returned from a global economic conference in Dubai. The conference had been titled, "Where's the Recovery?", and had focused on the question of why growth, or even stability, in the global economy was proving so elusive. He began by explaining that the economic downturn that had begun before Janice was even born still persisted despite steady advances in technology, energy, communications, and general productivity. He produced some graphs and figures about country GDPs that was rather lost on Janice, but the gist was clear: no nation had ever completely recovered from that blow. Furthermore, Charon explained, this long-running period of economic doldrums defied all theories and models. There were plenty of ideas and obvious points of failure, but nobody could explain why the whole world was still struggling.

Hence the Dubai conference and its goal of stepping back to get a broad view. Too much economic and political effort was focused on particular crises – what to do about European debt, for instance, or how to shift Asia's economies from export to domestic orientation. The hope of the organizers of the Dubai conference was to detach from the particulars in order to grapple with the whole. This, Charon explained, had forced them to reengage with the very fundamentals of economics.

Janice was intrigued by this. She'd never been very interested in economic or politics, but Charon kept the pace even and the material reasonably accessible. At times she got a bit lost in the sequence of scatter plots, trend lines, and population pyramids that Charon was flicking through as he spoke, but she did her best to keep with him. She wanted to at least appear attentive, unlike some of those around her who were checking their tablets and phones. It was a lot to absorb, but two critical points stuck in her mind.

One point was that wealth had to move around to do any good. This was a new concept to Janice, who realized that she'd always thought of wealth as piles of bullion locked in vaults or stacks of high-denomination bills secreted away in safe deposit boxes. Charon emphasized that wealth only brought prosperity when it moved around. Spending purchased goods and services, which kept people employed. Investment provided capital for new ventures, which caused more movement of wealth. In fact, if people were to tuck all their wealth away in safe deposit boxes, the economy would grind to a halt.

The other point was that the economically productive elements of any population were the working age members, from the late teens to the early sixties. Members younger and older than that were net drains that the productive members had to work to support. Society was willing to accept the burden of younger members, since they represented an investment in the future, but older members that were beyond their productive years simply drained resources.

This had been the lens through which the attendees at the Dubai conference had examined the world economy: where was the wealth that should be circulating and generating global prosperity? Unsurprisingly, it was concentrated in the hands of those in the older age groups, those beyond their productive years. These people constituted a disproportionate percentage of the world's population, due to demographic trends over the past several generations, and it was in their hands that much of the wealth lay.

Charon then plunged deep into a technical exposition of government borrowing and the international debt market. Janice found herself lost in all this, but presumed it had some relevance to the topic. She was able to reconnect when Charon moved into the summarization and conclusion phase of the presentation.

The Dubai conference had concluded by drawing up a set of recommendations for action. Foremost among these was breaking the hammerlock that the older, unproductive groups of the population had on the vast share of the world's wealth. This was apparently a more difficult problem than it might seem, due to a number of interlocking factors such as the political activism of older citizens and what Charon called 'outmoded ethics and archaic policies'. But this, he concluded, only heightened the urgency of exploring alternatives.

Janice applauded enthusiastically as Charon finished, and thought she saw him glance at her and smile. But he was mobbed by other attendees, and Janice thought he wouldn't appreciate being pestered by a strange woman wearing a yellow cord. But her mind was made up about one thing, and she pulled Kendra off to a corner of the room.

"Okay, Kendra," she asked frankly. "How do I get in?"

"Get in?" Kendra asked, a bit puzzled.

"You know – join. Sign up. Get rid of this," Janice pressed, fingering the cord. "There's a lot I still don't know, but it's clear this group is serious about addressing some of our most critical problems, and I want in. What does it take? Dues? Some kind of training? A rite of initiation? Enrollment? I'll do whatever it takes, just let me know what it is."

Kendra gave her an appraising look. "You're right. But it's not for the faint of heart. We recognize problems and take action where others shrink back in fear. As you've just seen, we're about far more than cocktail parties and rallies. We are dedicated to addressing some of the most trying problems our country – in fact, the whole world – is facing. But becoming one of us requires complete dedication. We aren't interested in halfway commitments or wavering intentions. If you want in, we'll take you, but only if you're willing to go all the way."

"I am," Janice replied, feeling thrilled. As she spoke the words, she realized that this was what she'd been looking for all her life: a good cause, something greater than herself to which she could dedicate her life. "Just tell me what I need to do."

"It is a rite of initiation, of sorts," Kendra explained. "The precise form varies by person and situation. You should talk to Melissa about it – she'd know exactly what a person like you would have to do."

"Have – you done this?" Janice asked.

"Oh, yes," Kendra confirmed, tapping the XCV pin on her lapel.

"Was it – difficult?"

"It was demanding," Kendra explained. "It forced me to examine what I thought was most important, and what I was willing to do for that."

"I'm up for that," Janice said.

"Good," Kendra replied. "Come on, it's about time for the gathering to begin."

The vast lobby had already taken on the reception atmosphere that Janice remembered from the prior week. This time she was less shy about going up to the bar and buffet, fetching a couple beers and a plate of canapés for herself and Kendra. They stood chatting about the gatherings – how often they were held, how large they were, what topics were covered. Janice spotted a couple people who'd been at the seminar, but everyone else was unfamiliar.

"Don't feel bad," Kendra reassured Janice. "It took me a while to get to know many people here. They come from a lot of different places."

"Are they all in the medical profession?" Janice asked.

"Many are. But there are others, too – lawyers, accountants, even a few legislative staffers. They're from all over the area, up to Bay City and over to – well, Port Huron. I'd guess that no more than a quarter of us are able to make any particular gathering, though everyone tries to get to at least a couple each year."

"Now, me," came a familiar voice behind them. "I try to make as many as possible, because I meet so many interesting people."

"Logan!" Janice cried excitedly.

"In the flesh," Logan replied with a charming smile. He was dressed impeccably, though his glasses were a different tint than the last ones she'd seen him in. "I was hoping you'd be here, Janice."

Janice flushed, not wanting to acknowledge even to herself that part of the reason she'd been so diligently scanning the room had been to see if she could spot him. "Logan, do you know Kendra?"

"You look somewhat familiar, though I don't think we've met," Logan said, extending his hand. "Logan Thompson."

"Kendra Myers," Kendra replied. "A pleasure."

"I notice your drinks are almost empty," Logan said. "A couple more of the same?"

The women nodded, and Logan ducked off. Kendra raised her eyebrows at Janice.

"'I was hoping you'd be here'? Whoa, girl!"

"He's just a friend," Janice insisted, blushing furiously.

"Okay, just a friend." Kendra winked. "Just leave some for the rest of us, okay?"

Never in her life had anyone said anything like that to Janice.

Logan returned shortly, rather clumsily bearing three beers and another plate of hors d'oeuvres. They found a couch and caught up, though it wasn't long before Kendra spotted someone else she wished to speak to and left. Janice told Logan about the talks she'd attended at the afternoon seminar.

"I wanted to make that," Logan said. "But I was lucky to even get here for this. My car didn't start, so I had to hitch a ride, and I've got shift first thing tomorrow, so I'll have to figure out what to do about that. But it means no late evening for me – I'll have to bolt right after the talk."

"I can – could I give you a ride home?" Janice asked.

"Would you? That'd be a big help," Logan replied with a glowing smile. Janice, who was well into her third beer, looked at her shoes and let her imagination toy with the possible developments that might follow driving Logan home.

But then the program was starting, and everyone was filing into the auditorium. There was a different guy making the announcements, and again Janice had to stand when the time came for guests to be introduced. She was the only one this time, and though she was warmly applauded, she felt her outsider status more keenly. Last week she'd just been a visitor evaluating things; this week she knew she belonged and desperately, fervently wanted in.

The speaker was Charon again, though he'd changed out of his suit into slacks and an open-necked shirt. To Janice's eye, he looked more determined, more fervent than he had last week. She guessed that this speech would be more impassioned, and she was not disappointed.

"How much are you worth?" Charon began firmly and without preamble or ramp-up. He gazed keenly around the room and repeated the question. "How much are you worth?"

"In certain contexts, that question would be immediately understood as a reference to your net worth: the total value of your assets minus any obligations such as loans. Your property, your investments, your retirement accounts would all be factored in. Now, I don't know for sure," Charon said with an understanding smile. "But I'd guess that if we totaled that kind of net worth for everyone in this room, it wouldn't be very much. Certainly less than two million dollars, possibly less than a million, given the aggregate amount of student debt you all could be carrying.

"Yet I was listening to a radio show recently where the guest, an investment advisor, was complaining about his newer clients who were coming in with such paltry portfolios. He remembered not long ago when his typical client would have an account valued at about a million dollars. That was his recommendation for people planning for retirement: a net worth of one million, with a mil and a half or two million being better.

"I stared at the radio in amazement, to the point where I almost drove off the road. A million dollars for retirement? I thought of you who gather here, most of whom are struggling to get enough hours to make a dent in your student debt and find a reasonable place to live and own a working car. You who would struggle to save a thousand dollars, much less a million. I thought to myself, 'this is a twisted definition of worth.'

"I don't know anything about investment advisors or million-dollar clients, but I know this: when I look out across this room, I see more worth than your balance sheets indicate. I see a room full of dedicated, hard-working people determined to help turn this society around. In fact, I see a more net worth among you here than among any number of retirees with million-dollar portfolios."

This brought a rush of spontaneous applause. Janice felt like Charon was speaking about her life specifically.

"It would be different," Charon began, trying to talk down the applause. "It would be different if those retirees had gathered those million dollars by working as hard, under such difficult circumstances, as you do. And, for all I know, some of them did. But know for a fact that some – perhaps many – did not.

"I recently returned from an international economic conference. Those of you who were able to make the seminars this afternoon got a lot of the technical details, but here I'll just summarize critical points.

"One thing the conference examined was the massive, out-of-control government borrowing that has marked recent decades. Our parents and their parents elected politicians who implemented policies that put this country trillions of dollars in debt.

"Now, to many of us, 'government debt' is just a number on a screen – we don't see how it affects us. But government debt is actually a tax on the next generation. Let me explain what that is by starting with what it isn't.

"In a recent election in my county, there was a ballot proposal to renew the millage for our county parks. Now, I like parks, and the amount wasn't that great, so I voted in favor. I was voluntarily taxing myself. I wanted it; I elected to pay for it.

"But government borrowing is getting money for yourself and handing the bill to your descendants. The parties doing the borrowing get the immediate benefit, but the next generation has to pay the interest. That's exactly what happened in the decades around the turn of the century: massive government borrowing gave the illusion of prosperity, and there was so much money sloshing around that people were able to skim off thousands and stash them in their accounts. No wonder the investment advisor grew accustomed to million-dollar clients.

"But it was all phony. Many amassed fortunes, or at least enough for a comfortable retirement, but then the bills started coming due. It's not that there weren't warnings. There were plenty of warnings, but they were ignored. One prominent economist of the day scoffed at the notion that the huge debt would be a concern, saying that we – their children – would owe it to ourselves. Well, here we are—and we're making the payments, but I'm not seeing any benefits – are you?

"Warnings were easy to ignore when the cash was flowing and the portfolio values were surging. After all, they got theirs, didn't they? Never mind that the next generation would be the ones paying. This was the main focus of this conference: where is the wealth that should be circulating and growing economies? One conclusion realized was that it had already been collected, and lay stashed in the portfolios and properties of those who had turned their governments loose to do such irresponsible borrowing. It was the largest instance of intergenerational larceny in history."

Charon paused dramatically to let that sink in. The room was stone silent. Janice was not even thinking about Logan's proximity.

"It would be different," Charon continued. "If those who had amassed that wealth at least used it responsibly. If you go back about 150 years, to the late nineteenth and early twentieth centuries, there were wealthy people, but at least they invested in their communities. They built factories that employed workers. They funded hospitals and universities. Even if they lived in opulent mansions, at least they hired tradesmen to build them and locals to serve as household staff! They spread the wealth around so others could benefit.

"Not so these modern wealthy. They spend their retirements on luxurious vacations, expensive cars, and second homes. They want dramatic and exciting experiences, because you only live once, right?

"I'll tell you a personal story. I've always loved watching big ships, and one day I found myself in Miami, so I decided to go down and watch the cruise ships come in. I'll never be able to afford a cruise myself, but at least I can watch, right? So I watched this big ship moor, and the passengers started disembarking down the main gangway. The vast majority of them looked like retirees, tanned and rested and full of themselves. They all got into expensive cars, or shuttles to high-end hotels, or buses to take them to the airports.

"From a rear gangway the crew was disembarking. They were much less well dressed, and looked tired. They got into older cars, or went to bus stops to await public transportation, undoubtedly heading back to simple apartments or small houses. In many ways they reminded me of you all – just struggling to make a living.

"I sat and thought about that for a long time. There were thousands of passengers on that ship, each one of them paying thousands of dollars to take a cruise that had lasted at most fourteen days. A little math tells you that the amount spent on that cruise was well into the millions – and for what? So that the passengers could dance and dine and take pictures of Caribbean ports to post online. No permanent value, nothing but a thrilling experience that lasted a few days. Multiply that by all the cruise ships and all the cruises, and you're looking at a staggering amount of money being dissipated on experiences instead of being reinvested into businesses or property or something enduring – and that's just the cruise industry!

"Personally, that's one of my biggest worries about the final conclusion of this conference, which had to do with where the wealth was concentrated. The studies found that an inordinate amount of it lay in the hands of the elderly. Now, some of this is normal and expectable. People work their whole lives to accumulate wealth to see them through their final years. When they die, the wealth returns to the community through inheritances and bequests, helping the next generation.

"What's abnormal – and dangerous – about our current situation is three things. First, the wealth accumulated in the hands of our elderly largely wasn't earned – it was borrowed, and the bill was handed to us. Second, today's elderly are living much longer due to medical advances, so this wealth isn't being returned to the next generation in a timely manner. And third, the wealth in their hands isn't being reinvested, but squandered on their transient experiences, so by the time they die, there could well be nothing left to pass on!"

Charon had been working up to a crescendo, and let that last threat echo in the room. There was a shocked silence as everyone grasped the implications of that. Charon had left his tablet on the lectern and was now striding about the edge of the platform, looking the audience straight in the eyes. Janice felt like he was talking directly to her.

"I hardly need to tell you this," Charon went on. "All of you know elderly people, and some of you work with them every day. Who has the large properties, the new cars, the nice clothes? Is it likely to be the young, your peers? Hardly! No matter what the profession, folk of our generation are in the same boat – jobs that barely pay, student loan debt, seedy apartments, third or fourth-hand cars. You can't get ahead, because you were robbed – robbed before you were even born!

"Those thieves – those thugs – those intergenerational crooks who stole your future are adept at hiding behind laws, politicians, family connections, and outmoded social conventions. They know how to protect their plunder. Even their kids are willing to protect them, though the kids are getting screwed along with the rest of us.

"But there's one thing they've forgotten, one thing they haven't reckoned on: us. The outcasts. The bastards. The petes. Those who have no family loyalty because we have no family. Where others have used their moral code to strip us of our lives, we will make our own moral code to take them back. We are still exploring new ways, searching for paths, but I guarantee you this: in the end, you will have your justice!"

This time the auditorium fairly exploded. People were leaping in the air, shouting, clapping, banging on chairs, whistling. Janice was howling at the top of her lungs and could barely hear herself. She turned to Logan, who caught and held her in his strong arms. When they stood apart, he looked into her eyes for a long minute, and she trembled in anticipation of what might happen next. But he turned away to rejoice with others, so she did as well.

Charon was standing on the platform nearly dripping with sweat from the passion of his delivery. Nobody seemed to be approaching him, and he didn't seem to be coming down to where everyone was celebrating. Silently he picked up his tablet and walked off.

"Well, that was quite something," Logan commented later when they were back out in the lobby, again transformed into a cocktail lounge.

"I know," Janice replied enthusiastically. "It's so clear when he explains it like that! It all comes together and makes so much sense. I just wonder what he meant by 'exploring new ways'."

"I'm sure we'll find out in time," Logan said with a yawn. "Y'know, it's been a long day, and I have an early shift. Does that offer to run me home still stand?"

"Sure," Janice said, her insides trembling a bit. They went out to her car and headed for Logan's apartment complex, which fortunately was east along the expressway, in the direction Janice was headed anyway. They talked casually until they pulled up in front of his door. He got out and came around to her door, and not knowing why, she opened it and stood to talk to him.

"Well, thanks for the ride," he said, looking into her eyes. "And for the fun – though short – evening. It was as good as the last time."

"Yeah," Janice stammered, tongue-tied. "Me, too."

They stood looking at each other until Janice began to feel uncomfortable. "Well – good night," she said.

"Good night," Logan replied, then he swiftly leaned over and gave her a kiss on the cheek, turned, and walked to his door.

Just inside the door, Logan stopped in the vestibule and watched through the peephole. Janice was still standing by her car, dumbstruck. Logan didn't know what she'd do. He had plans for any contingency, but wanted her to make the choice. Finally she got back in the car, but sat still for a long time.

"Come on, bitch, make up your mind," Logan muttered. Finally she started idling away, but even that wasn't definite – she might be pulling into a parking space and coming to the door. Only when she'd pulled out of the parking lot and onto the street did he judge that she was truly gone. He pulled out his phone and fired off a quick message.

Hook set. Up to you to reel in.

Then he keyed a number, stepping out of the door. "Yeah," he said to the party who answered. "She's gone. Come get me."

Eastbound on I-69, Janice berated herself for her cowardice. Tonight could have been it – her first night with a man. But she'd chickened out. Maybe next time. Rats – she still didn't have his number. She realized that she'd again driven off wearing the yellow cord. She fingered it and resolved that she'd worn it for the last time. Whatever it took, she was getting in. She felt like her life was just getting ready to really start, and that cord was the only thing tying her down.

Secrets

Derek awoke Saturday anticipating a busy morning with the youngsters. The hay being in and the corn still drying, the crop of the day was grapes – jam grapes, not wine grapes. Elizabeth, Tabitha, and Jude had made him promise to help them pick because Philip and Martha had "gotten him" the prior weekend.

"Hey, Derek," Philip said at breakfast. "Sam was wondering if you wanted to help him do the monthly cutover test at 1:00."

"Sure," Derek said. "I promised I'd pick grapes and help make jam this morning, but I don't know how long that will take. They tell me there are only four vines."

Philip just smiled.

After breakfast Derek found out why. The kids dragged him, in his new broad-brimmed hat, to where four gigantic concord grape vines were stretched out on trellises, each of which was easily fifty feet long. His jaw nearly dropped at the rows of vines festooned with broad leaves and heavy with dark purple clusters. 'Only' four vines?

"It's been a good year for grapes," Elizabeth explained. "They all come ripe at about the same time, so we have to gather them in quickly before the birds and mold get them. C'mon, they're already cooking down the first batch at the Big House."

Derek thought he was doing well with the pruning shears he'd been given. But then Jude came behind him and, trimming away some of the big leaves, uncovered at least as many clusters still on the vine as Derek had in his bucket. Clearly, he had much to yet learn about harvesting grapes.

When all the buckets were full they brought all the grapes to the large deck at the back of the Big House, where they washed and sorted them in big tubs of water. Nobody got out of that quite dry. They brought the cleaned grapes into the big industrial-style kitchen, where Derek met Ruth Winters, a salt-and-pepper haired woman whom he dimly remembered seeing at the funeral, along with her daughter Cathy, and Harmony

165

Peterson from the next house over. They were busy boiling grapes in huge pots and stirring them with great paddles.

Ruth groaned at the fresh load of grapes, and shooed the children out to keep picking while retaining Derek where his height and muscle could be most useful. So he helped measure and stir and dump and strain the grapes through the various stages of jam-making until they were ready to portion the jam into the sanitized jars. At this point, they had Derek pour the boiling hot jam mixture into a hopper which looked like it held about five gallons. This was then hoisted by a pulley hung from chains that were fastened into a track anchored to a beam overhead. Derek was amazed as the teen girls hoisted the hopper easily, slid it over the large island in the middle of the kitchen, and began filling jars from a spigot in the bottom of the hopper.

"Like that?" Ruth asked. "Sam rigged it up for us. Much easier than ladling the jam into jars with funnels. It's no end of handy, because we're always having to portion out quantities of things – jam, batter, juice, whatever."

"Oh, Sam," Derek said. "That reminds me, I'm helping him today – cutover, or something like that. What time is it?"

"Oh, that's today, isn't it?" Ruth said. "I'll have to remind Jan when she brings lunch. It's a monthly thing – every third Saturday at 1 p.m. we test our emergency generation system. It's just eleven now, so you have plenty of time. You can head over after lunch."

Lunch was sandwiches and lemonade on the deck, brought over by Jan Peterson. Afterwards, at about 12:30, Derek walked over to the back of Sam's shop where a two-seated UTV waited outside the door. He stuck his head inside to find Sam at a workbench, writing in a notebook.

"Ah – here," Sam said, looking up. "Ready? Let's go. Carry these, please?" He pointed to a pile of notebooks on the table, which Derek swept up while Sam clunked out the door with the help of his canes.

"You drive this?" Sam asked, pointing at the UTV.

"Um – yeah, I think so," Derek said with excitement. He never had, but it looked like fun, and how hard could it be, right?

"Just like car," Sam said dismissively. "Go slow first, until used to it. Here – notebooks in back."

It was fun driving the UTV along the farm trails, following Sam's pointed directions. They finally came to a structure surrounded by bushes that looked too large to be a shed but too small to be a barn. Some large oblong tanks stood nearby, and Sam pointed out that it had two sets of power lines running to it – one set from some nearby poles and another stretching back toward the houses.

"All power for campus come through here," Sam explained. "In from grid, through boards, out again."

"Um – 'campus'?" Derek asked.

"Houses, stable, workshop – you know," Sam said impatiently. "Bring notebooks, please."

Inside the shed was a large diesel engine and a wall full of switches and dials. The clock on the wall said quarter to, and Sam proceeded to start looking at various dials and writing things in a notebook.

"Please call, warn of cutover," Sam said, pointing at a phone on the wall. "Big House is twenty-two."

"Oh, I warned the Big House, and Jan Peterson," Derek said.

"Okay – Kent and Linda then – twenty-seven," Sam said. "Then come start engine."

Sam showed him the green button that would bring the diesel to life, and after checking a few gauges and throwing a switch or two, signaled Derek to punch it. The engine fired up with less noise than Derek had expected.

"Good, good," Sam pronounced, examining the gauges. "Look at generation levels. At one exactly we cut over." He jotted a few things in his notepad, adjusting a dial here or there.

"You – write all this down?" Derek asked, looking over his shoulder.

"Yes, yes, write everything down," Sam muttered. "Else nobody can follow. I explain all after cutover. There – " he pointed to a large switch on the side of a grey box mounted on the wall. "You throw at one o'clock by that clock – exactly, to second. Three positions: currently down, middle is all off, up is local generation. Throw all the way up."

"Just – up?" Derek asked, grabbing the switch.

"Yes – fifteen seconds," Sam said, watching the clock. "Three – two – one – now!"

Derek rammed the switch up with all his strength. The lights dimmed then flared again, and the engine grumbled in a lower key as it took the load. Sam inspected the gauges with satisfaction.

"Good, good. Now check outside," he said, hobbling to the door. Outside they examined the industrial sized electric meter, which was now still. "See? Off grid now – local generation only."

"How long will you run locally?" Derek asked.

"Two hours. Burn off older fuel. Try to rotate stock. Truck coming by next month," Sam explained.

"I'm amazed at how quiet it is," Derek commented, looking at the large muffler which hung under the eaves of the shed. Out here, the engine was barely audible, even standing almost beneath the muffler. Sam chuckled knowingly.

"Yes, nobody hear, nobody see," he waved his cane at the tall bushes surrounding the shed. "Nobody know. Come, let me explain all this."

For the next couple hours Sam showed Derek all about the generation station – how the fuel was fed to the engine, how to check the oil and coolant, how to monitor the current flow, how to watch for spikes and sags. He explained all the notations in the various notebooks, pointing out anomalies and what he'd done about them. Derek saw everything about the preventative maintenance schedule for both the engine and generator.

Derek found this brief, intense lesson immensely interesting. Sam expected him to learn and think, challenging him as few of his teachers ever had, and he rose to the challenge. He learned things he'd always wondered about electricity and engines and fuel. He was utterly intrigued and got immense satisfaction from Sam's congratulations for his insightful questions.

It wasn't until later that Derek realized that he'd ceased being made uncomfortable by, or even noticing, Sam's disabilities. Following his slurred and jerky speech had become second nature, and Derek was beginning to pick up on his nuances and inflections. His clunky movements were just how he was. Derek was even beginning to decipher Sam's facial expressions, such as the difference between a joking scowl (such as he made when he spoke of having given up a promising career in professional soccer to come do this) and a scolding scowl, which Derek got when he tried to pretend to know more than he did.

The two hours passed by quickly, and as three o'clock approached, Sam made Derek read him all the gauges and explain their meaning. Then Derek pulled down the cutover switch, verified that they were back on external power, and shut down the engine.

On the way back to the shop Sam looked at Derek suddenly. "You drive your car?" he asked.

"Sure – it's in front of the Schaeffer's," Derek replied.

"Go there," Sam said, pulling a phone out of his pocket. "We fix."

Mystified, Derek drove to the tree where he'd parked. Sam scrambled out and worked his way around the car.

"What is this – eight years old?" he asked.

"Just about nine," Derek replied.

"You use GLN much?"

It took Derek a moment to decipher what Sam had asked. The Global Location Network had been slowly supplanting GPS for about a decade now. Most new cars came with GLN navigation systems built in.

"No, I mostly drive locally," Derek said. "And I don't mind using maps – I'm not totally inept."

"Can I fix car?" Sam asked, pulling a cable out of his pocket and plugging it into the phone.

"Um – sure," Derek said, clicking the locks open. He didn't know exactly what that meant, but he trusted Sam, who opened the car and plugged the cable into a port beneath the dash. Then he pecked at the phone for a bit before grinning, pulling the cable back out, and pocketing everything.

"You mind telling me what you just did?" Derek asked as Sam scrambled back into the four-wheeler.

"About twelve years ago, federal law, all vehicles must have position transponder. When receive signal, must respond with GLN position. I fix yours."

"You mean," Derek asked. "You just disabled my position transponder?"

"Oh, no. Can't do that. Illegal to disable – federal crime," Sam said gravely, then broke into a mischievous grin. "But that doesn't mean coordinates transmitted must make sense."

"So – my transponder will reply, but it'll send garbage data?" Derek asked.

"Yes – but only if sent interrogation signal. Likely never happen," Sam replied.

"How did you do that?"

"Secret program," Sam said, patting the pocket where the phone resided. "Lots of secret programs, if know where to look. You bring phone and tablet?"

"Mine? No, they asked me not to," Derek explained.

"Next time, you bring," Sam announced. "I fix them."

"But Kent and Linda said –" Derek began, but Sam cut him off.

"I talk to Kent and Linda. We fix your devices, make them safe. You bring next time."

Derek drove Sam back to his shop and carried the notebooks inside for him. "Thanks for help," Sam said, giving Derek a firm shake with his strong, calloused hand.

"Thank *you*," Derek replied emphatically. "It was really interesting to learn all that."

"You like learning?" Sam asked.

"Sure," Derek assured him. "Most of my study has been in medicine, but I like learning all sorts of things."

"Okay. You come back, I teach you," Sam said decisively.

"Teach me what?" Derek asked.

"Everything," Sam replied, waving his cane around the room at the walls hung with gear. "You want to learn, I teach. Electrical, metal, mechanics, computers, communications. All of it."

"Wow," Derek said, impressed and a little intimidated. "That – that'd be great, Sam."

"Next Thursday," Sam pronounced. "You come in evening, help set up rig. Friday, Saturday, we drill."

"Drill what?"

"Well. Water well. At another house – friends," Sam explained. "Ever drill well?"

"No," Derek admitted.

"Good experience. Next Thursday," Sam assured him.

Derek's route back to the house took him past the stable. When he heard excited voices within, he poked in his head to see Martha and Chris saddling up the horses. Martha almost squealed when she saw him.

"Mr. Derek, Mr. Derek," she gushed. "We finished all our chores and they said we could have a short ride before dinner! Do you want to come along?"

"Sure," Derek grinned, tensing his almost-not-sore muscles just a little.

"No more than ten miles," Christopher assured him.

So Derek accompanied them on a ride that took them along different trails that were straighter and smoother. The youngsters congratulated him on his new attire and taught him how to urge the horse faster, and steer him, and 'ride with' the various gaits of the horse. To Derek's satisfaction – and slight alarm – they galloped the last half-mile, and he didn't find it unmanageable.

They got the horses stabled just as the dinner gong rang. The meal was the usual cheerful cacophony, with everyone filling in everyone else on how the day had gone. Elizabeth and Jude expressed disappointment that he hadn't been around for the afternoon's picking, but the greatest reproach by far came from Matthew, who had been waiting *all day* for Mr. Derek to read him books. This omission was rectified immediately after dinner while everyone else cleaned up, followed by all going out to a bonfire at the burn pile. Many children and youngsters were there from all the households, casing Derek to wonder just how many people lived on what Sam called 'the campus'.

The next morning Derek woke late to find the house empty. However, in the middle of the kitchen table was a jar of grape jam, an unsliced loaf of homemade bread, and a note saying "The fruit of your labors." Derek tried some of the jam and was enraptured – he had never tasted such jam, or such bread, for that matter. He stuffed himself with thick slices thickly smeared, not stopping until nearly half the loaf was gone.

The Schaeffers returned presently, and Derek was pressed into reading books and passing judgement on dresses and school projects. Eventually he pried free to take a walk outside. The sky was clear and the temperature was reaching a pleasant level – summer's last gasp before autumn closed in. He wandered around the bar and along Sam's shop. Things seemed quiet, but he knocked and stuck his head in.

Sam was seated on a stool at a workbench, pouring over a book in front of him and occasionally jotting something in a notebook by his elbow. He looked up at Derek questioningly.

"Hi, Sam," Derek said, getting the impression he was intruding. "Any projects today?"

"No projects," Sam said. "Sabbath. Day to worship and study and pray." He tapped the book, which had a battered leather cover.

"Fair enough," Derek said, closing the door. He wandered across the great yard feeling oddly displaced – he didn't want to be anywhere else (the very thought of returning to his apartment filled him with bleak emptiness), but neither did he feel like he exactly fit anywhere here. He kept wandering, catching a glimpse of the house beyond the Big House, where the Petersons lived.

Turning back toward the Schaeffers', he saw some activity by the wing that stuck out from the side of the Big House. He'd wondered about that when he'd been washing grapes on the deck. There was a yard area mostly overshadowed by great trees, with a gazebo in the middle and pavilions pitched here and there. Now there seemed to be people milling about in that yard, many people, and from the way they were moving they looked to be elderly. This was interesting – he hadn't yet seen any older people around. Maybe these were them. He angled his walk to get a little closer.

Sitting in a couple of chairs in the shade, the two sentinels had spotted Derek when he'd come along the stable and had been watching him ever since. They'd been on special alert, having been warned that there was a guest on the property.

"Here he comes," one said, spotting Derek's trajectory toward the yard.

"Yeah," the other confirmed. "Apparently, he's quite smart, and very inquisitive."

"Better get to it, then," replied the first. "You want to head him off, or should I?"

"You do it," the other said. "You've got more distraction value."

"You must be Derek," came a musical voice from behind him. Startled, Derek turned to see a woman with long, wavy brown hair framing an oval face with sparkling brown eyes and a warm, welcoming smile. She wore a smocked dress with a tiny floral pattern which, though it covered her from neck to knees, displayed her femininity perfectly. Derek had never seen a woman so beautiful.

"I – uh – yeah," Derek stammered.

"I'd heard you were here visiting, but we haven't yet had the chance to meet," she continued, extending her hand. "I'm Felicity Peterson. You've met my parents, ridden with my brother, and worked with my sister Harmony yesterday. She told me about you."

"A pleasure to meet you," Derek managed to get out. "What – what did she say?"

"That you were nice, and that you didn't get mad when she splashed you," Felicity said with a silvery laugh. "Though mother scolded her for treating a guest like that."

"I hope that she didn't get in trouble," Derek said. "We were all just having fun."

"No, no – everyone understands that grape harvest is like that," Felicity assured him. "So, how far did you get?"

"How far?" Derek was puzzled.

"With the grapes," Felicity replied. "How much did you harvest?"

"I – ah – I'm not sure," Derek said, desperate to keep the conversation going but finding himself tongue-tied. "I got pulled away after noon to go help Sam."

"Well, then," Felicity said with a sunny smile as she slipped her arm into his. "Let's go take a look, shall we?" She led him off toward the grape arbor.

Felicity seemed to be interested in everything about Derek – where he'd grown up, what he'd studied, what his life was like. They inspected the grape vines, which were mostly stripped, though they found a couple stragglers that they shared. Then they walked along the edge of the hay field, where Derek told of his first venture at haying and its painful aftermath. They stopped in on the horses, where Felicity seemed every bit as comfortable with the great beasts as Martha was. They strolled past Sam's shop and talked about what a strange but wonderful character he was. They discussed John Holmes' funeral, which Felicity had been unable to attend due to other responsibilities.

Derek couldn't believe his good fortune. He'd never had any woman pay this much undivided attention to him, much less such a beautiful and charming woman. And – Derek found it hard to put his finger on this – she didn't seem to be flirting or toying. She was genuinely interested in him, and once he got over his initial shyness, he was talking and laughing with her easily. He found no difficulty coming up with topics to discuss, for everything seemed interesting in her presence. He preferred topics that let her do most of the talking, just to hear her gentle voice. He had no idea why she thought him so interesting, but he wasn't going to question it.

The dinner gong sounding from the Schaeffers' brought an end to this idyllic interlude, much to Derek's regret.

"I have to go," Derek said. "It's been delightful talking with you. I – I hope to see you again sometime soon."

"Oh, you will," Felicity assured him with a smile. "If you're around, we'll bump into each other."

Derek headed in a bit saddened that the time had ended but with a lighter heart than he'd had in a long time.

Felicity rejoined her companion at their chairs.

"Well, that took rather a while," the companion commented.

"Given that he was the only known caution, it seemed acceptable to spend my time keeping him occupied," Felicity answered.

"And gaining another admirer in the process," he grinned.

"Stop it!" she slapped his arm lightly. "I'll have you know that he was very pleasant company and a perfect gentleman throughout. I'm sure he'll make a wonderful friend."

"You always bring out the best in people, Felis," the guy commented. She narrowed her eyes at him in suspicion. "Hey,

I meant that as a compliment! Angie says I should work on being more positive, so I am."

"In that case, thank you," Felicity replied. "Come on – he's in for dinner at the Schaeffers', and by the time he's done, they'll be inside. I think we can wrap up here."

After a delicious dinner, Derek again found himself on the front porch with Linda and Kent, enjoying the fading afternoon.

"Nice to see you a little less stiff," Linda commented.

"I only felt the riding a little bit when I woke this morning," Derek said, flexing a little.

"You did less of it this weekend," Kent explained. "And your muscles were more toned. Keep it up, and eventually you won't even notice."

"I hope to," Derek said. "I want to thank you both for your gracious hospitality these past weekends. Work and sore muscles notwithstanding, it's been – it's been great," Derek cut himself short, surprised at how close to tears he was.

"It's been a delight to have you, Derek," Linda assured him. "It's like you fit right in with our family."

"That's what it feels like," Derek replied huskily. "Is it always like this out here? So peaceful and – I don't know – harmonious?"

"No," Kent replied. "We're people, just like everyone else. We have our trials and struggles and heartaches. You may not be seeing much of that because you're a guest, but it's there."

"Also," Linda added. "You may be getting things here that you've never gotten before. You don't have any siblings, do you?"

"No – nor aunts nor uncles nor cousins," Derek said with just a trace of bitterness. "Just my mother, who's back in New York pursuing her own interests."

There was a minute of quiet before Linda spoke gently. "I'm sure your mother loved you as best she knew how – it's just that a lot of us weren't taught very well."

Derek didn't feel like he could respond to that while keeping his voice steady, so he cleared his throat and changed the subject. "I don't mean to be an imposition, but Sam was hoping I could come out Thursday evening to set up some kind of a drilling rig, and then for the weekend to help him with it. Something about a well somewhere."

"Oh, of course, you're always welcome," Kent assured him.

"In fact," Linda added cautiously. "If you'll be coming up Thursday afternoon, could I prevail on you to do another run for us? I could give you the money in advance."

"Oh, nonsense," Derek waved. "Happy to. It's easier for me to put it on my card and let you know how much it was exactly." He made a mental note to deposit the cash she'd given him first thing tomorrow – he wasn't accustomed to dealing with it, especially in those quantities.

"Thanks so much, Derek. It's a huge help," Linda assured him.

"Is this for all those people?" Derek asked.

"All what people?" Kent replied.

"The people behind the Big House this afternoon," Derek said. "There looked to be a few of them."

There was the slightest pause before Linda responded. "Some of it. Mostly it's just for the families – as you can see, there are a lot of us across all the households, and buying in bulk is always economical. But we have friends come to visit occasionally, and stay a while. On fine afternoons we entertain them in the back yard."

"Okay," Derek said. "Anything you need, I'm happy to help. For that matter, I'm coming up Friday, too, so I could do two runs, if you needed. Just e-mail me the lists."

Derek finished his beer and ducked into the house to pack his gear. Kent and Linda looked at each other.

"Smart, and observant," Linda pointed out. "We're going to have to tell him sooner or later, especially if he's going to be around as much as it appears he will be."

"I know," Kent acknowledged. "But we barely know him, and that's a lot to entrust to a near stranger."

"He's going to start piecing things together," Linda countered. "And some of his guesses might be more dangerous than him actually knowing."

"That's true," Kent admitted. "Maybe next weekend."

On his way back to town, Derek kept reviewing the weekend. He savored every moment of the time with the family, with Sam, out on the horses – and, of course, with Felicity. He sighed – a girl like that almost certainly had a boyfriend, probably some strapping farm lad. He'd best not dwell on her, lest he get his hopes up in vain.

But still.

"I want in," Janice said. "Whatever it takes, I want to be part of it."

It was midweek before Janice's shift schedule coincided with Melissa's, and the first chance she got she cornered her by the nurse's station.

"I thought you might when you saw what was at stake," Melissa said, pulling Janice aside into an empty room. "The gatherings are great pep talks, but the seminars really drive it home, don't they?"

"No question," Janice responded. "It boils down to whether we have a shred of a chance or descend into chaos."

"Some would argue that the descent has already begun," Melissa answered. "The only question is whether we can pull out in time, or if all this comes crashing down."

Janice felt solemn and determined. "The stakes are high, aren't they?"

"None higher," Melissa said. "Which is why every foot soldier is important. Are you free after shift?"

"Anywhere, any time."

"Jack's at five. You know where it is?"

"Sure – just downtown, right?"

The rest of shift was frustrating for Janice, as had all her shifts been since the weekend. She'd slip into fantasies about Logan and what that evening could have been, but kept getting dragged back to the maddening reality by complaining patients or demanding families or brusque doctors. She recalled from the seminars that it had been people like this who'd been so fiscally irresponsible, who'd made their fortunes at the expense of her generation, who cost so much per day just to keep alive. Every day it had been harder to come to work and meet their shrill and niggling demands. By the end of each shift she was almost screaming with frustration. She couldn't wait to get back to her apartment and a couple of beers to settle down.

Today, she was going to take the step, she thought with determination as she yanked open the door of Jack's Bar. Today she was going to stop just talking about it. Today she'd cast her lot with those who saw the problem clearly, those who were willing to take action. She spotted Melissa in a booth. There were already four shot glasses on the table.

"Have a seat," Melissa said, waving Janice down. "I took the liberty – I hope you like vodka."

"Sure," Janice said, not wanting to admit that she'd never had it straight up.

"To the Cause," Melissa said, raising one of the shot glasses. Janice lifted one, and Melissa shot hers. Janice followed suit, forcing herself to keep a straight face and not gasp.

"To those who seize the future," Melissa repeated, and Janice again followed, finding that the second shot went down easier, since her throat was already numb. Melissa knocked on the table and signaled for four more shots. Thankfully the waiter brought glasses of water as well, which Janice drank readily.

"Keep yourself hydrated, kid," Melissa said. "So, you're serious, then?"

"Deadly serious," Janice replied.

Melissa smiled at that. "There's a measure of risk," she said.

"Not compared to the risk of doing nothing," Janice countered.

"Good answer," Melissa said. She took one of the shots and sipped it, to Janice's great relief. She would have been willing to knock back another shot, but hadn't been looking forward to it. "Here's the deal—we call it an acceleration."

"An acceleration?"

"Yes, because that's precisely what it is: accelerating the inevitable," Melissa explained. "You remember how important it is to get those financial resources freed up before they're dissipated?"

"Yes."

"And how much it costs to keep one of these patients alive for one more miserable, futile day?"

"Yes," Janice replied more quietly.

"Our culture, in its folly and sentimentality, insists that we do everything we can to extend these meaningless, expensive days – and we, the medical industry, have been complicit in this. With our treatments and procedures and care, we're simply delaying the inevitable." Melissa finished her shot.

"Therefore, it's proper that we should help rectify the situation we've helped create. We have ways of identifying specific patients by a variety of demographic and clinical criteria. We know what their conditions are and what treatments they're receiving. This tells us exactly how to neutralize their medications. This lets nature – the inevitable – take its course. We simply remove the artificial delays we've introduced and let things accelerate naturally. See?"

"Yes," Janice said without emotion.

"We have the criteria, we know the patients. We have access to them that nobody else has. What we need are people to administer the neutralizing serum. That's where you come in. That's the test. That's the initiation. In or out?"

"In," Janice replied firmly.

"Good kid," Melissa said, raising the fourth shot.

Sam didn't like disorder. This wasn't immediately obvious to those who visited his workshop, but it was true. All they might see was a busy space hung with random cables and cluttered with stuff, but the items along the walls had a careful layout, and everything was properly labeled. Even the cables were hung in just the right places to facilitate his getting around. To Sam, disorder was like a stone in his shoe or wind whistling through a crack in a window – a situation just begging to be rectified.

Which was why the situation at the old factory troubled Sam. Sure, it was over ten miles away, across the county line. But Sam considered it within his purview, which meant that it should be in order, and it wasn't. There were plenty of vacated buildings in the area, and most of them were in order. Vacated factories that stood vacant were, in their way, in order. Vacated factories that were demolished were in order, too, though in a different way. Vacated factories that were reoccupied, with workers parking outside and trucks coming and going and machines clanking – they were in order as well.

But vacant factories that appeared vacant but were in some kind of use – that wasn't in order. Somebody was driving right into the factory and closing the door behind them. Somebody had turned the electricity back on and set up a discreet camera, probably motion-activated, above the factory door, pointed down the driveway.

Out of order. Just begging to be set back in order, or at least investigated.

Sam's first step had been to place a radio receiver by the factory door, which was a lift door like those on loading docks. The surveillance camera was easy to avoid, since it was pointed at where the driveway came off the road, and he never came that way. The receiver was on the ground near the door, disguised to look like a rock, and was connected by a fine wire to an old phone, which was wrapped in a ratty old plastic bag that looked like a piece of litter. Sam loved old phones. People discarded them when their glass cracked or new models came out. Sam had boxes full of them – little computers, with all manner of handy programs already written for them. Like the program that captured the frequency and pattern of the remote signal that opened the factory door. There it all was, ready to read, when Sam returned a week after placing it to collect the receiver.

It was equally easy to program a transmitter to duplicate the signal that opened the door. Sam studied the signal pattern and judged when the factory was least likely to be occupied, then one morning he threw some tools into a bag, hopped on his scooter, and went to pay a visit.

Coming out of the bushes at the trail head, he drove carefully around the building, staying well clear of the driveway. He angled up to the door and keyed the transmitter. The factory door grumbled open, and he zipped inside, hugging the wall, and keyed the door closed.

Guessing that the only camera was outside, Sam searched for the main light switches. They lit up big banks of industrial fluorescents hanging from the ceiling that illuminated the large empty area which had once been the factory floor. Sam could see the spots where the machinery had stood, and the great power cables that still hung down from the girders overhead, dangling over the empty stations. Good – those would prove handy.

Sam examined the floor. Lots of tire tracks, all running over each other. Could be several cars. He took quick measurements of the factory area with his laser meter, made some rough sketches, and located the breaker boxes and major power runs. Then he went down the short hall to the offices. Not much along the way – a janitor's closet on one side, a bathroom on the other, both empty. He checked a faucet, and yup, there was water, which meant someone had gotten the pump running. No hot water, but there was toilet paper, and a couple of spare rolls. He clanked his way to the offices.

'Office' would be a better term, since there was only one large room with a couple of desks and some chairs. There were a couple of space heaters tucked into a corner, idle over the summer but indicating how long the place had been in use.

This made even less sense. Who would be using this place, and why? No phones, but that didn't mean much – most people just used their mobiles. But no computers, no network, no storage, not even any serious heat. What on earth was this remote, empty building being used for?

Definitely out of order.

The office door that led directly to the outside had a new lockset, both knob and deadbolt, of a standard make that could be found at any home supply store. In no time Sam removed both locks and tapped out the pins using his portable drill. There. Once he swept up the mess and reset the locks in the door, everything looked just as it had. The keys would even work – but so would any other key that would fit the lock, including a blank.

Sam took a few measurements in the office, snapped a few photos, and made some rough sketches. Then he departed, leaving everything as he'd found it. Motoring back to his shop, he laid out the sketches, pulled up the photos, and pondered.

Somebody was using that factory. Somebody who didn't want to be seen. Somebody who wasn't using that factory for what factories were supposed to be used for.

Hmm.

Somebody wanted watching.

Deeper In

"So – how does it work?" Janice asked quietly, leaning over the desk where Melissa was seated. "What's the next step?"

"One way it works," Melissa replied, glancing around to ensure nobody was near. "Is that we normally don't discuss matters in environments that are under surveillance."

"Oh – sorry," Janice said, instinctively glancing at the plastic camera dome embedded in the ceiling.

"It's okay this time, just a matter of operational discipline," Melissa said. "We have a research team that's always evaluating admissions. When they find a case that fits a certain profile, we run a deeper analysis. If the case looks likely, we have one of our pharmacists work up the neutralizing serum. That's given to a floor worker – someone like you – to administer at a specific time. Your work is only the last step in a lengthy process, and only takes thirty seconds. But for a variety of reasons it is precisely timed. We might get thirty minutes notice, and have a three minute window in which to execute. That's why you always have to be ready for the call."

"Count on me," Janice said.

"Great. Like I said, ours is the last step, and in a way the simplest," Melissa said. "We get the serum, wait for the go-ahead – usually a text message – duck in, administer, duck out, dump the syringe, and get back to our routine. Nearly impossible to screw up."

"All right," Janice said. "Let me know."

Sam examined the items on the table. They were nearly ready to place at the old factory. Two of them were standalone units, motion-activated audio/video monitors with extra-length batteries. The one for the office was camouflaged as an old thermostat and the one for the hallway was done up to look like an old light switch. There was also a wide-angle video only monitor for mounting in the ceiling girders over the factory floor. Because of the distance, he didn't need to camouflage that one quite so well, and he could wire it for power.

None of the monitors needed to transmit very far. When activated by motion, they'd stream what they captured to a "server" unit tucked into the drop ceiling of the office – again, just a reconfigured older phone sandwiched between a storage unit and a big battery pack. Altogether, the server unit was about the size and weight of a ham sandwich, and could store up to 36 hours of audio and video, though it would probably never approach that. Whenever it received the download signal, it would relay whatever it had stored since the last download then reset itself to collect more footage.

Which brought Sam to the challenge of transferring the captured video back to his shop. The long-distance transmission wasn't the problem – he did that all the time to facilitate communications between the ranches. What was dicey was the transmission rig, which had to sit atop the factory in line-of-sight back to his shop, and had to be wired into the building's power. Placement and camouflage could make it less noticeable, but somebody who knew what they were looking at would recognize it immediately for what it was, and its orientation would point them back in his direction. He could only do the best he could, and pray these people didn't police their facilities too often or too carefully.

Sam had tested the setup by rigging everything up in the stable – all the cameras, server unit, and transmission antenna. Everything had functioned perfectly. The motion activation had worked, the cameras had captured and transmitted footage to the server which had stored everything until requested. The transmission antenna had caught the request signal and downloaded the stored footage from the server back to Sam's workstation, at which point the server had cleared and reset. Sam now had about twenty-eight video hours of cows mooing, jostling, eating, and pooping, taken and stored within the stable and transmitted on demand to his workshop at 2:00 every morning. At the end of the multi-day, high-usage test the batteries were still showing above sixty percent. This rig was ready to plant.

Sam replaced all the batteries with fully charged ones, packed all the electronics in a padded box, and put his tools and supplies in his work bag. He considered carefully what he might need – this was going to be touchy enough without him having to run back to the shop for some forgotten item. This installation would keep him on the site for a dangerously long time – perhaps up to two hours – making for a higher risk of detection.

Sam packed his scooter and headed out. It was about 10:00 AM, and the usage patterns indicated that nobody visited the site until late afternoon at the earliest, so he hoped to have plenty of time. But he was still cautious when he arrived, circling around the building and checking the radio receiver by the factory door. It showed only two activations since his last visit, and none within the past six hours. He was probably safe. He packed up that receiver and went back around to the office door, where he let himself in with a blank key.

Planting the standalone units in the office and hallway took mere minutes. The faux-thermostat had been painted to match the wall color and was positioned where it could view the entire room. The camera in the hallway monitored most of that space as well as a good portion of the factory floor. He'd put the best microphone on this one in hopes of catching conversations people might have near their cars.

Then came the fun part – working up among the girders to place the wide-angle monitor in the ceiling. He was able to snag one of the dangling power cables with his whip and climb it to the girders that supported the roof. Here he could do what he wanted. Cables and overhead fixtures were just backdrop – nobody really looked at them. He scrambled about, pulling up the power cables and knotting them around the iron rafters so they'd bear climbing weight. Some he let drop back down, while others he strung from girder to girder, strongly anchored at both ends. There were several large I-beams traversing the width of the factory which made it easy to move around up here, twenty-five feet above the floor. When he was finished he could clamber almost anywhere among the rafters. Hopefully, this would be the last time he'd need to do it, but you never knew.

Sam placed the overhead monitor in a discreet place near the center of the room, tapping into a nearby junction box for power.

He looked all over but couldn't find a trap door that led to the roof. He hadn't expected to, but it would have been handy. But he did spot some likely penetration points, and measured them off carefully.

Time for outside work. Sam tied his work bag and the padded box together, placing the bundle by the main wall of the factory and tying a long, strong twine to them and to his belt loop. It took a bit of searching to find good purchase points for his whip, but he eventually located some, and soon was standing on top of the factory.

The good news was that the roof was just as he'd imagined it – weathered black tar all over, including vents and power boxes. The bad news was that work up here would be him at his clumsiest – no walker, no overhead cables, only his short canes for support. He hauled up the bundle and hobbled over to what seemed like the best place for the transmitter.

The next hour was just hard, gritty work – drilling and placing and feeding yards of cable through holes and spray painting, all the while crawling around the tarred roof in the hot September sun. He aimed the antenna as best he could, homing on the signal he'd left transmitting from his shop. When he was finished, the transmission unit blended in reasonably well with the rest of the rooftop clutter. On the off chance that somebody did come up here, hopefully they'd not notice it at all, or if they did, they'd write it off as reception equipment.

Back in the office, Sam risked some precious time taking a breather, realizing that there was one item he'd forgotten: drinking water. He had to make do with tepid, brackish water from the bathroom tap, scooped with his dirty hand. When he'd rested a bit, he set about the final, most critical steps: powering the transmitter and wiring it to the server unit.

Wiring the transmission unit power cables into a junction box was the easy part. Discreetly threading the signal cable from the factory ceiling to the office was much harder, particularly for someone with Sam's limitations. By the time he was done he was more exhausted than he'd been in a long time. Fortunately, all that remained was turning on the server and plugging in the cabling. Sam stood on a desk to wire in the unit and tuck it up into the drop ceiling.

The system was now, theoretically, operational. Sam tidied up his gear then stood in various places around the office and recited things. Then he clanked out to the hallway, talking as he went, and wandered around the factory floor from here to there, speaking in a normal voice. Then he did one last sweep and, satisfied that he'd collected everything, headed back to his shop.

Once there, Sam washed up thoroughly and made himself a sandwich. Sitting at his workstation, he transmitted the signal for an on-demand download. This was the moment of truth: if he'd made any mistakes in that complicated setup, particularly up on the roof, here is where it would show.

Everything worked. The workstation received three video files, one from each camera. Sam watched footage of himself wandering around the office and was gratified that even his muttering in a far corner was reasonably audible. The hall cam video showed him moving from just outside the office door to the factory floor. The video was good, though expectably audio quality dropped off in the cavernous space. The bird's-eye camera in the factory ceiling covered every square foot of the floor and captured him packing up and leaving.

Sam grinned with satisfaction. He keyed the clear code and then initiated another download. This time, nothing – just like it should be. He set up a schedule to download each day at 2:00 AM. Most days there would be no footage to transfer, but on the days that there were, he'd get audio and video of what was going on inside that factory. He nodded decisively and finished off his sandwich. Ignoring the message light blinking on his phone, he headed for a shower and a rare midday nap. Even his gear got left on the table. That could wait till later – he'd already put in a full workday.

Thursday couldn't come too soon for Derek, who stopped to pick up more supplies on his way out of town. Again, a greeting party was waiting to unload his car and escort him in to dinner, where Sam joined them. Afterwards Sam had Derek bring his powered-down electronic devices back to the shop, where he put them in something that looked like a box made of wire mesh which had armholes through which one could reach to manipulate the devices.

"Faraday cage," Sam explained as he powered up Derek's phone and tablet. "No signals in or out. See? Zero bars." Sure enough, Derek's phone was showing no reception. Sam plugged both devices into cables and then turned his attention to a workstation beside the cage.

"First, do like car," Sam explained, pointing to the workstation screen, which displayed two columns of numbers and specs, which Derek guessed represented the two devices. "See here – always know location. If triggered by signal, will transmit. FCC regulations. If you wish, I can make transmit rubbish."

"Yeah, go ahead," Derek confirmed.

"Make units useless for positioning. No location, no navigation, no finding pizza joints. You sure?"

"Sure," Derek grinned, and Sam keyed a few commands.

"There," Sam said, pulling the devices out of the cage and handing them to Derek, fully powered. "I put other utilities on there, too – explain later. Now safe to bring. Nobody track you."

"That's great," Derek responded. "But why would anyone want to track me?"

"Basic precautions," Sam said cryptically.

There was a truck parked in front of the Big House that was clearly for drilling. Philip came with them, driving the truck while Sam rode along, with Derek following in his car. They drove several miles to a property that had the shaggy, overgrown look of a vacant house, but had a couple of cars parked in the drive.

"People live here?" Derek asked.

"New people," Sam explained. "Vacant for years, now fixing up. Well was shot – cloudy, bad water. We drill new one – deeper." Philip backed the truck up to where Sam directed him, and the two men unloaded the items Sam pointed to. A young man, who introduced himself only as Richard, came out from the house to greet them but didn't stay to help. Sam didn't seem to think this unusual. The last thing they did as the light faded was dig down to where the water main fed from the existing well toward the house.

"Tomorrow, you come, we start drilling. Hope to tie into that by end of Saturday," Sam explained, pointing at the exposed water main.

The next day Derek cut out of work a little early with Shaundra's complicity, again stopped at the warehouse club to load his car, and headed out-country in what was becoming a new and cherished pattern of life. He was welcomed like a family member and supper was on the table, but Matthew was going to have to be disappointed because work awaited – they hoped to get a couple hours of drilling in this evening.

That evening and all day Saturday, Derek learned more about well drilling than he'd been aware there was to know. It was hard work, and when they struck good, clean water at midday on Saturday, he hoped they might be close to finished. But there was still much to do, and it wasn't until well after dark that the job was substantially completed. Derek was grateful for the long, hot shower that evening, and collapsed into bed sore, exhausted, and gratified.

Derek awoke the next morning much earlier than usual, but felt rested and refreshed. Hearing the family bustle outside the door, he threw on his bathrobe and went to see what was up.

"Oh," said Linda when she saw him. "You're up early – I hope we didn't wake you."

"No, no, woke on my own," Derek assured her. "What's going on?"

"Just preparing to head over to chapel at the Big House," Linda explained.

"Chapel? When's that?"

"About forty minutes," Linda said. "There's a big brunch afterwards today. We were going to leave you a note."

"Do – do you mind if I come along?" Derek asked. "Is that a problem?"

"What, to chapel?" Linda replied, slightly surprised. "No, not at all. You're more than welcome. It's only a short walk, and you've plenty of time."

The chapel at the big house was a side room that had been set up with rows of chairs to seat about forty. Derek sat in the back, and was soon joined by Sam, who slipped in as quietly as he could and nodded to Derek. The families tended to sit in the middle rows, but the front rows and those along the side were occupied by elderly people. Derek wondered if they were the same people he'd seen in the yard last weekend. He presumed they were relatives, but if they were, there were a lot of them. Men and women were tending to them, and Derek wondered if one of the attendants was Felicity – he only caught a side glimpse of her face, and couldn't be sure.

The service was a Mass, like the funeral but simpler. The priest used a table that had been set up for the purpose, and Derek stood and sat and knelt when everyone else did. He felt a little less out of it when he saw that Sam didn't know some of the responses by heart either, and didn't go up for Communion.

When Mass ended there was an interlude which gave Derek a chance to talk to Sam.

"So you're not Catholic either?" Derek asked.

"No. Raised Baptist," Sam replied. "But worship on Sabbath – always good."

"So, what's next?" Derek asked, looking around at the bustle.

"Brunch," Sam grinned. "Every few weeks, all families. Also always good. Ladies set up soon."

As they were chatting, Kent came over with a white-haired woman whose eyes were creased with smile wrinkles. "Derek, let me introduce Helen Markham, a friend of ours who also works at the hospital. Helen, this is Derek."

"Good to meet you," Derek said, shaking her hand. "On which floor do you work?"

"None, really – I'm administration. I work in personnel," Helen explained. "And, if you don't mind my asking, how long have you worked at the hospital? I don't recognize your name, and I know pretty much everyone there."

"Well, I work at the hospital, but not for the hospital," Derek replied. "I work on the first floor, in the morgue. I'm the deputy ME, so I'm a county employee."

"So that explains it," Helen laughed. "Kent mentioned your name and I was going crazy trying to figure out who you were and where you worked."

Soon there was a general movement of people into another big room, large enough to be a dining hall, where a long table was set with steaming plates and heaping bowls. Derek was corralled by the enthusiastic Schaeffer children, but this time he definitely spotted Felicity, who grinned and waved back at him. Everyone was quickly seated, and an elderly man at the head of the table stood and introduced the priest to say grace.

"That's Grandpa," whispered Tabitha at Derek's elbow, pointing at the elderly man. Derek nodded, presuming the white-haired woman at Grandpa's left was Grandma.

After the opening prayer, the brunch began, and a noisy, merry affair it was. Derek loaded his plate with pancakes and sausage and fresh fruit smothered in rich cream. The coffee was strong and plentiful, and more of everything was constantly being fetched.

As the meal wound down and people began wandering around the room to chat with each other, Derek made his way over to Felicity. She greeted him warmly and introduced him to her younger brother Andrew, who looked to be about eight. Harmony and Christopher he already knew, and Christopher invited him for a ride that afternoon. Felicity was invited, too, but she had to decline.

"We'll have to get her sometime, though," Christopher assured Derek. "She's a fantastic rider."

So Derek went riding with Martha and Christopher, though their time was cut short when the rain which had threatened all morning finally moved in. So back to the house it was, for an afternoon of baking and reading and playing board games with the youngsters. Dinner was sandwiches set out for the taking, which Derek munched on the front porch with Linda and Kent in what was becoming a Sunday afternoon tradition. He asked a few questions about chapel, and inquired about the Peterson family as obliquely as possible, and mentioned how many elderly people there seemed to be at Mass. When it came time to leave, he headed back to his apartment feeling increasingly like that was where he just bunked these days – the farm was where he lived.

Flushed

On Monday morning, Sam checked the overnight download from the surveillance setup at the old factory. To that point there'd been nothing, but this time he hit pay dirt.

The videos were timestamped from the afternoon before. The bird's-eye cam caught four cars pulling into the factory in the fifteen-minute period right around four o'clock. A tall, dark-haired man got out of a sleek foreign sedan. A thin guy with brown hair came in a sports car. Two older domestic sedans arrived almost together, one bearing a stocky woman with short-cropped brunette hair and a flushed countenance, and the other driven by a thin hatchet-faced woman with spiky black hair.

The four met in the office. They all seemed to know each other, so there were no introductions. The black-haired guy seemed to be somewhat in charge, though the others weren't shy about contradicting him or speaking frankly.

The meeting wasn't out of control, but it was strained and contentious. The dark-haired guy plunged right in, saying that "they" weren't happy with progress. After all the resources expended only thirty percent of the units were even close to meeting quota, and another thirty percent were barely making half their quota. He implied that the "field units" needed to "deliver" more reliably.

The women bristled at this, particularly the brunette, who pointed out how hard it was to recruit and retain candidates. She explained how she'd gotten two all prepped and productive, only to have one take a job out of state and the other get married and quit. She'd been "working" a new recruit, who was ready to "come on", but she could only use what she had. This line of argument didn't impress the black-haired guy, who countered that these were "low-level" problems, and that she'd been given the position on the assumption that she could solve them without assistance. This did nothing to improve the tenor of the meeting.

The hatchet-faced woman, who hadn't taken a seat but hovered about nervously behind the brunette, protested in a twangy voice that they weren't being given enough cases. Even if they had a ready and willing candidate on every floor, they couldn't meet quota if they weren't given cases. She asked if the selection criteria could be adjusted to broaden the pool.

The brown-haired man answered this one, spreading his hands and stating that the criteria were "set" and couldn't be modified without "approval". This evoked a storm of protest from the women, who contested that the quotas were based on potential cases being drawn from a population pool, and the pool wasn't large enough.

Sam was having difficulty deciphering this without the full context. They could be talking about anything. But then the hatchet-faced woman said something that caught Sam's attention. He scrolled the video back and replayed it a few times to ensure he'd caught every word.

"Word's getting out, I tell you," she said. "People are refusing admittance. If the provider wants to admit them, they don't go. If the provider insists, they stop using that provider. Word's getting out."

"That's ridiculous," scoffed the brown-haired guy. "Half this operation is devoted to covering tracks. How could word be getting out?"

"Doesn't matter." Hatchet-face shrugged. "Word of mouth, online networks, anecdotes, whatever. Doesn't matter. The quotas assume a certain percentage of the OPEL population being admitted. That isn't happening, for whatever reason. No other factors have changed, so I'm guessing word is getting out."

Sam stopped the video and pondered. Providers, admissions – that was medical industry talk. But the rest didn't seem to fit – the talk of selection criteria, and quotas, and recruits. He restarted the video and listened again in light of this new context. It was still obscure, but Sam was starting to make some dark and horrible guesses about what the quotas were, and what the recruits did. He had no idea what an "OPEL" was, but it didn't matter. Put that together with other things that he knew, and he began to wonder – had he hit the jackpot here? Was he listening in on the clandestine counsels of those against whom they'd been contending for years?

He re-cued the video to where he'd stopped it and watched more. The brunette was now complaining about discharging too quickly and "too many ninety nines". That seemed to mystify the brown-haired guy, who sat forward and tapped some things into a tablet. The black-haired guy started going on about how all these problems made it practical to start looking more seriously at the second phase. This seemed to threaten the women, who objected and began listing all sorts of problems with this. Not knowing what the second phase was, little of this made sense to Sam. But he did catch one snippet that made him sit up sharply. It was when the brunette almost taunted the black-haired guy.

"Besides, your test case didn't go as well as you'd hoped."

"What do you mean?" the guy replied. "The test went perfectly."

"The case was much better known than you'd estimated. He was given a funeral at his church that was well attended."

"The official ruling was suicide, there was no investigation – so what if he had a funeral at his church? That's where people have funerals."

The brunette shook her head. "Not if you're Catholic. Suicides don't get buried from Catholic churches and he was. I overheard a couple of girls talking about it."

"So?" scoffed black hair.

"So somebody didn't think it was a suicide, and was able to present enough evidence to convince the pastor," the brunette explained caustically.

Black-hair dismissed this, but Sam stopped the video and pondered, a deep chill battling the hot fury rising within him. He couldn't be sure of anything, but this was a suspiciously large number of coincidences.

Might he be listening in on John Holmes' murderers?

Sam played out the rest of the video, which wasn't much. The people made some final comments and made plans to stay in touch, possibly to meet again in another week. They left within half an hour of arriving.

Sam archived the videos and deliberated. Even if these people had nothing to do with John's death, they were up to no good.

"Philistines," Sam muttered. He pulled out a notebook and began to make a list. These developments called for preparations.

Definitive, forceful preparations.

Selfridge Air National Guard Base lay near the western shore of Lake St. Clair, about fifteen miles northeast of Detroit. A small operation by the standards of military bases, it boasted a unique distinction: for decades it had been the only base in the nation that was home to all five military branches. Members of the Army, Navy, Marines, Air Force, and Coast Guard all shared the base in a minor but meaningful fellowship of the services, and on a good day you could catch sight of five different uniforms.

For that matter, within the past decade, six.

By executive order, certain members of the Department of Homeland Security were entitled to wear a uniform and be accorded the honors due military rank. In this regard they were like the Coast Guard, another branch of the DHS, with a mission that included law enforcement, border security, and surveillance.

But nobody was buying it – least of all the Coast Guard.

When Captain Chad Collins stepped out of his car and donned his gold-strapped combo cap, he saw the results immediately. A couple of airmen on cleanup duty suddenly remembered responsibilities elsewhere. Some Coast Guard petty officers who'd been loitering around in front of a building along his path promptly ducked inside. Anyone in uniform who spotted him coming did their best to turn aside or make themselves scarce, and Chad knew exactly why.

Because "real" military didn't salute DHS pukes.

He'd heard the jokes and endured the innuendo. Just because he hadn't attended an academy or gone through ROTC or OCS, he'd never be 'in'. Because it had been an executive order that had granted him rank, he'd never really belong to the exalted brotherhood of commissioned officers, no matter what his sleeves said. He saw it in their surly expressions and caught it in their salutes, when he was able to corner one of them. They were either insultingly sloppy or exquisitely, precisely correct, but they always communicated the same thing: contempt and derision.

He'd show them, Chad mused as he strode to the newly constructed DHS building. Yes, the newest, most high-tech building on base belonged to the despised Border Security and Domestic Terror Division. He might not get respect, but he got the budget. Also, by executive order, he could command cooperation from any of the branches. They might not salute him, but they had to give him any personnel or asset he demanded.

Today, that wouldn't be necessary. He strode into the control room and got a status update from the duty sergeant: one drone was prepped for launch and another was on standby. Where to fly today? They'd patrolled the Detroit River so often recently, and it was just drab and dismal. A flight north today, perhaps, along the blue, tree-lined St. Clair River. The Canadians would be annoyed by a drone skirting their border, but what could they do?

"Launch when ready," Captain Collins authorized. "Patrol north to lower Lake Huron."

Out on the runway, the techs made the final adjustments and pulled the chocks. The drone taxied and took off. Many eyes watched its trajectory until it passed out of sight. Stealthy though it was, it couldn't escape the experienced eyes of the base radar techs, who noted the direction the drone turned. Over a dozen messages went out from private phones, and within ten minutes the notice was posted on several hidden sites:

"Flying fish heading north from Selfridge."

"Today," Melissa whispered to Janice as they stood close, comparing records on their tablets. "Research indicates a promising case. We'll know shortly. Be ready."

Janice just nodded, her heart pounding. This was it. In or out. Fish or cut bait. She went about her duties, wondering if one of the patients she was tending would turn out to be the case.

About forty minutes later her phone buzzed. It was a message from Melissa.

"Case approved. Serum ready. Meet me by elevator."

Melissa was waiting by the elevator with a small pharm bag. She slipped it to Janice in passing, muttering, "Room 318. You'll get a text within ten minutes, then you'll have a three-minute window."

The pharm bag contained a pair of exam gloves and a capped syringe half-full of serum. Accelerating the inevitable. Serious or not. Janice pulled on the gloves, pocketed the syringe, and ditched the pharm bag. Using her tablet as camouflage, she ambled down the hall toward Room 318. The case had been admitted last Friday, respiratory complications, possible pneumonia, no visitors, next of kin was a Texas address. Only patient in the room.

Janice had been glancing up from time to time and hadn't seen anyone enter or leave the room. Nobody was working this end of the hall just now. After breakfast, before lunch, rounds completed – the timing was perfect.

Janice's phone buzzed. The message was simple: "Go." She was only a few doors away. Now or never. She strode through the door, her eyes on her tablet, trying to look as routine as possible. Only when she was inside the room did she pull the syringe from her pocket and uncap it. Just locate the injection port on the IV line, fifteen seconds, and out.

Janice looked up and was shocked to see not a case in a bed but a young woman standing by the bed with some items in her hands. Janice didn't recognize her – she was petite, with wavy brown hair and bright blue eyes. Her scrubs didn't quite look like those of a nurse – maybe an aide or a med tech. Her name tag said "Marie", and she was clearly tidying up. There were only a few items lying around, a couple of bundles of sheets and some kind of duffel on the floor, and a garbage bag tied up and ready to dump.

Janice felt naked and exposed. If this woman knew anything about anything, it would be glaringly obvious that Janice was violating every med administration protocol. One didn't just walk into a room and uncap an unlabeled syringe, obviously preparing to administer it, without proper verification and documentation. She felt like the woman could see right through her – what she'd come for, why she intended to do it, and for whom she was working. She stood paralyzed for a long moment, holding the syringe and staring at the woman, before recovering some composure.

"Sorry, I was just – " Janice stammered, then glanced at her tablet. "Oops – wrong room." She clumsily turned and fled.

Janice fairly ran down the hall, her heart pounding. She'd blown it. She'd blown it, and had gotten caught. She ducked into a restroom. Realizing that she was still holding the syringe, she squirted the serum down the drain and dropped the needle into the sharps disposal. Stripping off the exam gloves, she buried her face in her hands and leaned against the wall. What could she do? She'd blown the acceleration – her first one. She was in trouble with Melissa. That woman in the room had seen her clearly, and would tell someone, and she'd be in trouble. Her job, and maybe arrest! What could she do? Somebody had made a mistake. The case was supposed to have been there, yet that had looked like a post-discharge cleanup. She rocked back and forth, pressing her hands against her forehead, paralyzed with fear and indecision.

Back in the room, Grace was startled into paralysis as well. It was sheer bad timing, the strange nurse walking in during the cleanup window, and when she was almost finished, at that. Another minute and she would have walked into a tidy, empty room. Sheer bad timing.

The nurse's clumsy exit brought Grace back to herself. She was as surprised as the nurse, but she wasn't stunned. She'd discussed and pondered and trained for this possibility. She knew the drill.

Dropping what she was holding, Grace grabbed the small duffel at her feet and swift-walked out of the room. She turned a different direction than the strange nurse had gone and went briskly to her primary refuge – the one-person restroom near the stairs. Fortunately, it was empty, so she didn't have to worry about making it to her secondary. She ducked in, locked the door, and pulled out her phone. She texted a one-word message:

Flushed

SB came the immediate reply. Standby. Grace stood staring at the screen, the seconds feeling like hours. Please let the team be safe. In the grand scheme, she was small potatoes, no matter what her pulse and respiration told her. Please let the team be clear.

Back at the ranch, Gil was manning the comm console with his nephew Gary. The snatch was in progress, and everyone's nerves were on edge until all were home safe.

Gil nearly jumped when his phone chimed. He looked at the text.

"Damn."

"What?" asked Gary.

"Grace has been flushed," Gil answered tensely, keying a quick response and reaching for the phone. "Verify the team." Punching a number into the phone, he spoke briskly. "Yeah, we just heard from the cleanup. She got flushed. Who've we got standing by in town? Good – alert them." He tapped up a map of the hospital area.

"Team's still in the open, estimate ten minutes," Gary reported.

Damn. Too much at risk.

"SCRAM her," Gil decided, then in to the handset, "We're going to SCRAM. Tell the standbys to prep for Route B, but let them know we could go with A."

Gary had grabbed Gil's phone and texted a one-word message.

SCRAM. The message came back within a minute. Grace had been expecting it, reviewing the steps in her head.

Speed. Maybe two minutes burned already, she wanted to be away from the hospital complex within another five. Pulling the insulated water bottle from her duffel, she unscrewed the shell from the lining. There, in the carefully concealed compartment, were the two things Sam had prepped for her. One was an ID badge which looked identical to the one she was wearing – only a reader could tell that the internal circuitry was different. She unclipped her ID from her lanyard and clipped on the new one.

The other was a new phone chip. Grace popped the chip out of her phone and inserted the replacement. Old ID and old chip got screwed back inside the lining of the bottle, nametag went into the bottle, which was half full of water.

That was a minute. Grace left the bathroom and walked to the stairs. Fortunately, the stairwell wasn't yet monitored, but the lobby and main entrance would be. That was fine – the plan presumed it. Grace exited the stairwell into the moderately bustling lobby, walking calmly but briskly through the crowd, remembering to smile. She waved at the coffee shop ladies and greeted the security guard cheerily as she waltzed out the big sliding glass doors of the main entrance.

That was another minute, but she wasn't clear yet. She walked along the edge of the parking lot and past the ER entrance, bristling with cameras. No matter – she was just another hospital employee headed out for an early lunch, or over to an office to get some samples. Nothing to see here, folks. She walked briskly around the cancer center and turned left, toward the medical office building.

She entered the office building by the south entrance door and walked right through to the north door. Again, right through video surveillance; again, part of the plan. But just outside the north door she didn't walk directly out into the parking lot. Instead she turned sharply right and walked along the north face, beneath the leafy trees that stood alongside the building.

Cover. Her biggest danger now wasn't surveillance cameras, about which she could do nothing anyway, but eyes overhead. The trees were her friends. She knew the route to her immediate destination – she'd walked it out yesterday – but it required crossing the five open lanes of Pine Grove Avenue. Her head knew that it really wasn't much exposure, but her gut hated being under open sky for even that long. She walked along the face of the building, beneath the trees, lingering under the final one while watching for a traffic break along Pine Grove.

Back at the communications center, Gil wrestled with alternatives. Should he steer Grace toward the more open northern escape route, the bolder path that would extract her more quickly, or the more covered southern route that took her toward the downtown area, with its risks of cameras and surface detection? Plus, he'd heard reports of a fish in the air this morning – where was it? Would it make a difference?

Gil looked at the clock. Time was everything. The team was almost in, and probably would be by the time Grace remade. That was the vital thing. His gut told him to risk it.

"We'll send her the north way – Route B. Tell her that when she checks in," Gil told Gary. "Be sure the team notifies us the *minute* they're in." Gil picked up a phone and keyed a number. "Yeah, Brady? We got flushed."

"How far along?" Brady asked.

"Not sure, but the team was well away, so I'm presuming in the final stages," Gil explained. "It was the cleanup worker – we're scramming her right now. She has yet to be extracted. The team is almost in."

"Okay, I'll check the patient out and cut the camera back over," Brady said. He had all the scripts prepared; the tap of a key executed them. That part was routine. The next part was touchier.

A well-executed snatch could be done in five to seven minutes. The problem was that it had to be done right under the nose of a surveillance camera. This would intimidate most people, but not Brady. He knew that in the hospital's network-based security system, a camera was just another network device – a network address that was the source of a video stream.

And lots of network devices could stream video.

In preparation for a snatch, Brady tapped the video feed from the room and recorded the guest doing something innocuous, usually napping. Shortly before the snatch went down, Brady did a little network wizardry, giving the real security camera a dummy address and his recording device the camera's address. Then he just played the recorded video back into the security network for as long as necessary. As far as the security system was concerned, everything was kosher – it was still getting video feed from the expected address.

Cutting the video back to the camera was the slightly dicey part. Brady could either do it instantly, with only a brief video flicker, or he could throw a few seconds of snow into the process. The first option drew less attention to the feed – unless someone was looking directly at the monitor when it happened, in which case it looked like the patient literally vanished before their eyes. That tended to cause shrieks of fright. Putting a little static on the line lessened that impact, but could call attention to the image when it came back.

Brady opted for the instantaneous cutover, which he executed immediately. Eyeballing the live feed, he saw that the room was mostly in order, with only a bit of debris, a garbage bag, and the piles of bedding. Hopefully, that would be written off as a sloppy cleanup after an orderly discharge.

Grace waited almost a minute to catch a traffic break that would let her cross the street at the right pace. Swiftly, but not looking hurried – just another medical worker enjoying her break in the park on a fine autumn morning. Grace got across the street and onto the concrete path that ran alongside the baseball diamond. There were open patches overhead here and there, which made her nervous, but she kept on toward her destination. Don't look up. Whatever you do, don't look up.

She made it to the gazebo in the middle of the park, which fortunately was vacant. She messaged her position – now to wait for instructions. In the meantime, Remake.

First things first. Grace took off her ID badge, then unscrewed the water bottle again and extracted her old ID and the old phone chip from the liner. All these went into the water inside the bottle. Then she reached into the side pocket of her duffel for the two plastic packets that Sam had given her – the packets that looked like those used for take-out condiments, except these would never adorn a hot dog. She tore one open and emptied it into the water in the bottle. Then she added the contents of the second packet. Then she closed the bottle tightly and shook it a few times. No more drinks out of there! Sam had explained that it was a binary agent. Each packet by itself was inert, but combined in water they made a powerful corrosive that would quickly destroy the circuitry of the ID badges – thereby breaking at least two federal laws.

Before she was finished, the phone chimed with a simple message: *Route B.* The northern route. Crouching down, she pulled off her scrub pants to expose the running shorts she wore beneath. Her scrub tunic came off, revealing a cropped running top. It was just cool enough to justify the running pants and jacket. Her work shoes went into the duffel, replaced by a pair of running shoes with fluorescent pink and green stripes. Her hair went into a tight bun topped by an equally fluorescent hat. Fitting her phone into an armband holster, she grabbed the bottle and kicked the duffel under a bench. Let the park punks make of that what they would.

Now it was time to Assimilate – hide in plain sight. Grace started jogging out to the main running path down here, which was the walkway along the river. Right under the open sky without a shred of cover, almost a mile of naked exposure – that was her path to extraction. She kept jogging, reminding herself that she didn't look a bit like the girl who'd left the hospital – particularly from five thousand feet. Just another runner along the river walk, blending in with the bikers, dog walkers, skateboarders, and fishermen.

Back at the hospital, Janice recovered enough to go looking for Melissa. She didn't want to call and didn't know what to text, so she wandered until she located her, and pulled her into a vacant room.

"So – how did it go?" Melissa asked eagerly.

"I – it never happened," Janice tried to explain.

"Never happened?" Melissa interrupted. "Why not?"

"The room was empty, except for this girl I didn't recognize. She saw me – I think she knew what I was there for."

"What?" Melissa asked, turning white. "That's impossible. Nobody should have been in that room for another hour."

"She was there, I tell you – standing right by the bed," Janice insisted. "She got a good look at me."

Melissa was staring at the wall now, the muscles in her jaw flexing.

"Melissa, I – " Janice began.

"Shut up!" Melissa barked. "Just shut up! I give you a simple task – one simple task – and you blow that. Why did I even ask you? I should have done it myself. Did you go back? Did you give it a couple minutes then go back?"

"Go back to what?" Janice asked in tears. "I'm telling you the room was empty. The case was gone."

Melissa blinked a couple of times. "Don't be stupid – what do you mean the case was gone?"

"Gone. Not there. The bed was empty, and the girl looked like she was cleaning up."

"That's ridiculous," Melissa said, pushing past Janice and heading for the nursing station. "I checked that beforehand." She stormed to a monitor and punched up Room 318. The video showed an empty bed. Melissa rushed down the hall to the room, where she saw the same thing the monitor had shown.

"She was standing right there," Janice said, pointing. "She was holding those things, and that garbage bag was right there."

Melissa stared around, dumbfounded. Then she bustled back to the nurse's station where she keyed some things into a workstation.

"Discharged," she muttered. "Discharged as of nine this morning. Code 99. But – that's impossible. I saw – she was still here after that – how could she be – ?"

"Melissa, I – " Janice came up timidly.

"When?" Melissa rounded on her fiercely. "When did this happen? How long has it been since you found the case gone?"

"I – I don't know, exactly," Janice stammered. "Ten, maybe fifteen minutes. I was shaken, and then it took a while to find you – "

"'It took a while'?" Melissa echoed. "Dumb bitch! Stupid, inept fool! You bungle a simple job, and then you take fifteen precious minutes to report your failure!"

"But, Melissa," Janice wailed. "She wasn't *there*!"

"Get out of my sight," Melissa snarled. "This is a crisis, and I don't have time to coddle failures."

Janice wandered off while Melissa pulled out her phone and keyed a number. "We got a problem. A case went missing right under our noses. Yeah, missing, gone, vanished. That's the weird thing – the system shows a discharge."

Down at the riverfront, Grace was endeavoring to look like a typical runner. She jogged for a while, then stopped to look at the river. She put the straw of the bottle to her lips, being careful not to sip. Steadily she worked her way northward toward the twin spans of the Bridge.

She was awaiting final instructions. This route had three possible pickup sites, and they had yet to tell her which one to use. One thing she could do while waiting – get rid of her water bottle. Sitting on the concrete and dangling her legs over the river, she casually put the bottle down beside her, a little too close to the edge. When she got up, a discreet nudge with her foot toppled it in. A little feigned dismay, a grin from some nearby anglers, and the ID cards were safely drowned in sixty feet of water.

Grace's phone chimed again with another message: GPW. Gratiot Park, west side. North of the bridge and west a few blocks. She got jogging – they must be moving the pickup team into place.

The park looked seedy and run-down, as well as thin on cover. Grace couldn't see many good sites for Morphing, unless it was near those big trees along the west side. She worked her way around the edge of the park, and when she turned north she saw that there was a couple lounging beneath the trees near a motorcycle. Perhaps? She jogged along the broken sidewalk toward them.

As Grace came under the shade of the trees, the girl spoke. "Grace!" She turned to see the girl pulling off her leather jacket and stepping out of her jeans. Taking the cue, Grace kicked off her running shoes, handed over her hat, and quickly traded jacket and pants. Within a minute the girl jogged on, out from under cover, wearing Grace's running outfit, while Grace was strapping on a motorcycle helmet.

"Give her a minute," the guy said. "I'm Todd, by the way – that was Angie."

Grace's phone chimed again. "Team in. Come back."

"Thank God," Grace whispered. "The team's in safe."

"Now it's our turn," Todd said, starting the motorcycle. Grace climbed on and they sped away.

Ron Porcher wasn't at the Port Huron site, but he didn't need to be. He could remote into anywhere, which was how he dealt with the surveillance cover for the accelerations.

Porcher had the same problem Brady had – insuring that his team's actions weren't captured on camera – but he handled it a different way. All of the security cameras in all the hospitals had a feature whereby they would perform a self-test at random intervals. It was either a short test, which lasted about thirty seconds, or a long test, which took about three minutes. No video was transmitted during these tests, and the security staff got accustomed to cameras cutting out at irregular intervals, attributing the interruptions to self-tests.

But a command could also be sent to the cameras to initiate a self-test, which was precisely what Porcher would do when he sent the text to clear an acceleration. He'd trigger a long test, so the camera would go wonky for three minutes, which was plenty of time for a worker to get in, inject the serum, and slip out. Nobody thought anything of the interruption, and the acceleration didn't get caught on camera.

Except this morning. When he'd sent the command telling the surveillance camera in Room 318 that it should take a three-minute vacation, nothing had happened. At first, he'd been afraid that the candidate would walk right in with the camera still functioning, but he hadn't seen that either – he'd just seen the case continue sleeping. Then after a few minutes the screen did a little flicker, and suddenly he was looking at an empty bed and a mostly cleaned up room. Thus, it didn't surprise him when Melissa called in a panic about missing cases and strange women and aborted accelerations. He hadn't seen any of that, but he wouldn't have expected to.

Someone had hijacked the video feed.

Porcher had to admire the elegance. Slick as a whistle. But it meant that there was someone working the systems, someone from the other side, someone very clever and undoubtedly very versatile. This explained a lot, oh yes. Like the inordinate number of Code 99 discharges they'd been seeing. That meant database manipulation, certainly at a very low level.

Some party or parties were very deep in, and very good at working silently and hiding their tracks. Very good, indeed. But now Ron knew they were there – and they didn't know that Ron knew.

Time to get over to Port Huron.

Philistines

"One more time, Grace," Helen asked, handing the girl a steaming mug of tea.

Grace took a deep breath, sipped her tea, and closed her eyes. Willing to calm herself, she once again replayed the events in her head. It helped that Helen was there – she worked at the hospital and ran the "inside" of the operations, and had helped get Grace the job.

"I was on the floor below, awaiting the signal message. It came, and I moved quickly into the room. I didn't see the team or the guest. They'd done a good job of removing all personal effects – all that remained were service items. I bagged them and stripped and remade the bed. I'd just finished that, and was standing on the far side of the bed tidying up the last few items, when this nurse walks in.

"She had curly reddish hair, closely cut. I didn't recognize her. She didn't notice me when she first walked in – she was looking at her tablet. Then, still without seeing me, she pulled a syringe from her pocket and uncapped it. The syringe looked about half full of something. Only then did she look up and notice me.

"Thinking back, it seemed that she was more than just surprised to see me – she was stunned. She froze, and her eyes got really wide. Of course, I was surprised, too, but I tried to calm myself. My cover was good – I was just an aide cleaning up a room. I didn't say anything, but she looked at her tablet and said something about the wrong room, then left."

"How did she leave?" Helen asked.

"How?" Grace asked, not understanding.

"Did she leave like someone who'd just happened to walk into the wrong room? Did she storm out angrily? Did she back out cautiously?" Helen prompted.

Grace thought for a minute as she sipped her tea. "Y'know, that's the funny part. It was like she fled. Even at the time I remember thinking, 'she just ran away'. But then I had other things to think about – I knew I'd been flushed, so I had to follow the procedure. Do you want me to go on?"

"No, we've got it all from there," Helen assured her.

"Thank you for being patient with us, Grace," Gil said. "You understand why we keep asking, don't you?"

"Sure," Grace assured them. "If I keep going over it, you might spot some detail I missed earlier."

"But I think we've heard all there is to hear, which isn't much," Helen said.

"I'm guessing that we pulled our guest out just in time," Gil said, looking at Helen with raised eyebrows. "By a matter of minutes."

"Has this happened before?" Grace asked.

"Exactly like this? No," Gil responded. "We've had teams who've had to deal with hospital personnel during a snatch, but this is the first time we've had someone walk in to do an execution when we've just removed the guest."

"Of course, you understand what this means for you," Helen said with quiet sympathy. "We can't send you back out in the field."

Grace dropped her head and stared at her tea mug. "I was afraid you were going to say that. What rotten luck."

"I know," Gil acknowledged. "Your first job, which you'd waited and trained for, and you get flushed. Has to be disappointing."

"But," Grace protested. "Couldn't I go somewhere else? Maybe Lapeer? I've trained so hard – "

"Grace," Helen said. "Realize where you stand. You had to walk past at least five cameras to get out of there. You broke several federal laws. The circumstances of the flush will have called attention to the snatch, and you'll be associated with it. Your face is out there, and they'll be looking for it. You won't even be able to go to Wal-Mart for a long time. You can't risk getting anywhere near a medical facility."

Grace dropped her head and nodded.

"If you don't mind my asking," Helen continued gently. "Why do you place such importance on field operations? Why do you consider that the only way you can help?"

Grace looked up, sniffing and blinking several times. "You really want to know?"

"Sure, if you want to tell us," Helen replied.

Grace wiped her eyes with the back of her hand and sipped her tea. "They got Grandma Del."

"They got who?" Helen asked.

"Grandma Del," Grace replied. "She wasn't my grandma, really – we weren't even related. She was just a good family friend, and was like a grandma to me and my brothers. She took my real grandma into her home when she got cancer, and cared for her until she died. Grandma Del never had any children of her own, so we were like her family. She lived in a big old house up in Lexington, and we'd go and stay with her for weeks during the summer.

"She was in basic good health – mild diabetes, but nothing unmanageable. She came down with the flu, and got a light bout of pneumonia following it. Her doctor admitted her for overnight observation. She – never came back. I had a welcome home present all ready for her."

"How long ago was this?" Gil asked.

"Maybe two years," Grace replied.

"She must have been one of the first," Gil said.

"She was. It wasn't long after her that the rumors started circulating. I knew that was what had happened to her – it was just too quick. When I got wind that there were people who were doing something about it, I sought you out. I swore that nobody would ever do that to someone's Grandma Del, not if I could help it."

The room fell quiet for a while before Gil spoke.

"That's tragic, Grace. But it's never wise to make settling an old score the main motivator for anything, least of all one's whole life. I'm sure Grandma Del would agree."

"Probably so," Grace nodded. "Sounds like the sort of thing she'd say."

"And there are plenty of spots among the ranches where you can be just as useful, in different ways, particularly with your medical training," Helen assured her. "You have your mother's kind and sympathetic temperament. Caring for the guests once they're safe is just as worthwhile as getting them to safety."

"I – I suppose so," Grace acknowledged.

"I'm proud of you, Grace," Gil said, standing. "You're our first operator we've ever had to SCRAM, and you executed perfectly. Things would have been a lot worse if you hadn't kept your head and followed your training."

"Thanks," Grace said.

"You must be hungry," Helen said. "Ruth will have some lunch for you." Grace took her tea and left, leaving Gil and Helen to look at each other with furrowed brows.

"Good thinking, having her use her middle name while working there," Gil said. "It may have provided an extra level of cover for her."

"It was her idea," Helen said, glancing at the time. "I'd better get going back. Can you give Fitz a heads-up? This one's going to be hotter than usual."

"I'll take care of that," Gil replied. "You'll be able deal with your end of things?"

"As best I can," Helen said. "Though I may not be able to clean up as much as we need – the system has some built-in safeguards that I can't override. I may need Brady's help."

"You'll have it, if you need it," Gil assured her. Helen headed off, both of them still somber and concerned.

Just because things could have been worse didn't mean they weren't plenty bad.

Kendra found Janice in a corner of the cafeteria with a cold cup of coffee in front of her.

"Hey," Kendra said, sitting down.

"It wasn't my fault," Janice said, not lifting her eyes from the table. "There was no case there. I went as soon as I got the text, and the bed was empty."

"I know," Kendra said. "Melissa's just – under a lot of pressure right now, and this was just one more thing."

"Yeah, well," Janice said, picking up the cup of coffee and putting it down again. "I suppose this means that I'm through, then?"

"Not necessarily," Kendra replied. "But it would help if you could come look at some videos."

"That's her," Janice said, pointing at the blurry freeze-frame of the security video. It was taken by the main entrance camera, and the subject was just passing by the welcome desk. Her chin was well down, but her face was recognizable.

"She's not wearing a name tag," Porcher observed, pointing at the picture.

"She was. On the left side," Janice insisted. "I remember that. It said 'Marie'."

"Okay, how about this image?" Porcher asked, tapping some keys to bring up a blurrier shot. "This was from the camera on the corner of the building just by the ER entrance."

"Can't be sure," Janice said. "The hair looks right, but I can't see enough of her face."

"How about these?" Porcher brought up a split-screen which showed videos of a young woman moving briskly down a hallway.

"That's her," Janice confirmed.

"These were taken in the medical office building not eight minutes after the incident," Porcher explained. "You can see her exiting through the north door."

"Where did she go from there?" Janice asked.

"We don't know," Porcher said. "As far as surveillance is concerned, she vanished. The parking lot cameras never picked her up. Now, just a couple last images. Do you recognize this woman?" He flashed what was obviously an ID photo on the screen. It was of a middle-aged woman with black hair.

"Never seen her. Who is it?"

"She works at the hospital, in Pediatrics, and was on shift at the time. It was that woman's ID that the Jane Doe's badge squawked when she walked out the door," Porcher said.

Janice was confused. "But – how did that girl get that woman's ID?"

"She didn't," Porcher said. "You remember how your badge works, right? How the RFID chip responds with your data when you pass a scanner, be it at a door or station or window?"

"Yes," Janice said.

"Our Jane Doe's badge was set to respond with that woman's identifying data when interrogated. That later triggered a security anomaly for her in Pediatrics, because according to the system she'd already left the building."

"Is that – legal?" Janice asked.

"No," Porcher replied. "It's a federal crime. Now, one last thing: do you recognize either of these women?" He flashed up two more pictures of women that Janice couldn't identify.

"No – who are they?"

"The only two Maries in the work area. There are eight working for the hospital, of which only three are assigned to this site, and only two of which were on shift. Neither look familiar?"

"Nope."

"Go finish your shift," Kendra said. "Melissa's gone off on business. It'll be okay." The nurses wandered off, leaving Porcher to think. This was sophisticated. Very sophisticated.

Where had the girl gone? Once out the north door of the medical office building, the options were limited. Straight ahead took you to the parking lot and into the range of those cameras. A sharp left along the building took you back toward the parking structure, which had its own surveillance. A sharp right took you toward Pine Grove Avenue, the park, and ultimately the river.

The river.

Porcher grabbed his phone and keyed a number. "Yeah – how do I get hold of Selfridge?"

Sam had noticed the low-key tension and excitement around the campus on the day that the team barely got away and the operator had to be scrammed. But that was nothing compared to the excitement he felt the next morning when he checked the overnight download and found a new set of video files. They were timestamped just after 4 p.m. the prior day, when the brunette drove into the factory followed shortly by the brown-haired guy, who unloaded a good sized portable computer along with some other device. They went to the office, where the guy set up the equipment while the woman kept talking about the incident at the hospital – clearly continuing a conversation that had begun earlier. Then the dark-haired guy showed up. The brunette was all ready to start talking to him, but he waved her down until yet another guy arrived.

The next arrival was about ten minutes later, when a car with government plates pulled in. The driver was wearing a uniform of some type, and pulled some technology from the trunk. Dark-hair came out to greet him and brought him into the office, which he clearly didn't think much of.

Introductions were made, which gave Sam a chance to get names for the first time. The brunette was Melissa, the brown-haired guy was Ron, the guy in the uniform was Captain Chad something, and he didn't quite catch black-hair's name – it sounded something like "Sharon", which Sam knew couldn't be right.

Then Melissa launched into an explanation of what had happened that day. Sam knew most of the story, but it was interesting to hear it from the other side. He nodded in grim satisfaction: his suspicions had been correct. They were admitting on record what he'd only suspected until then.

After Melissa finished, Ron set up his portable and projected some images on the wall. He explained how these had been identified by the nurse, and about the spoofed ID card, and how the suspect had just vanished from the surveillance sphere.

"Vanished?" asked the captain. "How could she just vanish?"

"We don't cover every square inch of the hospital campus," Ron explained. "There are ways to avoid security cameras. In this case, there was only one way – which is where we hope you can help us."

"I'm sure I can," the captain replied. "Where do you think she went?"

"Into a park across the street from the hospital," Ron explained.

"Ah, a public space," the captain chuckled. "That's good."

"And it's right along the river," added Ron.

"Ooh, even better," Captain Chad gloated. "Ladies and gentlemen, you're in luck – I happened to have a bird over that area at just about that time." He was setting up his portable which had a very large screen. "I brought along a complete dump of the entire run, but I presume you want a specific time?"

"Times, we can give you," Ron said. "She would have left the office building and bolted across the street within five minutes of 10:18". The captain cued the video to that time and displayed the area of interest. "Right in there – that's the office building. Can you see the street?"

"Yes, but it's at a bad angle. The trees are in the way."

"Can't you zoom in?" Melissa asked anxiously.

"I can, which would give you a closer view of the leaves," the captain said. "Sorry, but the angle is just too poor. The bird is too far down the river. In the next few minutes it curves around and gets a much better view of the area – see?"

Everyone nodded as the image squared satisfactorily, giving a good overhead shot of the park area.

"So now, point out your target and we'll track where she went," Captain Chad said.

"Well, by this time she'd be in the park proper, somewhere in there," Ron explained, pointing to the central part of the screen. The captain's face fell.

"There's – ah – lots of cover there. We can't see through cover."

"But – that's where she is," Melissa protested.

"We'll just have to wait for her to come out," the captain said. They all gazed at the screen in silence while the he fiddled with a joystick.

"So – where is she?" Melissa finally asked sharply.

"What are we looking for?" the captain responded testily.

"You saw – woman, petite frame, shoulder-length brown hair, hospital scrubs," said Melissa.

"I don't see anyone matching that description."

"Well, she's got to be there somewhere!"

"There's an entire waterfront full of people," the captain pointed out. "Even if we narrow it down to women, that still leaves dozens of walkers, bikers, runners, roller-bladers, and sitters. Tell me which one to track and I'll track her."

Melissa searched the faces with growing impatience. "Can't you get the images any clearer?"

"It's zoomed in as far as it can go. That's the best we can do from five thousand feet."

"Can't you fly any lower?"

"We can, but then people spot the drone and start shooting at it," the captain replied, drawing looks of amazement.

"Really? Is that legal?" Ron asked.

"No – but they do it anyway. "

"What – from the U.S. side?"

"U.S. and Canadian both. I think it's the only time the Canadian government lets its citizens play with guns."

"Besides, it's a moot point," Ron said. "We aren't looking at real-time. This video was taken hours ago, and it's all we have."

"But – I don't see her here anywhere!" Melissa cried. "I thought this overhead surveillance stuff was supposed to track everyone!"

"You provide us a target to track, and we'll track it," the captain said coldly. "But don't expect us to magically find your targets for you."

"What good is this billion-dollar eye-in-the-sky stuff if it doesn't help when you need it?" Melissa fairly shrieked.

"Listen, lady, you let this target walk right out of a hospital – which is the next best thing to a prison when it comes to monitoring and security," the captain shot back. "If you can't track and contain her under those circumstances, don't expect us to come along afterwards and do miracles."

"Which is a good thing to remember," the dark-haired guy intervened before things really got heated. "Whoever did this had the resources and presence of mind to get away from the hospital cleanly. We seem to be dealing with a party with discipline, focus, and probably training. We can hardly expect casual, after-the-fact surveillance to counter that."

Melissa fell silent, but glowered at the screen, while the captain busied himself with his technology.

"I think that's the important thing to draw from this," Ron pointed out. "Sure, this party escaped us for now, but we caught them almost in the act. We've suspected for a while that there is a subversive movement around here, but all we've had to this point has been hints and rumors. This proves not only that they're active, but they're surprisingly sophisticated. Look at it! Planted personnel, falsified IDs, operational discipline, thorough planning – I think we can also assume a sophisticated

communications and support staff. I'm already investigating
things on the technical end."

Sam noted that – he'd better warn Brady.

"Can we get more regular overflights up this way?" the dark-
haired guy asked the captain.

"Sure – what do you want watched?"

"The hospital area, clearly – and maybe the streets around?"

"I can do it, but be aware that this is a high-cover area," the
captain explained. Seeing their looks of confusion, he went on.
"Lots of trees. Like that park – almost half of it pretty much a
loss. Look at the streets in the area – plenty of shade, but that
hinders surveillance."

"How far inland can you go?" dark hair asked.

"Legally? Five, maybe seven miles. Beyond that, it has to
be the FBI. We're border security. If we get too far from the
border, we catch hell with Congress."

"If they find out," dark hair pointed out.

"If they find out," echoed the captain.

The conversation moved into planning technicalities, which
Sam could review later. He had enough to ponder for now.

It was clear he was listening in on the enemy. These were
the ones who began it all, the reason the ranches and the snatches
and the guests all existed. And not just foot soldiers, either –
these were the officers, the planners and decision-makers.

The leaders of the Philistines.

Sam pondered. He could strike a blow. It may not be much,
and wouldn't set them back far, but it would be a blow. The last
of his shipments were due in soon. Then he'd be ready.

"'You shall utterly destroy them'," Sam muttered from
memory. "'The Hittites and the Amorites, the Canaanites and the
Perezites, the Hivites and the Jebusites, as the Lord your God
has commanded you. Not one stone shall be left upon another.'"
He watched the Philistines as they plotted to destroy the work of
the Lord, to persecute His people so they could kill with
impunity.

Oh, yes. He could strike a blow.

Philistines.

Commitment

Janice couldn't understand why she was so restless. She cracked a beer in hopes that it would calm her. Usually, she could settle down to a show, or a game on her tablet, but not tonight. Everything she watched seemed tinny and flashy, and got on her nerves – but so did the silence. Her walls seemed too cramped, but she couldn't get out – her neighborhood wasn't the kind you could walk around, and she couldn't afford gas to drive anywhere and had nothing to spend once she got there. She had nobody to call or visit. It was just her.

She had to do this. They had to give her another chance, and this time she wouldn't fail. She wondered if there would be another gathering this weekend – oh, that's right, it wouldn't matter if there was. She was going on afternoons for five days starting Wednesday. She drained her beer and hugged herself, remembering the excitement of the talks and the friendly intimacy of the social times. She tried to recreate the thrill, the sense of mission and purpose, but couldn't – there were only jitters and loneliness.

Reaching for another beer, Janice's eye fell on the yellow guest cord, that badge of exclusion, which she'd hung on her mirror. She never wanted to wear that again. Next time she went, she'd go as a member.

Whatever it took.

The next day Janice went through her duties mechanically, still feeling jittery. Her patients annoyed her more than ever. She didn't know where Melissa was; Anna had taken over supervisor duties for her.

As noon approached, her phone chimed. It was a message from Kendra, asking if she'd like to take a walk at lunchtime. Janice thought this odd, but assented, though it was cold and overcast outside. She met Kendra in the lobby and they headed to the park across the street.

"Melissa's still tied up with stuff," Kendra explained. "But we may have another chance for you, if you're still interested."

"I am," Janice confirmed, her heart leaping but her insides tightening. "However, I'm going on afternoons tomorrow."

"I know," Kendra said. "That actually makes it easier. If things come together, we'll get you what you need."

"All right," Janice said.

The next day as Janice was coming on shift, Kendra sought her out.

"I'm just getting off," Kendra said quietly by the stairwell. "We've got a case selected. Keep your phone with you. Here are the supplies." Janice felt the familiar form of a pharm bag being pressed into her hands.

Throughout her shift Janice tried to focus on her work but found it nearly impossible. Her phone sat in her right pocket, and she kept touching and checking it. She grew more and more anxious, wondering when it would chime, and what it would say. It came to feel like she was keeping a small venomous snake there, one that would lie in wait until the opportune time to leap out and bite her.

The pharm bag she kept in her left pocket, and it also grew in her mind as she worked. It came to feel like that pocket was full of darkness that would chill and cling to and stain her hand when she reached in. Periodically she shook her head to clear it of these silly images, but they kept creeping back in.

The shift wore on. Dinner was served, evening visitors came and went, bedtime orders were carried out, and still the phone did not chime. Finally, when the hall lights had been dimmed and most of the patients were asleep, the message came. Janice started as if she'd been bitten, but gritted her teeth and looked at the screen.

The message gave the number of a room two floors up. Thankfully, it was right near the stairs. It also said *appx 5min*, so Janice casually moved toward the stairway. There was nobody in sight when she reached it, so she slipped through the door and up the steps. Mentally mapping where the room would be in relation to the stairway, she worked out a route that would get her there without passing a nursing station.

When she reached the floor, she still hadn't received the go-ahead text. She pulled on the exam gloves and mentally rehearsed how she'd execute the acceleration. Her phone chimed again: the go-ahead. Trying to look like she belonged there, Janice stepped out on the floor and followed the route she'd planned. There was nobody in the halls, and everything was quiet and dim. She arrived at her destination within twenty seconds, double-checking the number to ensure she had the right room. She entered quietly, easing the syringe from her pocket and keeping it hidden in her hand.

It was a two-bed room, but there was only one occupant. He was sleeping in the bed nearer the door, his head turned away. The IV stand was by the bed, the green and amber lights glowing dimly. Without thinking or wondering or looking around, she slipped the cap off the needle and injected the serum into the injection port. Capping the needle, she turned to leave.

Only then did Janice notice that while she'd been intent on her task, the man had turned his head and was looking at her. He was completely bald, which seemed to make his eyes larger. They were both wide open, clear blue, and gazing at her with steady calm.

Janice froze, wondering whether the man would move or cry out or reach for the call button. He did none of those things, but lay still, fixing her with his placid gaze. After a moment, she turned away and quietly left the room.

On her way back to the stairs, Janice ducked in to the single bathroom near the stairway. She dropped the syringe into the sharps container. Suddenly, unexpectedly, she turned and vomited into the toilet. She knelt on the floor gagging and retching until her insides felt knotted. Pulling herself up by the sink, she washed her face and tried to rinse the foul taste out of her mouth. She was trembling so violently that she had to prop herself on the sink just to remain standing. She gazed with loathing at the pale, drawn reflection in the mirror. How weak she was! This had been the simplest of assignments – and besides, she'd only neutralized his medications. This was just letting nature take its course, accelerating the inevitable. But she couldn't control the trembling, and nearly dropped her phone when she withdrew it from her pocket. She managed to message *done* to the number that had texted her, then erased the message stream.

She was past due to get back on her own floor. Straightening herself, she took a couple of deep breaths to calm the trembling in her middle that threatened to start her retching again. She needed to toughen up. There was a future to be salvaged and it wouldn't be done by those who were unsettled by making a simple injection. Squaring her shoulders, she stepped out of the restroom and headed for the staircase.

From behind her, at the nurse's station around the corner, came the muffled keening of a monitor alarm. Someone punched it to silence.

"That's Room 512," said a voice.

"Wait," interrupted another voice. "We have an NI on that bed."

"Requested or ordered?" the first voice snarled.

"Ordered, but it doesn't make any difference," the second voice cautioned. The alarm started keening again and was again punched into silence. The first voice muttered something inaudible.

"Don't, LeeAnn, don't," the second voice pleaded. "If you intervene against an NI, you'll get in trouble! You could lose your job!"

The first voice said something in response and there was the sound of someone sitting down heavily in a chair. The alarm sounded again and was quickly killed. Janice headed down the stairway.

Back on her floor, toward the end of her shift, it was the work of a minute for Janice to check the status of the case in Room 512. She didn't concern herself with the name or diagnoses or any of that – she was only interested in the disposition code. There it was: 95 – expired under care. The case had already been removed. He must have been right on the edge, Janice thought – the neutralizing serum had taken almost immediate effect.

At dinner the next day, Janice nearly jumped out of her skin when Melissa suddenly sat down across from her.

"Hey, kid," Melissa said heartily. "Sorry, didn't mean to startle you."

"It's okay," Janice assured her weakly, feeling uncomfortable in light of how Melissa had treated her at their last meeting.

"Are you all right?" Melissa asked. "You look a bit peaked."

"Just – didn't get a good night's sleep last night," Janice replied.

"Yeah, rotating shifts are hell on the sleep schedule. Hey, sorry for getting so sharp with you the other day. I've been under a lot, and all that just made more mess on top of it all."

"It's okay," Janice waved her hand.

"Also," Melissa added in a conspiratorial whisper. "I wanted to congratulate you on your first acceleration. Quick and clean. Just like I told you – nothing to it, right?"

"Yeah, nothing," Janice mumbled, staring at her tray.

"You've earned this, and I'm glad to be the one giving it to you," Melissa said, extending her hand and dropping something onto Janice's tray. Janice saw that it was a small gold pin made of the letters XCV. It was unadorned, but otherwise just like the one Melissa wore pinned to her ID.

"You get a gem for each successful acceleration," Melissa went on. "There's a scheme to them – you start with white, and so many of those earns a red, and so on. I'll explain it to you sometime. The point is, you've started. You're in. You're one of us."

"Great. Thanks," Janice said flatly, fingering the trinket and looking at Melissa's pin, encrusted with red and blue gems. She wondered how many accelerations that represented.

"Hey, don't sound so excited," Melissa gibed. "Speaking of assignments, we may have a line on another one soon – interested?"

"Sure, whatever," Janice replied. "Just let me know."

"Okay, then," Melissa said, rising to leave.

"Melissa?" Janice asked.

"Yeah?"

"At one of those talks, the speaker mentioned online sites where you could read more about the topics they presented on.

Do you have any of those links? Not that I have much time for reading, but I thought I'd like to do as much research as I could."

"Sure, I do," Melissa replied. "I'll send them along."

"Thanks," Janice said, pocketing the pin and clearing away her tray.

The lights across the campus were out, but the windows of Sam's shop still glowed. This was unremarkable – Sam often worked late into the night, and at times was found in the morning sprawled on a worktable, sleeping amidst the debris of some urgent project.

Had anyone known what this project was, there would have been some concern.

Things were almost ready. Sam was testing the detonators now. Each one was standing in a cup of water. They were two-stage devices – they had to receive an arming signal from one source, and a triggering signal from a different source. In this case, the arming was done via wireless network like the one already installed at the factory. Sam keyed the command into the workstation, sending out the proper signals, and the LEDs on the detonators glowed amber as the capacitors started to charge. Sam gave them a few minutes. Then he took the triggering device and, gripping it tightly, turned the small key switch at the end. The LED on the top of the device went from amber to red, but nothing happened yet. It was only when he let go of the device, dropping it the few inches to the table, that the spring-loaded levers were released to send the triggering signal. On the detonators, the charging LEDs blinked off, and soon the water in the cups began to bubble and mist as it absorbed heat from the coils.

Sam nodded grimly and switched off the trigger. Deftly replacing the batteries on all the detonators, he packed them away. All was ready; it was time to get going.

The box of white powder was kept in the freezer, and the gallon of red liquid stayed in the refrigerator. Sam packed them both into midsized coolers and worked them out to the four-wheeler. Alone, either of the two ingredients was safely inert. But within an hour they'd be mixed together to form a thick paste that would be poured into carefully prepared molds. The paste would be a heat-triggered explosive that was perfectly safe at room temperature. But Sam didn't take unnecessary chances, so he kept the ingredients as chilled as possible for as long as possible.

The ingredients to make the two components of the binary explosive were supposedly available online, but Sam didn't even consider that option. Why engage in risky and potentially traceable online activity when you have a wide array of industrial and agricultural sources, as well as a fully equipped chemical lab right in your shop? Sam had concocted the components from innocuous ingredients he'd ordered from several different sources. He'd also determined the size, number, and placement of the charges. He'd even researched the optimal shape for each charge given its placement, and had constructed molds to form them. The detonators had been the final components. All was now ready.

The drive to the factory took about forty minutes, given how slowly he had to go to avoid disturbing his load. Once there, he drove the four-wheeler in through the factory door, being careful to avoid the surveillance camera watching the drive. Spreading out the gear on the floor, he mixed the binary components in a plastic trough then poured the resulting mixture into the molds. Placing the detonators firmly into the putty-like substance, he left it to set while he cleaned up. He took the opportunity to replace all the batteries on the components of his video monitoring setup.

Once the explosive had set, Sam wiggled the charges free of their molds and camouflaged them. Some got spray painted, others were fitted into plastic or metal cases, all ended up looking like ordinary devices found around factories and offices.

Then came the most tedious and nerve-wracking part of the task: placing the charges. A rough blueprint of the factory and some research into explosive demolition had told him the optimal placement to realize maximum effect. The problem was that the sites were all over the building, sometimes up near the ceiling. Sam was able to make use of his cables and whip, but it was dicey work when he was already tired. Eventually he was finished, and after carefully tidying up any traces of his visit he headed back.

It was nearly 4 a.m. when Sam returned to his shop. He was ready to topple into bed, but he wanted to do one final check. From his workstation he transmitted the arming code to the factory, and was gratified to see the return signals from all ten detonators indicating activation. He sent the disarm signal and cut the connection. All that remained now was to rig up a triggering device. He had to think that out – he wanted to engineer a totally different control mechanism. That should be simple enough, but he'd had enough complexity for one night. The hard part was done.

Hopefully he'd never have to send those signals. Hopefully the day would come when he'd ever-so-carefully remove the charges and take them to some empty field for safe detonation. But for now, they were in place, ready to smite the Philistines if the need arose, once he got that triggering component in place. But he'd think about that tomorrow. Right now, it was bedtime.

Later that same morning, Ron Porcher leaned back in his chair and shook his head in grudging admiration. His queries had taken a long time to construct, but the tale they told was astonishing – staggering, in fact. Even though this was the enemy, he couldn't help being impressed by the scope, sophistication – hell, the sheer audacity – of what they'd pulled off. And all of it completely beneath detection. Whoever these guys were, they wrote the book on covering their tracks.

Two years. Ten major hospitals and several smaller facilities. Hundreds – maybe as many as a thousand – OPELs smuggled out of the facilities, right down to the manipulation of the system to cover their departures. Code 99, supposedly one of the most rarely used codes. Discharged to external facility, no return expected. This code was usually used for things like discharges to hospice care, but they'd used it to cover all those missing cases. And that didn't count the deflected patients, those who'd been warned off admission and had just vanished into whatever underground operation these people were running. He guessed that count was at least double the Code 99s, probably more, but he had no way of querying for that. Both Melissa and Deana had been somewhat correct.

Damn. No wonder the pilot project hadn't been meeting quota.

Porcher wryly reflected that not long ago – twenty, maybe even fifteen years – it would have been impossible to do this. Back then, if Mrs. Fidget wasn't in her bed, someone would ask around to find out where she was. But these days, the computer system was the primary reality – the patients were incidental. Reality was what the computer system told you it was. If the computer system said to administer estrogen therapy to the patient in Room 300, you did so, even if the patient was a man. If the system said there was nobody in Room 508, there was nobody there, even if "nobody" kept leaning on the call button. And if the system said that Mrs. Fidget had been discharged with a Code 99, and the room was in order and ready for the next patient, you didn't question it. That's how modern medical care worked, and these people exploited it.

Well, then. This was a challenge. Porcher was certain these people were breaking all sorts of laws, but he'd let the lawyers and agents worry about that. He just wanted to catch them. He'd never been formally trained in information technology – he'd just drifted into it when it became clear that his career as an x-ray tech was going nowhere. It all seemed to come naturally to him, across the spectrum: servers, networks, databases, security systems. He loved watching the trained techs, the professional geeks, disregard him because he was "just" a jumped-up med tech. Let them – it just made it that much easier for him to outflank them.

But tracking down this crew, whoever they were, would take effort and ingenuity. They'd run a major operation across an entire region for years, all under the radar. They had to be good, and they had to be agile. Porcher had one critical advantage: he knew they were there, but they didn't know he was here. He had to keep it that way, because the moment they detected someone sniffing around, they'd fold right up and vanish. You could do that in the tech world. He not only had to find them, but remain invisible while he did it. That was a tall order.

Porcher grabbed a pad and began sketching out what kind of traps and tripwires he could set up.

That afternoon as she came on shift, Janice received a text saying that there might be a case, and that she should stand by. About an hour afterwards inter-floor delivery handed her an envelope addressed to her but with no sender listed. It contained only the now-familiar pharm bag. Janice slipped the syringe and exam gloves into her pocket and went about her duties.

It was after general bedtime when the prep text came. The case was on her floor this time, Room 308, within five minutes. Taking her tablet, she began working her way toward that end of the floor. When the go-ahead text came, she was only two doors away. Walking briskly into the darkened room, she pulled out the syringe, slipped it into the port, and was gone within thirty seconds. This time she was careful not to look at the sleeping patient.

She arranged her work to take her to the other end of the floor for about twenty minutes. She thought she heard some minor commotion around the nurse's station, but she blocked it out. No concern of hers. By the time she returned, one of her coworkers remarked offhandedly, "Lost one." Janice nodded and shrugged – it was a common enough statement on the geriatric floor. A short while later, the removal team arrived to take care of Room 308.

When Janice got off shift that night, she went home and did something she hadn't done since high school. After downing a couple of beers, she stripped to the skin and stood in front of her full-length mirror so she could look over every inch of her body. She turned this way and that to expose everything to examination. She didn't do this because she enjoyed what she saw – indeed, quite the opposite. But she forced herself to gaze, to scrutinize the bulgy shape and pasty white skin until she was nearly gagging with revulsion. All the while she was feeling the old urgings, the horridly familiar compulsions. Over the years she'd learned how to silence them, to resist, but tonight she was too weak. Her hands reached for the bottom drawer, groping in the back for that which she'd never quite had the strength to discard. There it was. She gazed in grim fascination as she drew out the slip case that held the Exacto knives.

Her old friends.

Shadows

As Janice was going on shift the next day, Derek was getting ready to head west for another weekend – with the obligatory stop at the warehouse club to load up with yeast and nuts and coffee and detergent. He wondered what this weekend would look like. The autumn chill was setting in, and clouds and rain were forecast. But there was nothing frosty about the reception he received at the Schaeffer household, where he was greeted with excited cries of "Mr. Derek!" and willing hands to help unload the car. He delighted Matthew with a brand-new book, which meant that he had to read it about eight times after dinner.

The next day dawned cool and rainy, so Derek ambled out to Sam's workshop, regretting that the temperature this weekend reduced his chances of bumping into Felicity. Maybe at chapel on Sunday.

Sam seemed both tired and a little subdued, but was glad to see Derek. There weren't any big projects needing attention, but Sam had a lesson plan ready: they were to learn about phone systems. Sam had entire sets of older phones lying around – perfectly good, but retired from businesses and organizations. Derek got thoroughly trained in network-based telephony, covering voice-over-data, routing, and short- and long-range wireless transmission. Sam sketched out how several sites could set up their own self-contained voice and data communications network, using some basic equipment and a few transmission towers. Derek even learned how to "gate" the self-contained system into the outside phone network, permitting both internal and external communications. Sam coached Derek as he set up a small system from the shop to one of the far outbuildings.

"Gee, Sam," Derek commented as he packed away the gear from that exercise. "Now I could rig up a phone between here and the generator shed."

"You could," Sam confirmed with a grin. "But I beat you to it."

229

"But I'm wondering," Derek asked. "Isn't this all sort of reinventing the wheel? Isn't the system that supports these," he held up his mobile phone, "taking care of all this? Why rig up all this extra equipment? Why not give everybody one of these?"

"Some people like their privacy," Sam answered.

Back at the Schaeffer household, dinner was being readied. Family members were scattered all over the house, including Martha chatting and giggling in the living room with Harmony Peterson. Upon seeing Derek, Martha called out a question.

"Will you be going, Mr. Derek?"

"Going where?" Derek responded.

"To the dance next Friday night," Martha explained. "The autumn dance, up by Marlette."

"It's the last big social event before Christmastime," Harmony added. "Just after harvest and before the cold sets in."

"I – ah – don't dance very well," Derek admitted.

"Hardly anybody does," Harmony said. "But they always have good music and a good caller, so everyone does all right."

"Do you – need tickets or a reservation or anything?" Derek asked. The girls broke into peals of laughter.

"Now, girls," chided Linda as she came into the room. "Don't laugh at Mr. Derek just because he's unfamiliar with the circumstances. You're more than welcome, Derek – it's kind of an open event. I'll give you the address. People start arriving between four and five, and it lasts well into the night. You could bring a dish to share, but please don't – everybody always brings too much. There'll be a pig roast and plenty of fun."

"Sounds good," Derek said.

Dinner was the usual noisy time with all the good food that Derek could wish for, but he couldn't help but pick up on a subtle change in the atmosphere of the home. Everyone, most notably the older ones, was a bit more subdued, as if distracted by something. There had been more quiet conversations in the corners all day, and Kent and Linda wore a concerned look about their eyes. Once or twice, Derek heard Linda speak sharply to some of the children, which was totally uncharacteristic of her. Philip wasn't around for most of the day, but he came in partway through dinner and whispered something in Linda's ear. She abruptly stood and left, while Philip sat down and filled his plate hastily.

Derek was curious and a little concerned. He could hardly ask flat-out what was going on, but something was clearly stressing the little community. From a few hints he inferred that something unusual had happened earlier in the week, something that had unsettled everyone. This unsettled Derek in turn, causing him to more deeply appreciate just how precious this haven of peace and love had become to him. He didn't like the thought of anything disturbing it, but he didn't know what he could do.

Sunday morning, Derek woke early and made his way out to the kitchen. He asked when chapel would be.

"Oh, we're not having chapel today," Linda explained. "Fr. Gabriel isn't available. Some people drove up to Yale for early Mass, but that's well underway by now. We'll be having family prayers and Scripture class shortly – you're welcome to join us."

Over in his shop, Sam had just finished his morning devotions and simple breakfast when he got a surprise of his own. He checked his workstation as a matter of course and found that there had been a visit to the factory the night before at about 9 p.m. It was just the brown-haired guy – Ron, apparently – and the captain. They arrived within about five minutes of each other, and each brought a portable.

"Why do you meet in this scruffy place?" the captain asked as he walked into the office.

Ron pointed at the ceiling. "The only wires coming into this place are electrical. No phone, no cable, right on the fringe of wireless coverage – there's about zero chance of surveillance."

Sam grinned.

"We have another place like it between Flint and Saginaw," Ron went on. "Middle of nowhere, all approaches monitored, plenty of room for inside parking. Admit it: unless you saw us drive in, would even a close flyover tell you anyone was here?"

The captain grudgingly admitted that he probably wouldn't spot anything. Then they set up their technology and talked a little shop – clearly they were meeting to brief each other on familiar subjects.

"We've been increasing flyover patrols of the area – not so much the waterfront as the streets and roads in and around the city. Rather than tracking one particular threat, we've been covering everything," the captain began.

"Everything?" Ron asked skeptically.

"Well – traffic in particular," the captain explained. "People are creatures of habit – even if they're trying to be elusive, they still tend to follow the same patterns of life. If you watch long and carefully enough, you can always discern the patterns."

"Okay," Ron said slowly, still fishing for understanding. "So – whose patterns have you been watching?"

"Everyone's."

"Everyone's?"

"Working from the hospital outwards," the captain qualified. "Without a particular target, we just film everything. It comes in handy when you finally get a target you want to track. Then you can look back through footage to see what he's done in the past."

"Ahhh," Ron said, beginning to grasp the principle.

"It's actually the best way to learn about targets, if you have the resources to expend," the captain went on. "People who know they're being watched do unpredictable things. People who don't know they're being watched just do what they normally do – which, eventually, is just what you want to know, especially in cases like this."

"Sounds like a good start. Anything else?" Ron asked.

"This tree cover is a serious hindrance, so I'm working on getting low-level assets to work beneath it."

Sam's blood ran cold. The ranches were going to have to step up precautions, and even that might not be sufficient. All their protocols assumed high-level threats. There was almost nothing they could do against low-level surveillance, which could not only get beneath cover but was completely unpredictable.

Sam refocused on the video. Apparently the captain had finished his briefing, because now Ron was talking. He was explaining the results of his investigations, how he'd uncovered all the Code 99s throughout the region. He explained how the tracks had been carefully erased at the system level, and how the cases had practically vanished.

"Altogether?" the captain asked.

"Well – just from the medical system," Ron said. "I don't know about out there in the world. But vanishing from the medical system is a big deal – it means you can't get care anywhere."

"So, then," the captain asked, "is this a conspiracy?"

"You could call it that," Ron replied. "Whoever this is, they're sophisticated, skilled, subtle, and entrenched. They're determined, and have resources and expertise."

"And they're breaking federal law," the captain growled. "Which makes them a threat to national security."

"Quite possibly," Ron acknowledged. "Truth is – and you didn't hear this from me – word is the hospital is going to get a shaking up soon, and that's only the beginning."

"How so?" the captain asked.

"I can't talk about it much," Ron said. "HHS investigative stuff. It'll be public soon enough – probably this week. Let's just say when you set the house on fire, the rats run out."

The men fell to discussing details, which Sam could review later. For now, he just sat staring at the screen, his guts churning. This was bad. This was very bad. So far, he hadn't let anyone know about the videos, and how he'd bugged the old factory. Now he was going to have to – Gil and Kent and Ruth and Fitz and Shelly from Lapeer at least, and probably more. Everyone had hoped the flushing earlier in the week would be quickly forgotten, a passing ripple in the river of events. Now it was starting to look like the tumbling pebble that triggered an avalanche. This was a major threat.

The pencil Sam was gripping in his hand suddenly splintered. He had to get that triggering mechanism in place. He may not be able to strike much of a blow, but something in his heart told him that the time was approaching for him to do what he could. The time he'd been anticipating his entire life.

"Philistines," he muttered, looking at the image of the two men on the video screen.

Later that morning, after the rain had ceased, Derek went out with Martha to help with the horses. Having assisted with the basics, he left Martha to brush them while he wandered away. He decided to drop in on Sam just to say hello.

He found Sam sitting at a worktable with his Bible closed and a notebook opened on the table in front of him. He seemed to be in a somber, almost gloomy mood. His brows were knit in thought, and from time to time he'd scribble something in the notebook. Derek had never seen him so pensive.

"Hi, Sam," Derek said cautiously. "If I'm disturbing –"

"No, no," Sam said sharply, looking up at him. "You come in. Come in."

"Is there – something I can help with?" Derek asked. Sam shook his head but slowly extended his hand. Puzzled, Derek took it, and found his hand gripped in the strongest handshake he'd ever known.

"Derek," Sam said.

"Yes?" Derek replied. There was a long pause before Sam spoke again.

"Derek."

"I'm right here, Sam," Derek replied, beginning to get a little unnerved by this curious behavior.

"Derek, listen," Sam said coarsely. "If I fall –"

"If you fall?" Derek laughed, looking at the rafters overhead. "Sam, you're not going –"

"*If* I fall," Sam interrupted sharply, squeezing Derek's hand to command his attention. "Remember this: love the Lord your God with all your heart, and soul, and mind, and strength – and love your neighbor as yourself. *That*," he slammed his free hand down hard on the Bible at his elbow. "Is all the Law and the Prophets. Do you understand?"

"Um – yeah, Sam," Derek assured him.

"Will you remember?"

"Of course," Derek answered, wondering what was causing this strange mood.

"Go now," Sam said, so Derek did, leaving him to his meditations and scribbling.

Derek wandered for a while in confusion and distress. It seemed like a shadow had fallen over his adopted home. The

Schaeffers seemed subtly disturbed, Sam was acting odd and – fatalistic? What was going on?

Back in the house, another odd thing happened. He was standing by the phone – a desktop phone like he'd worked on with Sam the day before – when it rang. Nobody was around to pick it up, so he did.

"Hello?"

"Hi, this is Allison up at Beaversdam," came the voice. "To whom am I speaking?"

Derek was taken aback. "At where?" he asked.

"Beaversdam. This is Rivendell, isn't it?"

Now Derek was even more confused. "I'm sorry, this is Derek, and I'm a guest. This is the Schaeffer's house. Can I find someone for you?"

"Yes – is Linda there?"

"She is – I'll fetch her," Derek replied, at last getting something he could work with. He summoned Linda, who took the call, leaving Derek to wander off and puzzle over all the strange things that day had brought.

The rain blew away by late afternoon, and though the air that came behind was cool, it was not too cold to sit out on the porch with Linda and Kent after dinner. They chatted quietly, looking out over the damp, darkling fields while the wind tattered the clouds overhead, showing strips of blue-black sky in which the occasional star could be seen. Even though this weekend had been different from the others, Derek still felt very settled and welcome, and was already dreading his return to the city, his job, and his bleak little apartment.

"Well, Derek," Linda offered. "You're becoming quite a fixture around here. The kids are now regularly talking in terms of 'when Mr. Derek comes', so your presence is now assumed."

"I know," Derek replied. "I've been starting to wonder if I shouldn't start paying rent. You've been so hospitable – I just hope I'm not intruding on your family."

Linda dismissed that. "Oh, pshaw. I was about to say that I hope we aren't imposing on you by asking you to do all our supply runs for us. You have no idea how much trouble it saves us to have you taking care of that."

"As far as the kids are concerned – and us, for that matter," Kent added. "You're no burden at all – in fact, it's a joy to have you around."

"Thanks," Derek said, his heart warmed to hear that. They were all quiet together for a minute before Derek spoke again. "I've been wondering something, though."

"What's that?" Kent asked.

"Where's Beaversdam?"

Out of the corner of his eye Derek caught Linda and Kent exchanging sharp, almost wary, glances.

"Why do you ask?" Kent responded.

"On the phone earlier today," Derek explained. "The call that was for you, Linda – the lady said she was calling from Beaversdam. I've never heard of the place. She also asked if this was – something – Riverdale? I know it was the right place, because she was looking for you, but the names were strange to me."

Linda was looking intently at her beer bottle, and Kent shifted in his seat and cleared his throat.

"I think," he said. "It's time we explained a few things to you. You're clearly finding out – and probably figuring out – some things for yourself, so we'd best just come out and tell you, so you aren't making mistaken guesses."

"Okay," Derek said slowly, gratified to be getting some answers but feeling a little nervous – was he about to learn some dark or horrid secret about the wholesome-seeming farm?

"Best to start at the beginning," Kent began. "A couple of years back, some disturbing rumors started to circulate, especially among the elderly. People began to speak of older people being admitted to hospitals, even for minor issues, and never coming back out. It didn't receive any official attention – after all, old people do die, sometimes unexpectedly – but it was starting to scare people.

"After a couple people we knew died suddenly after being admitted – people we knew were in reasonably good health – and we were unable to get any satisfactory answers, we decided to do some digging on our own. It was hard, because the government controls the health statistics, so you only see what they want you to see. But with some persistence, we got our hands on the raw data and analyzed it ourselves."

"Wait – who's 'we'?" Derek asked.

"Myself, Gil, a friend of ours who's really good with computers and health care data, and a lawyer we know named Fitz. A very clever young lady named Anastasia – she lives in northern Indiana now. A few others helped. The results were clear: the elderly were dying at a higher rate in this area, and the rate was increasing. Though the details were cleverly disguised, the increase was almost completely found in acute care facilities – hospitals."

"Don't most people die in hospitals?" Derek asked.

"Fewer than you might think," Kent explained. "Especially the elderly. They do die in hospitals, but being more prepared for death, they also die in care facilities, hospices, their own homes – the distribution is pretty consistent.

"Except in this area, beginning a couple of years ago. That's when we began to see a spike in hospital-based deaths among the elderly. But it seemed to depend on more than just age – there were other factors that seemed to play in. From talking to those who'd known them, a clearer picture emerged. The increase in hospital deaths was almost completely among elderly with either no dependents or who were estranged from their relatives – in short, those who had nobody to care for them. There are a distressingly high number of people like this, especially in this area, considering the economic upheavals of the last couple of generations."

"You keep referring to 'this area'," Derek interrupted. "What do you mean by that? The Blue Water area?"

"The entire Thumb," Kent replied. "If you can picture a map of Michigan, you know that this eastern portion is aptly nicknamed 'the thumb', because it looks just like the thumb of a mitten. It's roughly bounded by two expressways – I-75 to the west and I-69 to the south. It is all or part of five counties, and is largely rural, especially the areas north and east of the expressways.

"This is what made us suspicious as we dug through the data. You know how the medical system works these days: you can't go to any provider you want, you have to go to the ones designated for you. If you need hospitalization, that provider can only send you to certain hospitals. In most situations, that's not a big geographic limitation. Where did you grow up?"

"New York," Derek said. "Near Syracuse."

"That's right, you told me," Kent said. "Where you lived, given the providers you would have used and the hospitals they worked with, you could have been sent anywhere within, say, a hundred-mile radius, right?"

"That'd be about right," Derek confirmed.

"But in the Thumb area, patients end up getting sent to a much more restricted set of hospitals. In fact, the hospitals are found in the communities that lie along the expressways, like beads on a string, from Bay City down I-75 through Saginaw to Flint, then east along I-69 to Lapeer and finally to Port Huron. If you live in the Thumb and need inpatient care, you'll go to a hospital somewhere along that arc.

"That's precisely what made us suspicious. Not only was this area seeing an increase in deaths of elderly who fit a particular profile, but that increase was completely found in the hospitals bordering the Thumb – including those in Port Huron."

"But – wow," Derek mused, trying to digest this. "I mean, does that mean someone in there is killing them? Who? And why?"

"Very difficult questions, and all we have is speculation about the answers," Kent replied. "The deaths are so skillfully done that they look like, and are documented as, natural deaths. That makes us suspect it's the medical personnel themselves. If you think about it, two or three unscrupulous caregivers could do a lot of damage even in a large hospital."

"That's hard to comprehend," Derek said. "What are we talking? Physicians? Nurses? PAs?"

"That's one of the most puzzling things," Kent admitted. "As you know, most people go into medical professions in order to help people. From the specialists down to the nurses' aides, there's a strong ethic of care. What could breach that and cause people to violate their convictions and even their oaths, we can only guess. We've heard rumors of what sound like secret societies, and have even caught wind of meetings over near Flint, but have nothing firm.

"Which brings us to the other question – why? We have three plain facts that are very disturbing, especially taken together. One is the sophistication. So many deaths couldn't just be a few providers getting happy with the dosages – that would have been discovered and stopped quickly. So much effort for so long bespeaks a coordinated effort at many levels.

"The second thing is the deliberate silence. Again, you know how carefully health trends are monitored and publicized. Let there be a pertussis outbreak in some township, or a region's diabetes incidence spike, and it's all over the sites and airwaves. Yet here was a disturbing increase in senior deaths, and not only was it not discussed, it was buried so cunningly that we had to do our own analysis to find it.

"But the most disturbing thing of all was the synchronization. This uptick in deaths commenced at about the same time, to about the same population, almost universally across the area. With little temporary variances, we saw it occurring in acute care facilities from Bay City to Port Huron.

"Put these factors together and you have what looks like a concerted effort – a conspiracy, if you will. I know it sounds like something from the tinfoil-hat crowd, but we were staring right at the facts and considering the implications. We have no idea who, or precisely why – other than social and philosophical commentary predicting such things. But there was no denying the effects."

"Wow," said Derek, stunned.

"We also found – " Kent began, but Linda gently interrupted him.

"Kent – Rivendell? Beaversdam?"

"Oh – right," Kent said. "Once we figured all this out, we realized we had to do something about it. Not only had we lost some friends, but people were making their own guesses and starting to panic. So a few of us families began taking in elderly folk, particularly those who fit what seemed to be the profile. We hid them and provided what care we could."

"Medical care?" Derek asked.

"Well, that to some degree, but other care, too – housing, food, comfort."

"Wait a minute – those old people at Mass, and out behind the Big House. Were those – them?"

"Some of them," Kent confirmed. "We only have a few here – I was getting to that. We worked out ways so that people could put their assets in trust and appoint trustees, so they could effectively vanish. No providers to send them to hospitals, just friends to care for them in their final years."

"But what about serious medical care?" Derek asked. "How do they get that?"

"Often they don't," Kent admitted with a shrug. "That's the situation you find yourself in when your care facilities start to become execution chambers. Sure, something like renal failure is serious, but is seeking care worth a pillow over your face while you sleep, or whatever might happen if you were admitted to the hospital? We're managing some things with pharmaceuticals and equipment like portable dialysis units, but all that's outside the law and somewhat risky.

"As word got out, we started getting so many people coming to us for help that we began spreading them out. We found families who'd be willing to take in these elderly folk and care for them. We were able to buy up foreclosed and abandoned properties all over the area – there are thousands to be had. Young families needing housing would take in older people needing care, and everyone would benefit. In fact, that well you helped Sam drill the other week was for just such a house."

"Really? I only saw the one guy, and a couple of kids through a window," Derek said.

"Sometimes the elderly keep out of sight, sometimes they're too frail to come out much. Anyway, we have a network of these sites all across the Thumb and beyond. We give them code names – Beaversdam and Rivendell are from classic tales we know well – for use within our own communications network."

"That's why Sam has the whole internal phone setup!" Derek exclaimed, realization dawning.

"Exactly. Secrecy and seclusion are important – we don't want our guests to be found. Our communications, our living facilities, even our travel patterns have to be discreet and indirect, lest anyone trace us back to them. In this area, we have an extra burden to be concerned with."

"What's that?" Derek asked.

"Overhead surveillance," Kent answered, pointing at the sky. "Being a border community, we never know when there might be a drone overhead. Ostensibly, it's for border security, but we know for a fact that they're increasingly sweeping them further and further inland to observe ordinary citizens. This is under the pretense of combatting 'domestic terror' – a vague and very pliable term – but in practice it is used to look for any activity the government might consider suspicious."

Derek pondered this for a while. "But – I don't understand why your activity would be considered suspicious. Can't people live where they like, and with whom they wish?"

"Supposedly they can – and if it was that simple, it wouldn't be so pressing," Kent replied. "But the situation gets trickier and more legally dubious because of what we sometimes must do to get people to safety.

"A best-case scenario is that someone approaches us while they're still reasonably healthy and free. We set up the legal framework and move them to one of our sites – which we call ranches. Thereafter, all external entities deal with them through their trustees. Essentially, they vanish.

"But things aren't always so easy. Sometimes people are considering the step, but something happens – a minor mishap or a doctor's orders – that lands them in the hospital. People have even come to the realization of the danger they're in while in the hospital. Whatever the reason, they're inside and they need help. In that case we have to do a snatch – a covert, unauthorized removal of that person from that facility. As you know, doing that involves breaking laws – federal laws, these days."

Derek looked skeptical. "That sounds a little – "

"Melodramatic? Cloak-and-dagger?" Kent completed. "I know – and I wish it wasn't necessary. Snatches are difficult and delicate and dangerous, and we don't like having to do them. We wish people could just demand to be released and walk out the door. But you know how entangling bureaucracies can be, and how easily people can be intimidated into compliance, particularly by medical personnel. And if there is a conspiracy targeting these patients, there'd be a strong incentive to keep them in the facility until they could be killed. We've lost patients while we were planning snatches to rescue them. Just this past week, we barely got one out before the nurse showed up with the lethal injection.

"I don't have to tell you how many laws we have to break to get these people to safety. They're the ones who have to truly vanish. If they were ever found, they could be prosecuted, and would certainly be questioned, which would lead back to us, and then to all the others. We're still maintaining a tenuous legal framework to protect them – our lawyer, Fitz, is a canny and courageous guy – but we suspect it's only a matter of time before they penetrate that and we have to go truly underground.

"That's one reason for the heavy precautions. They are excessive – for our current situation. But we have to always be ready for the next level of threat. That's why we're already –"

"Kent," Linda said warningly, tapping her bottle. He glanced at her then shook his head.

"Right. Clearly, I can't unpack everything that's being planned – we don't even do that among ourselves. But if you're going to be around, you need to be aware of what you're in the middle of."

"Well, it certainly explains a lot," Derek replied. "Several curious things I'd noticed make more sense now."

"Needless to say, we're entrusting a lot to you by telling you all this," Linda said. "But we trust your integrity and discretion. We know you wouldn't deliberately betray us, and we are confident you won't get careless with this knowledge. But we also wanted you to know what you were involving yourself in, just in case you wanted to – draw back."

"Oh, I don't want to do that," Derek assured her quickly. He thought back over the circumstances that had so swiftly drawn him into the life of this family. Something suddenly occurred to him. "You know, these criteria that seem to identify the likely targets – don't they fit John Holmes as well?"

Kent stirred in his seat and his expression grew darker. "You're right – and what happened to John worries us deeply. It also shows the limitations of our adversaries. By all the metrics that can be tracked by computer, he was a prime candidate: elderly, widowed, no descendants or near relatives, victim of a deadly and incurable condition. The only problem was that he wasn't yet in a hospital. We've concluded, largely based on evidence that you provided, that he was executed in his home, probably by the same parties who are coordinating the hospital executions.

"But this is also where they're out of their reckoning. John and Angie did have a family – a family of love which they'd built over the years. I was one of their children, as were many others that you saw at his funeral. His death mattered to us. And though justice has become so corrupt in the land that there will be no official action taken on his death, we are taking action of our own. Though we may not be able to bring his killers to justice, there are other things we can do to thwart them.

"If John's death was what we suspect, it represents a dangerous precedent. It means they're getting impatient to the point that they're unwilling to wait for their victims to come into their power – they'll risk seeking them out and killing them in their homes. This is not impossible. Keep in mind that these would be people who live alone, often in neighborhoods where they have no connections. Who's going to even notice the appliance repair truck that's briefly in their driveway, especially when their death looks just like a suicide? This represents a whole new level of threat for these defenseless citizens."

"Do we have any idea who's responsible for all this?" Derek asked.

"Anybody's guess," Kent admitted. "The level of sophistication and depth of resources indicates government involvement, but it could be private industry – or some unholy alliance between the two."

On the way home that night, Derek struggled to absorb everything he'd learned. At times his reason rebelled, scoffing at the whole thing as the biggest cock-and-bull story he'd ever heard. But the urge to dismiss it all as craziness went against his experience with these people. He'd known hare-brained conspiracy theorists, and they were the polar opposite of sober, grounded realists like Kent and Linda – or Ruth, or Gil, or Sam, or any of the rest of them. No, the whole world might be crazy, but they would be sane and stable. Plus, he had the witness of

John Holmes' death and the aftermath. How could he dismiss that?

As he drove and pondered, Derek came to realize what lay at the root of his desire to scoff at and disregard what he'd heard: fear. If that was all nonsense, then he could just keep living as he'd been living, pretending everything was okay. But if it was true, then the world was much less predictable and far more dangerous than he'd imagined.

That frank realization brought another aspect into sharp relief: he was terrified. To dismiss Kent and Linda as fanciful fools was the easy path. To acknowledge that they might be right meant having to choose sides, to decide where he'd stand. Of course he couldn't stand opposed to them, but there was another place he couldn't stand – off to the side, watching in indifference. That wasn't an option, not when he knew what he did, and what they were standing for.

But to stand with them? Confronting whatever forces might be arrayed against them, forces that might even now be seeking them out? Could he face that?

Resolve clarified and hardened within him. To hell with it all. He'd rather stand beside them, even if it meant falling, than live a safe, comfortable life of willful ignorance. He'd always valued courage and longed for an opportunity to be courageous, like the characters he played in his games.

It looked like he was going to get his chance.

Interrogations

It was at lunch on Monday when Derek caught up with Janice. He was startled, almost shocked, at her appearance. She was sitting at a table with a tray in front of her, looking – Derek had a hard time putting his finger on it – defeated? Crumpled? Her shoulders drooped and her face looked puffy and vacant. Her eyes were sunken and stared blankly at nothing in particular. Part of him was revolted, but a greater part was gravely concerned. He walked over to where she was seated.

"Mind if I join you?" he asked. She almost startled at his voice, but looked up and smiled at him.

"'Please do" She gestured to the seat across from her.

"Janice," Derek asked as he put his tray down. "Are you all right?" It probably wasn't a tactful thing to ask, but he'd never seen anyone's appearance change so dramatically so quickly.

"Oh, yeah," Janice replied listlessly. "I've been on afternoons for a few days."

Wow, thought Derek – if this was what afternoon shifts did to a person…

"And then you've had the business with moving," Derek added. "And your dad leaving and all."

"My dad?" Janice asked, puzzled. Then realization dawned. "Oh, right – that, too."

"So – how's the new place working out?" Derek asked, though it was clear Janice's mind was on other things.

"Oh, fine, fine," Janice said distractedly, and proceeded to chat about that while Derek took bites of his lunch. As he watched her talk, he noticed something about her collar.

"So – you decided to join, then?" he asked.

"Join?" Janice asked, puzzled.

"The pin. On your collar," Derek pointed. "Like the one Melissa had for that professional association or whatever it was."

"Oh, that," Janice said, touching the pin but pulling her fingers away quickly, as if they'd been burned. "Yeah, I went ahead and took the plunge. Professional development and all that."

"So, what's it like?" Derek asked.

"It's – okay," Janice said, toying with the remains of her lunch.

"What do you do?" Derek prodded. He'd noticed how vague Melissa had been about the topic, and now fresh recruit Janice was being equally reticent to open up about this mysterious group. He found this rather odd – usually new members of any organization were bubbling with enthusiasm for it.

"Oh, we have meetings and stuff," Janice replied. "I went over for some seminars. There are chances to socialize. It's mostly medical stuff – you wouldn't find it interesting."

"Well, I am a physician's assistant, even if I do work in the morgue," Derek said. "Do you have meetings here in town? Down Metro Detroit way?"

"Actually, over by Flint. I guess they're sort of irregular…"

Derek tuned out the rest of what Janice said because the first part caught him.

By Flint.

"I'm sorry?" Derek came back to the present, aware that Janice had asked him something.

"I asked, what have you been up to? I haven't seen much of you since you helped me move."

"Oh, I've been doing great. I've been hanging out with some new friends. I met them through – that is, I met them around. They're great, and I've been learning a lot."

"Must be nice," Janice said a little morosely. Derek figured he was hearing a bit of residual pain over the Brenda situation, but he thought it odd that someone who'd newly joined a professional association would be short of friends. But maybe Janice was like him in the sense that she didn't make friends easily. He sympathized with that, and his heart went out to her. Whatever was going on, it was clear life wasn't treating her well. He wanted to help, and got an idea how he might do so.

"It is nice," Derek said. "In fact, there's going to be a big social event this Friday evening. It's a barn dance. I'd have to check, but I think it'd be okay for you to come. We could go and you could meet some of my friends."

"A – barn dance?" Janice asked, taken aback. "I – I don't dance very well."

"Neither do I," Derek admitted. "But I've been assured that isn't a problem – they'll have a good band and an experienced caller, whatever that is. There'll at least be good music and good food and good friends."

Janice was experiencing a surprising amount of internal turmoil. She'd only been asked to one dance in her entire life, by a guy she found distasteful but went with anyway because he was the only one who'd ever asked her. This situation was totally different – Derek was just a friend, and it wasn't anything like a date, and it certainly wasn't high school, but – a guy just asked her to a dance. A barn dance, granted, but she did love live music and it had been so long – plus Derek's honest, friendly face was like a ray of light to her heart.

"It's – Friday night?" Janice asked. "I'm on day shift Friday."

"It'll be a blast," Derek assured her warmly. "You don't have to bring anything, and the people are the most fun. I'll drive."

"Well…" Janice wavered. The thought of meeting fun people was enticing.

"Hey, kids!" A familiar voice called, and suddenly Melissa was sitting down beside them. Derek noticed that Janice seemed to shy away from her just a little.

"Hi, there," Derek said flatly. In truth, he was a little put off by how Melissa's affected intimacy had interrupted their moment of friendship.

"Hey, Derek, Janice was telling me recently that you're a Castor," Melissa said.

"I'm a what?" Derek asked.

"A Castor," Melissa explained. "As in Castor and Pollux, from Greek mythology. The god Zeus fell for the human queen, Leda, and came to her in the form of a swan. He raped her, though there's some dispute over how much fight she put up. She conceived and bore Castor – some say as a twin to Pollux, who was the son of her husband the king."

"Okay," Derek said cautiously. "What does that have to do with me?" He noticed that Janice's hand had flown to her mouth and her eyes were wide, but there was no stopping Melissa now.

"That's why we use the term for people born from fathers they don't know. Unusual birth circumstances. Not to worry – we understand. It means you'll fit right in, doesn't it, Janice?"

"It does, does it?" Derek asked sharply, looking at Janice. He felt stung and betrayed, but saw that tears were standing in Janice's eyes and she was shaking her head slightly. Clearly, she hadn't intended this, but still...

"Sure it does," Melissa continued, oblivious to the side drama. "In fact, we're having a gathering this Saturday night, and I want to invite you, if Janice hasn't already. Lots of people like you, with common goals and interests. People who understand your struggles, and want to make the world a better place for people like us."

"'People like us', eh?" Derek answered with a harsh edge. What did this woman know about him?

"Yes – just like us," Melissa replied, apparently missing Derek's tone. "Janice will tell you all about it. You'll have a great time, won't he, Janice?"

Derek bit back an even sharper response, figuring it was no use discussing anything with this boor. "I'll think about it," he said tersely, picking up his tray. "I've got to get back to work. See you, Janice."

As Derek walked off, Janice turned to Melissa. "Why did you say that? I'd told you that about Derek in confidence!"

"It's nothing to be ashamed of," Melissa countered. "That's precisely the kind of prejudice we're fighting. It's a vestige, kid, a vestige of the old moral order that needs to be swept away."

"But that's very personal information," Janice emphasized. "I should never have said anything. He probably thinks I'm a complete jerk."

"He needn't worry – his secret's safe with me," Melissa replied casually. "And he really would fit right in. Make sure he comes – offer to drive. You were planning on coming, right?"

"Well, I – " Janice began. She hadn't known there was a gathering this weekend, and if she had, she would have been ambivalent about attending. For some reason, the prospect seemed flat and insipid.

"It'll be your first chance to show off your shiny new pin," Melissa pointed out. "Which reminds me – it's already out of date. I need to get you a new one – but how about a chance to leapfrog to the next level? We may have a line on an acceleration that might come through this afternoon. You could go from no jewels right to two."

"Fine – just message me the details," Janice said with resignation, feeling beaten down and discouraged.

"That's my girl," Melissa said, rising to leave. "And don't forget – I really want to see your buddy at the gathering. Don't let me down."

"How am I supposed to get him to come if he doesn't want to?" Janice pleaded. From his response, Janice guessed that Derek would want nothing to do with Melissa, or her – and she could hardly blame him.

"That's your problem," Melissa said bluntly. "Use your feminine charms – just be sure he's there." With that she walked off, leaving a dismayed Janice alone at the table.

A little while later, Derek's phone rang. When he saw it was Janice he was tempted to let it roll to voice mail, but on the fourth ring he reluctantly answered.

"'Hello?" he said flatly.

"Derek, Derek," came Janice's frantic voice. He could tell she was sobbing. "I'm *so* sorry. I am *so* sorry. You have every right to be furious with me and never speak to me and I couldn't blame you a bit. But I hope you don't and please forgive me. Please, *please* forgive me."

It was hard to remain angry in the face of that kind of contrition, but Derek felt he had to be a little indignant on principle.

"Okay, okay – but why did you tell that harpy?"

"I don't know, I don't know," Janice replied through her tears. "We were just talking one day about unusual birth situations, and she used artificial insemination as an example, and I said I knew someone like that, and she asked who, and without thinking I just blurted your name right out. I regretted it the minute I did it and would have taken it back if I could, but I had no idea she'd – oh, I'm such an idiot and I've ruined everything. Please, *please* say you'll forgive me and still be my friend. And here you'd just asked me to a dance and *please…*"

By now, Derek was feeling so sorry for her in her dismay that he couldn't remain angry. "Okay, I forgive you, and I'll still be your friend. And the invitation to the dance is still open, if you like." He hoped that there wouldn't be a complication with his bringing her, but he couldn't imagine one.

"Derek, thank you, I don't deserve a friend like you. But – but it gets worse. Melissa wants me to get you to come to the gathering on Saturday night, and is really pushing me. I told her you probably wouldn't, but she won't take no for an answer."

Derek felt upset again, a little bit at Janice for being so weak, but mostly with Melissa. Who did she think she was, pressuring his friends to try to make him do something? "Listen, I'm a little busy – " he began, but Janice interrupted.

"Please, Derek, I know I have no right, especially after what I did, but it's only an evening," Janice pleaded. "There's a social time and a talk and we can leave right afterwards. You don't have to do anything but show up and we can leave right away, and if you don't come she'll be so mean to me – "

Okay, this was getting bizarre. Why would it matter so much to Melissa that Derek show up at a meeting? What Derek really wanted to do was ask Janice why she hung around with such manipulative people, but he figured it wasn't the time for that discussion.

"Tell you what," Derek said. "I'll think about it. We can talk about it later. No promises, but I really will think about it."

"Thank you, Derek, thank you," Janice breathed, her relief palpable. "It's not a far drive at all, just this side of Flint, only an hour."

There it was again, that detail that Derek had caught before, but which had slipped away. Near Flint. He scoured his memory for why that should matter, but couldn't recall what it was.

"Okay, I'll get back to you. Got to go," Derek assured her. What was it about Flint? He also had to check with Kent or Linda about Janice attending the dance.

Later that afternoon, the messages came to Janice's phone, and she did her third acceleration. It was becoming routine, mindless. On her way home, she used her dinner money to buy a case of cheap beer.

Janice's stomach and head were still feeling delicate at the beginning of shift the next morning, so it wasn't helpful that everyone seemed edgy.

"What's going on?" Janice asked her colleague Gina, looking at the clusters of staff whispering in corners.

"Haven't you checked your e-mail?" Gina asked.

"Not yet," Janice admitted, pulling out her tablet.

"You'll see," Gina assured her. Janice flipped through the message headers until she saw an all-staff message from the hospital president. Scowling, Janice opened it to find the expectable flowery organizational rhetoric about relentlessly striving for excellence and superlative performance. Filtering out the fluff, she zeroed in on the information that mattered. Her heart started pounding.

"What the hell is a personnel auditor?" Janice asked with a suddenly dry mouth.

"No idea," Gina admitted.

"'Will be interviewing select employees'," Janice quoted. "Which employees? How will they be selected?"

"Again, no idea," Gina said as she turned to go. "I think that's what's got everyone worried."

Figuring that she had more reason to be worried than most, Janice tapped out a message to Melissa: *Need to talk asap. Urgent.*

The reply came back quickly. *3rd floor by stairs.*

Janice was impatiently waiting when Melissa showed up.

"What's all – " Janice began, but Melissa waved her to silence and motioned her into the stairwell. Puzzled, Janice then recalled that there were no cameras in there, so ducked in behind Melissa.

"What is it?" Melissa asked sharply.

"Have you seen this?" Janice asked, thrusting the tablet toward her. Melissa took it and read the message, visibly relaxing about halfway through.

"Oh, that's all," she said, handing the tablet back. "I thought it was something about the acceleration. That's nothing to worry about."

Janice was dumbfounded. "'Nothing to worry about'? Nobody knows what a 'personnel audit' is, or who is going to be interviewed by this auditor for what reason. What if this is about the accelerations?"

"Listen," Melissa assured her with a smile. "This isn't about the accelerations. You have nothing to worry about."

"How do you know?" Janice pressed, her heart pounding. "What if that girl who saw me went and told someone? What if they're spotting the accelerations?"

"This has nothing to do with the accelerations," Melissa repeated.

"How can you be so certain?" Janice asked in a panic.

"I can't tell you that, but trust me," Melissa said. "It does have something to do with that girl, but not what you think. Nobody suspects you. In fact, you probably won't even have to talk to her."

"I don't know how you can say that," Janice said, pacing in anxiety. "Nobody knows who this is, why he's coming, or what criteria will be used to select employees for 'auditing' – whatever that is."

"Her name is Kimberly Scriver, she's from the Department of Health and Human Services, and she probably won't be interested in interviewing you," Melissa said.

Janice pulled up short and stared at Melissa. "How do you know that?"

"I can't tell you," Melissa repeated. "But those are the facts, so you can calm down. I expect she'll be here no more than a week. I can't guarantee you won't be called, but if you are, just answer her questions. If it'll make you comfortable, we can hold off the accelerations until she's gone."

"It would," Janice admitted.

"Speaking of which, I have this for you," Melissa said, pulling a small envelope out of her pocket and tipping something into her palm. Janice saw it was an XCV pin with two white stones embedded.

"We've never had anyone go directly from one to three without getting a two pin," Melissa said in a congratulatory tone as she undid Janice's pin from her collar and affixed the new one as if she was awarding a medal.

"Yeah," Janice said absently. "Melissa, I'm so nervous."

"I keep telling you, you've got nothing to worry about," Melissa assured her. "But there's one thing you might want to watch."

"What's that?" Janice asked anxiously.

"Ease off the sauce, especially if you have shift the next morning," Melissa admonished. "I can smell it all over you."

Later that morning, in an office in a small strip mall just north of Port Huron, two men walked into an office that had "Gerald K. Fitzgerald, Attorney at Law" emblazoned on the door. They presented their request to the receptionist, who buzzed the back office.

"Two guys from DHS to see you, Mr. Fitz."

"Thanks, Kelley. Be right out," came the answer. After a rather long wait, a thin man with wire-rimmed glasses and bushy brown hair came out. He shook the agents' hands with gusto and ushered them into his small conference room.

"Now," Fitz said as he sat down across from them. "How may I be of assistance?"

"Did you, this past Monday, file a transfer of deed with the register, placing property belonging to Mrs. Joanna Wilcox into a trust?" one of the agents asked in a severe tone.

Fitz blinked. "Are you asking me questions pertaining to one of my clients?"

"Yes," the agent affirmed.

"May I see your badges, please?" Fitz asked. The agents pulled out their ID wallets and handed them over. Fitz snapped pictures of them with his tablet, at the same time performing about a dozen signal scans of the chips embedded in them. Sam or Brady might be able to do something with the scan results. Then he tapped up an app and spoke into the tablet's camera, "Interview regarding the trust of Mrs. Joanna Wilcox," then set the tablet on a cradle, the camera pointed toward the men.

"Could you please repeat the question?" Fitz asked, nodding toward the tablet, so they did.

"Yes, I did. That being a matter of public record, Agent – ah – Sanderson."

"May I ask by what authority you filed that transfer?" Agent Sanderson said.

"You may certainly ask," Fitz said with a smile. He waited for a while in silence then shook his head. Dullards. "As the trustee, I filed on her behalf."

"May we see the authorization appointing you as trustee?" Agent Sanderson asked.

"Of course," Fitz said, tapping his tablet. "Kelley, could you bring in the Wilcox file?"

They waited in dead silence for what seemed an inordinate length of time. Fitz sat with a quiet smile on his face, offering neither small talk nor refreshments. Finally, Kelley appeared and placed a folder at Fitz's elbow. He flicked through the contents, extracted a letter, and laid it on the table in front of the agents, who scrutinized it carefully.

"This letter was signed last Thursday!" Agent Sanderson announced with glee. "Three days after she left the hospital!"

"I believe she mentioned being discharged from the hospital," Fitz said casually.

"We'd like to talk with Mrs. Wilcox," said the other agent.

"I'll be happy to convey your request, Agent – ah – Harris, but I can't guarantee it will be honored," Fitz answered.

"Why not?" Harris barked, but Sanderson intervened in a conciliatory tone.

"We just want to ask her a couple of questions. She's not in any trouble."

"That's good to hear," Fitz said. "However, in your excitement regarding the date on this letter you've overlooked the contents. Mrs. Wilcox has placed all her assets in a revocable trust and appointed me the trustee to address all external matters on her behalf. Simply put, she's elected to retire from public life. If you wish to write down your questions, I will present them to her, though I can't guarantee that she'll choose to answer them."

The agents looked at each other. "That – that wouldn't do," Agent Sanderson replied. "We need to speak to her directly."

"Is Mrs. Wilcox being charged with, or suspected of, engaging in some illegal activity?" Fitz asked calmly.

"No," Sanderson replied hastily. "We just want to talk to her."

"We've established that," Fitz said. "The question at hand is whether she wants to talk to you. The presumptive answer here is 'no', though again, I will happily convey the request."

"Look, we're from the federal government," began Agent Harris hotly, but Sanderson swiftly shut him down. Fitz just looked at him calmly for a minute before speaking.

"I understand. If Mrs. Wilcox is being charged with violation of a federal law, or being summoned as a witness in a federal case, please present the indictment or subpoena – I will ensure it is delivered to her with all dispatch. Otherwise, your contact with her remains at her discretion."

The agents looked at each other, stymied. "Look," Agent Sanderson offered. "It isn't even her we're interested in. We want to talk to – parties – involved with her departure from the hospital. Do you know anything about them?"

Fitz looked convincingly puzzled. "'Parties involved with her departure'? Do you mean the friend or friends who picked her up at the door?"

"Well – maybe," Sanderson conceded. "But we're more concerned with the parties inside the facility."

"'Inside'? You mean hospital staff?" Fitz asked. "I'm not sure I understand – surely you can speak with hospital staff at your leisure?"

"They may be staff," Sanderson said. "It seems there were some – irregularities – regarding her departure."

"Agent Sanderson, you surprise me," Fitz said with a straight face. "Are you implying that one of our medical facilities, in full compliance with all pertinent federal directives, could have irregularities in its procedures?"

"Look, we don't know how the old lady left the hospital," Agent Harris blurted out, clearly at the end of his patience. "How do we know she wasn't kidnapped? That's a crime."

"Indeed it is, though usually one investigated by local authorities," Fitz conceded. "However, in this case, you can set your concerns to rest. Mrs. Wilcox simply chose to stop receiving treatment and was discharged."

"Can you prove that?" Agent Harris rejoined hotly.

"In fact, I can," Fitz answered calmly, withdrawing another letter from the folder and placing it on the table beside the first.

"This is a witnessed and notarized letter from Mrs. Wilcox stating that she elected to receive no further care at that facility. It is dated last Thursday."

Again, the agents looked at each other in befuddlement. Agent Harris looked to be on the verge of saying something, but Sanderson quieted him.

"Clearly, we must consult with our legal staff," Sanderson said, rising. "May we take images of these documents?"

"Of course," Fitz replied.

"Thank you for your time," Agent Sanderson said while Harris busied himself taking the pictures. "We'll be back in touch."

"I'm sure you will," Fitz said genially. Once they were gone, he picked up his tablet and tapped out a message. That hadn't been as bad as Gil had warned him about – but it was certainly only the first attempt.

Brady was getting a little nervous, and he couldn't put his finger on exactly why. Since the snatch last week, where the cleanup operator had been flushed, they'd all laid low. Brady wasn't doing much more than was normal for his work, and staying well away from databases. But even so, he was still encountering odd things. Password changes on network devices. Remote sessions that would take just a little too long to fire up. Plus the uncanny, undefinable feeling that he wasn't alone as he prowled the networks and instances of the medical facilities – that someone was watching for him.

For his part, Ron Porcher was reasonably satisfied. Some of the low-level flags and tripwires he'd set were being triggered. No smoking guns just yet, but activity that was beyond normal operations and randomness. What little he was detecting indicated that his quarry might not be in the hospital at all – the threads seemed to run in the direction of the Regional Medical Administration facility.

As much as he longed to get more aggressive with his monitoring, Porcher knew that stepping up the activity now would risk betraying his presence. Best to be patient, difficult as that was, and wait for his quarry to come to him.

In the meantime, he'd refined his other queries and sent the reports on up the chain. The evidence was indisputable, and in plain sight if you knew where and how to look. Within a year of the pilot program's institution, there'd been a significant increase in Code 99 discharges at the participating facilities. He'd even spoken to some of the staff who had authorized the Code 99s – at least, according to the audit trail. They (of course) couldn't recall particulars, so invariably referred him back to the computer system – in other words, if the system said I did it, then I did it. He'd also cast his net more broadly and verified that, indeed, none of the cases who had been Code 99 discharged had ever sought medical care anywhere thereafter. Additionally, there were a significant number of elderly across the area who'd simply ceased going for medical care. No record of death, no services elsewhere that would indicate a move, they just stopped going to the doctor.

According to Porcher's loose calculations, the number of elderly who had thus vanished numbered well into the thousands, possibly as high as four thousand over the past two years. But people didn't just vanish. Those old people were somewhere.

And Porcher intended to find out where – and who was hiding them.

In an office in one of the innumerable glass-sided Bauhaus office buildings that dotted northern Virginia, Dr. Kevin Tasker slammed the file folder on his desk in fury. He'd spent the morning being briefed by his staff on the implications of the data that had been sent down from Michigan. They'd cross-matched it with other data sets and summarized the results. The evidence was clear and the conclusions were inescapable.

Damn them! It had been Tasker who'd originally sifted through the reams of economic, geographic, and demographic data and identified that corner of the nation as being ideal for the pilot program. He'd pushed for the funding and chosen the personnel. And when results had consistently fallen short of what the models had projected, he was the one who'd nearly lost his position.

Now, it appeared, it had not been his projections and efforts that had been at fault. The pilot had been derailed – sabotaged – by interfering parties who had no idea what they were meddling in. They might have set the country back by decades, perhaps endangering its very existence. Bastards! Self-righteous, intruding fools! Who did they think they were?

Tasker dropped into his chair and brooded on his injury. These self-appointed vigilantes had to be dealt with before they caused further damage. They were subversives, a shadow government accountable only to themselves, who played by their own rules. They were certainly guilty of violating federal protocols, and were probably providing medical care outside designated channels and smuggling pharmaceuticals as well. Who knew what else they were capable of? This was treason – this was insurrection – this was sedition – this was domestic terror, that's what it was.

He grabbed the phone and punched up a contact over at DHS. His staff was already following up what leads they had. Surely they'd ferret out something, and when they did, it would be the thread that would help unravel the whole cloth. They'd better be ready to move swiftly when they found that thread.

Time to see if the Fast Response Units at the new Fort Wayne Center were everything they were billed to be.

Barn Dance

Despite Melissa's assurances, Janice was one of the first to be summoned for an audit interview. A messenger found her on the floor during shift, informed her that she was wanted for an interview, and stayed with her until she wrapped up her work and came along. She was torn between panic and grim resignation, but there was little she could do, with the messenger walking beside her. She was taken right to the office door and left there. She knocked tentatively.

For all Janice's fears, the interview proved anticlimactic. Ms. Scriver was a short, somewhat stout woman with grey hair cut in a bob and a severe face. She had a thin-lipped mouth that neither smiled nor frowned, but briskly instructed in what she wished done. She interrogated Janice about the day she'd found the strange girl in the room, asking all manner of questions about the incident. Janice kept bracing for the worst question, which was what she'd been doing in the room in the first place, but that question never came. Ms. Scriver showed her the shot from the security camera at the main door which Janice had already seen, and Janice confirmed that it was the girl in question. She then asked many questions about who else had been around, and whether the girl had used any communications devices, and the like. Janice wasn't able to give her any good answers, but she didn't seem to expect her to. When it seemed that Janice had told all she knew, she was abruptly dismissed with an injunction not to discuss the interview with anyone. Janice found herself outside the office feeling surprised. Melissa had been right – the interview hadn't even come close to any of the topics she'd been dreading.

On Thursday afternoon Derek did a supply run for the farm, since he wouldn't be coming out on Friday. Dinner was the usual merry mayhem, and Derek ensured he had good directions to the dance site. Then he wandered out to drop in on Sam, who was busy with a metalworking project, so he got drawn into that. He got his first chance to do arc welding, brazing, and cutting, all under the supervision of a first-rate instructor. Derek was continually amazed at how adept and agile Sam was within the confines of his shop – swinging himself around by his cables and grips, hooking things with his cane, and flicking things down with his small whip. Sam's larger whip was woven of some kind of plastic wrapped around a core of flexible metal cable, but the smaller whip was shorter and more like a buggy whip, with a springy handle about eighteen inches long topped with a foot-long cord. With this he could extend his reach to nab tools from across a work table, or deftly pull items down from high shelves, or give Derek's hands a warning smack when they too-eagerly reached into a danger zone. Derek headed home rather late, having put in a full workday on top of the one at the hospital, but happier and more self-confident than he'd ever been.

The next day Derek, messaged Janice to ensure they were all set for the dance that night. She was, but asked him a question for which he was utterly unprepared: what should she wear? He'd planned to wear his jeans, boots, and a shirt with some decoration about the shoulders that he'd picked up at the tractor place. Thinking back, he realized that most of the women out at the farm wore dresses to social events like chapel. So he advised Janice to wear a dress, only to be told that she didn't own many dresses and maybe she shouldn't come. This puzzled Derek, who'd been given to understand that women loved dances of all types. He messaged back encouraging her to wear whatever and come anyway.

When Derek picked Janice up after work, he understood a little better why she'd been concerned. She was wearing snug pants and a tank top with thin straps and sparkles. The outfit looked more suited to a nightclub or cocktail party than a country dance, but he complimented her on it regardless. He was concerned about her – she still wore that harried look about her eyes. He hoped a little music and dancing would lighten her spirits.

Derek tried to chatter lightheartedly as they drove out through the country, but Janice seemed subdued. She told him about the personnel audits, of which he hadn't heard. He asked her how hers had gone, and she couldn't go into much detail, but allowed as how it hadn't been too bad. But the prospect of the interviews hung like a pall over the whole hospital. Derek wondered if that was what was so weighing on Janice's spirits.

"Who did you say was doing these interviews?" Derek asked.

"Health and Human Services," Janice answered.

"Odd," Derek mused. "Wonder what they're looking for?"

"That's the big question," Janice said. "Nobody knows, but everyone's nervous as hell."

By the time they reached the address Linda had provided, Derek was very hungry. This was clearly the place, a large farm with many outbuildings that was already crowded with cars.

"Are we late?" Janice asked as she surveyed the dozens of vehicles.

"No – it's kind of an open format," Derek explained. "You come and go as you please. People have been arriving since about four, bringing food to the dinner tent. Most families are having dinner here, and the ones with small children head home early. Come on – I'm starving, and there's supposed to be at least one pig roasting."

"Sounds delicious," Janice said in a flat voice.

They walked through the farm past groups of people chatting merrily. It was clear where the dance action was going to be – a large concrete-floored pole barn was off to the left, brightly lit and with all doors slid wide open. Bales of straw were stacked about, and music could already be heard coming from inside.

The dinner area was also clearly visible – an open pavilion covering long tables groaning with dishes and baskets. What looked like two fifty-five-gallon drums on their sides stood on legs nearby, smoking and being tended by chefs, and the aroma wafting from them was heavenly. There was no order or protocol – one just grabbed some silverware, filled a plate, and found a place at one of the tables littered about. The chefs were bringing fresh platters of roast pork just as Janice and Derek were passing through, and advised them on which sauces were best to apply. They got a couple of beers from a cooler and sat on some bales. The ravenous Derek was in heaven – he'd heaped his plate and every bite was delicious. Janice had been more sparing, and picked at her food while looking about nervously. She wrinkled her nose when the wind shifted about to carry some odors from the clearly-occupied stable off to their left.

"Is there some kind of – program?" Janice asked.

"Linda said the main dancing begins about 7 p.m., which is in about ten minutes," Derek explained. "Have you tried this cornbread? It's fantastic."

"No, thanks," Janice said. "How many people do you think are here?"

"Supposedly it's families from five counties, so there could be quite a few – possibly a couple hundred. There's certainly food enough for them all, and Linda said there'd be a dessert tent somewhere. Oh, sounds like something's starting."

The music from the pole barn concluded to applause and whistles. People began to tidy away their dishes and head for the barn, so Derek and Janice followed. Inside the huge structure were so many people that Derek wondered if his estimate might be low. There was a stage area for the band with a microphone in front of it, and bales piled about the edges. People were milling about and chatting merrily. Derek felt a little overwhelmed, and Janice stood close by, looking about nervously.

"Derek! You made it!" came a delightfully familiar voice from behind. He turned to see Felicity with a smiling young man in tow.

"We did! Been looking forward to it all week," Derek forced out, smiling at them both. "Felicity, this is my friend Janice, who works at the hospital."

"Janice! How delightful to meet you!" Felicity said warmly, taking both of Janice's hands. "I'm so glad you could make it. This is my friend Chuck Garrity from over by Caro. Chuck, this is Derek Stevens, a friend of ours, and his friend Janice."

Chuck removed his hat and actually bowed to Janice, who stared at him, amazed. Then he gripped Derek's hand and greeted him so warmly that Derek almost forgave him for escorting Felicity.

"So, this is our first time at one of these," Derek admitted. "We just grabbed dinner – what comes next?"

"Well," Felicity began, but just then someone walked up to the microphone and called "good evening" several times until the hubbub died down. The guy welcomed everyone in the name of a couple families that Derek didn't know, and thanked yet another family for hosting the celebration. He said a couple words about the harvest, which had apparently been good, and suggested they all join in a prayer of thanks. At this the room grew quite still, the silence disturbed only by those who'd been seated rising to their feet and the men removing their hats. The guy offered a brief but eloquent prayer. From the corner of his eye Derek could see that Chuck – and every other man in sight – took all this quite seriously.

The guy finished to a murmured chorus of 'amen', and the men all put their hats back on. Then he introduced someone whose name appeared to be 'Chigger', and the place broke into raucous applause and cheers.

"'Chigger'?" Derek asked Felicity, who was fairly bouncing with excitement.

"I know," she replied with a wry smile. "Musicians always seem to go for the strange nicknames, don't they? But he's the best caller in the Thumb – it'll be a fun evening."

"What's a caller?" Derek asked.

"Someone who calls square dances," Felicity explained. "Line dance, contra dances, and the like. They all have someone calling the steps in time to the music."

"Y'know," Derek admitted shyly. "Janice and I don't know how to dance like that."

"That's okay," Felicity assured him. "Chigger's a good instructor, and everybody assumes the first dances will draw plenty of novices. Listen!"

Chigger had finished his greetings and now called out, "How many here tonight have rarely or never square danced?" Derek was surprised at how many hands went up, including his and Janice's. Chigger then invited all these onto the floor for the first simple dance.

"Oh, let's find two other couples and dance the first set together, shall we?" Felicity gushed, seizing Derek's hand. "Chuck, you don't mind, do you?"

"Not in the slightest," Chuck replied courteously, turning to Janice and bowing again. "If I may have the honor."

Janice looked flustered, but could hardly refuse, and took the proffered arm with a blush. Derek offered his arm to Felicity and they proceeded toward the dance floor together.

"So this is the custom?" Derek asked. "You dance with different people than you came with?"

"Oh, yes," Felicity explained. "It's all part of the fun, meeting new people. I promised Chuck the first dance, but since you're guests, hospitality comes first. I'll dance with him later."

"It's very gracious of you both," Derek said. "I think Janice is feeling rather out of place."

The 'set' went rather well, with Chigger giving nice, slow instructions and the more experienced dancers demonstrating patiently for the beginners. As Derek began to shed his nervousness and get his feet under him, he found himself being almost swept along by the lively music. He'd never been much of a dancer, but the thump of the drums and the lilt of the fiddles almost had his feet moving by themselves. He was nearly out of breath when the music finished to general applause.

Then followed a bit of bustling about as everyone arranged for a reel. In this dance, men and women formed two lines up the middle of the floor, facing each other. Felicity ended up somewhere else, but Derek was happy to face Janice, who still looked nervous.

This dance was also simple, though Derek was glad to see other rookies bumbling from time to time, to general laughter and encouragement. After that dance was finished, he spotted the Schaeffers, who'd just arrived, and took Janice over to meet them. Martha was anxious to get on the floor, so as the squares were forming up, she hooked Derek's arm and dragged him out.

Derek was glad that Martha was experienced, because this dance was faster and had less coaching. He was still feeling clumsy, but the music was carrying him, and the girls in the square would nudge and steer him at the proper times. At the end of the dance, the band and caller took a break, to Martha's disappointment and Derek's relief. No wonder these country folk stayed so fit and trim – not only was their work physically demanding, their recreation was exhilarating! Ducking outside to cool off, he spotted Cletus and Philip by a large cooler of water. They drew him a big cup and asked him how he was holding up. He just panted in reply.

"You just wait until the later dances," Cletus ribbed him. "If you're just learning, I'll give you two, maybe three more sets before you're out of your league. Gets to the final dances and most of us just stand by watching in amazement."

Only then did Derek notice that he'd lost track of Janice. It was okay – everyone seemed to mill around at these things. When the musicians reassembled, Cletus introduced him to a pleasant girl named Emily with whom he danced the next set. Following this was another contra dance where he ended up across from an older woman who was an excellent dancer. He kept an eye out for Felicity, whom he noticed was dancing merrily with several different guys, all of whom were clearly better dancers than Derek. He tried, almost successfully, not to feel jealous.

The contra dance left Derek completely winded, so he skipped the next set to duck outside and cool off. He opened a nearby cooler to find it full of iced beer, one of which he cracked open as he plunked down on a straw bale, trying to catch his breath.

"You Derek?" came a voice from over his shoulder. A bit startled, Derek turned to see a beefy looking guy with an easy smile who looked to be about his age.

"Yeah," Derek replied, puzzled.

"I'm Gary," the guy said, holding out his hand. He had a firm handshake. "Mind if I join you?"

"Not at all," Derek replied, still mystified. Gary fished a beer from the cooler and sat down on the bale beside him.

"I – ah – couldn't help but notice," Gary began hesitantly, as if approaching the topic obliquely. "That you've been watching Felicity a fair amount."

"Yeah," Derek replied slowly, his hackles rising a bit. Who was this guy? He glanced nervously at Gary's broad arms and thick neck, and looked quickly around to see if anyone was near.

Gary picked up on Derek's nervousness and chuckled. "Relax," he grinned. "You're in no trouble. You'd have to be blind in one eye and couldn't see out of the other not to notice

Felicity. She's the prettiest girl in the region, and every guy from Richmond to Port Austin knows it. The only thing like competition she's got is Kitty Jenkins from Deckerville, who knows she's beautiful and thinks everyone else should know, too. Felicity, now, she doesn't just have a pretty face – she has a loving heart and a kind spirit and a gentle demeanor toward all. She's beautiful to the core."

"Yeah," Derek agreed, appreciating the assessment but wondering where this was going.

"Me, now, I'm her first cousin, so I stand a bit too close," Gary said. "But if I wasn't, you could be certain I'd be lining up like all the rest. It's a testimony to your good taste that you appreciate Felicity – but I'm warning you that you have a lot of company."

"That's not surprising," Derek said.

"I thought it might save some confusion and possibly heartache if I explained how things work out here," Gary went on.

"What do you mean, 'how things work'?" Derek asked.

"Between guys and gals," Gary explained. "Felicity, now – in fact, most gals out here – won't be anybody's girlfriend."

"They won't?"

"Nope. They don't do 'relationships'. If they're interested in marriage, they'll allow a suitor to court them, but until then, they'll just be friends," Gary said.

"Really?" Derek asked.

"Yup," Gary affirmed. "Saves a lot of trouble. If you wanted to court Felicity – not saying you do, just making an example – you'd ask her if she'd let you court her. If she said yes, then you'd go to her parents and ask permission to court her. If they granted it, you'd court her with an eye to marriage. If things didn't proceed along those lines, the courtship would be broken off with no hard feelings."

"I see," Derek said. He'd never thought about marrying, but he could see how this would make sense, especially in this intriguing subculture.

"Simple, really," Gary said, then he looked at Derek almost apologetically. "Of course, you'd have a tougher row to hoe with almost any girl."

"Why's that?"

"Well," Gary responded reluctantly. "Nothing against you personally, of course, 'cause you seem like a square guy, but you don't have any family around here, do you?"

"No, I don't," Derek admitted. "I'm from out of state."

"I'm not saying it's hopeless, just harder," Gary said. "If a suitor comes to their door, most parents want to know what family he's from, and if they're the right kind of folk."

"Well, I doubt mine would qualify," Derek said.

"Again, I'm not saying it's hopeless, just harder," Gary reassured him, rising to go. "Well, that's all I had to say. Just wanted to explain the ropes to you, in case you wanted to take things further than a dance set, with Felicity or any other girl."

"Thanks," Derek said sincerely, gripping Gary's hand. "Thanks, I really appreciate it."

Gary wandered off, leaving Derek to think. Marriage. He'd never considered it, but had to admit that if anyone could make him do so, it would be Felicity. But then he thought glumly about all the guys between Richmond and Port Austin, most of whom probably came from solid and well-known families, and were certainly better dancers. What chance did he stand? Best not to dwell on that or he'd get depressed. He finished off his beer and headed back in. It sounded like the set was just wrapping up.

Back inside, the caller and musicians were breaking up for another rest. But instead of everyone scattering, one of the musicians set a chair on the floor by a couple of microphone stands. She had a violin, and sat in the chair while Harmony and Felicity stepped up to the microphones. The woman tapped a count and then started with her violin, drawing out a beautiful but plaintive melody that filled the barn. Then the sisters joined in with a crystalline harmony that soared to the rafters, transfixing everyone in the place.

Derek barely heard the lyrics. They had something to do with holidays at home, and a brother leaving, and a sick grandmother. But the lyrics weren't the main thing – the themes and melody were what touched Derek to his depths. He felt yearnings for things he'd never had, and longings more precious than anything he'd ever possessed. He stood still as stone, tears streaming down his face. He'd trade the entire sterile wasteland that was his life for the briefest glimpse, the lightest whisper, of the world which that song provided a hint of. He'd been searching his whole life, never realizing it, for whatever that melody captured, whatever it reflected. He could not bear that it continue; he could not bear that it cease.

But cease it did. The final strains from the violin hung quivering in the air as the girls touched the closing notes. There was a moment's silence before the barn erupted with thunderous applause. Derek did not join in. He watched as the violinist rose and bowed while the Peterson sisters curtsied, then he wandered away into the night. All his concerns, including Felicity, were forgotten. He found a dark and quiet corner, well away from the lights and cheery bustle, and sat gazing at the stars, weeping and pondering his life.

Janice was trying to find a corner in which to hide, but there weren't any. The people were everywhere, laughing, chatting, hanging out. She eventually settled for sitting on a bale by a door and trying to blend into the background.

She should never have come. She'd known that from the moment she realized she had no dresses. Oh, she had that stupid bridesmaid one with the fussy back, but she wouldn't wear that, and all her other dresses were short cocktail numbers that showed too much of her thighs. That would never do, under the circumstances. Derek had made light of it, so she'd worn this party outfit. Just like a guy. When they'd arrived, she'd realized with horror that *every other woman* was wearing a dress. She was the only woman at the dance – possibly for twenty miles around – in pants. Not only that, but a spaghetti strap tank top that looked totally out of place. She'd been so mortified that she'd been tempted to go sit in the car, but then Derek's friend and her dancing partner had showed up, looking like they'd stepped out of a Norman Rockwell painting, and dragged them out on the floor to do that stupid country dance. And then – *then*, before she'd had a chance to slip away – everybody had lined up for *another* stupid country dance. Only this one had entailed parading down between two lines of dancers – essentially everyone in the place – so they all could see how freakish and out-of-place she was. She'd wanted to die.

They were watching her, she just knew. They were whispering about the oddity, the misfit, the woman with bare shoulders who wears pants. She'd seen a few of them glancing in her direction. Why had she come? She put her head on her arms and willed herself to be invisible.

Derek didn't know how long he sat there gazing at the stars, beholding the vastness and majesty of creation. He felt himself opening up and expanding in response, the long-closed drawers and cupboards of his heart swinging wide to reveal – nothing. Empty dustiness was all his life had been. He'd gone to school to get a good job. He did the job to earn money. He spent the money on diversions to distract himself from the hollow darkness within. Games and shows and concerts – anything so that he didn't have to sit in that empty apartment that only reminded him that he was as empty as it was.

This sky, though – this was worth looking at. His mind knew that it was mostly emptiness as well, but it was a rich emptiness, a magnificent immensity that overwhelmed with its greatness. If he could pour himself out into that, he would. That would be a fate worth being unmade for. If he had to be empty, let him be caught up in that glorious expanse and dissipated across the galaxies.

But – suddenly, but with sure certainty – he knew that dissipation was not what he was made for. Void might call to void as he gazed up at the starry vastness, but that end was not for him. The glory of the skies might be their immense openness, but his void was made to be filled. But with what? He thought over the past few weeks, as he'd been drawn into the family life of the farm. He had an odd image of himself as a hollow plastic mannequin clunking around the house amidst real, flesh-and-blood people. ("Hollow here. Listen – you can hear it if you knock on my chest.") They were not hollow. They did not live to fill their hours with distractions. There was something there, something that seemed to whisk out of sight whenever you looked for it, something that ducked behind the curtains or chuckled from beneath the couch, something that filled the house with life.

The song had captured that elusive something, causing it to pierce his heart so swiftly that he knew it only in its departure. He was left with only loss, but a loss whose sweetness and poignancy outweighed all the empty distractions with which he'd filled his hours. Even now, the blessed yearning was fading from his mind, but he knew he would take that longing over every sensory pleasure the world had to offer.

He realized that his legs were starting to cramp and he was getting chilly. He felt like the sky had said all it could to him, so he levered himself to his feet and headed back to the barn – evoking a curious mental picture of the cupboard doors and empty drawers of his soul, somewhere in the center of his chest, swinging and banging as he walked along.

As Derek entered the warmth of the barn, he saw that the musicians were reassembling. He also saw something that he hadn't before: at the far end of the barn, set apart from the general bustle around the dance floor, were two elderly couples. One he recognized from the breakfast at the farm the other weekend – it was Grandma and Grandpa. The other couple, who had darker hair, were about the same age. They were back in a little alcove formed by bales, with the mothers enthroned on chairs and the fathers standing or leaning on bales behind them. They were chatting merrily among themselves, but every so often a couple would approach them. Usually it was a young couple, and the man would bow and the lady would curtsey, and they would speak to the elderly folk. There were smiles and handshakes and laughter, then the young couple would again bow and curtsey and move on.

Suddenly Derek realized what he was seeing: partners, probably intended for marriage, were being introduced to the clan matriarchs and patriarchs. Not just partners, though – as he watched a couple came forward to present a baby, who was laid on one of the grandmother's laps with much excitement and joy. He felt like he had stepped back centuries – millennia – in time, yet it was fitting and proper here, too. The ancient phrase 'paying respects' came to mind, as if respect was a debt that was owed to these venerable couples who had sacrificed so much for their descendants. They had earned respect, and now it was being paid to them. Once, he might have scorned this as an empty and archaic ritual, but now he saw it as a proper and suitable expression. It was like – like – the musicians on the platform playing a set, or the dancers on the floor twirling and circling under the caller's guidance. It was freedom within order. Nobody was forcing those couples to present themselves, but it was fitting and proper that it should be done. This was a way of seeing things that Derek had never considered before.

Speaking of order, Derek noticed that the musicians were tuning up and some – not many – dancers were making their way toward the center of the floor. The room also seemed to be segregating, with the ladies moving toward the far half of the barn and the men gravitating toward the near half. Within that, people were sorting out, with some forming a great circle with women on the far side and men on the near side. In the center of the circle were forming four squares of eight dancers each. Most of these were middle aged couples, but Derek saw Felicity in there – with yet another guy. Everyone else lined the fringes of the barn in a wide, loose ring.

"I take it this is one of the dances I was warned about earlier?" Derek asked a fellow who stood nearby.

"Yup," the guy grinned. "If you know what you're doing, you might line up with the circle there – they do some nice line steps. But the squares are the very finest, competition grade dancers."

"I think I'll stay out here," Derek said.

"Yeah, we clap and stomp and look on in awe," the fellow laughed.

Chigger was joined at the mics by another caller, a bright blue-eyed woman with a flowery dress and a straw hat. Chigger said a few words about the dance, then the musicians started up a lively base tune. Both callers got the bystanders like Derek clapping and stomping in time with the music. Once that rhythm was in place, the lady caller began a singsong chant to which the inner circle of dancers responded. This was something to watch in itself – the dancers stepped and turned in graceful unison, the guys sometimes slapping their boots and the girls twirling their skirts.

Once the line dance was well along, the band added a vigorous tune atop what they'd been playing and Chigger began calling the square dance. Now Derek was truly amazed as the dancers in the squares stepped and twirled in response to Chigger's rapid-fire, almost inaudible calling. Derek had never seen such grace and precision, all done while the line dancers kept perfect pace with their caller. He just raised his eyebrows and looked at the guy, who grinned back.

On the ladies' side, Janice had seen when the dance was setting up that it would be more conspicuous for her to remain sitting on her bale than to stand with the other girls. Of course, that eventually required her to clap and stomp, which she did grudgingly. Hopefully when this dance was over she'd locate Derek and find out if he'd had enough of this yet.

Grace was only along as a driver. She normally loved the autumn dance, but she'd had a hard day and needed to be up early tomorrow. But she'd agree to drive Keith, who'd wanted to come, and Mom, who was *of course* wanted for the band, besides accompanying the duet she had been rehearsing with the Peterson sisters for weeks. But Grace had made both of them promise they'd head out right after this dance. She stood on the fringes, clapping with the rest, loving the music and appreciating the dancing but dreading the long drive home.

Grace casually glanced around to see who she could recognize. She looked to her right and gasped sharply. Abruptly she stepped back behind a bale, to the surprise of her neighbor.

"Grace, what's – " the neighbor began, but Grace motioned her to silence.

"Judy, listen – don't make a fuss about it, but glance down to the right. See the girl in black pants and tank top?"

"The one with the reddish-brown hair? Yeah, she'd kind of hard to miss," Judy said.

"Is she looking this way?" Grace asked.

"No, not particularly," Judy replied. "She's looking all around – she seems kind of bored."

"Does it seem like she spotted me?"

"Hard to tell, but I don't think so. Grace, what's this about?" Judy asked.

"I can't tell you, Judy," Grace replied. "Do you know if Gil is here? Or Ruth?"

"I think I saw Jan around, so Gil is here somewhere. Why?"

"Listen, find Gil, tell him to meet me out behind the silos. I have to disappear."

"Grace, what's all this – " Judy began, but Grace cut her off again.

"I'll explain what I can later, Jude – just do it, please, as quickly as you can. And keep an eye on that girl!" Grace backed out of the barn and took a circuitous route to the silos. Shortly afterwards, the dance broke up to cheering and applause, which made Judy's job easier – she just started passing the word through the crowd that she was looking for Gil. He was found within five minutes.

Janice was glad when the clapping and stomping ended, and began to work her way across the barn in search of Derek. She found him by following the crowd out one of the barn doors to where the dessert tent was located. People were crowding around the laden tables, and Derek was standing by a water cooler chatting with some guy and munching cookies.

"Hey, there you are," Derek hailed her. "I was wondering where you'd gotten to. Having fun? How'd you like that dance? Wasn't that something?"

"Yeah, something," Janice said. "Look, Derek – "

"Oh, this is Mike. Mike, Janice. She works at the hospital, too. Mike was helping me keep time there. Hey, you've got to try these brownies, if there are any left – "

"No, thanks," Janice replied. "Derek, have you had enough? Because I worked a full day and am getting kind of tired – and I have a headache."

"What? Oh, yeah," Derek responded, glancing at the time. "It is getting a little late, and I'm tired, too. I guess the dancing from here on is kind of intricate, so maybe we beginners better call it a night. Let me hunt down Kent and Linda to thank them for inviting us."

But at that moment Kent was joining Gil behind the silos where Grace was waiting.

"Gil, she's here," Grace blurted out. "Right in the barn – I saw her."

"Who's here?" Gil asked.

"The girl who walked into the room," Grace explained. "The nurse with the needle. From the day I got flushed. She's here, at the dance."

"What – are you sure?" Gil asked.

"Positive. I got a good look at her, and clearly remember her face. She's easy to spot – she's wearing black pants and a tank top with sequins."

"Wait a minute," Kent interrupted. "Black pants? Are you talking about Janice?"

"Who's Janice?" Grace asked.

"Derek's guest," Kent said. "He brought her over and introduced her. Later Linda said she felt sorry for the girl, because she'd stick out like a sore thumb, being the only woman in pants."

"Sounds like her," Grace said. "Reddish-brown hair, pale complexion, just a little taller than me?"

"Sounds right," Kent replied.

"How does Derek know this girl?" Gil asked.

"He works with her," Kent said, then paused. "At the hospital."

Blasted Heath

Derek spent a pensive Saturday tidying his apartment. He did his laundry and, for a change, folded it and put it away instead of leaving it in baskets. Rather than eating his lunch out of the wrapper while standing over the sink, he ate it off a plate using silverware seated at the table, after which he washed all the dishes and put them away. In the course of his tidying he found a book he'd never finished, so he spent the remainder of the afternoon reading – something he hadn't done for pleasure in years. He enjoyed it immensely, and resolved to get back into the habit. When the time came, he drove over to pick up Janice and thence toward Flint.

Melissa was already at the gathering site, briefing Logan, which was never one of her favorite tasks.

"So – how's little Janice doing?" Logan asked, sipping his beer.

"She's doing well – three so far, and it's starting to look like she'll be good for at least one a week," Melissa replied.

"You still feeding them that line about how the serum just neutralizes the medication and lets the case go naturally?"

"I tell them whatever helps them become more productive," Melissa said. "And speaking of productivity, you got my message about the guest she's bringing, right?"

"Yeah, yeah," Logan said impatiently, glancing at his phone. "So what is this guy, a male nurse?"

"I guess he's a physician's assistant by certification, but he's the deputy medical examiner for the county. He works in the morgue," Melissa explained.

"The morgue?" Logan asked skeptically. "What good does that do us?"

"Think ahead, numbskull," Melissa shot back. "He performs all the autopsies and effectively fills out the death certs for any deaths discovered by first responders. If we had him, he'd be worth five nurses."

275

"All right," Logan said grudgingly. "Does he like boys or girls?"

"Girls, I'm assuming," Melissa said uncertainly.

"Better be right," Logan warned. "I'll contact Ashley – she knows how to handle guys."

"Where are you going to be?"

"Working on a project visiting from Saginaw," Logan said smugly, pocketing his phone. "She was here last time. None too bright, but decent-looking with a fantastic rack. I'm giving her a little private attention."

"Bastard," Melissa muttered toward his back as he wandered off toward the lounges.

When Derek picked Janice up, she looked a little better rested but still uneasy. As they drove west, Derek asked a few questions about the nature of the organization. Janice started gushing about how it was this forward-thinking group that understood current issues and wanted to get out ahead of problems. She explained how they had the social times for networking, but also how they conducted research and offered seminars. She went on in this vein for most of the drive. To Derek, it sounded as if she was trying to convince herself as much as him. In the end, he was left as unclear about the organization as he'd been before.

"An interesting-looking building," Derek commented as they pulled into the parking lot.

"It used to be a church," Janice said. "They got it for a song because it was standing empty."

For some reason, this made Derek a little sad. "What happens now?"

"Well, there's a reception, with drinks and snacks, and then a talk – sort of an informational/motivational time – and then some more socializing afterwards, with dancing and such," Janice explained.

"Gee, dancing two nights in a row," Derek grinned. "We're turning into real high-livers." Internally, he was dreading the reception – he'd never been good at such things. Maybe he could find a quiet corner where he could sit and chat with Janice.

They entered, and Janice, with her pin, just tapped her hospital ID on the reader. Derek swiped his driver's license and was handed a yellow cord. They moved into the mingling area. "If you're hungry, I could get us some nibbles," Janice offered.

"Sure," Derek said, looking around at the people chatting in little groups. Janice headed for the food line while he looked for somewhere to perch.

"Ooh, a guest," came a voice at his elbow. He turned to see a young woman in a tight-fitting, low cut outfit. She stepped right up to him, almost brushing his arm with her breasts. "Welcome to our little gathering."

"Uh – thanks," Derek replied, stepping back a little. "We – ah – I'm here with a friend, who went to get some food."

"We're glad to have you," the girl said, fixing him with an intimate gaze. "I'm Ashley."

"I'm Derek," he replied, holding out his hand. She held it for longer than necessary, tracing her fingernails across his palm as she withdrew.

"Can I get you a drink, Derek?" Ashley purred. "And your friend, too, of course."

"Ah – sure," Derek said. "A couple of beers, thanks."

Shortly thereafter, Janice returned with plates, and Derek was just telling her about the woman he'd met, when Ashley herself returned with the beers. She nodded when introduced to Janice, but almost plastered herself against Derek, to his discomfort and Janice's infuriation. They found a spot to sit, where Ashley sat beside Derek with her thigh up against his, gazing at him and asking him all manner of personal questions.

When the signal came for the talk, Ashley looped her arm in Derek's and started walking in, clearly intending to sit with them, or at least with Derek. He didn't know what to do. This was unique in his experience – he'd never had to deal with a clinging woman before. He didn't want to tell her bluntly to go away, because he was a guest and she was free to go wherever she wished, but she was assuming an intimacy that wasn't appropriate. He could tell that Janice was fuming, but she probably didn't know what to do, either. If Ashley thought she was being seductive, she was greatly mistaken. In comparison to Felicity's wholesome beauty, or even Martha's fresh young prettiness, Ashley's heavily made up visage nearly revolted Derek. He almost felt sorry for her – her eyes had a flatness to them, and the stylized enthusiasms of her speech sounded like she was reciting lines rather than conversing.

For her part, Janice was nearly boiling over. She had no idea who this floozie was, moving in and flashing her cleavage at Derek, but she resented being treated like she wasn't even there. Why didn't Derek tell her to buzz off? They made their way into the auditorium where Derek let Janice sit first so he could sit on one side of her, without Ashley between them. Of course, Ashley sat on his other side and laid her arm on the armrest in such a way that her fingertips brushed the top of Derek's thigh.

The MC greeted everyone and made some announcements, then asked the guests to stand, which Derek did. When he sat back down, Janice noticed that Ashley had insinuated her arm inside his. Janice tried to think of other things – it wasn't like she had any claim on Derek – but her frustration kept intruding. She looked across the room for a familiar face, then realized that she didn't know anyone. Unless she spotted Melissa or Kendra, the only person she knew here was Logan, and he was nowhere in sight. She might be a member by virtue of her initiation, but socially she was a stranger.

A guy stepped up to give the talk. It wasn't Charon, and Janice settled in to try to attend to him. She tried to muster the enthusiasm she'd once felt for the vision of the group. She tried to catch the spirit, the camaraderie. She tried to ignore the fact that Ashley was now caressing the inside of Derek's thigh and whispering intimacies in his ear.

She failed at all of these.

It had been a difficult day for the leaders back at Rivendell. Most of it had been spent being briefed by Sam on his espionage project at the old factory. During this, Kent, Gil, and Ruth often glanced at each other, clearly wishing that Sam would clear these little initiatives with others first, but they all knew he had a special status. Technically he wasn't under anyone's authority, and though he cooperated readily, he knew it was usually easier to get forgiveness than permission.

But there was no denying that the videos Sam had gathered were valuable intelligence, even if they were distressing to watch. They went over them several times and discussed the implications, most of which were grim. Even when carefully followed, all their precautionary protocols could only hope to deflect casual detection. A focused search, especially by an entity with the resources of the federal government, would sooner or later succeed. They began discussing the various contingency plans they'd drawn up for evacuating the ranches and moving the guests.

Halfway through the day, their morale took another hit when they got a call from Fitz reporting that his office had been broken into sometime early Saturday morning. It had been a sophisticated job – the alarm had been disabled – and a few things had been smashed to make it look like clumsy burglary, but they'd taken all his paper records.

Of course, something like this had been expected, and all records pertaining to Mrs. Wilcox and any other guests had long since been removed to safe locations and any electronic files scrubbed. The 'burglars' would spend their time sifting through records of trusts and accounts for long-dead clients, but it was a frightening reminder of what they were facing.

"And Mrs. Wilcox got away safely, correct?" Fitz asked.

"Yes," Gil assured him. "She was moved to Northfarthing a couple of days ago, and we initiated the cutover then."

"Good. Just be sure I get that paperwork, because I think I'm going to need it," Fitz replied.

With one thing and another, it was evening before they got around to discussing the disturbing incident at the dance the prior evening.

"And Grace has no doubt this was the same woman?" Ruth asked.

"None," Kent assured her. "She was able to get a good, clear look. The memory of the flush is still vivid in her mind. Plus, her description during the debriefing exactly matches the woman that Linda and I met. We also know that she works at the hospital."

"So," Gil said, "if we know that this is the same woman, that raises the question: why did Derek bring one of their operatives to one of our events?"

"Rather, did Derek bring a party he *knew* was an operative to one of our events?" Kent corrected.

"Kent, this isn't personal," Gil replied. "I know you like Derek. I do, too – a lot. But we have to examine objective facts. How much does Derek know about our operations?"

"Not many details," Kent replied. "Just last weekend we gave him the broad overview because he was noticing too many oddities. He's smart and observant, and he's been getting around with Sam. I don't know what Sam may have spilled, but he's pretty discreet."

"Okay," Gil said. "Someone has to play devil's advocate here, so it looks like it's me. Making no assumptions about Derek's motives or character, and making no hypotheses about anything, let's look at the sequence of events.

"We first come into contact with Derek in the aftermath of a suspicious death, which looks like a field kill. He starts coming to visit, and shortly thereafter we have the first flush we've ever had. He starts noticing things, and gets the operation broadly explained to him, and the following week the hospital announces a personnel audit by HHS. He shows up at one of our events with someone known to be one of their operatives. That's a disturbing number of coincidences."

"It's also patent nonsense." Kent laughed. "Any theories spun from that would have holes big enough to drive a truck through. We encountered Derek in conjunction with John's death because *he* was suspicious, and wanted to call our attention to facts his superiors were hushing up. As far as the flush – I hardly need to tell you how tight operational security is around those. Almost nobody beyond the team knows when a snatch is going down – how could Derek possibly know? And that personnel audit at the hospital may have been announced last week, but that would mean it had been being planned well beforehand. It just doesn't hold water!"

"We know all that, Kent," Gil replied. "And nobody is accusing Derek of anything or trying to build a case against him. I'm just trying to assess risk. We have enough risk all around us.

We need to evaluate if, for whatever reason, having Derek around increases our risk."

"I'll buy that," Kent conceded.

"Do we know where he is, and what he's doing?" Ruth asked.

"You mean – today?" Kent said.

"Yes," Ruth replied. "This is the first weekend in several he hasn't been out here. We know he was at the dance with this woman last night. Do we know where he is today?"

"When Sam disabled the built-in locator ability of his phone, did he plant some of our custom apps on it?" Gil asked.

"He usually does," Kent said.

"Including our locator program?"

"Don't know," Kent replied.

"Why don't you check?" Gil asked. As Kent pulled out his tablet and tapped up the program, Gil went on. "We have word that they're having one of their rallies this evening."

Kent busied himself with the tablet for a minute. "Derek's phone is responding," he said, then a minute later. "It's showing his location in Burton. Just east of Flint."

Janice had slid down as far in her seat as she could, and sat with her arms crossed, staring at her feet. Whoever this speaker was, he wasn't anywhere near as good as Charon. He was droning on about moral order, and how different social orders called for different social norms, but he was doing it like a college lecturer rather than a motivator. Janice could sense that other listeners were growing restless and impatient for the party portion of the evening to commence.

To Janice's left, Ashley was still clinging to Derek, who seemed to be wearying of it. A couple times he'd physically removed her hand from his leg, and he'd shot Janice a couple of embarrassed and apologetic glances. Janice knew it wasn't his fault, but it was still hard to be patient. It seemed that Ashley was not to be deterred no matter how often she was rebuffed. Even now, she was pressing against Derek's arm and leaning her head on his shoulder.

The droning speaker finally ended to polite applause, and everyone stood to head for the exits. Of course, Ashley wanted to drag Derek away, but he stalled long enough to ensure Janice was coming along. They made their way out to the lobby, where people were already starting to get drinks and break up into their little groups. Ashley, holding tight to Derek's arm, seemed like she was almost frog-marching him toward the corridor where the lounges lay.

"Wait!" Janice called sharply, confused. "You can't take him back there!"

"Who are you to be making up rules?" Ashley spat back over her shoulder.

"But – I didn't make that up," Janice cried. "He's a guest! He can't go back there!" People about were starting to look at them, and one of the guys from the security table was bustling over.

"He can go anywhere he wants, bitch!" Ashley snapped, clinging possessively to Derek's arm.

"Now, now," the security guy was saying. "Everyone calm down."

"You know, Ashley, you're right," Derek said, pulling away from her. "And right now, I want to go home with my friend." He looped the yellow cord from around his neck and handed it to the security guy, then grabbed Janice's hand and walked out to the parking lot.

At the desk in the security closet, Porcher and Melissa were watching this meltdown on the monitor that covered the lobby.

"That went well," Porcher observed snidely.

"Logan's an idiot," snarled Melissa. "Just because he likes painted whores doesn't mean every guy does. She came on way too strong, and probably spooked him off. He may be lost to us."

"At least through this channel," Porcher admitted. "What about the girl? Could we work through her? What's their relationship?"

"Friends, best I can tell," Melissa said. "They meet for lunch. He helped her move recently."

"'Meet for lunch'?" Porcher asked quizzically. "Really? He works at the hospital?" He started tapping at his keyboard.

"Yeah, didn't I tell you that?" Melissa said. "He works at the morgue."

"Hmm – he's not on the list," Porcher mused. "Odd. What do we know about him?"

"He's the deputy medical examiner, a physician's assistant by training, and he works on the first floor of the hospital."

"Hmm," Porcher said again. "Probably a dry hole, but I'm going to check him out."

The silence in Derek's car was pregnant and awkward as he pulled out of the parking lot. Janice was half-curled against the door, staring at her feet, while Derek navigated back to the expressway. Once they were comfortably back on the highway, Derek ventured to speak.

"Janice, I'm – I'm sorry about what happened back there. I didn't mean to slight you at all. I have no idea who that girl was, or why she latched onto me like that. I tried not to encourage her – "

"It's okay, Derek, it's okay," Janice reassured him in a dull voice. "I don't blame you. If anything, I blame myself. I know just what she was doing there." *I know*, she continued within herself, *because it was done to me – I was just too blind and narcissistic to recognize what was happening.*

It was all crumbling and falling to pieces. Sure, Melissa had pressured her, but she'd also invited Derek in hopes that he'd see what she'd seen, that he'd glimpse the sweeping vision of the future. Hell, she'd wanted to recapture that vision herself, to again touch the core of what she'd aligned herself with in hopes that it would bring meaning to the terrible things she'd done. She'd hoped to be encouraged and feel the camaraderie and know where she belonged.

There had been none of that. No fellowship, no encouragement, no grand vision, no purpose, no belonging – just a tart clumsily trying to seduce Derek just like Janice had been seduced. Only he'd been perceptive enough to see it while she'd been a fool – a complete, blind, gullible fool.

"Ahhhhh!" Janice cried out, bending over and hammering her knees with her fists. It was all coming apart; her whole life was coming apart. She was falling into the hollow dark –

Derek was alarmed but kept his head – and his lane – as the car sped down the almost empty expressway. Janice was stressed by something he didn't understand. He reached over and caught one of her fists in an attempt to stop her striking herself.

"Janice, Janice, calm down," he said, clasping her hand. "It's okay." He worked his fingers inside her fist and grasped her palm.

"Let go, Derek, let go," she replied weakly, pushing at her hand. "You don't want to touch me."

"Yes, I do," Derek insisted, gripping her hand. "I'm with you and I'm your friend. Please don't hit yourself. Squeeze my hand as tightly as you need to, but please don't hit yourself."

She clung to his hand, bending over it and muttering. He could feel her breath and her hot tears falling on it as she rocked back and forth. "It's all falling apart, falling apart," she crooned.

"What's falling apart?" Derek asked, but she gave him no answer. He tried another tack. "Listen, if this group is so stressful for you, just quit. If it's a professional association, just stop going. It's not like you're required to belong or anything, is it?"

"Just quit," Janice murmured. "Just quit. If only it was that simple. I can't quit. Not now, not after what I've done. Not now."

Derek was mystified. "But – why can't you quit? What have you done that makes it so you can't quit?"

"What have I done?" Janice muttered, staring straight out the windshield down the road. "What have I done? Just quit? Yes, yes," her voice grew frantic, almost hysterical. "I'll quit and be done with it! It's all crumbling anyway!" She fumbled with her collar, then lowered the car window and hurled something out into the night. Puzzled, Derek saw that the pin she'd been wearing was gone.

Janice gazed out the window for a minute, then turned to Derek with panicked eyes. "My God, Derek, what have I done? What have I done? They'll see that it's gone, they'll ask where it is. What will I say? What will I say?" She clung to his hand as if it was a lifeline.

Derek was beginning to wonder if he should drive straight to the hospital's psych ward. Something was pressuring Janice badly, and he had no idea what it was. She seemed to hate this group but felt she couldn't leave, she was terrified of 'them'; she dreaded some dire things she'd done to the point that she felt contaminated. What on earth could that be?

Then the pieces started to come together. The meetings near Flint – Kent had mentioned that in passing. The secret corps of medical professionals infiltrating the hospitals. The unexplained patient deaths.

The pin.

XCV. Ninety-five.

The NUMCS code for expiration while under care.

Derek looked out of the corner of his eye at Janice. She was bent over his hand, sobbing, deep in some internal agony. Was it possible? Could she have taken a patient's life? Was that the requirement for membership, the entrée into this society?

Not Janice. No way, not Janice.

"I never wanted to be a nurse, you know," Janice said in a low, dead voice.

"You – didn't?" Derek asked, wanting to encourage any conversation that would move her back from the edge of frenzy.

"No. I was interested in other things. I especially loved theater," Janice said flatly, staring at the dashboard. "I was good at it, too. I got roles in school plays. I went to workshops over at the Shakespeare Festival in Stratford. I learned about costumes and sets. I even landed a role in a drama club production of *Macbeth*."

"Which role?" Derek asked.

"Lady Macbeth."

"Ooh, the big one," Derek said. "How did you do?"

"They liked me. They said I brought 'vibrant life' to the role. 'Out, damned spot! Out, I say!'" Janice abruptly cried, raising her hands and rubbing them fiercely. Derek was taken aback by this sudden outburst, and hoped it didn't mean Janice would veer again toward hysteria. But she quickly settled down, whispering to herself as she stared ahead catatonically and kept rubbing her hands.

"So – what happened?" Derek asked.

"My mother didn't think it was a good career option," Janice replied. "She thought I wouldn't make a good actress – which was her way of saying I was too gross, clumsy, and ugly. Since she was petite and graceful and pretty, I was always a disappointment to her. Of course, I knew that I could never act professionally – I wasn't in that league. But I would have been happy to work at the grocery store and do local theater in my spare time, just for the love of it. There's much more to the theater than just acting – there's casting and directing and producing, and even wardrobe and makeup. I loved it all. But as far as my mother was concerned, if you weren't making money doing it, it wasn't worth doing. She thought nursing would be a good profession, so she badgered me and pressured me until I finally caved just to get her off my back. And look where it's gotten me."

They drove for a long time in silence, the mile markers flicking by. Derek gripped Janice's hands tightly, somehow knowing that she needed to not be alone. She clung to his hand gratefully, but still seemed trapped in her own world. She muttered quietly to herself from time to time, or put her forehead down on her hands and quietly sobbed. He had no idea what was going on inside her, and felt impotent, but wanted to help as he could.

As they closed the final miles toward home, Derek spoke. "Janice, I want you to know – whatever happens with that group, or your job, or your family, or whatever, I want to be your friend. If I can help in any way, you just call me, okay? You aren't alone, no matter what."

Janice said nothing in response, but nodded and leaned over his hand with tears streaming down her cheeks. Derek's heart nearly broke – he'd never seen a more lonely, desolate person.

Derek dropped Janice at her apartment and drove home, gravely concerned for his friend.

Suspicion

The next day was the first Sunday morning in several weeks that Derek woke in his own apartment, and he didn't like it much. Between his distress about Janice and his speculations about the meaning behind her dark hints and desperate statements, he'd had a tough time getting to sleep. He felt lost and confused, and longed to touch base with the environment that had anchored him so well of late. He was lamenting his state when it occurred to him how silly he was being. Sure, he hadn't gone out on Friday evening and stayed the weekend, but that didn't mean he couldn't hop out for the day. It wasn't like it was far. He dialed the Schaeffers' number.

"Hello?" Linda answered.

"Hi, Linda. Derek here. I was thinking of swinging out today, if that's okay, and wondered if I could pick anything up for you."

"Oh – ah, Derek," Linda stammered. "It's – ah – maybe today – here, let me let you talk to Kent."

Derek was mystified. That didn't sound like Linda at all. In a moment Kent came on the line.

"Hello, Derek?"

"Yeah?"

"Listen, about your coming out today – we'd love to see you, but we're dealing with a bit of a situation here. Nothing I can explain over the phone, just a bit intricate. Might be best if you held off your visit for now."

"Okay, sure," Derek replied. "Maybe next weekend?"

"Um – maybe," Kent equivocated. "We'll see. How about I give you a call?"

"Sure, sure," Derek said. "Bye." He rung off and stared at the wall. That hadn't sounded like Kent, either. Had he done something wrong? Maybe they'd heard about his attraction to Felicity from that Gary guy. Whatever it was, it was clear that his standing invitation had been rescinded.

287

There wasn't much for Derek to do around the apartment –
his burst of tidy efficiency the day before had taken care of it all.
Neither games nor shows appealed to him. He had a lot to think
about – the nearly mystical events of Friday night, the upsetting
debacle of the meeting in Flint and the drive back, the
uncharacteristic response of the Schaeffers. He ended up
walking around his neighborhood and all the way down to the
river. The autumn air was chilly and the leaves were getting
ready to turn. He called Janice and got her voice mail, but
another try later got her in person. She sounded weary and
discouraged, but assured Derek that she'd make it.

Derek walked along the river, watching the deep blue water
roll by and pondering. Eventually, the wind chilled him enough
to send him home. He opened a can of soup for supper and ate
it with peanut butter crackers, feeling lonelier than he had in a
very long time.

At work the next day, even in her emotionally battered state,
Janice could feel the tension and fear. The personnel audit
interviews were continuing and everyone was living in dread.
There seemed no rhyme or reason to them – people would be
summoned, by messenger, to come in for an interview. There
was no advance warning, no delay, and no pattern. It wasn't like
they were being conducted by floor or department or discipline.
It seemed the auditor was working from an arbitrary list to which
only she had access.

The effects of the interviews on morale was devastating.
Those who returned from them were shaken, and some had red
eyes. Janice remembered being told not to discuss the nature of
her interview; everyone else seemed terrified to do so. Some
people broke down in hysterics shortly after their interviews and
had to be sent home. Others never came back from them. At
least two people were escorted to the doors by hospital security,
but others simply – never returned. Nobody had any idea what
happened to them, or why. Janice just put her head down and
did her job, wondering what all this was about.

Later that morning, over at the county building, Medical
Examiner Dr. Stout was finishing off a firmly worded e-mail to

the hospital president. In the hospital's newly released budget, which took effect today, they had revealed they were increasing the rent they were charging the county for the morgue space by twenty percent. That wasn't even close to realistic in these financially constrained times. He copied the county treasurer on the message for good measure.

At his office outside of Flint, Ron Porcher was feeling very satisfied indeed. For one thing, the patient, low key audits he'd been conducting around the St. Clair County medical systems had borne good fruit. He'd eliminated candidate after candidate, finally narrowing the field to just one suspect. The suspect worked at the Regional Medical Administration, the nature of his job gave him far-ranging access to many different systems, and he had the requisite skills to do what had been done. He also had the skills to cover his tracks, which he'd done very, very well.

But once Porcher knew exactly who he was tracking, there was nothing the suspect could do about it. The suspect's only cover had been anonymity. Without that, his every move could be watched without him ever knowing. It was just a matter of time until they caught him.

But that could wait a few days. The immediate excitement was about the results of his queries on Derek Stevens. Of course, he wouldn't have shown up on the lists – he wasn't even a hospital employee. He worked for the county, so he would have sailed right under a hospital-wide personnel audit.

Wouldn't that have been a shame.

Close investigation of Derek's records had revealed some very interesting changes recently. Radical, unusual, inexplicable changes. Porcher wanted to crosscheck these with other data, particularly overflight records, but the patterns were distinctive and damning.

Porcher fired off a message to Captain Collins and Melissa, requesting they meet him at the factory the next day at 1 p.m. He asked Collins to bring overflight records for a very specific list of dates and times. Then, taking a deep breath, he typed up a message to Washington with the summary and the good news:

They may have found the smoking gun.

At ten the next morning, Agents Sanderson and Harris showed up at Fitz's office looking official. Fitz, who'd left the mess of the "burglary" mostly untouched, ushered them past it and into the conference room.

"Have a bit of a problem?" Agent Sanderson asked, looking around.

"Oh, yes," Fitz replied cheerfully. "We were burglarized over the weekend."

"Burglarized?" Sanderson replied with just a little too much surprise.

"Yes – some people must think that we filthy rich lawyers leave bags of cash lying around our offices."

"Was anything taken?" Sanderson asked.

"Some dismally archaic computers, some office equipment, and several boxes and drawers of documents," Fitz explained.

"Documents? Why would anyone take documents?"

"Your guess is as good as mine, Agent Sanderson," Fitz shrugged. "I understand that personal records can have some transactional value among identity thieves, but in this case the malefactors are doomed to disappointment – almost all my records are of dead people whose trusts have been closed. But enough of my problems. How may I help you gentlemen?"

Sanderson nodded to Harris, who withdrew a sheaf of papers from his pocket and lay it ominously on the desk.

"Under Chapter Twelve, Section 125 of the Domestic Terror Act, you are required to provide us with the last known whereabouts of a person who is part of a domestic terror investigation. That is not protected under attorney-client privilege. We are hereby requesting that information," Agent Sanderson said formally. "There is a copy of the relevant statute and a request document naming Mrs. Wilcox."

"I see," Fitz said, unfolding and examining the documents. "So – septuagenarian Joanna Wilcox is a suspect in a domestic terror investigation?"

"Just – a party of interest," corrected Sanderson. "It says so right there. But the law still applies."

"Of course," Fitz said. "You are aware that this law is being challenged and has a good chance of being overturned?"

"But it is, for now, the law," Sanderson replied. "And you are required to comply, or suffer the penalties listed there."

"Certainly," Fitz answered. "And I will comply, to the degree that I am able, which isn't much."

"Why not?" Agent Harris growled.

"Because I'm no longer Mrs. Wilcox's representative," Fitz explained. "I've been fired."

"Fired?"

"Indeed," Fitz said, keying his tablet. "Kelley, can you bring in the Wilcox file, such as it is?"

Kelley brought in a very thin file folder, containing only two documents, both of which Fitz lay before the agents.

"Yesterday afternoon I received these. The first was a document removing me as trustee of Mrs. Wilcox's trust and terminating all relationship with me. The second document revokes the trust completely. Needless to say, I was crushed, but we lawyers learn to soldier on."

Agent Harris eyed Fitz suspiciously, but Sanderson gaped and stammered. "But then… where…"

"What this means, Agent Sanderson, is that I have no professional relationship with Joanna Wilcox, and thus do not fall under the provisions of the law you referenced. As her one-time counselor, I will help you as I may. Her home address you know. This office address you know – this is where she signed the papers I showed you last time. I have no idea where she signed the documents firing me and revoking the trust, but she was not required to provide me that information."

"But…what happened to the assets in the trust?" Sanderson asked.

"I presume she rolled them into another trust," Fitz shrugged.

"Who helped her do that? Who's her new trustee?" Agent Harris asked belligerently.

"She didn't provide me with that information," Fitz replied smoothly. "It's a matter of public record, of course. Such documents are filed with county courts and registers of deeds."

"Which county?" Harris pressed.

"No idea," Fitz answered. "There are eighty-three in Michigan, but plenty of other states, too."

"You're obstructing justice!" Harris barked, slamming his fist on the table.

"If you make clear the nature of the obstruction, I will rectify it to the best of my ability," Fitz said coolly.

Sanderson patted his partner's arm while he poured over the documents and then the printout of the law. At last he shook his head and stood up.

"Counselor, thank you for your time," he said.

"But...he...we..." Harris stammered.

"Always happy to help my government fulfill its constitutional responsibilities," Fitz said. "Kelley will show you out."

About 1 p.m., three cars converged on the old factory. Captain Collins came up from Selfridge in the south. His pride was still stinging from a humiliating encounter in the clubhouse the evening before. A Navy lieutenant had calmly but emphatically promised to break Collins's nose on the bar if he ever heard Collins use the term 'jarhead' again. Arrogant bastards. He'd show them who wielded the power in today's America.

Ron Porcher came in from the west. He'd spent the morning refining his queries and gathering everything he could about Derek. He was convinced that Derek would be the key to unlock the gate that would enable them to clean this up for good. He'd kept Washington abreast, and they had the unit at Selfridge and the center at Fort Wayne on standby.

Melissa drove in from the east. The tension at the hospital was increasing under the relentless pressure of the audits, but nothing useful had turned up yet. They'd found some credentialing irregularities, and a couple of cases of outright fraud, but not what they were actually hunting. It was making her impatient.

The factory was still dusty and beginning to get chilly to a degree that the space heaters couldn't eliminate. The men set up their portables and keyed up their data.

"So, our friend Derek led a boring life until recently," Porcher began. "Lives alone, no romantic entanglements of any variety, doesn't get out much, only sporadically contacts his single mother over near Syracuse. No relatives to speak of, works alone with dead bodies, pretty much a recluse.

"Then, a few weeks ago, things changed. I'm not sure why, but his spending and travel patterns altered on the weekends. Weekend network usage at his apartment drops to zero. No card use at restaurants or bars either locally or anywhere else. Not even any phone usage – it's like he drops off the face of the earth."

"Going home to visit Mom?" puzzled Melissa.

"No border crossings, and going through Canada would be the sensible route," Porcher answered. "Also, no trace of activity you'd expect for trips like that – fuel purchases, phone records, and the like. It truly is like he vanishes for two days – and then dutifully turns up at work again the next Monday.

"However," here Porcher began to get excited, "there is a very unusual spending pattern that starts shortly after this change began. On Friday afternoons – and occasionally on Thursday afternoons – the last thing before he vanishes, he stops at the local warehouse club and loads up on stuff. And when I say 'loads up', I mean 'packs his car'. On one recent visit he purchased sixty pounds of nuts, four cases of coffee, twenty-five pounds of spices, twenty pounds of yeast, forty large jars of olives – the list goes on. The bill for that visit topped five hundred dollars, and he had a similar spree the following weekend."

"On his salary?" Melissa asked skeptically.

"Here's the weird thing – early the following week he makes a large deposit at his bank – exactly enough to cover the pre-weekend purchase. A large, cash deposit."

Porcher stopped to let that sink in. Collins just looked puzzled, but a wicked grin spread slowly across Melissa's face.

"He's making supply runs for them," she said.

"Sure looks that way," Porcher agreed. "What a single guy living alone is doing with sixty pounds of nuts and four cases of coffee is beyond me, unless he's delivering them to someone."

"That sure looks like a smoking gun," Melissa said.

"That's what I thought," Porcher replied. "It isn't much, but it's consistent, traceable, and very out of pattern for someone in his life circumstances. But I wanted to see what aerial surveillance might show. Captain?"

"I extracted the records for the times you provided and had them scanned for vehicles matching your description. The results seem to match the pattern you described, though the records are spotty because we were covering such a wide area.

"Three weekends ago we got a good series of images. Here you can see the end of a workday – we were almost right overhead. There's the car heading out of the hospital lot. A little while later, if we speed through the frames, we can see the car parked outside his apartment. See – you can just catch it through the cover. Then the platform loops away to cover other areas.

"When it comes back around, it's working the west end of town, by where the expressways converge. You can catch a glimpse of the warehouse club complex there, and if you look here, you can see not only his car, but him loading it."

"Look at that platform cart!" Melissa exclaimed. "It's heaped!"

"Sure is," Collins confirmed. "That appears to be an instance of what Ron was talking about. We have a few other records, not as good, but indicative."

"So," Porcher asked. "Where does he go from there?"

"Only thing we can tell is that he heads west," Collins replied. "He doesn't take either expressway – if he did, we could track him to Lansing in the west or the Ohio border to the south. Instead, he takes surface roads and passes quickly out of range of our sweeps. We can't tell where he goes. He could drive anywhere in the state."

"Highly unlikely that he'd go very far," Porcher shook his head. "A couple of times he's done these supply runs back-to-back, on both Thursday and Friday nights. He's always at work on Fridays, so wherever he goes is within commuting range."

"But – all those supplies," Melissa exclaimed. "Week after week – it has to be for large numbers!"

"True, but that's what makes me suspect it's a distributed operation," Porcher replied. "Fort Wayne concurs. Any single site with that many people would leave a very detectable footprint. We're not seeing that, which indicates distribution, possibly across the entire region. That's the strategic assumption we're working with."

"So, he's followed this pattern for weeks?" Melissa asked.

"So far as we can tell, with one exception: last weekend," Collins replied.

"Of course," Melissa said. "The gathering Saturday night."

"Well, he did pick up someone on Saturday evening, and drove to Flint – we tracked him all the way there," Collins confirmed.

"The pickup would be Janice," Melissa said. "He gave her a ride."

"But," Collins added. "He picked up that same person the prior evening at about the same time – and headed west via his usual routes and out of our range."

"Oh, *really?*" Melissa asked, her eyes lighting up.

"That's all we know. They returned after dark, because his car was back at the apartment the next morning. It was there Sunday, too," Collins said.

"We definitely need to interview this guy," Porcher said. "I'm guessing he's the key. Get him, odds are we get some kind of coordinating center in the area, and then the whole network is ours."

"We've got the auditor at the hospital, and Stevens works on the first floor – just an elevator ride away," Melissa said.

"There is the issue of his being a county employee, but a phone call should resolve that," Porcher said. "He's at his office until the end of the workday, and doesn't suspect anything, so we can safely assume he – and what he knows – will be ours by the end of the day.

"So here's my question to you two: I've alerted D.C., and they're waiting for my confirmation. If I think we're poised to make definitive progress, they'll hit the button and unleash the troops. If we're going to get the critical information today, we don't want to give the enemy time to respond. We want to hit them hard, fast, and everywhere. D.C. is willing to commit on our say-so, if we think the situation warrants it. Do you think it does?

"The evidence is convincing," Collins confirmed. "The opportunity to strike before they can respond is unbeatable. I say go."

"So do I," Melissa agreed.

"Then it's done," Porcher said. "I'll send the message now. In the meantime, you get back to Selfridge and get high- and low-level assets in the air. Be prepared to cover the entire Thumb. Melissa, you get back to the hospital and stand by to bring our boy in."

"And in the meantime," Melissa snarled. "I know someone else I can talk to."

Dr. Tasker was in a meeting with his chief of staff when the message came. Glancing at his tablet, he stood to leave.

"This is what we've been waiting for," Tasker said. "An intel source that should open the whole thing. Notify the field units to deploy to the staging area and get me some bodyguards. Is that plane to Selfridge ready?"

"Standing by, sir," the chief of staff replied.

"Then we're on our way."

Dr. Stout was catching up on his golf articles when his e-mail chimed. It was a routine message from one of the hospital administrators. They were doing some kind of review over there and were requesting to include Stevens, since he worked on the premises.

Stout chewed on that. Bureaucratic bastards – what the hell was a 'personnel audit', anyway? He hadn't yet received any response to his e-mail regarding the rent increase on the morgue space. Hmm. He returned to his golf articles. He'd get around to their request shortly. What he'd say, he didn't yet know. Maybe it depended on what he heard from the hospital president.

Janice was working her shift when Melissa walked up and beckoned her into an empty room. "In here," she said briskly. "We need to talk."

Mystified, Janice went into the room. Melissa closed the door and motioned Janice to take a chair. "So," Melissa said in a sharp tone, looming over her. "Your buddy Derek. Where has he been going on weekends?"

"What?" Janice asked, puzzled. She'd expected some questions about the gathering and how it went. She looked up at Melissa's fierce, hard eyes. Janice didn't know what this was about, but that look didn't bode well.

"You heard me. Derek has been skipping town every weekend for the past several weeks. Surely he's talked about his trips during your lunchtime heart-to-hearts."

"Why don't you ask him?" Janice asked, beginning to be frightened.

"Oh, we will," Melissa said with an ugly smile. "But I thought I'd give you a chance to tell me what you know."

Janice did remember Derek mentioning his friends in the country from time to time, but he'd never mentioned specifics. He talked a little about things he'd learned, like well drilling and power generation, but he hadn't discussed the circumstances under which he'd learned them. But even if he had, Janice wasn't about to relay any of it to Melissa. The older nurse's face wore a feral expression that frightened Janice, and she wasn't about to betray her friend to that.

"He – he hasn't said much," Janice offered timorously. "Just that he visits friends. He doesn't mention who or where."

Melissa looked down at her with narrowed eyes. "All right, then – last Friday night he picked you up and took you somewhere. You were gone all evening. Where did you go?"

Janice started and tried to hide her alarm. How did Melissa know about that? "You – you mean to the gathering? We went – "

"Not Saturday night, you idiot. Friday night. Where were you?"

"We – we just went out for drinks and conversation," Janice stammered. "Down Metro Detroit way – this place Derek knows – "

Swift as a striking snake, Melissa grabbed Janice's wrist and squeezed with astonishing strength right on her carpals. "Don't lie to me, you little bitch. You went west – nowhere near Detroit. Where did you go?"

Janice's vision was narrowing with the pain, which felt like spears of frozen acid lancing up her arm. She couldn't even cry out she was gasping so badly, fighting against the agony to catch her breath.

"We – a dance," Janice breathed. "A barn dance. In the country. Melissa, you're hurting me!"

"Where?" Melissa persisted, twisting Janice's arm. Sparks were dancing before her eyes.

"I – I don't know – I didn't ask. A farm, in the country. Ahhhhh, Melissa!"

"What routes did you take? What towns did you pass through?" Melissa pressed, still squeezing and twisting.

"I don't know, I don't know," Janice sobbed, trying to turn so as to relieve the pain. "It was all fields and woods. We came back in the dark. Please, please, Melissa, please stop!"

"This farm – what town was it near? Who was there?"

"I don't know, he didn't say, I don't know! Lots of people, dancing, lights, bales sitting around. I only met a couple – Linda and her husband – ahh, Melissa, *please!*"

It seemed like Melissa would continue to press her brutal interrogation, but just then her phone rang. Keeping her grip on Janice's wrist, she pulled her phone out and glanced at the caller. Scowling, she threw down Janice's arm and took the call.

"Yeah? What? He said what? That...that arrogant prick! Oh, yes, I'll be right up."

Whoever it was had done something to anger Melissa more than she already was. Janice cowered in the chair, terrified that her heightened fury would goad Melissa to further cruelty. Indeed, it seemed to be starting that way, as Melissa stood over Janice and slapped her brutally across the face.

"You! I'm not through with you, but I have other business right now. You get back to your shift, but don't leave this floor, and don't contact anyone. Understand me?" Melissa barked.

Gasping, Janice nodded weakly as she cradled her wrist, which was throbbing and burning. Muttering curses under her breath, Melissa stormed from the room.

Stunned with shock and terror, Janice stared at the floor. Any lingering illusions were totally shredded. Melissa didn't care about her; she'd never cared about her. The joking, the sham friendship, the whole big-sister-looking-out-for-you had been one big act, a massive scam to manipulate her into doing what Melissa wanted – executions.

Janice looked down at her hands, one of which was already starting to swell. She was seeing it all the time now in her dreams, and the image was beginning to intrude on her waking hours: the black, scaly rash that covered her hands and was creeping up her forearms. Oh, to the natural eye her skin still looked white, but when she closed her eyes she could nearly feel the stiff, dry coating. It had begun as flaking on her fingers and palms, and had spread from there to the back of her hands and was now working its way up her wrists. How far it would get, she didn't know – and she didn't plan to find out.

Oh, yes. Without thinking or moving from the chair, she pulled her phone from her pocket and keyed Derek's number.

"Hey, Janice," Derek responded.

"Derek, listen – they're after you. Melissa was just her asking me questions about you – where you've been going on weekends, where we went last Friday."

"Janice!"

"I didn't tell her much, because I don't know much. But she was serious. She got really mad and – they mean it, Derek."

"Janice, you sound terrible! What did they do to you? I'm going to come up – "

"No!" Janice said fiercely. "Forget about me! Get out! Derek, get out now. They'll kill you. I'm not kidding." She rang off and switched off her phone. There – let them do to her what they would. She'd warned her friend. Soon they wouldn't be able to do anything to her. She'd go home tonight and cut deeper than she ever had. She knew where the femoral artery lay. She knew how deep she'd have to go to reach it. She'd been tempted before, sorely tempted, but she'd never quite dared. Tonight, she'd dare. What difference would it make? Everything was in shambles now, crumbled at her feet. It may as well end.

Down in his office, Derek's heart was hammering. He had no doubt that Janice's warning was legitimate. He also had no idea what to do. His apartment was no safer than here, and he didn't know if he was welcome at the farm – and he certainly didn't want to lead any danger to them! Almost panicking, he pulled out his backpack and began stuffing his gear in.

But – what about Janice? He didn't know what had happened, but from her voice it seemed clear that Melissa had done more than just 'get mad'. That bitch! If she'd hurt Janice – but what could he do? If Janice was right, it was him they were after. Here, in his office, he was two doors from the outside. If he went deeper into the hospital, even with the best of intentions, he could be trapped there. What good would that do him or Janice?

"Yeah, Melissa?"

"Hey, Ron. Listen, I'm here in Scriver's office looking at an e-mail from Stevens' boss, a Dr. Stout. He's denying the hospital permission to interview Stevens. Goes on about spheres of authority and proper channels. Mentions something about a dispute regarding some rent the hospital charges the county. Insists on speaking with the hospital president."

"Dammit," growled Porcher. Dr. Tasker was already in the air. "Let me handle this. I'll call D.C. and then send some agents over there to rattle his cage."

"Agents? Where are you going to get agents?"

"Think, Melissa—Port Huron is a border town. The place is crawling with Border Patrol agents. I know a supervisor, I'll have him send his most intimidating guys. Give me a few minutes – this won't take long."

"Medical examiner's office, this is Shaundra."

"Hi, Shaundra, is your boss in?"

"Sure, Mr. Talbot, I'll patch you through," Shaundra knew the voice of the county administrator, and after she transferred the call she muted her handset and picked up the line. She couldn't do her job if she didn't stay a step ahead of Dr. Stout, who never told her anything.

"County medical examiner."

"Dale, this is Jim. I just got off the phone with Washington, having some DHS bigwig chew on my ass for ten minutes about you not letting the hospital interview one of your employees. What's all this?"

"I...but..." Dr. Stout stammered. "They didn't follow channels – why would Washington care about that?"

"I don't know and I don't care. You know how much of our budget depends on DHS! They expect cooperation, and if that means you cooperate with the hospital, you cooperate with the hospital!"

"Ah...sure, Jim, no problem," Dr. Stout began, but just then two big guys in suits and dark glasses came in the door, so Shaundra had to hang up.

"Dr. Stout?" One of the guys asked. Shaundra just nodded and pointed at the inner door. The two walked through without knocking. Shaundra wasted no time. She picked up the handset and dialed.

"County morgue," came Derek's voice.

"Derek, this is Shaundra. Listen: the county administrator is getting leaned on by Washington, and he's leaning on Stout, to let you be interviewed by someone over there. And two DHS goons just walked in to talk to him, too. Someone's after your hide, kid."

"I'm gone," said Derek. "And Shaundra? Thanks – I love you."

"Love you, too, kid. Now get going." Shaundra hung up just as the two agents reemerged with Dr. Stout babbling apologetically at their heels.

Derek hung up, threw his ID badge in the drawer, grabbed his backpack, and walked out the door. He didn't need a third warning. The company he'd been keeping over the past weeks had inculcated a sense of constant wariness. He had his exit thought out, and was at his car within two minutes. He toyed briefly with the idea of swinging by his apartment but rejected it. He headed north, avoiding the main traffic arteries in favor of tree-shaded residential streets that took him longer but provided cover. Within fifteen minutes, he was clearing the city and making his way out toward the country.

Derek knew where he was going – he only had one place to go – but he wanted to be very circumspect about getting there. The fact that the farm hadn't yet been hit indicated that they didn't know where it was, so they hadn't been tracking him that closely. He could only hope he'd given them the slip in time, and that they weren't tracking him even now. Even so, he took a different route – one that took him far north and allow him to approach the farm by coming south rather than west. The route would require him to pass through open, field-lined stretches as well as woods, risking exposure, but there was no option. He drew hope from the idea that they couldn't watch everywhere yet.

As Derek was passing through Avoca, the two Border Patrol agents burst into his office, Melissa close on their heels. They stared around at the empty space.

"Where is he?" one asked.

"Yeah – it's like a tomb in here," the other replied.

"Obviously, he's gone, you imbeciles," Melissa snapped, pulling out her phone and dialing Porcher. "Ron? Yeah, he's gone – nobody's here. Yeah, maybe, or maybe someone tipped him and he bolted. Can you tap the hospital security videos? There's a camera right here – has to be something."

"Gimme a minute," Porcher said, tapping a few keys. Melissa waited impatiently while he isolated the camera and accessed the archive.

"Damn – not much here. The camera is fixed on the service counter, not his work area. Occasionally you catch him flicking through the video field. There – a little over an hour ago he came in through the main door, but there's no video of him leaving."

"Wouldn't need to be," Melissa said. "There's a back door leading to a service hall that opens directly to the outside. Wait – can you get the entry/exit log?"

"Just a second – " Porcher muttered. "There – shows him checking in this morning, but no record of departure."

"That doesn't mean he didn't leave, just that his badge didn't leave," Melissa pointed out.

"Wait, wait," Porcher said with relief. "No call to panic just yet. He has his phone with him, right?"

"I'd guess so, but he probably has it turned off," Melissa replied.

"Doesn't matter," Porcher said. "So long as it has a battery in it, it'll respond to a locator ping. You have his number?"

"Not on me, but it'll be in the personnel records."

It took Porcher a while to locate these, by which time Derek was getting about to Yale and preparing to turn west.

"Okay, got it," Porcher announced. "Here goes – his phone is about to tell me where he is." There was a moment's pause. "Wait – that can't be right."

"What is it?" Melissa asked anxiously.

"According to his phone, he's in southern Greenland," Porcher growled.

"What?"

"It happens," Porcher explained. "Phones get dropped, overheated. But that jogged my memory – his car also has a locator beacon. That's going to take me some time to connect, so let me call you back."

Porcher was starting to get nervous. He tapped away frantically, trying to connect to the FBI's vehicle locator site. He understood how much was at stake. Dr. Tasker's chief of staff had explained that far more than just the outcome of the pilot program was riding on this effort. They not only had to prove that the pilot had been sabotaged by a conspiracy, they had to deliver the scalps of the conspirators – nothing less would salvage the project. The vultures were already circling in D.C. If they failed now, not only would Dr. Tasker be removed but the office would be dismantled. That's why Tasker had pulled out all the stops, activating the Domestic Terror Division's Fast Response Units out of Fort Wayne.

All this had been done because Ron Porcher had assured them that the critical intelligence was essentially in hand. He didn't want to have to explain how the asset had slipped through their fingers even as they'd closed in.

There – he was in the FBI site now. Tapping in Derek's car information, he clicked in the locate button, confident that his problem was about to be solved.

"Dammit!" he swore, slamming the table. He quickly called Melissa.

"Any luck?"

"None," Porcher snarled. "According to his vehicle locator he's 500 miles west of Perth in the Indian Ocean. This guy's had help. One bad result may be a malfunction; two bad results is almost certainly tampering. Have we checked his apartment?"

"Not yet. Should we call someone?"

"Yeah – those guys standing right there. I'm messaging you his address," Porcher said. Melissa scribbled it down and handed it to the agents, who headed off.

"Won't they need – a warrant, or something?" Melissa asked.

"Nah," Porcher said dismissively. "In the unlikely event that someone gives us a hard time, we just say it's part of a domestic terror investigation. That satisfies everyone."

"I'm new to this end of things," Melissa replied.

"Can you get to a workstation?" Porcher asked. "I want to conference Collins in. We need overflight footage. Call you back."

He dialed Collins as he worked his portable, wishing he had a faster data connection. But that had been the point of this old factory, hadn't it? Remoteness and isolation?

Derek checked his map. He'd come about the proper distance on this road, so that bank of trees ahead must be it. He saw a turnoff just before it and pulled off, parking in the shade of a small tree at the edge of a soybean field. He grabbed his backpack and paused, then left the keys in the ignition. With any luck, someone would find his car and drive off with it. That, more than anything, drove home how completely he was having to break with his life. Hunted by the government. Questions about where he'd been and who he'd been meeting. They were after the farm and had somehow discovered that he was a possible avenue. He wondered how, but it didn't matter. Maybe that's why Kent and Linda had been so cautious about him – but how would they have known?

He slung his pack on his shoulder and headed for the bank of trees. One of the shrouded trails that led to the farm passed through them. It was the most camouflaged way he could think of to approach the farm – half a mile under complete cover. Within fifteen minutes, he should be at their back door. What happened then was up to them.

He hoped they'd shelter him, because he had nowhere else to go.

Melissa and Porcher were in a three-way video conference with Collins in Selfridge. They were watching footage that showed a distant view of what looked like Derek's car pulling out of the parking lot of the old medical office buildings just behind the hospital.

"Why did he park back there?" Melissa wondered.

"Because he's been learning," Porcher said with exasperation. "It's about the same walking distance, but he knows the hospital parking lots are under video surveillance while those older ones are not. Where's he going now?"

"You can see the target pulling away here – turning here – crossing this street into this neighborhood – " Collins explained, marking the video as it played.

"Wait – why didn't he turn onto Tenth?" Melissa asked.

"Because he knows better," Porcher said dismally, his insides going completely dead. "He's heading for cover."

"Exactly," Collins said. "Right here is where we lose him."

"Does he show up somewhere later? There are only so many outlets," Porcher asked in near panic.

"I can set my techs to scanning the records in search of his car, but no guarantee we'll spot him," Collins explained. "Might get lucky, though."

"Dammit, I thought you were putting all your birds up! This is top priority – how can you say it's up to luck?" Porcher shouted.

"First off, you don't just throw these things into the air," Collins responded heatedly. "I've got two up, and my techs are prepping the rest on an accelerated schedule, but it'll be two more hours before they're all aloft. Secondly, you're not getting how this works. We can fly sweeping overflight patterns, or we can actively track a target. Give me a specific target, and I'll track him to the ends of the earth. But if we're running sweeps, we may catch your target – as we did here – and you may get lucky and catch him in later footage if his route happens to match your pattern. But no guarantees – it's an odds game. And if the target is canny about using cover and nonstandard routes, as this one seems to be, the odds are tougher."

"Oh, God," Porcher groaned.

"By the way, if this guy's so important, why aren't you running his tracer?"

"We've tried.   Both phone and vehicle.   They've been tampered with," Porcher explained.

"Well, then, you may have lost him." Collins said.

"Can't have," Porcher moaned. "We can't have. Too much is riding on this."

"Well, we may get lucky with the footage, but I wouldn't bet on it," Collins said. "Other than that, I don't know what you're going to do."

Porcher's phone chimed – it was Tasker's chief of staff. They'd landed.

"Collins, Tasker's in your back yard," Porcher explained. "You might want to greet him. I don't know what you're going to say."

"Don't lose hope, Ron," Melissa said. "There's still one avenue we haven't yet exhausted."

Derek showed up at Sam's workshop and was greeted with warmth but grave concern.   Shortly thereafter, he was sitting with Sam, Gil, and Kent explaining why he was there.

"You have no idea why they might have chosen now to target you?" Gil asked. "Have you said or done anything differently over the past couple of days?"

"The only thing was going to a meeting with Janice on Saturday evening," Derek replied. "She's been going to these things for a while, and suggested that I might like them. So did Melissa, who's this coworker of Janice's – I think she's a supervisor. I don't like her very much. She seemed to think I'd fit right in with this group at the meeting."

"What does she look like?" Gil asked.

"Who, Melissa?" Derek asked, puzzled by the question. "Kind of tall for a woman, stocky but not fat, short brown hair, kind of a scowling expression."

"Is this her?" Gil asked, leafing through a folder he'd brought and extricating a printout.   It showed a couple of people, including Melissa, in a sparse and rather dirty office.

"Yes, it is," Derek said in surprise. "Where is that? How did you get that?"

"Doesn't matter," Gil said. "Do you recognize any of the others?"

Derek scanned the grainy print and shook his head. Gil took the photo back.

"So, at this meeting you went to," Kent continued. "Did you say anything about visiting here, or about us?"

"Not in the least," Derek assured him. "Even driving to the dance, I didn't say anything. I mean, I'd mentioned a while back that I had some friends, and that you lived in the country, but that was the extent of it. Especially after what you told me, Kent, I've been careful to keep quiet about details. When I introduced Janice to you and Linda at the dance, I presume she understood you to be the friends I'd spoken of, but I gave no details about where you lived or what you did.

"As far as this meeting in Flint, we didn't even get on the topic. All the way over Janice was talking about the group, and how great and visionary it was. Once we were there some...stuff happened...that kind of upset Janice, so the drive back was talking about her."

"Okay," Gil said decisively. "We can speculate that either something happened at the dance, or something happened at this meeting, or maybe something happened that we don't know about, but the upshot is that they're suddenly very interested in talking to Derek."

"Wait a minute," Derek said in confusion. "What do you mean, the dance? What could have happened at the dance?"

Gil and Kent looked at each other nervously before Kent answered.

"I don't know how to tell you this, Derek, but your friend Janice might be a murderess."

"Yeah, I figured that," Derek said dismally.

Gil, Kent, and to some measure Sam were all stunned and looked at each other in amazement. "You...you did?" Kent asked. "How?"

"Based on some statements she made on the way back from Flint," Derek said. "I also pieced together a few things. When she invited me to this meeting over by there, something kept nagging me until I remembered what you'd said about this shadowy group having meetings near Flint. Also, there are these little pins – XCV – that they wear. Melissa's proud of hers, but she's cagey about what it's for. All I knew was that it had something to do with this group. Then Janice starts wearing one, though she tore it off and threw it out of the car. I think I know what it means – ninety-five."

"Ninety-five?" Gil asked.

"It's the Numchucks code for death while under care. They're subtly boasting about what they do," Derek explained. The men looked at each other in horror.

"And – and your friend earned this – ah – distinction?" Kent asked.

"Yes, but I'm sure she was pressured and manipulated into it – possibly seduced, too," Derek replied. "But she deeply regrets it now, which worries me all the more."

"Worries you?" Gil asked.

"We have to get her out of there," Derek said. "It's tearing her apart. She's turning from them, warning me. She's in serious danger right now."

"Probably true," Gil said. "But I don't see what we can do."

"C'mon, you guys are the experts at extracting people from hospitals," Derek countered. "You do it right under their noses."

"Well, sure, but that's not while everybody's watching," Kent said. "And we coordinate with the person being extracted."

"That part will be easy," Derek said. "I'm sure she'll jump at the chance to escape. What if she could get away from the hospital? Her shift ends in an hour or so – can we pick her up somewhere if she manages to get clear?"

Gil and Kent looked at each other. "It would greatly simplify things if she could get away, but it's not the only problem," Kent explained. "We're tied up right now preparing to deal with worst-case scenarios. We don't have the manpower to throw together a snatch team."

"You don't have to," Derek said. "I'll do it."

"You!" barked Kent. "Derek, you're the most wanted man in this part of the country right now! You have no business doing anything but hiding!"

"I'd love to, but I have no choice," Derek replied. "I'm the only one she'll trust – she doesn't know any of you. Besides, an hour ago I slipped away from the hospital on nothing but my own wits. Surely, with your experienced planning, if we can get her away from the hospital, I should be able to direct her to safety."

"Risky, Derek," Gil cautioned. "Damn risky."

"I know, but we have other no option," Derek said. "They'll kill her – or she might do something to herself."

"Other problem," Sam chimed in. "Communicate with her. She's only known contact with you – her phone probably monitored."

"And we can't risk one of our people couriering a message to her," added Gil. They mused for a minute. "Wait a minute – you mentioned she was on shift, right?"

"Yes, for about an hour yet."

"Then she'd have a tablet checked out, right?"

"I presume so," Derek confirmed.

"That's how," Gil grinned. "Kent, get in touch with Brady. Sam, can you think out and prepare what gear he'll need?"

"Wait," Derek said. "How are you going to communicate with Janice using one of the hospital's tablets?"

"They're not the only one with resources," Gil replied. "C'mon, Derek, let's look at a map. We have an hour to prepare the snatch and move you into place."

Janice felt detached, as if she was observing her body from some distant place, mechanically executing her duties while she watched through remote optics.

Her coworkers avoided her. They'd seen Melissa take her into that room. They'd certainly heard the cries and sharp words. They'd seen Melissa storm away in fury, and Janice emerge favoring her wrist and crying. They knew she was in trouble. They looked away from her, and moved off when they saw her coming. She couldn't blame them. Who could tell when Melissa might come storming back to resume her interrogation? Nobody wanted to be near when that happened. Better to avoid the object of misfortune, lest one be caught up in it. So Janice worked in conspicuous isolation, a pariah among her coworkers.

She looked down at the unblemished white skin of her hands and arms. She knew that was a lie. Maybe the remote Janice, the shell, had pure white skin, but the real Janice knew what her hands looked like. They were black and shriveled, and the blight was now well up her forearms. It was the clean skin that was the illusion. All she had to do was close her eyes to see the true image. Black, scaly, hideous, unclean.

Not for much longer.

The shift wore on and Melissa did not return. Everything was routine, except that half an hour before shift ended, a little message popped up on her tablet.

After work head home drive past 13ᵗʰ & Chestnut turn right on Chestnut slow down – Castor.

This puzzled Janice. Castor – why did that ring a bell? The streets were familiar – the intersection was just a little beyond her apartment. There was no way to respond to the message, so she memorized it and cleared it.

The shift ended and Melissa still had not reappeared. Janice was unsure what to do. Melissa had told Janice to stay on the floor, but her shift was over and she wasn't allowed to stay. She decided to go. Melissa would do what she would do, and in less than an hour she wouldn't be able to do anything to Janice ever again – and neither would anyone else.

Mechanically, Janice made her final notes, returned the tablet to the cradle, and headed home. She half expected a screaming Melissa to intercept her in the lobby, or to have her badge trigger an alert at the entrance. But none of that happened, and Janice proceeded to her car as if a normal workday was ending.

As she drove home, Janice pondered the mysterious message. What did it mean? She was disinclined to do it, to do anything out of the ordinary. It would take effort, initiative, and she was going to need all of that for what she intended to do when she got home. But then – it was only a couple of blocks further, and it might solve the mystery. She could see, then loop back home. So she made the usual turns, but drove past her apartment, down 13ᵗʰ to Chestnut, turned right on Chestnut, and slowed down.

Just as she was passing beneath the overhanging boughs of some great trees, a figure stepped from behind one of the trees and stood in front of her car. She gasped – it was Derek! What was he doing here? He was wearing a broad-brimmed hat like he'd worn to the barn dance and held something flat in his hands. He walked around to the passenger side and held the thing up to the window. It was one of those portable dry-erase boards, and it had three messages written on it.

Assume car bugged. Say nothing. Let me in.

Derek could see how shocked Janice was, and he hoped she was just shocked enough to obey without making a fuss. She fumbled with the button and the door unlocked. Without a word Derek jumped in and flipped the board over to display the message, *Give me your phone.*

Janice pointed to her purse on the seat, and Derek fetched the phone out. It was a sealed model, so Derek pulled the gadget which Sam had given him from his pocket. Plugging the gadget into the phone's charging port, he pitched the phone into the back seat – the battery would be drained in two minutes.

Glancing at his own phone, Derek saw a new message from Gil. In silence, he scribbled it on the board for Janice: *Drive west on Chestnut.*

Derek was executing what Gil called the fastest snatch on record – so fast that it was being planned as it was happening. Given the short timeframe and inexperienced operator, the key principle was simplicity. There had barely been time to get Derek equipped and into position; Gil and the planners were back at Rivendell making it up as they went along, messaging the steps to Derek one at a time.

They drove west on Chestnut in silence. Derek's phone vibrated, and he transcribed the message to the whiteboard.

Turn left into alley between 22nd and 23rd. Park under tree. Get out of car. Open hood.

Janice did as instructed. There was a large tree overshadowing the alley, and as soon as they'd stopped, Derek hopped out, threw up the hood, and snipped a battery cable with the heavy cutting pliers Sam had given him.

"Derek, what did you do to my car? What's all this about?" Janice asked, getting out of the car.

"Only way to kill your locator beacon," Derek explained. "We're getting you away, Janice. Your life is in danger."

"Oh," Janice said, taken aback. "What – what do we do next?"

"Wait for instructions," Derek said, watching his phone. A message came through, but it simply said, *Stay under tree. 3min.*

"About three minutes, stay here, under cover," Derek relayed.

"Three minutes until what?" Janice asked.

"Further instructions," Derek replied. "Gil didn't have time to explain much, just that we break up the pattern – do unpredictable things – and stay under cover as best we can."

"Under cover?" Janice asked.

"Under trees, buildings, anything to shield us from overhead surveillance," Derek explained. "It's a skill I'm learning."

"From whom?" Janice asked. "Who are you communicating with?"

"My friends in the country," Derek said. "They're good at getting people out of dangerous situations.   Ah – our instructions." His phone buzzed and he read the screen. "Okay, this is it. We go to the bus stop at Court and 24th and take the #12 bus. It should be there in about four minutes, so we've just enough time."

"But, Derek," Janice asked. "My car? My phone?"

"Forget them," Derek said, holding out his hand. "Forget them and walk away. This is your life we're talking about. Cling to those and they find you. When they find you, they'll kill you – you know that. Walk away and live."

Glancing back at her car, Janice took his hand and allowed herself to be led along. They stayed on the sidewalks, under the trees as best they could. The journey to the bus stop was brief, and they had to walk the last half block under the open sky, but then they were inside the bus stop shelter, for what cover that afforded.

Derek was jittery. He felt exposed, naked. Looking down 24th, he saw the bus coming up the street. A minute or two and they'd be gone. Come on, traffic! Rats – it got caught by the light at Oak. Another minute. He glanced at his phone. No further instructions yet. He tapped his foot, watching the traffic light and willing it to turn green. There, at last! Only a few blocks now.

Suddenly a black SUV pulled right in front of the shelter and stopped with a squeal of brakes. Behind it, another one jumped the curb and came to rest half-blocking the sidewalk. Janice shrieked as men jumped out, brandishing pistols. Derek heard a strange whirring noise, and looked up to see an aircraft that looked like a miniature helicopter dropping down to hover above the street.

Out of the SUV in front of the shelter stepped another agent and – Melissa? She looked at them with a malicious grin.

"Hey, kids – need a ride?"

The Temple of Dagon

The first vehicles had started arriving in at the fairgrounds on the north side of Sandusky at about 4 p.m., mostly vans and SUVs, all black and official. Nobody thought much of them, not even the groundskeeper. There was always someone or other using some corner of the vast grounds.

But when, a little over an hour later, the Bearcat IIIs and command panel vans came barreling up M-46 to turn north on Dawson and start assembling inside the big loop on the grounds, Sheriff Alex Corrigan's phone started ringing off the hook. Particularly concerned was Violet Buchanan, fairgrounds manager.

"They're all over, just pulling in and pulling in," Violet exclaimed. "Fred just went out to talk to them, but those guards in helmets and sunglasses told him to go away. They had machine guns!"

"Okay, Vi, I understand," Al said soothingly. "I'm sure there's some explanation. Sue is on her way up right now to check it out – in fact, that may be her right now." Al hung up and checked his cell – it was Sue all right. Why would she be making an official call on his private phone?

"Yeah, Sue, what's up?" He asked.

"Well, chief, it's a bit of a mess up here," Deputy Sue Morris explained. "I was stopped by a couple guards with loaded assault gear, and some guy came out and handed me a piece of paper authorizing them to requisition the space under the Domestic Terror Act and demanding full cooperation from us. Then he just walked away – no questions, no discussion, nothing. These things are still pouring in – gotta be twenty vehicles here already."

"Okay, Sue, stay up there, if you would," Al said. "I want eyes on that site and someone ready to respond if necessary."

"Ah – okay, chief," Sue responded.

"Can we get the State Police? Do they know anything about this?" Alex called across the room.

"Just called 'em," Chet replied. "They say it's some kind of DHS/DTD operation and that we should stay clear. Apparently, they've been tearing up I-69 from the Indiana border."

"DHS? Domestic terror?" Alex asked, mystified. "Around here?"

"That's what they said," Chet affirmed. "They also said that this was just the first wave."

After outfitting Derek with the minimal gear he needed for the snatch, Sam retired to his shop to tidy up some details. It was nearly suppertime, time to wash up and fix a sandwich. But first, he thought he'd check the video from the old factory. He'd checked it this morning as a matter of course and there'd been nothing from the night before, but with all the activity it never hurt to check again. He sent the download signal and was surprised to see footage start transmitting. He let some of it transfer and then started playing it. The timestamp said about 1 p.m., and that Ron guy, Melissa, and the captain were meeting.

Sam listened in as Ron explained how he'd tracked Derek's purchases. Sam smacked his forehead – of course, how could they have not considered that? Something as innocent as supply purchases would stand out like a sore thumb against Derek's history and life circumstances. He'd have to advise Gil about that. Sam continued watching as Collins confirmed the findings from his overflight data, and their decision to get Derek in for an interview. So that was why they'd suddenly decided to haul him in. Good thing Derek got out when he did. Sam's brows furrowed as he listened to them talk about notifying Washington, and troops, and "hitting them fast, hard, and everywhere". That sounded very bad, and something that Gil and Kent and a few others should know about immediately.

Sam paused the playback and was preparing to dump the video to storage so he could play it back in the house when he noticed something alarming:

The video was still downloading.

Between finding transport at Selfridge, and some traffic slowdowns, and other delays, it was 5 p.m. before Tasker made it to the old factory. Since he'd made it known upon landing that he wanted the entire pilot program team in attendance, the delays had given everyone time to drop what they were doing and get there. By the time Tasker pulled in, they were all on site, from as far away as Bay City, and the factory floor was getting a little jammed with vehicles.

Melissa was with the Detainment Team that was hoping to bag Derek. Of course, the first thing that Tasker had asked was where the intel asset was. Porcher answered, nervously and somewhat truthfully, that they were closing in on him at that moment. Tasker harrumphed and muttered something about thinking he was already in hand, but let it go. His chief of staff was pinning a large map of the region to the wall and Tasker went over to talk to Charon, Deana from Lapeer, and the rest of the area managers. Tasker's two bodyguards with their cyborg helmets and rifles stood against the far wall looking ominous.

Porcher's earpiece was tapped into the chatter between the detainment team and Collins' people, who were controlling the helidrone that was shadowing Janice's car. He got close to desperation when it seemed like Janice was just driving home as usual, but cheered up slightly when she drove past her apartment and turned onto a street that wasn't one she'd normally use. He almost crowed when Selfridge reported that she'd slowed down and an unknown party had jumped into her car. It could only be one person, but Porcher didn't want to speak until he was safely in custody. He was on tenterhooks listening to the banter between the team and the drone controllers, and nearly sobbed with relief at the flurry of chatter that accompanied the move-in and takedown. They had him. The effort would not be in vain.

Tasker's chief of staff sidled over and asked for a status update. Porcher explained that the asset was in hand, but he wanted to wait for a firm ETA before making an announcement. The chief nodded at the wisdom of this. Tasker was busy in conference with his managers – the good news could wait until it was imminent. It wasn't until nearly twenty minutes later, when the detainment team was nearing the exit that would take them north to the old factory, that Porcher had the nerve to make the statement.

"Dr. Tasker, I'm pleased to report that the intel asset has been apprehended and is expected to arrive at this site within thirty minutes."

"Good job, Porcher," Tasker said, walking over to the map. "I've just been explaining to everyone the importance of this evolution. We've concentrated heavy field assets in a location central to the region." He tapped Sandusky on the map. "As Mr. Porcher has assured us, we expect the intel asset within half an hour, which should mean we'll know the critical data within 45 minutes. The asset may not know the full scope of the operation, but I'm assured he knows about at least one vital component, possibly a headquarters. Once we hit that, we can expect to learn everything we need and provide the field assets the necessary data to take out the entire network.

"I wish to thank Mr. Porcher for his diligent work, as well as Captain Collins of Border Security down in Selfridge, and Ms. Bateman, who I understand also played a vital role." Tasker looked around the room. "Where is Ms. Bateman?"

"She's with the detainment team, sir," Porcher explained. "Bringing in the asset."

"You had us worried, you know," Melissa said to Derek. "Giving us the slip so smoothly. We thought we'd lost you."

Derek stared out the heavily tinted window of the SUV and said nothing. There was nothing to say. He'd failed. Not only was Janice in their hands, but now he was, too. Just what Gil had feared.

"But, we figured we had one chance – your archaic code of chivalry. You couldn't leave your lady fair. You just had to rescue her," Melissa gloated. "All we had to do was tail her, and sure enough, you came right to us."

Derek remained silent, watching the road go by. Of course, they'd put him and Janice in different cars, sticking him with this loathsome hag.

"That's why you'll lose, you know," Melissa taunted. "You've lost big and you're about to lose bigger. You could have had it easier. You could have talked to me or Scriver, or maybe even Porcher. Just told us what we wanted to know and had done with it. But no, you had to make a big escape, and then try a daring rescue on top of that. So now you get to talk to Tasker himself. He's never very patient, and is probably extra testy about being dragged all the way up here from D.C. to resolve this little regional problem. He has the power to make your life very difficult. You might want to consider cutting a deal quickly – save yourself a lot of pain."

That, he wouldn't do, Derek resolved. He wouldn't betray his friends to these murdering monsters. He just wished he felt stronger. What he felt was weak and alone and impotent. He couldn't even protect himself, much less Janice. Here was his chance to be heroic, to stand strong against evil. But there was no virtual saber in his hand, no belt pack with vials of All-Heal, no spare lives to draw on. There was just him, and he knew he wasn't enough. Though his mouth was dry, he kept on swallowing, and felt like he was going to be sick.

The SUV slowed and turned as if it was exiting. He looked at the signs. Why were they getting off the expressway at Imlay City?

It had been Todd who'd dropped Derek off for the ill-fated rescue attempt. Of course, he hadn't driven away, but had remained in the vicinity, monitoring the instructions sent to Derek and observing from a safe distance. He witnessed the takedown at the bus stop and immediately called Gil and Kent.

Gil promptly transmitted the deactivation code to Derek's phone – a special trigger to one of Sam's apps that wiped all data and most other apps from the device, leaving only a handful of programs running. One of these was their own locator, by means of which they tracked Derek's progress westward on I-69.

It was hard for Gil and Kent to watch this without despairing. Derek's flawless escape had been completely undone, and both he and Janice were in the worst possible place. With increasing frustration they discussed options, but none of the ideas bore any fruit. Finally Kent barged from the room to pace the front porch in agitation. Gil knew what that meant – Kent needed space to think and pray, which he did best by himself. For his part, Gil watched the slowly-moving dot on the screen that marked Derek's route in the hands of his captors, turned over alternatives in his mind, and did a little praying himself.

Kent paced on the porch, struggling not to be overwhelmed by the implications of all this. They'd always allowed for the prospect of discovery, but had only ever planned for some small corner of the operation being uncovered, something that could be isolated and shut down. But this was the possibility of complete exposure. Yes, Derek only knew of Rivendell, and had visited only one other ranch. Yes, they had taken precautions and had safeguards in place to isolate their operations. But this was the federal government, who had effectively unlimited resources. Despite the precautions and safeguards, they'd somehow traced Derek to the ranches. If they were to find Rivendell, what else could they not discover, no matter how carefully the tracks were covered?

Ahhh! Kent pounded the porch railing in anguish. So much was at stake, and their fate lay in the hands of a young man who wasn't even one of their company. Kent struggled to force his attention back where it belonged, to trust, but it was difficult. His imagination thronged with disastrous images which he struggled to thrust away. They might be able to get a signal out to the ranches in time, but flight was a desperate option that could easily be traced – their fallback plans were not that sophisticated. The guests were in the most danger, for their lives, certainly. As far as the government systems were concerned, they'd officially vanished from existence. Was there any doubt that the forces hunting them would want to make that status lethally permanent? But what of the host families, the ones that knew of their guests and would be able to publicize their fate? Would they not also be subject to silencing of some nature? And what of their own families?

While Kent was fighting these worries, struggling to offer them up, Gil stuck his head out the door.

"Kent, the convoy with Derek has just exited the expressway and is northbound on M-53."

"M-53? I wonder where they're headed?" Kent replied. They'd speculated on where Derek was being taken, guessing either Lansing or the DHS Ops Center at Fort Wayne. Turning north at Imlay City didn't fit either of those alternatives.

"So do I, which got me wondering: do you think Sam has some kind of audio program on Derek's phone? Something we could remotely activate to listen in on his environment?" Gil asked.

"Never thought to ask," Kent replied. "Let's check with him."

Sam was astonished that the video was still downloading. That meant that there was activity triggering the motion sensors – someone was still in the building. He paused the download, activated the local recorder, and keyed the video cameras to real-time transmission. That would drain the batteries within a couple hours, but he needed to see what was going on.

The three cameras showed in split-screen on Sam's monitor, with the ceiling wide-angle across the top, the hall camera in a smaller window to the right, and the office camera showing in the largest window. Sam had never seen the old factory so busy. The wide-angle lens showed the factory floor crowded with vehicles. The hall camera showed the side view of the same cars but no activity. But the office camera showed a room packed with people, most of whom were totally unfamiliar. There was some chatter among them, but mostly they were attending to a man who was standing before a map affixed to the wall. The camera angle allowed Sam to see that it was a map of the Thumb region, and the man was looking at it while he spoke. He seemed to be addressing the others, referring to things Sam knew nothing about, but a few critical phrases struck Sam like physical blows.

Concentrated heavy field assets in a central location.

Know the critical data within forty-five minutes.

A headquarters getting hit.

The necessary data to take out the entire network.

Sam's vision narrowed, and he clutched at his worktable. Philistines. Philistines! Attacking the Lord's people, assaulting the innocent!

"Oh, no, you don't!" Sam didn't even think, but swept the file folder from the shelf behind. He grabbed the remote door opener and the triggering mechanism, then tapped in the code to arm the detonators and watched as all the indicators glowed amber. "Oh, no, you don't!"

Tucking the devices in his jacket pocket and zipping it tight, Sam swung to the door. Grabbing his cane and long whip, he went to where his scooter was parked just outside the door. The clouds overhead were low, deepening the gathering twilight, and the wind was cold. But none of that mattered. Now it was forty minutes. He climbed aboard his scooter and headed up the trail toward the old factory.

Philistines!

He could strike a blow.

From the front window of his home along West Sanilac Road, Tony Bowers had watched the vehicles roll east for over an hour. Vans and MRAPs and Bearcats, all pitch black and bearing the logo of the Domestic Terror Division of Homeland Security. He'd started keeping count, and was exchanging texts with his cousin Chet over at the sheriff's office, with Tom Lehner in town, and with others. Occasionally Melanie would look in at him, worried, but she'd return to cooking dinner without saying anything.

Tony's phone rang. "Yeah, Tom?" he answered, then listened for a bit. Closing his eyes, he nodded, then said, "I'm in." Hanging up, he headed for the bedroom and his gun safe.

Melanie met him in the hall as he came back with his 7mm hunting rifle and some boxes of shells. "Where are you going?" she asked in a voice edged with panic.

"The old K of C hall. Tom is getting some of us together to make plans."

"Tony, what does any of this have to do with us?" Melanie asked.

Tony set his jaw and blinked a couple of times. "Honey, there was a time when this country was great. She didn't get that way because her citizens cowered in their basements while the soldiers marched by to take away their neighbors. Those are troops mustering at the fairgrounds – armed troops, without a foreign enemy in sight. I've seen the videos that Sue Morris took, and the footage from when Larry sent his little drone over. I know attack footing when I see it, Melanie, and those guys are on it. Assault weapons, body armor, even mortars and RPGs. I don't know what they're after, but I know who: Americans. Our fellow citizens. We can't just stand by."

"But why you? Why you?" Melanie pleaded, tears streaming down her face. "You have so much at stake! Think about me! Think about them!" She pointed toward the family room where the children were playing before dinner.

Tony looked at his wife soberly. "I am."

Gil was mystified. The phone to Sam's workshop rang and rang, and they knew Sam had just gone there to work for a while.

"Dinner?" Kent asked.

"He usually eats in his shop when he's working," Gil said. "And he never disturbs them at the Big House. Let me check with Jan." He keyed a quick message, which got a swift response. "Nope, not at our place."

"Curiouser and curiouser," Kent said. "Shall we go take a look?"

It didn't take them long to reach Sam's workshop, where they found the door standing open and his walker outside.

"Looks like he left in a hurry, wherever he went," Gil said edgily, wary of yet another disturbing development in an already distressing day.

"Indeed," Kent said, walking into the shop and looking at the file folder lying open on the workbench. "Matthew 10:27?" he asked, looking at the writing on the folder.

"We can look it up later," Gil said. He pointed to a rough map sketched on the inside of the folder. "That's clearly the route to the old factory. This must be the file he kept on the site."

"Including this?" Kent asked, pointing to an uncut key taped to the folder and labeled 'Office Door'.

"I presume so," Gil said, pulling the key away from the tape.

"But – it's blank," Kent objected.

"This is Sam," Gil offered. "If he says it opens the office door, it opens the office door."

"Gil – look," Kent said, pointing beyond the folder to the monitors, where the real-time video was still playing. They recognized the room from the videos Sam had shown them, but they'd never seen so many people in the office.

They watched the numbers increase as Derek and Janice were brought in.

"I wonder if that's where Sam went?" Gil whispered.

Kent said nothing, but dashed out to return a moment later. "It's a good bet – his scooter's gone."

"But – why? What could he do?"

Kent looked at the images with shock. The sound was confused but the video was clear. Janice was being shoved to the side, up against the wall near some guards wearing some sort of helmets, but Derek was pushed into a chair with people crowding around him. Now Kent knew how Derek had felt about Janice. They had to do something. Despite the danger and the long odds, they couldn't just leave them. Even if they didn't know how they were going to do it, they had to try to help.

"Where are the four-wheelers?" Kent asked.

"We're going, then?" Gil asked.

"We have to, don't we?"

"Yup," Gil replied, pocketing the key.

"We'll just have to trust to the outcome," Kent added.

"That's for sure."

The detainment team had traveled north for a while, then had turned onto some dirt roads that had a lot of turns. Derek wondered where they were taking him, whether he was under arrest, and a host of other things, but he didn't want to speak lest the quaver in his voice betray his terror. They hadn't handcuffed him or read him his rights, but he was definitely in their power. Finally, they turned onto a dirt driveway and drove through what looked like a giant garage door. At least, it lifted like a garage door, and the inside was jammed with cars – so jammed that there was only just room for the two trucks. The inside didn't look like a garage, though – it had a high ceiling with bare florescent bulbs washing the room in garish light, rafters of metal girders, I-beams spanning the roof, and cables hanging about.

As the door lowered behind them, Derek and Janice were pulled from the SUVs and pushed toward a hallway of sorts. Melissa took them into what seemed like an office space – a long, dusty room with no partitions, only a couple of desks, and just a few chairs. It was full of people, none of whom looked familiar to Derek, but from Janice's gasp behind him he wondered if she recognized a few. Along the back wall stood a couple of guards holding rifles and wearing cyborg helmets – what some called 'grasshopper helmets' because the silvered visors that came down over the eyes looked something like the compound eye of a grasshopper. Derek had read about those – they had sophisticated communications and sensory enhancement capabilities, and were integrated with their weapons. They also made the wearers look intimidating and inhuman.

"Bring them here!" barked a gruff voice from the far end of the room. Derek and Janice were shoved toward a balding man with a florid face who was glowering at them. Derek wondered if this was the guy of whom Melissa had spoken.

"Empty your pockets!" the man commanded, so Derek did, placing everything on the desk beside him. Janice's purse was dumped out, and someone began pawing through the items.

"You – sit," the man stabbed his finger at Derek and then at a chair. "Her – over there." He waved dismissively, and Janice was rudely shoved to the back wall where she stood beside one of the guards.

The red-faced man leaned over Derek. "Do you know why you are here?" he barked.

Still not trusting his voice, Derek shook his head.

"You have been implicated in involvement in a network of terror cells that have been operating in this region," the man snarled, poking his finger at Derek. "These groups have conspired to break federal laws and sabotage a vital national project. They have been undermining national security in this area for years."

Derek just stared at the man, wondering what he was talking about. Terror cells?

"You're being offered one chance to cooperate, and you'd better take it quickly! What do you know about these operations? How long have you been working with them?"

Derek just dropped his eyes and clenched his jaw. He wasn't going to say a word to this guy about anything.

"Damn you! We've no time for your foolishness!" the man nearly screamed. "You have no idea what you're meddling in! You have no concept of what's at stake here! If you know what's good for you, you'll – "

"Sir," interrupted a quiet voice. Derek looked up to see a red-haired guy with round-rimmed glasses standing at the man's elbow and talking quietly. They moved away across the room and spoke in low tones for a bit. Then the red-haired guy returned by himself.

"Hi, Derek," the man said, holding out his hand and sitting on the desk. "I'm Simon."

Derek just looked at the hand and said nothing. The man shrugged and withdrew it.

"Please forgive my boss," Simon continued. "He tends to come on a little strong, and he's been under a *lot* of pressure recently. I'm trying to explain to him that you can hardly be responsible for the actions of people you barely know, right? I mean, you've only been involved with them for a few weeks. Maybe you've done them a few favors, hung out with them – that doesn't mean you're deep in their counsels. Hell, I see you as a victim in all this – caught up in things you didn't know about, things that were going on long before you showed up."

Derek stared at the guy. He didn't know what he was up to, but Derek didn't trust him. Still, it was nice to hear a sympathetic voice after all he'd been through.

"So, look," Simon was continuing. "I know you can't tell us much – you probably don't know much – but even what little you know could help. That's all we need, then you're free to go. Just a few names and addresses for us to check out, and you wash your hands and walk away."

Derek looked down at the floor. Seeing the set of Derek's jaw, Simon continued.

"In fact, we could find you a job – a good job. You're only working in this little backwater because you couldn't find work in New York. We could find you work wherever you wanted – New York, D.C., Florida, southern California, you name it. Work with real people and real doctors, not corpses and petty county bureaucrats. We take care of our friends."

Derek looked up at him, not so much because he believed the blandishments but because Simon's gentle tones were so soothing. Perhaps sensing his weakening, Simon pressed in.

"After all, it's only an investigation. We just want to talk to people. Nobody's pressing any charges yet."

Derek looked at Simon, then glanced at the wall. There hung a map of the region with a cluster of ominous looking black pins concentrated in central Sanilac County. He didn't know what that was about, but it looked like preparations for more than just an investigation. He dropped his eyes and shook his head.

"That's enough, that's enough," barked the florid-faced guy. "Everyone out, everyone out, except you two and the girl." Simon grimaced, shook his head, and turned to crowd from the room into the hallway. Derek and Janice were left alone in the room with the guy – and his heavily armed guards.

The urgency pounding in Sam's veins was struggling against his prudence and caution. The weak headlight on his scooter couldn't cut far into the dusk gathering along the shadowed trail, so he had to travel more slowly than he wanted. He'd already gone off the trail once, toppling over and remounting with frustration and difficulty. He didn't know how far he had yet to go, but he begrudged every minute.

Sam's slower pace gave him time to ponder what he was going to do when he got there. His first impulse was to simply strike a blow, to protect his family, but he had to consider what that meant. Initially, he'd berated himself for not getting around to installing the remote triggering circuitry at the old factory. But now he wondered if he could have done that – wiped out several human lives with a few keyboard strokes. He'd placed the charges with an eye to demolition, denying the enemy a meeting place and maybe some equipment. Could he really have detonated them to kill?

But if he wasn't willing to kill, what was he going there to do? Ask them politely to leave while he leveled their building? How much would that deter them, anyway? Besides, this was war – a war in which the enemy had shown no compunction about killing. In war there were casualties. He certainly had the power to inflict casualties – but did he have the authority? By what office could he exercise lethal force? Simply the fact that he'd had the foresight to install the charges, and held the trigger in his pocket? Did might confer right? His mother would not approve. John and Angie would not approve. Jesus would not approve.

It should be the civil authorities. "'For he is the minister of God, a revenger to execute wrath upon him that doeth evil','" Sam recited from memory. But what to do when the civil authorities are themselves the transgressors?

There were also practical considerations. For safety, the triggering signal was very short range. Nobody could stand at a safe distance and manually trigger the charges – the signal wouldn't travel that far. To be certain the signal would reach, the trigger would have to be brought right up against the outer wall, into the blast zone – and even then, the signal might not reach all the detonators. The best place was inside the building, central to the detonators, which was where he'd planned to install one when he could. But now he wondered if that hadn't been Providence. Had he installed the trigger, it would have been far too easy in his panic and rage to send the signal to activate it without taking time to consider. This way, he had to address both the moral and practical problems.

There was no safe way to do this. An idea began to form in Sam's mind, an idea that would resolve his conundrum. He'd have to be quick, but he could do it. He'd even warn them, caution them about the danger. The choice would be theirs. If they did not heed his warnings, their blood would be on their own hands, not his. Of course, it would come at cost to him, which touched him with sadness for the loss. But if he was right, that was lost to him regardless – but perhaps not lost to all, if he succeeded.

And maybe it was time to avenge those lost. His mother. John. Grandma Del. God knew how many others. Maybe it was time for them to answer for all those lives.

Maybe it was time to see what kind of man he was.

After a brief delay to refuel one of the four-wheelers, Gil and Kent headed up the trail toward the old factory. Above the heavy overcast, the sun was nearly set, making the trails almost pitch dark, but the headlights cut the darkness easily. They sometimes used the four-wheelers for nighttime deliveries, so they were outfitted for the job.

Both men were mulling over what they were heading towards. They guessed they were following Sam, they knew that Derek and Janice were at the factory, but they had no idea what they would do once they got there. Only one thing was instinctively clear to them both: they had to get there as quickly as possible.

And sometimes you listened to your instincts.

The florid-faced guy was staring at Derek with steady-eyed malice. Derek forced himself to gaze back. He knew he wasn't up to defiant declamations and certainly not physical assaults, but at least he could keep his head up.

"Have you ever seen a rape?" the man asked.

Derek's mouth went dry. Not trusting his speech, he just shook his head.

"Because that's the least of what's going to happen to your little friend over there if you don't tell me what I need to know," the man went on.

On the periphery of Derek's vision one of the guards stirred a little. Derek glanced over to where Janice was shrinking against the wall, horror painted across her face.

"Now," the man repeated. "Are you going to cooperate, or do I have them start on her?"

Sam unzipped his jacket pocket as he cleared the brush at the end of the trail and came into the clearing surrounding the old factory. Without slowing, he thumbed the door opener. Sweeping around to the driveway, he turned and rode into the factory.

And nearly smashed into an SUV that was parked just inside the door. Boy, it was crowded in here! He'd expected a lot of vehicles, but this was wall-to-wall. No matter – he deftly steered between two of them and lay his scooter down against a tire. Thumbing the opener again to close the door, he cast it aside and climbed onto a car hood. There was one of his cables right within reach – how handy. He scrambled up it, reaching the I-beam overhead. Glancing down, he saw that there was a cluster of people in the hallway, just by the factory floor where the vehicles were parked. They were yelling in surprise and pointing at him – well, that was to be expected.

Glancing around, Sam decided that the next I-beam over would be ideal for his purposes. Uncoiling his whip, he flicked it around some rafters overhead and swung across. A quick estimate of distances told him that he was nearly perfectly placed. It was time.

Ignoring the people pointing and yammering on the floor beneath, Sam pulled the triggering device from his pocket. Squeezing it tightly, he breathed a quiet prayer and turned the switch on the bottom. The LED on top went from amber to bright red.

It was active.

Flicking his whip to loosen it from the rafter, Sam started swinging it toward the light fixture at the far end of the beam. Now he could attend to the people below.

"Hey!" one authoritative guy barked up at him. "What are you doing up there? Who are you?"

"I am," Sam bellowed, "your worst nightmare!" With a snap of his wrist he sent the whip crashing across the bulbs of the fixture, causing a cacophony of shrieks and splintering glass. "I am the one who got away!" Looping his whip over his arm, he unhooked his cane, reached up to the fixture almost directly overhead, and smashed one of its bulbs. "You tried to kill me, but I escaped, and I have returned as the messenger of judgement!" Smash! went another bulb, to the alarm of those below. "I am the wrath of God among you! I am the one who escaped your clutches and lived! I come with doom in my hands!" Smash!

The dreadful silence of the office was broken by a muffled hue and cry from the hallway. Puzzled and angered, the red-faced man was just turning around when the office door burst open and a dark-haired guy stuck his head in.

"Sir – you'd better come see this," the man said in alarm.

"What the hell?" the man said angrily, then rounded on Derek as if the interruption was his fault. "I'm not done with you!" Then he stabbed his finger at one of the guards. "You! Come with me. You! Don't let either of them move." He stomped from the room, leaving Derek and Janice alone with the faceless guard.

Sam had finished smashing the lights above him, and was repositioning himself to get his whip over to the banks nearest the door, when the red-faced man he'd seen in front of the map came bustling out to join the crowd. Beside him was a guard with a rifle. This, Sam guessed, was the leader. He pointed his cane right at the man.

"Did you think you could slay John Holmes and not have to account for his blood?" Sam called. "You may have hidden your crime from men, but do you think Jesus did not see from His holy throne? 'For Mine eyes are upon all your ways: they are not hid from My face, neither is your iniquity hid from Mine eyes'! Now retribution has come upon you, and you will answer for his death!" With a crack Sam brought his whip across one of the far banks of lights, totally darkening that corner of the room.

Down on the floor, Charon and Porcher looked at each other in shock. What did this howling maniac know about Holmes' death, and how had he learned? Overhead, Sam started swinging the whip toward the next fixture.

"Shoot this monkey!" Tasker ordered the guard.

The guard toyed with his rifle, hesitating. "Sir, he's just smashing light bulbs," he replied.

Sputtering with rage, Tasker grabbed the rifle from the man. "Damn you! Go back and guard the prisoners. Send out Wallace."

"Yes, sir," the guard said.

Sam connected with the fixture, smashing three of the four bulbs with one blow and getting the fourth with the follow-up. Seeing the rifle in Tasker's hand, he called down.

"You'd better not shoot me! If you shoot me, it'll be the last thing you do! Kill me, and the wrath of God will smite you swiftly!"

Gil and Kent stopped the four-wheelers at the end of the trail and peeked around the bushes. There was nothing but the light in the office windows, shielded by the drawn blinds.

"You see Sam?" Kent asked.

"No – let's check the door," Gil said, pulling out the key. They crept to the office door and put an ear to it.

"Sounds quiet in there," Kent said. "Should we risk it?" Gil nodded.

A couple of minutes after the red-faced guy left, his guard came back and gestured the other out into the hall. Derek had no idea what that meant. The guard who returned was without his rifle, but he still had a sidearm. Poor Janice was crouched down by the floor, staring around in wide-eyed terror. Derek wanted to say something reassuring, but didn't know what to say, and didn't want to say it with the guard there.

Then the last thing Derek expected happened – the doorknob on the outside door turned and the door slowly opened. The guard wheeled and reached for his holster. Then, of all people, Kent and Gil came through the door. The guard's pistol was out and pointed at them.

"No!" Derek cried. Kent and Gil froze, staring at the unearthly visage of the helmet. Kent reflexively made the Sign of the Cross.

To Derek's astonishment, the guard lifted his weapon. He removed his helmet to reveal a sandy-haired man with honest blue eyes.

"Are you here for them?" the guard asked.

"We are," Kent nodded.

"Take them and go," the guard replied. "I'll figure out something. I wasn't relishing what I was going to have to do if Tasker tried to make good on his threats."

"C'mon," Gil beckoned to Derek and Janice. Derek leapt up, but Janice lingered, cringing.

"Let's go, Janice," Derek ran over and grabbed her wrist, dragging her toward the door.

"Whom do you serve?" Kent asked the guard bluntly.

"I believe in America-That-Was," the man replied with grave simplicity.

"She is no more," Kent shook his head sadly. "She has fallen. You see what she has become. Come with us. Only the Kingdom will endure what is coming."

"I still hold out hope," the man said.

"There is no hope," Kent urged. "Come with us and live."

"No," the guard said. "It is my mission. I must keep trying until I die."

"Then God be with you," Kent said. From the hall outside there came a sharp popping.

"Gunfire," the guard said. "Fly!"

They fled. Dashing across the open space, they made it to the four-wheelers. Janice was almost limp, so Derek and Kent jammed her on the seat behind Gil, who took off while they clambered on the other and followed.

Back in the factory, Sam had just taken out the last fixture he could reach. More than half the factory floor was in darkness, and he was hiding behind girders while shots echoed through the room. Two agents and the guard were trying to take him down, but had been foiled so far by the darkness and the metal framing. It would be any minute now, but Sam kept shouting warnings.

"You'd better not kill me! The Lord will smite you quickly if you add that sin to all the others! Turn and repent, you bloody-handed Philistines!"

The four-wheelers were half a mile away when the factory exploded. Despite the distance and the buffering trees, the force of the blast nearly stunned them.

Sam's Story

"Holy crap, sir!" the tech exclaimed in alarm, recoiling from his monitor as if had burned him.

"What is it, Taylor?" Collins asked nervously. The last thing this operation needed was another complication.

"Their command site, sir, and it just – blew up!"

"Blew up?" Collins whispered.

"Yeah, right here," Taylor keyed the video back a little and played it out. There were two images side by side, normal and infrared, because the natural light was nearly gone. The building showed as a featureless blur, barely distinguishable from the dark grey surroundings, when suddenly it exploded in a flare that whited out both lenses, which struggled to adjust to the overload. Then the image rocked and bobbed as the blast shock buffeted the drone.

Collins swore quietly. They'd all been in there – Charon, Ron, Melissa, Deana, even Tasker. Hell, he'd even toyed with the idea of joining them.

"Get the field HQ on the line," Collins barked.

Derek felt like he was in another existence. The tension and terror of his arrest followed by the horror of the interrogation, then the stunning rescue and the shock of the blast had all left him feeling like he was observing someone else's life. But here he was, clinging to Kent's back as they raced along the pitch-dark trail at what seemed an alarming rate.

"What was that explosion?" Derek hollered in Kent's ear.

"I don't know!" Kent called back over the rushing wind. "But we want as much distance from it as possible! Oh, Sam, oh, Sam!"

"What about Sam?" Derek asked.

"I'm not sure, but I fear for him," Kent answered.

They were soon back at Rivendell. Gil had called ahead, so a party of worried and mystified women awaited on the deck of the Big House to take a shocked Janice into their care. Then Gil joined Kent and Derek in Sam's workshop.

The monitor was showing nothing but snow when they arrived, but Kent cued the video back. The men watched the footage in amazement. Derek relived some of the horror of his brief interrogation by Tasker, and they saw Sam arrive and clamber up to the rafters. Between the remote pickup and his slurred speech, Gil and Kent had trouble making out what he was saying. Derek, who'd been working more closely with Sam recently, was able to discern it.

"'I am the one who got away'," Derek said. "'You tried to kill me.' What does that mean?"

"Later," Kent waved off the question as they focused on the video. They watched Sam start to smash lights and call warnings down from the rafters.

"He keeps warning them not to kill him, that God's wrath will smite them if they do. What does he mean by that?" Derek asked. Gil and Kent did not respond, but looked at each other with grave expressions.

Everyone jumped when they started shooting at him. "No, Sam, no!" Derek cried through his sobs, and tears streamed down the men's faces. All they could do was watch the footage as the shooters maneuvered for better angles, while Sam sought shelter behind the girders.

"Why is he moving so funny?" Derek asked through his tears.

"Moving funny?" Kent asked.

"Yeah," Derek replied. "Normally he's fluid and graceful up where he can grab things. But he's moving clumsily. It's like he's not using his left hand. See him there? Has he been hit?"

"I don't know," Gil said. "But you're right, he's moving strangely."

They all cried out in anguish when they saw the shot that finally got Sam. Horrified, they saw him clutch at a strut, stagger, miss, and tumble from the rafters. Before he hit the floor, the screen went white.

"Wait, wait," Kent said. "Back it up just a little, to where he was falling." Nobody wanted to watch that, but Gil recued the video and slow-stepped it through the sequence. "There – just there," Kent said, pointing at the screen. "The light's terrible, but you can just see it as he falls. Something drops out of his left hand."

"Oh, Sam, Sam," Gil moaned.

"What is it?" Derek asked.

"We can only guess, but we could possibly piece it together from his records," Kent replied, waving at the folder open on the worktable. "But I suspect that was the triggering mechanism."

"Triggering mechanism?"

"Yes – called, appropriately enough in this case, a dead man's switch. It's a switch that activates when something is released, not depressed. So long as he gripped it, the charge wouldn't detonate. Only when he let go would it close the circuit." Kent explained.

"'If you shoot me, it'll be the last thing you do'," Derek quoted. "He was warning them."

"Knowing full well they'd ignore the warning," Gil added. The men all sat in stunned grief for several minutes.

"Well," Kent said. "I'm guessing that we have here some of the most coveted footage in the state."

"If not the nation," Gil confirmed. "But I think – hope – we can assume any traces were eradicated by the blast. This is far from over, but hopefully we won't have any visitors tonight."

"But – I don't understand," Derek said. "Why were there explosives in the factory in the first place? What did Sam have to do with that?"

"All we have for that is his records, which we'll go over tomorrow," Kent said. "Right now, you need to get some rest, Derek. You've had a hell of a day."

"I have," Derek agreed. "But I don't know if I'll be able to sleep after – after all this."

"Linda will have a pill to help," Kent said. "And you'd left some of your clothes out here, which she's washed. C'mon."

The blast site was a sea of flashing lights. County sheriff cars, state police, fire and rescue units from Imlay City to Brown City, even a couple of black DHS trucks clustered around the smoking ruin. There wasn't much for the EMTs to do – not only were there no survivors, there were no intact bodies, so thorough had the explosion been. There had been several secondary gasoline fires from ruptured fuel tanks, but the fire departments had foamed those down, to the frustration of the investigators who had to sift the now-slimy site for clues.

The sheriff was receiving the report of the state police explosives expert who'd arrived half an hour before and had just finished his preliminary walkaround. Annoyingly, a couple of DHS guys were hanging at the sheriff's elbow, acting as if they were the ones being reported to. The sheriff longed to tell them to buzz off, but one didn't antagonize the Feds.

"We sure this building wasn't being prepared for demolition?" the explosives guy asked.

"If so, I hadn't heard of it – and permits go through my office," the sheriff replied. "Why do you ask?"

"The nature of the blast. An industrial accident might have damaged part of the structure, but this blast was amazingly thorough. It was clearly from several precisely placed – and possibly shaped – charges that were detonated simultaneously."

"Shaped?" one of the DHS guys asked.

"Yes," the state policeman replied. "Molded in a particular shape to direct the force of the blast. It's the sort of thing demolition people do to optimize their explosives when they're taking down a structure."

"So – this was deliberate?" the DHS guy pressed. "Maybe domestic terror?"

"Deliberate, certainly, but probably not terror. Terror blasts are usually one-point affairs, like IEDs or car bombs. Multiple blasts might be timed to coincide, but wouldn't be as precisely detonated as these were. That's why I wondered if this was a demolition blast, but even that doesn't make sense."

"Why not?" the sheriff asked.

"First off, a building this size wouldn't need explosives – a crane would do the job," the expert explained patiently. "But even if you did use explosives, if they were properly placed and detonated you'd need no more than two pounds to level this building. Based on the blast circle and debris, I'd guess that we're looking at more like twenty pounds. Massive overkill – there isn't an intact cinder block on this site. No demolition team would be so wasteful."

"So then – it *could* be domestic terror?" the DHS guy insisted.

"An empty factory in the middle of nowhere?" the expert replied with scorn. "To terrorize what? The birds? The nearest house is three quarters of a mile away."

"But it's possible, right?"

"Remotely possible, but far from likely," the expert conceded.

That seemed to be enough for the DHS guys, who walked away tapping on their tablets.

"I'll be taking pictures and measurements," the explosives guy said. "I may be here for a couple of days before I have enough for my full report. Any idea why all those vehicles were inside the building? Over half an acre of parking out here, but the interior was jammed with nearly a dozen cars. So much scrap metal now, and it's going to make recovery a lot harder."

"Another mystery about this whole thing," the sheriff said. "Whatcha got, Steve?" This was to one of his deputies who had approached with some items in hand.

"Not much," the deputy admitted. "I've put the paramedics to work combing the shrubbery for debris. Lots of dust and concrete shards, but precious little else. Found these, though." He handed over a piece of a helmet, a laminated ID card, and a scorched wallet.

"Well, it's something," the sheriff said, turning the wallet over and opening it. "A couple of IDs at least. May not get much else. See any – remains?"

"No, thankfully," the deputy replied. "One of the firemen was telling me that there seemed to be a group of people standing right in front of one of the charges when it detonated. Won't be finding much of them."

The sheriff walked over to where one of his men was supervising some firemen removing debris under a bright field light. In the background, a newsman was talking into a microphone in front of a camera with the steaming wreckage in the background. Shortly, they'd call him over to ask what he knew about the blast, and he'd have to admit that he didn't know much. Nobody did.

But at least they had the names of a couple of the victims.
That always sounded like progress.

It was after midnight when the phone in the home outside
Syracuse rang, waking its owner.

"Hello?" the woman answered groggily, glancing at the
clock.

"Hello, Ms. Stevens?" a strange, official sounding voice
asked.

"This is Julia Stevens," the woman responded, looking at the
number and seeing it was from Michigan.

"This is Sheriff Jeff Murray of the Lapeer County Sheriff's
Office," the voice said. "I'm – I'm afraid it's about your son
Derek."

It was nearly 4 a.m. when Tony walked back through the
front door. Melanie, who'd been dozing fitfully on the couch,
sprang up and ran to him, holding him in silence for a full
minute.

"What happened?" she finally asked as he hung up his
jacket.

"A whole lotta nothing, as it turned out," Tony answered,
collapsing onto the couch. "The units seemed all ready to go,
with command vans ready, but apparently the word never came.
They just sat there with their engines idling. About 7:15 last
night, a couple of SUVs tore out of there with lights flashing, so
we braced for something, but that's all that ever happened. The
SUVs never even returned. About an hour ago, the big units
started rolling out, caravan style, not like they were deploying.
Some of our gutsier guys followed them, but they just went over
on M-46 and down to M-53 to the expressway, where most of
them headed west."

"I wonder if the SUVs leaving had anything to do with that
blast down by Imlay City," Melanie wondered. "That was early
last evening."

"We wondered the same thing," Tony said. "We caught
word of that on the local sites. But – a blast at an empty factory
in the middle of nowhere? Sounds more like an industrial
accident to me. Why would DHS care?"

"Dunno," Melanie shrugged. "Want some coffee?"

Derek awoke the next morning feeling physically rested but emotionally numb and battered. It took him a moment to recall why he felt so empty – Sam. He rose and dressed mechanically then headed for the workshop.

A short while later, Kent found him there, sobbing, watching the footage of Sam's last minutes of life over and over again.

"I only knew him for a few weeks," Derek said. "But I feel like I've lost a brother."

"We all do," Kent assured him.

"One thing I don't get, though," Derek said, cuing the video back to where Sam climbed to the rafters. "This part at the very beginning, where Sam says something like 'I am the one who got away', and 'you tried to kill me, but I escaped'. Do you know what he meant by that?"

Kent sat down on a stool and rubbed his face. "Yeah. Gil and Ruth and I talked about that at length last night after you went to bed. We think it's a vital clue to what Sam thought he was doing there, and how he understood his actions.

"There are some things you should know about Sam. His mother came to the area almost thirty years ago. She never said exactly where she was from, but it was somewhere west of here – possibly Minnesota. She was a pastor's daughter who found herself pregnant and had either fled or been driven from her home. She just got on I-94 and took it to where it ended in Port Huron. She probably lived in shelters and cheap apartments until she went into labor, when she was taken to the emergency room and dumped.

"She had a long, hard labor with Sam. When she finally delivered, they gave her a sedative to knock her out."

"Wait – this was a normal delivery, right? Not a C-section?" Derek asked.

"Yes."

"If she made it through, why sedate her?"

Kent rubbed his face again and looked at the table, as if reluctant to continue. "Have you ever wondered why you see so few people like Sam around these days?" he asked.

"You mean – with cerebral palsy?" Derek replied.

"That, and other developmental or genetic disabilities like Down Syndrome," Kent said. "When I was growing up they were – well, not common, but seen enough. Now you hardly see any."

"Why is that?" Derek asked.

"Couple of reasons," Kent continued. "More sophisticated prenatal testing means that more are detected *in utero*, and aborted there. They never see the light of day. But those who make it to birth are often set aside to die – sometimes with their parent's knowledge, sometimes without."

Derek just gaped. "Really? But how...I thought..."

"They're written up as dying due to complications of childbirth, or as stillbirths," Kent explained. "That's what happened to Sam. When they saw the extent of his handicaps, they decided his was a life not worth living. They wheeled him into a supply closet and left him to die. They sedated his mother so she wouldn't make a fuss about it until it was too late.

"But somebody must have miscalculated, because she awoke before she was supposed to, when nobody was around. Frantic about her missing baby, she tore out the IV and rushed about the floor looking for him. His guardian angel must have guided her, because she found him in the closet, still breathing. She gathered him up and fled the hospital with nothing but him and the gown she was wearing."

"So, he was like – an early 95, or very nearly," Derek said.

"Precisely," Kent confirmed. "An ugly little secret about the medical profession is that this sort of thing has been going on for forty or fifty years now. Handicapped newborns, severely injured, terminally ill – all were at risk of being quietly shoved to the side and either left to die or actively killed. Anyone who was inconvenient or expensive was a potential target. The struggle you got caught up in is only the most recent expansion of a trend that's been building for decades.

"Fortunately, Sam escaped that fate – as you heard him declare. But he wasn't in much better shape after being rescued – his mother had only the clothes on her back, and was wandering the streets of a strange city.

"It was John Holmes who found her. He took her home to Angie, and they all but adopted the two. They provided them a home until she got her feet under her, and were like grandparents to Sam his whole life. It was John who instilled such confidence in Sam, teaching him to view his disability as a challenge, not a handicap. Thanks to John, Sam didn't see himself as limited in any way – just unusual. John taught Sam almost all he knew about handiwork.

"Sam's mother, poor woman, was never quite right after that ordeal. She got it fixed in her mind that Sam's brush with death, and his condition, were God's punishment for her sins. John and Angie worked to free her from that mistaken idea, and sometimes they seemed to make progress, but it was an ongoing struggle. They – and Sam – thought her constant self-condemnation contributed to her early death. She struggled with numerous health problems and died when he was in his teens.

"But one thing she did was to raise Sam in the tradition from which she'd come. Lots of Bible stories and Scripture memorization. Like many from a fundamentalist background, he majored in the Old Testament, which is the biggest portion of the Bible. He took in with his mother's milk the tales of howling prophets and dreadful judgment. The days when God's heroes would go out and physically strive with the ungodly – David and Goliath, or Gideon and the Midianites – loomed large in his imagination."

"And you think that outlook contributed to what he did at the factory?" Derek asked.

"Almost certainly," Kent said, pulling Sam's Bible off the shelf and opening it. "Unlike most people nicknamed Sam, his full name wasn't Samuel. It was Samson."

"As in Samson and Delilah?" Derek asked.

"The very one. A judge of ancient Israel renowned more for his physical strength than his moral constancy," Kent laid the Bible open on the table open before Derek and tapped the page. "He met his end in a particularly dramatic manner. You can read about it here at the end of the sixteenth chapter of the Book of Judges."

Derek did his best, struggling a bit with the archaic wording. Slowly his eyes grew wide, and he looked up at Kent in astonishment.

In the Big House, Gil and Ruth sat at the table sipping coffee and discussing the complications following the events of the prior evening. They'd just caught a rebroadcasted report they'd seen earlier from one of the Detroit news sites giving an update on what was being called the Imlay City Blast. The names of two confirmed victims had been released: Derek Stevens and Janice Boyd, both of Port Huron, whose ID cards had been found near the blast site. Other victims had yet to be identified and next of kin notified.

Gil and Ruth were hardly behaving like people who had seen a serious threat eliminated and dangerous enemies destroyed. Instead they looked gravely at the screen, which was displaying pictures of Derek and Janice, while the voice-over went on about the blast.

"This seriously complicates matters," Ruth said darkly.

"I know," Gil replied. "Derek won't be a problem – Kent's talking to him right now. But she's an unknown quantity."

"We've never had to deal with this before," Ruth said. "Until now, everyone who's come to us has known at least something about us, and has willingly joined. But she's just been landed in our midst, knowing nothing. We have no claim on her, and we can hardly keep her prisoner."

"*And* she's just been publicly declared dead," Gil added. "A casualty of suspicious events. If she were to walk out of here – which we can't stop her from doing – the media and government would be all over her, and then all over us."

"Perhaps we could persuade her," Ruth offered. "Where is she now?"

"Jan had some of the girls take her out to do some garden work," Gil said. "She was rested but still seemed stunned. Jan thought a little fresh air and sunshine – and company – might help her."

"Maybe we can get Derek to talk to her," Ruth suggested.

Back in the workshop, Kent was discussing the situation with Derek.

"You're officially, publicly dead now," Kent was saying. "It was on the news this morning. Apparently, yours and Janice's

IDs were blown clear of the building, so they assume you're buried under the rubble."

"Wow," muttered Derek. "This simplifies some things and complicates others. At least I won't have the Feds looking for me."

"We were hoping – " Kent began, but was interrupted by sudden shrieking coming from outside. Both men jumped to their feet and rushed out the door.

Numerous women were running screaming from the edge of a garden patch. Kneeling by the edge of the patch was a woman who was doing violent, frantic things. She seemed to be plunging her hands into the dirt, scooping up handfuls to rub on her face and into her hair.

Not all the women had fled. One hovered near, cautious but focused, awaiting a chance to dart in. But when she tried, the kneeling woman caught up a trowel and brandished it like a knife, taking great sweeping cuts at the other woman and forcing her to jump back. Then with terrible cries the woman began stabbing and hacking at her arm and hand with the trowel.

Derek caught sight of the frantic woman's face when she took a swipe at the other girl. "My God," he whispered. "It's Janice."

Without thinking, Derek sprinted for the garden. The other girl was still hanging back, awaiting her opportunity, but Derek bolted right past her. Knocking the trowel aside with a sweep of his arm, he tackled Janice, pinning her arms to her sides and dragging her to the ground. She struggled and screamed in his arms. "Janice!" he cried. "Janice, it's me! Derek!"

"The eyes! The eyes!" Janice cried. "They're always there, always watching!"

By then, Kent was there, and they pulled Janice to her knees. Derek kept a firm grip on her wrists and tried to get her to look at him.

"Janice! Janice! It's Derek! We're safe!"

For a moment it seemed to work. She blinked her eyes, white in a face begrimed with mud and tears and snot. "Derek?"

"It's me, Janice. Derek."

"Derek, the eyes. They're always there, looking at me. When I close my eyes to sleep, they're looking. All through my dreams. Around every corner."

Mystified by this, Derek looked up at Kent. But just then Janice looked down at her hands. She began to shriek and struggle again.

"Off! Off!" she shrieked, gazing in horror at her hands, covered with blood-stained mud. "Get it off me, get it off!"

"Janice, it's just mud, it'll wash off," Derek tried to assure her.

"It's spreading, it's spreading," Janice screamed, fighting Derek's grip. "Out, I say! I have to get it out!"

Ruth had now joined them, and was trying to help Kent. Derek was beginning to worry that they had a psychotic episode on their hands.

Just then, Martha dashed up, breathless and frightened. "Grandma wants to see her," she said.

"All right," Ruth replied. "Let us clean her up a bit."

"No," Martha said emphatically. "Grandma says now, just as she is."

Kent and Ruth and Derek all looked at each other. "Janice, Janice," Derek said. "We're going to see Grandma. Come on, let's go."

Curiously, this seemed to quiet Janice at least temporarily. She let herself be lifted to her feet and led along, with Derek holding one wrist and Kent the other. Derek was alarmed at Janice's erratic behavior but determined to stay beside her. He was also alarmed by the amount of blood mixed with the mud on her arm. She'd gashed herself badly; raw, ragged cuts with dirt driven deeply into them. That would need attention quickly.

Martha led them into the Big House, down a corridor, and to a door which she opened but did not pass through. Ruth and Kent went first, followed by Derek and Janice.

They entered a tidy little suite, with a sitting room and a bedroom beyond. Grandpa stood, tall and stately, beside a bookshelf, while Grandma sat on a rocker nearby. She was wearing a beautiful dress and a white apron with intricate embroidery.

When she saw Janice, Grandma rose and held out her arms, concern etched on her face. "Child, child, whatever is the matter?"

Janice stood stock still for a moment, staring, then fled to Grandma's arms and collapsed, wailing uncontrollably. Holding Janice tight, Grandma sank to her knees, letting Janice lean against her while she howled and sobbed.

Derek looked on in astonishment. Janice was shuddering in her grief, clinging to Grandma, who was cradling her head against her bosom, disregarding the drool and filth being smeared all over her clothes.

"I – I murdered them, Grandma!" Janice finally cried when she'd caught her breath. "I injected poison into their veins while they slept! And now the eyes follow me everywhere, all the time!" She collapsed into wailing again, while Grandma stroked her dirt-caked hair and kissed her forehead and whispered to her.

Derek felt he had to come to her defense. He knelt on the floor next to Janice and took her hand.

"They lied to you, Janice," he pleaded. "They lied to you and pressured you and manipulated you. It isn't all your fault!"

Janice looked at him as if she'd only just seen him. "Derek? Derek, you're alive?"

"I am," Derek assured her. "We were rescued."

"Maybe from that," Janice replied. "But not from this. Derek, nobody wants me. My mother left me and my mother left me and my father left me and now I'm all alone with the eyes, the eyes that follow me everywhere."

"Child," said Grandma gently. "I want you."

"You do?" Janice asked quietly, looking up. "Even after all I've done? And look – I've got your beautiful apron all filthy."

"It will come clean, child," Grandma replied lightly. "As can your soul come clean of all you have done. Today, if you wish. You can make a new start, and you can be my daughter."

Janice looked at her with wide eyes, and Grandma's smile glowed with love. Moved by an urging he did not understand, Derek spoke up.

"And I will be your brother."

Janice turned to him, bewildered. "My brother? But – why, Derek? Why would you do that?"

"Because he loves you," Grandma answered. "As do I. Come now, child – let us get you clean." With Derek's help, Grandma rose to her feet and helped Janice out through the door where Martha stood ready to assist.

A firm hand grasped Derek's shoulder and spun him around. He found himself face to face with Grandpa, who was almost scowling at him.

"Did you mean that?" he asked sharply. "Or were you just saying it? Will you be her brother through the hardest times? Will you stand by her when she seems to lose months of progress in a single day? Will you remain by her side when the darkness closes in?"

Stung by the skepticism in Grandpa's voice, Derek looked back with a bit of defiance. "Yes, sir – as best as I can."

Grandpa's expression softened, and he clapped Derek on the shoulder. "Then you will be my son," he said. There was a slight gasp somewhere behind him.

"Thank you, sir," Derek replied, not quite understanding. "May I go now?"

"Of course," said Grandpa.

Derek turned and walked past Kent and Ruth. "I'll want to look at those wounds, once they get cleaned up," he said to Kent, who nodded. He went outside, unsure of how much more drama his life could take. He wandered over to the garden and picked up the trowel, wincing at the blood along its dirty, rough edge.

"How is she?" asked a quiet voice behind him. He turned to see Felicity, dressed in everyday working garb. Only then did he recognize that she was the girl who'd braved Janice's fit to try to help her.

"Her body should be all right, once we get those wounds cleaned out," Derek assured her. "She'll need a tetanus shot for sure, and probably IV antibiotics for a few days. Her heart, though – "

"Oh, Derek, that poor girl," Felicity slipped her arms around his neck and laid her head against his chest. Derek wrapped his arms around her and they just leaned on each other. Derek's heart didn't take flight – he was just grateful for a human touch, someone else who cared about Janice, and about him.

"Is it true, the rumors?" Felicity asked. "That she was – one of them?"

"It is," Derek said, figuring it was public knowledge by now. "But I know a little about it. She was manipulated and pressured, really she was, and in the end, they were ready to kill her."

"I can imagine," Felicity replied. "Is it also true that Grandma said she'd take her as a daughter, and you said you'd be her brother?"

"That's true, too."

"Derek, that was a loving and courageous thing to do," Felicity assured him. "Not just that, but charging in to save her from hurting herself, and going into town to rescue her yesterday."

"Well, that didn't work out too well, did it?" Derek asked with chagrin.

"You were up against terrible odds, but that didn't stop it from being a heroic thing," Felicity said.

"I didn't know what else I could have done," Derek replied.

"That's my point. And – is it also true that Grandpa said he'd take you as his son?"

"He did, but I don't know what that means, exactly," Derek admitted.

Felicity took his hand and walked him toward the deck. "It means, should you choose to follow the faith, that he will be your sponsor for your formation. Do you plan to do that?"

"I do now," Derek said. "To the world out there, I'm dead. I've walked the paths of death long enough, and I've seen where they lead. I want to walk other paths now, the paths you all walk. If your faith is part of that, then that's what I want."

"It's the very center of it," Felicity smiled. "Once you're baptized, there's a solemn adoption ceremony where he takes you as his son. It doesn't have legal standing, though sometimes a legal adoption accompanies it. Since you're legally dead, that wouldn't apply to you, but so far as the families are concerned, you'd be his son, along with the rest of his sons. You can even take his name, if you wish."

"Wow," Derek said, sitting on the edge of the deck and pondering all that. "This takes – I'll have some time to get used to this, won't I?"

"Yes," Felicity assured him. "Preparation for baptism takes several months, and there will probably be other things, too."

"Good," said Derek. "I suspect I'm going to have to unlearn a lot as well."

"Unlearn?" Felicity asked.

Derek sighed, struggling with the words. "It's hard to explain. I barely understand it myself. It's not just what happened yesterday. Even during the weekends I was spending with Kent and Linda and the kids, delightful and restful as they were, there was still this quiet uprooting going on, an unearthing of things I'd thought long buried. Then at the dance, when you and Harmony sang that song – "

"The duet we did with Mrs. Kyle?"

"Yes. There was something about the song, or that came with the song, or whatever, that let me see myself as I really am. It wasn't very impressive. There's – there's nothing in here, Felicity," Derek said, tapping his chest. "I've lived my life on the surface, immersing myself in distractions and illusions. I'd fantasize about being strong and brave and manly, but when the crisis came, I was so terrified I couldn't even trust myself to speak. I crumpled like a cheap can. I have no depth, no root. Sam, now – Sam was hurling defiance at them even while they were shooting at him."

Grief at Sam's death overwhelmed him, and he curled over sobbing. Felicity lay her head on his shoulder, weeping freely.

"I know, I know, we all loved him," she sobbed. "But don't sell yourself short, Derek. There's more in here than you think." She lay her hand over his heart. "Sam would agree. He was given what he needed when he needed it; you will be, too. One of Grandpa's favorite sayings is that courage isn't not feeling fear; courage is doing what you must even when you're terrified. Just now, you had more courage than I did. When Janice started that fit, I wanted to help, but I hung back – certainly afraid of being struck, but also afraid of her frenzy. None of that deterred you. That was courage, even if it didn't feel like it."

"It didn't feel like anything," Derek replied. "It was just what I had to do, and I did it without thinking."

"That's my point," Felicity said. "Your love for her was what sparked your courage because love is what always sparks courage. I hung back because I didn't love her enough; you charged in because you did."

"Maybe," Derek said skeptically. "It's clear I have a lot to learn about love, and about myself."

"Don't we all?" Felicity said. "Something tells me the next few years are going to get darker and more turbulent. We're all going to need all the love, and courage, we can find."

***

Captain Collins's tablet chimed the distinctive tone that signaled the arrival of a secure communication. Pressing his thumb in the designated area, he waited while the scan confirmed his identity. He hoped this was what he suspected – there, the device gave a chirp and displayed the message.

"Yes!" he said fiercely. This was it. He'd been back and forth with Washington all week, advising them and providing information while the higher-ups had deliberated and discussed. Finally, the Secretary had issued the authorization. It was top secret, of course, but he still whispered it aloud just to hear the words:

"In light of recent developments which suggest a high threat of domestic terror activities in the region, overflights are now sanctioned as far as thirty miles inland – *with* preemptive strike authorization."

***

"Okay, Amy, I can take care of this. I'll get right on it and have it back to you by the end of work tomorrow."

"Thanks, Shaundra," Amy smiled as Shaundra gathered up the notes and papers. "You're a lifesaver."

"I may as well help you," Shaundra shrugged. "It's not like I have anything else to do." She headed back toward her office with the folder of materials under her arm. Amy was Mr. Talbot's admin, and was perpetually swamped in more work than she had time for. Shaundra, on the other hand, had all kinds of time, especially during the last week.

A week. Just a week. It seemed like an age had passed, so much had changed.

Shaundra had paid only casual attention when the local news sites had reported the explosion over in Lapeer County. She was glad it hadn't happened near a population center, but like many she thought no more of what appeared to be an industrial accident. That had changed sharply when the morning reports had named two victims: some nurse she didn't know and Derek Stevens. She'd driven into work numb and stunned. She'd never had the chance to get to know Derek very well, but he'd been friendly and likeable. His last words to her had been, "I love you", and she'd known it to be true. Given a chance, they could have been deep, lifelong friends.

She'd been almost to work before the other implications began to dawn on her. She must have been too slow with the warning she gave Derek – either that, or something else had gone wrong. He hadn't managed to escape, and neither had that nurse, whoever she was.

By the time she'd reached the office, she was well and truly frightened. She'd listened in on the call from Mr. Talbot, and she'd seen those men who'd come to visit Dr. Stout. She knew that Derek had been aggressively sought by federal agents just hours before he'd died. Given that, how had he ended up dying near a remote factory north of Imlay City?

She'd barely hung up her coat when the phone had rung with a call from Mr. Talbot's office.

"Shaundra, is Dr. Stout in?" Amy had asked.

"Not yet, girl," Shaundra had said. "You know how casual he is – "

"When he gets in, send him down to Mr. Talbot's office immediately," Amy had interrupted sharply. Shaundra had been surprised – normally she and Amy bantered easily, but this Amy had sounded tense and nervous.

"Sure, Amy. Is…everything okay?"

"I can't talk right now. As soon as he gets in, right?" Amy had replied.

This exchange had further upset the already unsettled Shaundra. She'd made coffee and checked the e-mail and tried to recite verses to calm herself. Finally, Dr. Stout had shown up, and as soon as he'd hung up his coat Shaundra had passed along Amy's message. He'd headed for Mr. Talbot's office, and after ten minutes she'd finally felt it safe to call down.

"Amy, what's going on?"

"Something weird," Amy had responded in a tense whisper. "When I got here this morning, two guys in suits were waiting in the hall. They didn't identify themselves but demanded to see Mr. Talbot. When he arrived, they handed him their IDs and went into his office with him. Three minutes later, he calls to have me cancel his morning appointments and to get Dr. Stout down here. They've been in that office with the door closed ever since. That's all I know. I'll keep you posted, but I gotta go."

This had alarmed Shaundra. Could anyone have discovered that she'd warned Derek? Would she be called down to Mr. Talbot's office next? Would they come and take her away for questioning? She'd tried to busy herself with petty tasks, but accomplished nothing – she was too distracted.

Over an hour later, Dr. Stout had burst into the office, grabbed his coat, and without saying a word to Shaundra had left for the day. The next morning he'd called her from the morgue, asking that all his calls be forwarded there. He'd been working down there ever since, not even coming to his office at the county building, thus leaving Shaundra with plenty of time on her hands.

So, she'd made herself useful to Amy and others while managing the minor work of the office. Unfortunately, one of those duties had been dealing with Derek's mother, which had made her feel even sorrier for the poor kid. His mother hadn't even come over from Syracuse, though she could have made the drive in a day. Of course, since there was no body, there were no funeral home arrangements, but Shaundra thought she could have made some minimal effort. But all she had done was arrange with a cleaning service to empty out Derek's apartment and ship his worldly goods back to Syracuse. There'd been no memorial service, no obituary, nothing other than a one-line death notice on the local news sites.

Shaundra stopped in the hallway, sitting down on one of the benches to wipe her eyes. Poor kid. He'd deserved better than to be swept away and forgotten, without even the slightest remembrance that was every human's basic right. After church last Sunday she'd asked Pastor Brent and Mother Gladys and her friend Clarissa to pray with her for Derek. The four of them had stood in a circle, held hands, and prayed as best they could. It was sad to think that would be the only memorial he'd get. She hadn't known how Derek had stood with the Lord, but he'd always been kind and friendly. She hoped for the best and trusted in the Lord's mercy.

Shaundra daubed her eyes and sniffed, then gathered up Amy's paperwork and turned toward her office. She was surprised to see a man in some kind of uniform step out of the door.

"Excuse me – can I help you?" Shaundra called.

"I hope so," the man replied. "Are you Shaundra?"

"Yes."

"Delivery for you," the man said. "The door was unlocked, but there was nobody there, so I just left it on the desk. I hope that's okay."

"That's fine – thanks," Shaundra replied. A delivery? She stepped into her office to see a large, colorful bouquet sitting beside a fancy travel mug. She picked up the mug, which was full of fragrant coffee, to find beneath it a gift certificate made out to her from the new boutique coffee place down on Huron Avenue. The flowers were also fragrant, and she searched through them until she found the card. All it had on it was her name, with a little heart beside it. She sat down in her chair, gazing at the card in bewilderment.

Who could have sent her all this?